CITY WOLVES

"Historical romance, pioneering feminism, rough sex, Inuit spirit guides, wolves, dogs, more wolves, real people mingling with fictional ones, a fresh take on the Dawson City gold rush—this is entertainment. An indomitable heroine takes city wolves into the wilderness and makes them howl. I for one could not stop listening."

KEN McGOOGAN, *Pierre Berton History Prize winner, author of* Fatal Passage *and* Race to the Polar Sea

"Over time, our instinctual, embodied way of knowing has been banished, rupturing our intuitive connection with nature. Now Dorris Heffron, in her insightful exploration of the profound and mysterious relationship between a woman and her wolf-dogs, offers us a metaphor for healing the terrible breach. In this larger than life novel, power/love, greed/sharing, vengeance/mercy are among the archetypal tensions spurring the plot along and the reader with it, as the author draws us irresistibly into a world where connecting with our fellow creatures means the difference between life and death. A marvelous work! I look forward to it becoming a Canadian classic."

ROSEMARY GOSSELIN, *BJ, MSW, NCPsyA, Jungian Psychoanalyst, Integrative Consulting Services*

"Dorris Heffron has illuminated a fascinating and little-known aspect of human behaviour—the degree to which humans have modelled their social structure on that of wolves—and turned it into story. *City Wolves* is a wonderful blend of fiction and history, natural and unnatural: high art indeed!"

WAYNE GRADY, *Naturalist, author of* The Nature of Coyotes

"*City Wolves* takes the insightful truth of good biography and runs with it, imaginatively rollicking into a gripping narrative. Dorris Heffron's meticulous research allows her to give life to a neglected theory about who really first discovered the gold that started the Klondike rush and to compelling portrayals of historical characters like Kate Carmack, Belinda Mulroney and their cohorts in Dawson City. This novel celebrates and breathes real life into the women of the gold rush, opening up a new vista in historical fiction."

JENNIFER DUNCAN, *writer, educator, author of* Sanctuary and Other Stories *and* Frontier Spirit, *biographies of women who went to the Klondike gold rush*

CITY WOLVES

HISTORICAL FICTION

Dorris Heffron

Blue Butterfly Books

THINK FREE, BE FREE

Blue Butterfly Book Publishing Inc.
2583 Lakeshore Boulevard West, Toronto, Ontario, Canada M8V 1G3
Tel 416-255-3930   Fax 416-252-8291   www.bluebutterflybooks.ca

For complete ordering information for Blue Butterfly titles, go to:
www.bluebutterflybooks.ca

First edition, hard cover: 2008

LIBRARY AND ARCHIVES CANADA CATALOGUING IN PUBLICATION

Heffron, Dorris, 1944–
City wolves : historical fiction / Dorris Heffron.

ISBN 978-0-9781600-7-4

I. Title.

PS8565.E33C48 2008   C813'.54   C2008-905564-0

Design and typesetting by Fox Meadow Creations
Text set in Fournier and Weiss
Historical photographs from Library and Archives Canada
Printed in Canada by Transcontinental-Métrolitho

The paper in this book, Rolland Envrio 100, contains 100 per cent post-consumer
recycled fibre, is processed chlorine-free, and is manufactured with biogas energy.

*No government grants were sought nor any public subsidies received for
publication of this book. Blue Butterfly Books thanks book buyers for
their support in the marketplace.*

This book is dedicated to Elizabeth Love Kane,
dear friend, great supporter of the arts,
choirmaster of the malamutes of Beaver Valley.

It is inspired, if not commanded, by our own Yukon Sally,
regal Alaskan malamute, yet definite wolf throwback.
She led the way.

CONTENTS

Part Two: DAWSON CITY

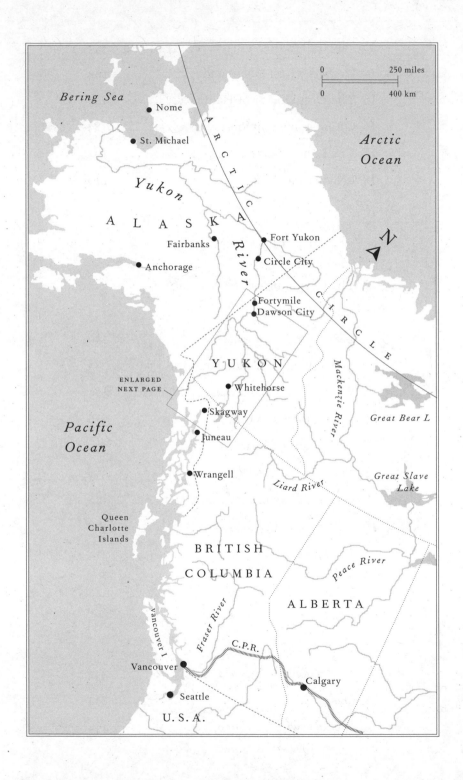

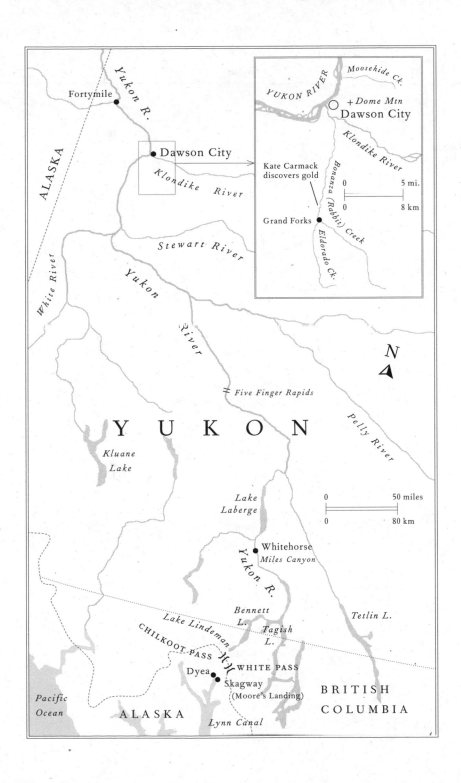

Some of the characters in this novel are fictitious and some are not. Those who are not, bear their real names.

PROLOGUE

Ike's spirit was restless, always had been, even before it left his worn-out body. For Ike was a man of good intentions who fulfilled his dream, created something good, useful and much sought after in society, but he suffered guilt at the cost and at his inability to control what became of it in the hands of others. He saw all of that come out in his lifetime. He was not at peace with himself in his lifetime and so, when his old body died, his spirit continued in restlessness, hovering through the years, through centuries, finding kindred spirits here and there, trying to influence like-minded people who instinctively loved wolves of the wild as he did and saw in the working dogs he created from them, the creatures of complexity, of greatness and greed, that are found in country and city, in wolves, dogs and people.

Ike's wife, Piji, was his equal partner in the original project. His partner in crime, he sometimes felt, though she did not always think as he did. In the end, they said she lost her sanity. But Piji's spirit found rest. Her body died clothed in malamute fur and her spirit carried on reasonably contentedly in the minds of breeders of the highest standards.

As for Ike, he hovered anxiously through many centuries. His story was handed down from generation to generation and eventually written down, though not published. Disgusted, often, Ike's spirit moved on and found its greatest hope in the birth of Meg Wilkinson who was determined to become the first woman veterinarian, though she began, like Ike, as a wolf hugger.

PART ONE

HALIFAX

1

The Origins of Meg

MARGARET ANNE WILKINSON was born in 1870 on a farm near Halifax, a city on the south-east coast of Canada. Margaret, dubbed Meg, was the seventh child of Emma and Herbert Wilkinson.

"Lucky number seven," said Herbert. "And born in '70. This calls for a cigar."

Exhausted from the strain of childbirth, Emma kept her thoughts to herself. She had a long habit of keeping silent, for her thinking was not always pleasing to others. Her thought on this occasion was ... let me have the luck of this being my last baby.

But it was not. Three years later, at age forty-one, she gave birth to another girl, Alice.

"Now, my dear," said Herbert, "you have two girls to help with the housework."

"That's enough," said Emma. "No more, Herbert. No more."

All very well for our Queen Victoria to have so many children, Emma had thought to herself, time and again, as she washed soiled diapers in buckets of cold water, bent over in her smoky, dark, log cabin on a lonely farm in the wilds of Canada. Our queen has a palace and servants.

Emma undid the top buttons of her flannel nightgown and expertly guided her new baby's head so that her mouth found the nipple ooz ing the first drops of nourishment. Ah, Emma sighed quietly as she relaxed against the goose-down pillows. This is the easy part. She smiled at Herbert as he turned to leave her with the midwife from Halifax. A smile from Emma was a rare thing.

"Good wife." Herbert nodded jauntily. "Good mother. My little Emma."

"He's a right gentleman," said the midwife after he closed the thin plank door.

"Yes," said Emma. "Always has been. He's the fifth son of the squire of Squirrel Hall. Back in Yorkshire, that is, in the old country."

"Squirrel Hall," the midwife laughed. "That's a good one!"

"It was very grand."

"Aye." And spare me the details, thought midwife McLarty. I've heard it all before. The grand life left behind. "My old country is Ireland. I'd a starved to death if I'd stayed there. Guess prospects weren't too good for a fifth son, either. But you've got yourself a fine-looking farm here, Mrs. Wilkinson. And a fine family, I must say. I've delivered some shockers, believe me. Especially to women your age. The dead ones are a relief. It's the ones born witless, or without limbs, or with cleft palate. You wouldn't believe ..."

"I believe you," said Emma. She closed her eyes as though too tired for further talk. And would you believe me if I told you I was a scullery maid at Squirrel Hall? That I saw more at age twelve than you think you know now? But I won't tell you, for I've learned that once you uncover yourself, people don't forget what they have seen and may use it against you. And you, my good midwife, have seen quite enough of me. Quite enough. She opened her eyes to shift baby Alice to the other breast.

"I'll be going now, Mrs. Wilkinson, seeing as you're managing well enough on your own."

"Thank you, Mrs. McLarty."

Three-year-old Meg then burst into the room, having escaped from her bed in her nightgown. She was tripping upon it as she forced her way around the skirts of Mrs. McLarty.

"Mommy. Mommy. Is this tomorrow?" Meg asked excitedly.

"Now that's what I call a sunny disposition!" Mrs. McLarty laughed. "Top o' the mornin' to you little Missy."

"Hello," said Meg, curtsying slightly as she had been taught to do, then she turned to her mother. "Is that the baby you promised me tomorrow?"

"Yes, my little Meg, this is your sister, Alice."

Alice struggled to open her eyes then cried at all she saw.

Is this tomorrow?

"It's an interesting question," said Herbert to Emma. "She should not be discouraged from asking it. She's a questioner and an optimist by nature. Like me when I was young." He smiled at Emma. "I knew you would marry me eventually. And come to Canada with me."

"Such a bright face you put on everything, Herbert. And still do." But you would have had your way with me, without benefit of marriage, had I let you, thought Emma. It is a great lesson to impart to our daughters.

Emma recalled Herbert trailing after her when he came home from boarding school. She was then fourteen and he seventeen. He was not at all like the handsome and mysterious Mr. Rochester, hero of her heroine, Jane Eyre, star of the runaway best seller *Jane Eyre*, the book that was passed or nicked, from upstairs to down, in every cultured household of the time. Squirrel Hall had been exceptionally cultured, thanks to Mistress Wilkinson, who kept the best library in the county. She was a great fan of Charles Dickens' novels and had entertained the man himself to a grand dinner at Squirrel Hall when Dickens was in the vicinity doing research for the boarding school background of his novel *Nicholas Nickleby*. That the novel turned out to reflect badly on local schools did not endear Mrs. Wilkinson to some of her neighbours.

But all that had occurred before Emma came to work at the Hall. Mrs. Wilkinson endured as a prominent hostess and defender of Dickens and other writers whom she called "forward thinking." She read *Jane Eyre* as soon as it came out but found the story of a modest young governess marrying the master of the house not very likely. She knew from her own household of a husband and five sons that a governess was more likely to be taken advantage of and then sent away on spurious grounds. But the need for governesses for her sons was long past when Mrs. Wilkinson loaned her copy of *Jane Eyre* to her head housekeeper, who soon passed it on to young Emma who read and re-read it.

During a re-reading at the servants' table in off hours, Emma suddenly had the feeling of being watched. She looked up and there in the doorway was young Master Herbert looking most intently at her. She was too fearful of what he might do, to speak.

"You like to read?" he asked.

She nodded.

"I'll get you any book you want."

Emma accepted with much trepidation the loan of books, since it was approved by Mrs. Wilkinson, but she would not converse with Master Herbert about the books or remain for more than a moment alone in his company. She knew about servant girls who were dismissed because they had got with child, or even become too familiar with a master. Mrs. Wilkinson treated her staff with respect and generosity. She had been involved in the abolition of slavery movement when she was young. She was a supporter of public education and she tried to raise her sons with a high regard for women. But when one of her sons got a servant "in trouble," it was the servant who was dismissed, albeit with payment. The baby was delivered to an orphanage and the fifteen-year-old girl was said to have ended up on the streets of London. Emma was determined not to end up in that faraway den of iniquity. She planned to marry at the mature age of seventeen or eighteen a sober, hard-working blacksmith, or the like, whose house she would keep in good order, and hopefully have a nice little family.

Thus Emma was terrified when Master Herbert waylaid her, alone, on the path back to her home in the village. It was in just such places that the ruination of a girl could occur. She stood paralyzed as Herbert lifted her hand to his lips. "You're the prettiest little thing in all the world."

She looked up at a window and saw Mrs. Wilkinson looking down upon them. She turned and fled to her home. She pretended illness, not daring to return to Squirrel Hall. A week later, Mrs. Wilkinson drove up in a carriage. She asked to speak with Emma privately.

"Our son, Master Herbert," she said, clasping her gloved hands tightly together, "wishes you to accept his apologies for frightening you. He made it very clear to us that you are not at fault. He has gone to look for a job in London and prays that you will return to your job at Squirrel Hall." Mrs. Wilkinson coughed, not used to the heavy cloud of coal smoke lingering in the small room. "As do the squire and I. Will you come now, Miss Emma?"

Emma drove back to Squirrel Hall in the carriage with Mrs. Wilkinson.

Herbert came home at Christmas and behaved with perfect decorum, though it did not hide the fact that he was still smitten with Emma, still trailed after her, still coveted her, with her carrot-coloured ringlets, sea-green eyes, healthy face and figure. Mrs. Wilkinson looked worried. The squire was disgusted.

"The lad has never had any common sense." The squire's raised voice could be heard from behind closed doors. "He's too much like you, my dear wife. Full of books, ideas, questions. His head in the clouds. How can he still be so damn moonstruck! All very well for a woman to be such a ... what did you call it?"

"Romantic?"

"It doesn't do for a man. A man has to get on with things. Why can't he be more like me?"

"George, I fear he is too much like you. A very determined young man who chooses just the woman his parents warn him against."

The squire laughed heartily. "But you were such another kettle of fish, my dear! Emma is a mouse, meek and silent as a mouse."

"I should think so, around you!" Mrs. Wilkinson's laugh was heard, followed by a pause for another sip of port. "I have spoken with her. She's a bright little thing. Understands what she reads. Though it's hard to understand her. She has the accent of her class, of course. Maybe we should encourage Herbert to converse with her. Allow more familiarity. Yes! Let us try that, George. Absence has served only to make the heart grow fonder."

Emma never forgot the offence she felt at hearing that conversation. It spurred her into a new direction. She had been promoted from scullery maid because she showed that she was diligent at any task set to her. Now she would learn to speak like a governess. Why not? And if Master Herbert spoke to her, she would answer. Yes she would. And if that got her dismissed from the household, she would find another position. If Master Herbert dismissed her ... so be it.

But Herbert was charmed, impressed, intrigued by her. She made him feel looked up to, admired, worldly, as though he had the attributes of a man like his father, though in fact he had no property or authority. Herbert went back to London, worked away at his dull, low-level clerking job. The fifth son of a not extremely wealthy squire of the hunt, the squire of Squirrel Hall, young Herbert was not a great marriage prospect. Interesting women like his mother did not surround him. He needed to make his own way in life. He devised a plan. Next Christmas he went home with a proposal for his parents and for Emma.

"I'm going to marry Emma," he said in a meeting with his parents, "She has given her consent. A small ceremony in the chapel. No expense. But I could do with a little help in the cost of getting across the ocean and acquiring some land in the Canadas."

"Are you serious, lad?"

"I am, sir."

The yule log in the large fireplace crackled and spat in the silence. The squire stood up and held out his hand to Herbert. "I congratulate you, my son. It sounds like a practical venture."

"Thank you, sir. And mother?"

"So far away, in such a dangerous land ..." she protested but then stepped forward to embrace him.

"Thank you, mother." He patted her back then drew away. "I would like to present my betrothed." Herbert went to the doorway and brought Emma in, holding her hand firmly.

She curtsied slightly then said, "I will look after him, to the best of my ability, ma'am. And sir."

Emma revelled, to this day, in the look of surprise on the face of her in-laws, that she should so speak up and in such a good accent.

Herbert had done well in the new country. He bought a hundred acres of land just a half day's journey outside the city of Halifax. A barn and a log cabin were already built near the creek that ran through it, though only half the land was cleared of woods. Over the years, Herbert established an apple orchard and put his six sons to work looking after the cows and pigs, the horses and plowing, the planting and reaping. He even managed to clear another ten acres, using some of the trees to add onto the log house a bedroom, bigger kitchen, and enlarged sleeping loft.

He called the farm Wolf Woods because he was fascinated by the sound of wolves howling at night in his woods. At first he worried that they might come close and do harm to his livestock, Emma's chickens, or even his children. He kept a gun over the doorway. But he never saw the wolves or their tracks outside of the woods. He liked to write home about the wolves in his woods, knowing what good table conversation it would provide for his parents and their friends.

Unlike his father, he had no desire or time to become squire of the hunt. He became interested in the politics of his new country, spent more and more time in Halifax, and got himself elected to the provincial legislature of Nova Scotia in 1876.

"This is the great epoch of my life," he said to Emma, his thumbs in his waistcoat. "Next to marrying you, of course. A man's life can become of real importance in a young country like this, helping with its development. We can change the course of history!"

Herbert was becoming quite an orator. He liked to practise in his own household with wife and eight children gathered round the long table.

"It's a pity your parents didn't live to see this," said Emma, seated at the other end of the table spoon-feeding baby Alice. "They would be proud of you."

"And of you, my dear wife."

I doubt it, thought Emma. I've grown from a mouse into a tired old workhorse. Worn out with childbearing and doing all the jobs of a full staff at Squirrel Hall. Washing, ironing, sewing, mending, gardening, preserving, cleaning, endless cooking and baking. Endless! Followed by endless washing up. I'm too tired to read a book, even if I had the time. And you have no idea how much I hate the very walls of this house. Made of undisguised tree trunks! It couldn't be more primitive. And never a friend to talk to within. Hedgeless fields without. Wild wolves howling in the night. How I miss the red brick houses, row upon row, in my Yorkshire village. Cobbled streets with people I know, coming and going. The smell of a coal fire. My poor old parents and my sisters. I'll never see them again. Nor the grandeur of Squirrel Hall. Oh dear. Oh dear.

"Momma's weeping!" Meg got off her place at the end of the bench and tugged at her mother's sleeve.

"Finish your meal," said Emma sternly, pushing Meg away. "You are talking nonsense. Keep your place at the table, or you shall have none." Emma stood up, carrying Alice. "I must see to the apple crumble."

Alice began to cry.

"My poor little one. My poor little one." Emma nuzzled her cheek into Alice's, transferring her tears and her self pity.

2

Tomorrow's Lesson

MEG FOUND MORE INTEREST in playing with small animals on the farm than in trying to play with baby Alice, who seemed always to be crying in one kind of frustration or another. Chickens and geese scattered as Meg toddled after them but soon ones more curious or brave would stand and observe her. Some eventually let her touch their head. Some followed her at a distance. Piglets offered her their snouts. Meg played outside with the cats and kittens since Emma had declared the house off limits to animals and no dogs were allowed on the farm after the collie got rabies and had to be shot.

Emma herself feared the outdoors, did not go beyond necessary trips to the outhouse, and refused to tend the garden because she hated snakes and feared coming upon them. They weren't poisonous or large, but it was enough that they slithered across one's path, hid in the wood pile, or curled up under her tomato plants. She had never seen a snake in England but she knew all about them from the Bible and other stories that depicted them as evil, slimy, aggressive, and generally poisonous. Early on, Emma gave up chasing outdoors after little Meg and told her older brothers to keep her out of danger in the barnyard. As Meg grew bigger, calves and colts became her companions.

"Peeeuuuw!" said Alice when Meg came indoors. "You stink like our brudders."

"Brothers." Meg wrinkled her nose back at Alice.

"She speaks well for her age," said Emma. "Stop picking on her."

Meg's main job when she was eight years old was to look after the chickens. Each evening she made sure they were all safely in an enclosed section of the barn. Each morning she let them out and fed them, pouring a pail of grain into one trough, water into the other. She gathered the eggs, cleaned them with vinegar, and sorted them into baskets of small and large, for home use and for sale. Weekly, she pitched out soiled straw onto the manure pile and put fresh straw in the nests and on the floor. She liked the work and particularly the pay-off, going with her brother in the wagon into Halifax to sell the eggs.

She loved the laying hens with their quirky gait and glances, their discernibly different characters, and their busy, productive lifestyle. But she had to steel herself to the short lives of the meat chickens, all the fuzzy little chicks that grew into plump chickens who would be scooped up, strung up on a hook, and then have their necks wrung and their bodies plucked of all feathers. There was a toughness, an emotional distance to be maintained with those you raised to kill and eat. Meg was relieved, glad that in her mother's rigid list of girls' work versus boys' work, it fell to her brothers to kill the chickens. But it outraged her that the boys were given almost all the outdoor jobs while she had to stay inside doing housework.

"It's not fair," Meg said to her mother one evening as she finished drying the dishes, while outside, her brothers made a game of pitching hay. And inside, five-year-old Alice was allowed to play with the mixing bowls. "When I was Alice's age, I had to help with the dishes, not just play with them."

Emma said nothing. She had just sat down to knit after washing the dishes. She was too weary to respond to Meg's questioning.

"I want the wooden spoon," said Alice, reaching to take it from Meg's hand as she dried it. "I'm making a pretend cake."

"You can't have it," said Meg. "I've just cleaned and dried it." She raised it above Alice's reach.

"Mommy! Meg is teasing me again!"

"Give Alice the spoon," said Herbert from his desk in the corner.

Meg made a face at Alice but handed the spoon out to her, holding it over the bowls Alice had arranged on the floor. Alice reached for it, tripping over the bowls, fell and scraped her knee. Meg helped Alice, screaming, to stand up then quickly gathered up the bowls, and shouted "Nothing broken!"

"No thanks to you, is it!" Emma stood up, losing her temper, railing at Meg, "Now look what you've done! Your little sister's knee bleeding. You could have broken her bones, along with all the crockery. There's nary a moment's peace around here, is there! Can you not just get on with the job and stop questioning your place and everything you're told to do? You'll never get on in life with such cheekiness."

"Emma, my dear..." Herbert stood by her but couldn't decide what to say.

"It's time for the hairbrush, Herbert. She has to learn her place and to obey. You told her to give Alice the spoon and she held it out of reach of the poor little thing."

"Prepare yourself, Meggie," said Herbert, looking pained.

Punishment for the young girls was the hairbrush administered to the bared bottom laid over the knee of the parent. Punishment for the boys was a strapping over the bared bottom in the privacy of a barn stable. Herbert did not enjoy administering the punishments but it was his place as a man and he agreed with his wife that children should be punished for wrongdoing. He had been strapped by his father. The hairbrush for little girls was Emma's insistence.

The problem in spanking Meg with the hairbrush was that it caused her to pee onto the lap of the spanker. Repeated experience of this taught the parents to take the child out to the outhouse before she was spanked. At eight years old, Meg was expected to go to the outhouse on her own. She met her brothers coming in for the night.

"Why such a long face, Meg?" asked Stewart.

"You're not getting the hairbrush again, are you?" said Dave.

Meg burst into tears as she ran to the outhouse. She heard her brothers go into the log house as she opened the door of the outhouse. She shuddered in the cold night air of early May as darkness was gathering. She lifted the wooden lid over the round hole and set it down. The fumes from the pit of human excrement far below ascended. Meg covered only half the hole with her small bare bottom and hung onto the edge of the board box, lest she fall in. She heard the sound of her urine landing far below.

Then, with the lid back in place and her hand on the outhouse door latch, Meg made a sudden decision. She would not go back into the house for her spanking. She would bolt.

She ran behind the lilac bushes and crouched at their edge out of sight from the house. Too cold in her blouse and pinafore, she decided to make for the barn. She would spend the night with her chickens. But as she reached the big pile of straw in the barn yard, she heard her father calling from the house, "Meg! Meggie, come inside now. You must."

Hiding behind the straw, Meg saw her father open the door of the outhouse then hurry back to the house. "Lads!" he shouted. "Get out here. We have to find your sister. Quick! Bring lanterns."

Meg dove into the pile of straw. She buried herself deeper and deeper into it, preparing to cover her face as well as her head in straw.

"She's probably in the barn," she heard her father say, "hiding amongst her blessed chickens."

As she lay hidden in the straw, she heard them calling for her and shouting at each other as they searched the chicken coop, the stables, the hay loft, the grain bins, even the pig pen.

"She won't hide out with pigs, lad!"

"You're right, Dad," Stew shouted back. "She ain't here. But I wouldn't put it past her. She thinks every animal's her pal."

"Don't say 'ain't,' lad. Sounds like you were raised in a barn."

"It's the sorry truth, Dad," said Dave. "Meg's not to be found in barn or yard."

"Come, then. We must take the news to your mother."

Lifting the straw away from her face, Meg saw that they had left the latch loose and the barn door creaked open. Raccoons, foxes, wolves, any creature could get in and kill her chickens. She made a dash for the barn and closed herself inside it. The hens began to cluck, cows to moo, pigs to snort. She went around soothing and hushing them. She climbed into the hayloft and took a perch on a beam where she could see the house through cracks in the barn boards. She saw her father come out with his arm around her mother, holding a lantern in his other hand. Stew, Dave, and Joe spread out in search-party formation. Andy was left inside minding Alice.

"She'll be eaten by wolves!" Emma was frantic. "Torn apart. Eaten alive. Meggie! Meggie, come home. Come out from hiding, wherever you are."

The boys searched up the lane and along the creek. Her parents searched the orchard.

"She could be hiding in the trees. You know how she likes to climb them. Oh that girl!" Emma cried as she passed near the barn, "How could she do this to me! When we find her I shall shake the living daylights out of her!'

"Now, now Emma. Talk like that won't bring her back."

There was silence and then talk too muffled for Meg to hear as her parents circled the barn and then came inside it. Meg sank down in the hay. Emma and Herbert looked in on the chickens.

"She's such a good girl, really." Emma was gently sobbing. "A hard worker, like me. Think of the money she has brought in from these hens. I haven't time, or patience, to tend them the way she does. I've been too hard on her, haven't I? If I had had more girls and less boys, more to help me out in the house, I wouldn't have asked so much of her. Wouldn't have driven her off . . . into the hands . . . or jaws, of Lord knows what. I'm better with Alice. Oh Lord, give me another chance with my little Margaret. Named after my own mother she was."

"We'll find her," said Herbert. "She'll be in your arms by tomorrow, if not sooner."

"Don't tell me that!" Emma cried. "A little girl can't last a night in this God-forsaken wilderness. And there is no tomorrow. Ever! We have to find her *now*! Margaret! Meggie!" she shouted to the rafters. "Come back, You won't be spanked, if you just come back. Now!"

Just as Meg was about to emerge, her mother screamed in desperation and fled from the barn to the house, to her bed. I'll wait until dawn, thought Meg. I'll go back into her arms, tomorrow.

She fell asleep for brief periods. She woke with the hay scratching her cheeks and looked out on the night. She saw deer come single file to the creek, moving cautiously, stopping in perfect stillness when they sensed something alarming, then moving on when they saw it was just a fox heading toward the barn. The deer drank and went back to the woods, leaping with a gracefulness that made Meg sigh in awe. Then she clenched her teeth as she watched the fox circle the barn, then creep to the door leading out from the chicken coop. She scrambled down from the hayloft and rushed through the coop to make sure the door was secure. It was. She stroked the heads and backs of her hens, mumbling their names. The rooster crowed. She cautiously opened the door onto the earliest light of dawn. Closing the door behind her, she headed for the house.

She stopped suddenly when she saw, not far away, three wolves facing down the fox. All four animals turned and stared at Meg. The fox took off. The wolves continued to stare. Grey wolves with white faces and mesmerizing ginger eyes, alert, staring at her.

"Meg! Lie low," her father shouted from the house.

Meg was too frightened to move. Gun shots were fired into the air as the wolves turned and ran, disappearing into the woods. Meg stood watching them.

Her father swooped her up, embraced her, set her down. She ran to the house where her mother stood in the doorway. "It's tomorrow, Momma. I'm back."

Emma pulled her inside. Slapped her hard on the face, with her forehand and then her backhand. She whacked her behind. "Don't you ever, *ever*, run away again."

"Emma!" Herbert yelled. "That's not the way ..."

Meg stood in shock, her face stinging. Alice came running, crying.

Emma bent down to embrace Alice. Then she extended her hand out to Meg. "Come, my little Margaret, let us begin afresh."

Meg burst into tears as she was pulled into her mother's arms.

3

MEG'S FIRST PATIENTS

MEG WANTED TO SEE THE WOLVES AGAIN. She was sure it was they who kept the foxes at bay and hence her chickens protected. She tried to wake herself before dawn in order to watch out the loft bedroom window for them, but she always slept through until the bright morning light and then there was no sighting of fox or wolf. Watching from the window in darkness after her siblings had gone to sleep was no more productive. Some nights she could hear the howling of wolves but they never came into sight.

There were different opinions within Meg's family as to what might have happened, had Herbert not fired into the air when Meg stood eye to eye with the wolves.

"They would have attacked," said Emma. "It's in their nature. That's why wolves were driven out of England."

"You never know," said Herbert, politically astute.

"Our Meggie faced them down," teased Dave. "Didn't you, Meggie."

"I want to see them again," said Meg. "It's the only way of knowing, for sure."

"You wouldn't dare!" said Alice.

"You'd better not!" Emma frowned.

It was another three years before Meg saw them again. Late after-noon, in the spring, Emma sent Meg fiddlehead hunting with Alice. "Go on. Scat! Get out of my hair." Emma handed them a pail. "Let me get on with the baking in peace. But don't be long. You have to peel the potatoes for supper, Meg."

"What about Alice?" said Meg. "Doesn't she have to do any-thing?"

"Don't be lippy," Emma warned Meg, then added, "Alice will help set the table."

As they set off, Emma called from the doorway, "Have Stewart or David accompany you. You are not to go into the woods alone."

"Stewart or David," Meg mimicked. "Joseph and Andrew. Robert and George. No one but our Mom calls them that."

"It's what they would be called in England. Momma said so."

"But that's not where we live, is it? If we called our brothers by such long-handled names, we'd be laughed out of the schoolyard. And so would they." Meg hoisted herself up onto the edge of the lower barn door and called out, "Hey Stew! Dave! You in there? One of you has to come with us. We're going into the woods, for fiddleheads."

"We're busy," Dave shouted back. "Go get Joe or Andy. They're plowing near the woods."

"Busy, my eye!" Meg landed back on the ground. "They're pipe smoking in there. Can smell it a mile away."

Dave came to the barn door, wielding a pitch fork. "Take your big nose elsewhere, little sister." He jabbed the pitch fork towards her. "Or I'll turn you into fish bait."

"That'll be the day!" Meg turned her back on him, pulling Alice by the hand in the direction of the grain fields. "Don't forget to put Dad's pipe back in his desk before he gets home, lads."

"Scrapper!" Stew appeared at the door and called out as Meg led Alice away, running. "How be we tell the parents what a scrapper you are? Eh!"

"They wouldn't, would they?" said Alice anxiously when they slowed down. She stomped her foot and whined. "I hate the way everyone makes fun of me."

"Of you!" Meg took her hand and made her continue on. "It's me who gets called the Scrapper. Just because I gave that Choyce boy a fat lip."

"But it was because he called *me* 'Fatty, Fatty, two by four, couldn't get through the kitchen door.' And I can! I'm not a fatty. At all!"

"Of course you're not. That's why I gave him a fat lip."

"You shouldn't have. It's very … unbecoming … to fight like boys."

"Guess that's why they also call me Tomboy. I don't mind. 'Sticks and stones may break your bones. But names will never hurt you.'"

Alice considered for several moments. "I think they're very hurtful. I don't like anyone calling me anything but Alice."

Joe and Andy were plowing behind two oxen in the field nearest the woods. "Can't stop now," they said. "We've only a few rows to go. We'll keep an eye on you from here. Don't go far in. There's plenty of fiddleheads in the damp parts near the edge. Just holler if you need us."

Meg helped Alice fill half the pail with ripe green fiddleheads and entangled weeds. Then she was bored. "I'll just climb this tree and be on the lookout for wolves, bears, and Indians," she said. "You pick a few more and then we're done."

"There aren't any Indians around here any more," said Alice.

"That's what you think."

"That's what Dad told Momma. They've 'gone the way of the buffalo.' That's what he said."

"You don't even know what that means … 'gone the way of the buffalo.'" Meg was now on the first big branch of the maple tree.

"Oh yes I do."

"Then tell me."

"You tell me."

Meg laughed. "Pick a dozen more fiddleheads and I'll tell you."

"There are no more buffalo."

"Right." Meg was now as high as she wanted to go. She peered through the branches.

"Dad says it's a cryin' shame."

Meg did not answer. She was looking a short distance away, behind big rocks, at three wolves tearing voraciously at the bleeding flesh of a freshly killed deer. She could see their large fangs as they looked up intermittently, snarling warningly at one another to keep to their own section. They looked fleetingly in the direction of the human voices, but kept on devouring the deer meat.

"Meggie. Why don't you answer me?"

Meg got down from the tree as fast as she could. She grabbed the pail in one hand, Alice's hand in the other. "Let's go. Or we'll be in trouble," she hissed.

Alice ran as fast as she could to keep up with Meg, twigs snapping loudly beneath their feet. At the edge of the plowed field, Meg stopped and looked behind into the woods. She could see nothing but trees.

"What was it?" said Alice. "What did you see?"

Andy was running towards them. Andy, the avid hunter and best marksman in the family, was carrying the rifle he kept with him in the fields. "What's up, kids? What are you running from?"

Meg knew that Andy was itching to shoot a wolf. He said they interfered with the deer supply. "Nothing," she said, stalling for time. "Nothing dangerous. Just a dead deer. All eaten apart. It was ... It was horrid."

In early autumn, the crops were harvested and stored, the apples picked and sold or laid away in barrels. The woods had turned orange and scarlet. Emma was indoors with Alice, stirring a kettle of relish to be preserved in jars and stored on the shelves alongside the preserved tomatoes, green beans, and berries. Two crocks of pickled cucumbers stood on the floor below. Nearly nine years old, Alice was good at preserving, baking, cooking, could knit almost as fast as her mother, and had learned to sew straight seams with the new hand-turned sewing machine. She was her mother's companion and protégé.

"You will make a good wife," Emma said to Alice, fingering the curls so becoming on her daughter's forehead. "You must save your-self for a good man."

"Save myself?" said Alice. "What does that mean?" Was she to be preserved, pickled for future use?

"You'll understand, soon enough."

"What about Meg? Will she make a good wife?"

"Where there's life, there's hope." Emma smiled. She tried not to show favouritism to Alice, but she was so much easier to share senti-ments with, particularly this sense of Meg being a "difficult girl." Alice smiled. It was satisfying to have her mother's preference, though there was something strangely unsettling about it at times.

Meg, now twelve, was glad to be outside in the sunshine, gather-ing up pumpkins, pushing them along in a wheelbarrow towards the shed. Then she heard the agonized cry of a cat. She ran to find their young black cat, Nightie, lying in the grass, bleeding at the mouth. Meg yelled for help. She could see it was choking on something.

"Open your mouth. Open your mouth, Nightie!" If I had gloves, thought Meg, so she won't bite through my fingers. If I had some-thing to prop her mouth open ...

The cat rolled over onto her side, her eyes bulging. Meg saw the small sharp edge of a snapped chicken bone, piercing through the cat's neck fur. Meg yelled again for help. Suppressing her own fear, Meg grabbed the cat's upper and lower jaw, prying open its mouth. She could see the bone stuck in the cat's throat. But she couldn't fig-ure out how to hold the mouth open while trying to pull out the bone. Then she pressed on the lower jaw with her left hand and reached in with her right hand. Her finger hooked the bone just as the cat went rigid and lifeless. Meg pulled her hand out of the cat's mouth and fell back onto the grass. She had extracted only part of the bone.

Emma and Alice came running from the house, Dave from the barn.

"Too late," said Meg. "Nightie is dead."

I might have saved her, Meg concluded when she went over and over the scene in her mind, if I'd had the right tools. Some tongs or tweezers. If I had more practice, I could do like the horse doctor who tends big animals. Meg resolved to get that practice at every opportunity.

Ice and snow were melting from the fields. The creek, suddenly overflowing, was rushing in torrents loud enough to be heard at the house. Meg liked to go to sleep and wake up hearing the sound of it. One night something woke her before dawn. She got quietly out of bed, Alice still sleeping beneath the quilts. Meg grabbed her jacket and went to look out the window, left open just a little to let in fresh air. Farther up the creek, she saw the three wolves. They had been drinking from the edge, one lying down, the others standing on either side. The two standing looked warily around.

Meg observed the wolves for what seemed a long time. There was something wrong with the prostrate wolf. The other two lifted their heads and howled. Meg's brothers stirred in their beds on the other side of the loft. Meg crept over to Stew and tapped his shoulder. She planned to ask him to go out with her to see what was wrong with that wolf.

"What the . . . !" Stew woke with a start.

"Shush up," said Meg. "I need you to go out to the outhouse with me. I'm scared and I got to go . . ."

"Use the dang pot," he whispered. "What's the matter with you!"

"I'm sick. Just come with me."

"What's up?" Dave spoke without moving.

"Would everybody shut up!" Joe whacked his pillow and sat up angrily. "Settle down, would you, Meg!"

The parents' bedroom door was flung open. "What in Tarnation is going on! Your mother needs her sleep. You lads . . ."

Meg came down the ladder. "Dad, please. It's me. Something's wrong with the wolves. Can you please come with me? Please."

When she went outside, with her father and Stew each carrying guns, the two standing wolves lowered their heads, ready to take on whatever came. Then the third wolf pulled herself up. Stew fired his gun in the air.

"Don't!" Meg tried to wrestle the gun from him. He held it above her head.

The wolves were running towards the woods. The third wolf staggered and fell to the ground. The other two stopped, crouched, and came back to sniff the fallen wolf. Meg, Herbert, and Stew watched, still and silent, from the other side of the creek. The wolves circled the fallen one, sat sentinel beside her, watched in the direction of Meg and company. They sniffed the fallen one again, then turning to the woods, they trotted then ran until they were hidden in the trees. But the sound of their howling in lament and decoy, rose loud and clear.

Meg ran to the fallen wolf, her father and brother behind her with guns, telling her to stop. They stood sentinel, ready to aim at the wolves in the woods while Meg bent down to examine the wolf. Her front paw had been severed. She was unconscious. Meg noticed her teats were prominent, her belly enlarged.

"Looks like she got caught in a trap," said Stew.

Meg hesitated then cautiously moved her hand to touch and stroke the wolf's side.

"Don't," said her father. "She might come to."

Meg continued to stroke the soft fur of her belly. "We have to help her. She's ..." Meg stumbled with her Victorian vocabulary. "She's, you know, like our mare ... in foal. If we stop the bleeding, maybe she'll live. Dad, please ..." she looked up at him. "Tell Stew to go get clean rags, a basin, hot water. Let's do what the horse doctor did when Nellie got that cut. Put a turn-key on it."

"This is a wild animal," said Herbert, feeling he was making a speech he didn't fully believe in. "She should be put out of her misery."

"Stew, give me your handkerchief," said Meg.

"What?"

"Your snot rag. Now!" Meg got up to grab it from his pocket.

"I'll do it," said Herbert. He drew out his own handkerchief and considered how he might approach the wolf to tie it on her bleeding leg.

"Let me!" Meg held her hand out. "Dad, please. We have to be quick."

He gave her the handkerchief and took up the more manly position of holding his gun to the wolf's head in case she revived and attacked his daughter. Stew did likewise from the other side of the wolf. Meg slid the cloth under the bleeding leg, formed a knot and tied it tight as she could. Then she did another one. "More rags. Hot water," she commanded Stew.

Stew stood stubbornly sentinel.

"Go, lad," said Herbert. "I've got the wolf covered." The muzzle of his gun was at the wolf's neck.

"Give me your hanky first." Meg held out her hand. "Hurry!"

"Bossy brat!" said Stew, but he ran to the house.

Meg examined the wolf as she lay unconscious, her mouth partly open. Not a young wolf. Her teeth were brown with tartar, two of the fangs broken. She had scars on her snout. Her fur was matted on her hind quarters, ready to be shed in the warmer season. There were burrs from previous autumns still lodged in the fur at the base of her neck where she couldn't reach to pull them out.

"Cold," said Herbert, speaking in hushed tone, lest the wolf be wakened. "It's cold you want to put on a bleeding wound. To numb it like. Gather some snow, Meggie, and cover the poor leg in it."

"You're right, Dad," Meg concluded. "It's hot water for birthing, isn't it?"

"You'll make a good midwife, Meggie."

"I'd like to be a doctor," said Meg, stroking the wolf, "of animals."

All the Wilkinsons were in attendance when the unconscious wolf was transported by wagon to be laid on a bed of straw in a corner of the drive shed. The buggy was moved outside where Emma hastily climbed into it demanding Alice sit beside her and the horse be hitched up, should the wolf wake up and escape. Meg set a pail of water near to the wolf, then was ordered out of the shed, the shed door locked. She and her brothers watched through cracks and knot holes in the board walls. They saw the wolf open her eyes and attempt to stand then sink down as her body began to contract. Meg flinched in empathy. Her father and brothers stood in watchful silence.

"What's happening?" Alice yelled.

"Quiet lass!" Herbert rushed to the wagon shaking his finger at her. "The wolf is birthing."

"I want to *see!*" She started to get out of the wagon as Emma tried to hold her back. "If Meg can, I can."

"Hush then!" Emma grabbed Alice's shoulder and climbed out of the wagon after her.

All had their hands and faces pressed up against the shed walls when the first pup was delivered by the mother wolf. She licked the glistening birth sack off the pup then chewed through the cord with her back teeth so it didn't bleed. Then she slurped up and swallowed the placenta before licking the pup again, encouraging it to nuzzle against her. She lay back briefly before a second pup and then a third were similarly born and taken care of, the placenta consumed.

It was at the swallowing of the placenta that Alice fled the scene, clamping her mouth as vomit arose. She didn't want to see any more births. Meg had to be wrenched away from the scene to come to dinner. She didn't want to leave the sight of this wounded wolf and the three suckling pups, ever.

"It's so icky!" Alice exclaimed, wrinkling her nose in the kitchen. "I hope it's not at all like that for humans."

"That wolf is a good mother." Emma was amazed at what she had seen the female endure. "But you must remember, Alice, animals are inferior to humans and birthing is natural and simple for them."

Inferior? Meg couldn't see anything inferior about this mother who gave birth to three, quietly, all on her own, having wakened in a nightmare place, with her leg severed. But Meg was taught not to oppose her mother. She kept her views away from her.

Ma Wolf, as Meg called her, accepted her confinement for a month. She had no real choice, since she couldn't dig her way out with no front leg. And when she attempted to gnaw her way through the shed boards, sheets of tin were nailed over the holes. Meg understood that Ma Wolf was terrorized by this strange imprisonment and by having a severed leg, though it was healing well enough and she was learning to hobble on three legs. Meg didn't want to add to the terror or endanger herself by entering into Ma Wolf's imposed cavernous den. She placed Ma Wolf's food and water in pails just inside the door, withdrawing fast, before the wolves made a move. She locked the door with new strong bolts. Gradually, Meg showed more of herself and talked to the wolves, but when Ma growled and bared her teeth, Meg got the message to back out of range.

All the Wilkinsons took an interest in the development of the mother and pups but it was Meg who observed and tended them every moment she was allowed, racing home from school, racing through all chores, in order to do so. She reported when Ma Wolf first cautiously tasted the meat in the pail, when she began to "wolf" it down and when she first fed chewed morsels to the pups.

"That means," said Herbert, looking down the table at Meg, "that soon you must release your wolves back into the wild."

"As soon as they can fend for themselves," said Emma, as she often had, pointing her finger at Meg. "That was the promise made. It's what's best for them."

"I know." Meg clenched her fists and bowed her head, holding back tears.

"Then maybe we won't be wakened every night with Ma Wolf howling for her pack," said Alice. "And them all howling back from the woods."

"And circling our house, ready to gobble up 'fraidy cats," big brother Andy scowled across the table at her.

"That's enough, Andrew," said Emma. "Alice is not unduly afraid of wolves. Nor, I must say, am I."

Everyone stared at Emma.

"Why do you all look so surprised? Haven't all of you seen the courage, the fortitude, the steadfast nature of Ma Wolf? And the faith of her pups? Are you so blind to virtue?"

Emma stood up and went to the oven. "But that doesn't mean," she concluded, donning oven mitts, "that they aren't wild animals and must therefore be returned to the woods."

This was the first clear memory Meg had of her mother coming round to any of her views.

On a Saturday, right after breakfast, Herbert and his sons took up their hunting rifles and marched out of the house like a small army, leading Meg to release her wolves. Emma and Alice watched from the garden gate. The pups were leaping up and scratching at the door as they did whenever Meg brought food, though they scattered and drew back when Ma Wolf growled and the door bolts were pulled back.

"Andy and Joe," Herbert commanded, "you lads guard the barn yard in case the pups take off in the wrong direction. Stew and Dave ... either side of the shed door. Meg and I will open it wide. Keep us covered."

"Little pups and a three legged mother against five armed men!" Meg scowled.

"You never know," said Herbert, "if someone gets between a pup and its mother ..." He kept Meg behind him as he unlocked and opened the doors, flinging one for Dave to catch as he held the other at an angle that let him and Meg stand behind it.

At first Ma Wolf would not come out. She hobbled around the pups trying to keep them encircled. But the pups were curious and adventurous. They scrambled out onto the driveway. Then Ma yelped and quickly took the lead, hobbling straight towards the meadow and creek. She looked back, seeing the Wilkinsons gathering in a line at the edge of the meadow but not pursuing further. She led her pups to the creek where she lay down for a drink and rest.

"It's too much," Meg cried. "Too soon. She's not strong enough."

Then Ma got up, considered crossing the creek where she was, but it was too rocky and fast-flowing. She led the pups to the wooden bridge and crossed over.

"See how smart she is!" Meg clapped.

In the meadow on the other side of the bridge, again Ma lay down.

The woods were another field away. The pups lay down near her, then got bored and began to romp around with each other.

"We can't stand here all day," said Emma. "There's bread to be made. And soap. Meg, the lye is ready."

"I'll do it," said Meg. It was outdoor work where she could keep a lookout for the wolves. "But please, Momma, just a bit longer."

"Yes," said Herbert. "Let's see what happens, Emma dear."

Ma Wolf let the pups play in the fresh spring grass while she hobbled around, testing her strength, looking sometimes to the woods, sometimes back to the shed and the family watching her.

"Maybe she'll come back to us," said Meg. "Maybe she knows we'll keep her pups safe and well-fed."

"Right!" said Dave. "Well fed upon your chickens and our livestock."

Ma Wolf stood still and howled. A small chorus answered then two wolves came out of the woods. Ma hobbled fast as she could towards them, her pups running with her. The pack, now of six, disappeared into the woods.

Late that afternoon, at the time she had usually fed the wolves, Meg, escorted by Herbert with his rifle, took a pail of meat and gizzards, to a pile of rocks near the woods. She set it down and howled in imitation of Ma Wolf. There was no answering howl. Meg and Herbert retreated to a distant stone pile and waited until Herbert lost patience and took Meg home. Meg lingered long at the garden gate, peering towards the rock pile near the woods. Yes! She could see Ma Wolf and the pups emerge. They were eating their food. Meg summoned her father and all to witness.

Soon Meg was allowed to leave food for the wolves, without armed escort. Each afternoon throughout spring, summer and into the autumn, she delivered their food to the rock pile. Sometimes Ma and the pups were visibly waiting for her, standing at the edge of the woods. Meg threw the meat from the pail into four piles on the ground, voiced a brief howl, then backed away. Always she stood out of range as they ran to the food and devoured it. They never approached her or tried to follow her home as a dog might. But they looked at her carefully, appreciatively. The pups grew into strong young wolves. They appeared less and less frequently with Ma who had become quite adept on three legs, but she could no longer hunt, and they were off, learning to do so.

One chilling cold and rainy afternoon in November when Meg was carrying a pail of chicken gizzards over the bridge, she looked towards the rock pile and saw Ma Wolf lying in its shelter. Meg talked to her as she drew cautiously closer. But Ma did not even lift her head. Her ginger eyes were still, her three-legged body lifeless. There were no marks of violence. Just a lifeless body.

Meg's brothers dug a grave near the rocks. Meg helped lower Ma Wolf's body into it.

Did she come here to die alone in a protected spot, Meg pondered through grief. Did she have an illness or a heart attack? The thought of poison did not occur to her until much later when she discovered the fate of the pups.

"Now what are you going to be," said Stew, "a wolf doctor?"

"There's no such thing," said Alice. "There's only horse doctors."

Ike's spirit hovered over the scene. He smiled upon Meg for rescuing the wolves but he approved even more her letting them go. As a child, he had loved wolves as she did though he had no fear of them, for he was familiar with their ways and wished only that he could be more like them. Then, out of love he created a vision of them which involved possession and ambition. It necessitated captivity and domination. But the end product was strong and handsome and very useful to people. He and Piji succeeded in creating a line of the most famous indigenous sled dogs of North America.

Discontented in life, Ike's spirit found reason for outrage in wandering through history. He saw his dogs, admired for their strength, intelligence, and supreme dedication, taken from the North Pole to the South, on voyages of important discovery. All very glorious, until he saw so many of them starved or driven to their death, some eaten by their human masters, who sometimes ate each other, to no avail, since they too soon died. In disgust and guilt, Iké slunk away from such scenes.

Seeing the dead body of Ma Wolf and Meg's grief, Ike was moved differently.

"That's nothing!" he wanted to shake Meg. "Nothing, compared to the pain and suffering I've seen inflicted upon wolves through the centuries that I've bounced around in my torment. Toughen up, girl. You're on the right track. You made it better for those wolves. Can you find your way to help my dogs?"

4

Parents First

Meg was fourteen when she graduated from the one-room local school. Her teacher was Jean Duncan, about to leave her profession to get married and become the wife of Dr. Atkins, a medical doctor in Halifax.

"I want to be a horse doctor," Meg said to her, lingering on the last day of school. "I mean a doctor of all animals, actually."

Jean thought carefully before responding, knowing her own struggle in becoming a teacher, which was an accepted and admired profession for unmarried women. "You are serious about this, are you, Meg?"

"Very."

"I have heard of women doctors, doctors of people, that is." She smiled. "They have a very difficult time, because people don't accept that they can be as good as men. They think they shouldn't try to be. They think a woman's place is in the home. Mind you, my fiancé doesn't think like that. He approves of women doctors. Though they have a tough go of it. It would be very hard to have children and be a doctor, of any kind."

"My mother's place has always been in the home," said Meg, then dared to add, feeling a sense of betrayal of her mother and her home life, but Miss Duncan was a woman she felt she could trust and might never have the opportunity to confer with again: "And my mother is as unhappy as can be."

"Oh dear, Meg, is that really true?"

"I think so. Maybe it's because she misses England and all that she had there. Or because she had six sons before she had me and Alice to help with the housework. She misses her sisters and other women to talk to. She doesn't like the farm but she won't go on trips to Halifax with my dad, because her clothes are old and out of fashion and don't fit right any more. She's over fifty now and says she's altogether too old and worn out."

Jean fiddled with her pencil, tapped its rubber head on her desk. "I see why," she said, "you want to be something different. A doctor of all animals." She reached for the big dictionary on her desk. "Let's look this up. I think there's a more correct word for this." She fingered through until she came to it. "Yes! Veterinarian. A surgeon of injuries and illnesses in animals." She showed the word to Meg. "Is that what you want to be?"

"I do," said Meg, feeling she must practise the pronunciation of this big word in private.

"I have never heard of a woman veterinarian, but there's always a first, at everything. Do you want me to talk to your parents about this?"

Emma was surprised to see Meg and Alice being driven home on the last day in their teacher's horse and buggy. She went inside to change her blouse and fix her hair.

"You must stay to tea," said Emma, standing on the porch. "We weren't expecting company but I do have a fresh strawberry pie, in honour of Meg's last day at school. It's not much compared to what we served at Squirrel Hall. But then, we're not in England, are we? Oh my, I'm a bit flustered. My husband and I have been making some plans in light of our daughter's finishing her schooling. Please excuse me. I'm overexcited. Meg and Alice, help your teacher down from the carriage. Miss Duncan, I'm pleased to meet you."

"Thank you, Mrs. Wilkinson. Thank you very much. I'd love to stay to tea." Jean glanced at Meg. *Is this the unhappy mother you described?*

"What's been going on?" Meg whispered to Alice.

"Don't ask me." Alice shrugged. "But looks like Mom is pretty happy about something."

Herbert emerged from the house and stepped quickly to the buggy. "Allow me." He shooed the girls towards the house. "Allow me, Miss Duncan. I'm Herbert Wilkinson. Most pleased to welcome you to our home."

Meg and Alice were instructed to set the table with the white linen cloth, silver spoons, and china cups brought from England. Cream was whipped into peaks which promptly sank in the heat of the afternoon, so it was left in the bowl and served "English style," clots of cream plunked onto the pie.

"Your daughter, Meg, has been consistently top of her class," said Miss Duncan, then noted Alice dropping her head. "Of course, Alice also does well."

"All our children do, if I may say so." said Emma. "Our sons have all moved on in the world."

"Yes. I've only had the pleasure of teaching your daughters. And now that Meg has graduated ..."

"She is to be commended," said Herbert in oratorical style as he raised his tea cup. "Here's to our Meg. She's always been an industrious lass. Turned a few hens into a right profitable business. And now that she's finished her schooling, we're willing to hand on to her the full responsibility of the household. Yes, Meg. You and Alice can feed and do for the lads while your mother and I take a long overdue vacation. Miss Duncan, you'll understand my good wife's excitement when I tell you, tell all of you," he nodded to Meg and Alice. "My dear Emma and I are taking a trip back to the old country."

"I congratulate you, sir." Jean said then turned to Emma. "And Mrs. Wilkinson."

"I only dreamed of it, over thirty years." Emma wiped the corner of her eye. "Over thirty years."

"When will you go?"

"In August," said Herbert. "I must come back in time for the autumn legislature but Emma may stay on over the winter. She has never enjoyed our winters, have you, my dear."

Jean looked at Meg who subtly shook her head and looked at the table. It was no use even asking.

"I hope you have a wonderful time abroad," said Jean. "I must be on my way now. This has been a lovely tea. Thank you. Thank you for including me in celebrating your plans. But there's something I want to put for your consideration. It has to do with further education for Meg. She wants to be a veterinarian. I would recommend her in applying for college entrance exams this September. And if this year is not possible, then she could use the year to study at home and do the exams next year."

Emma froze. Herbert coughed.

"It is a policy in our family," he said, "that one child is not given more than another. And certainly, a daughter cannot be favoured over a son. Our sons have managed well without further education, so too will our daughters."

Parents putting themselves first, thought Jean as Meg accompanied her to her buggy. How different they are from mine. My parents would do anything to give us the best education possible. As I intend with mine. How can there be any progress, with attitudes like theirs! That Mrs. Wilkinson was clearly to the manor born, and nothing here in "the colonies" will please her. She'll come back unhappier than ever. A natural-born snob if there ever was one. Oh well. Jean climbed into her buggy and looked at Meg. I musn't teach this bright young girl disrespect for her parents. I must give her hope, not despair. Jean, soon to be Mrs. Atkins, wrote her address on a piece of paper.

"This is where I'll be living in Halifax. I want you to call on me when you come to the city. I'll look into borrowing books for you to study at home."

The subject of further education for Meg was not raised again. Emma would not look Meg in the eye, though Meg felt her looking intently at her at times. Emma's manner with Meg was as though a distance must be maintained. But Emma was on no even keel in regard to their trip back to Yorkshire. The trip was on and then it was off. On again, off again.

The egg money was used to buy yards of cloth for new dresses for Emma. But Emma couldn't work the new sewing machine. She angrily pulled the cloth and broke the machine's needle. "Now look what I've done!" She cried and took to her bed. "I'm not a seamstress. I can make rough clothes for eight children but I can't make anything fine for myself. I'll never master that machine, let alone the dress patterns. And I can't go anywhere, looking the way I do. I'm *not going*!"

"I've put in a new needle," Alice called out to her then whispered to Meg. "And I bet I can follow this dress pattern." A passable wardrobe was assembled.

It was an unusually rainy July.

"The crops will be poor," said Emma. "We can't possibly afford to go now."

"The weather may clear," said Dave. "But no matter. The pork prices are good and we've got a bumper crop of pigs ready for market."

"It may be a good year for apples," said Meg.

"That's my little optimist," said Herbert, "always alert to a good profit. I'll put you in charge of the orchard this year. Let you see to the picking and the selling. With all your schooling, you could see to the bookkeeping too, couldn't you?"

"I've been doing that for years with the eggs."

"Now don't get lippy," said Herbert.

"She feels hard done by," said Emma. "She wanted that egg money for herself."

"Mother!" said Meg. "I never said that."

"You might as well have. The way you've been moping around ever since that teacher left. She put ideas into your head, didn't she? Well, I had to go to work for my living when I was your age. And I had to pay rent to my parents. You have it so much easier than I did. And you resent your father and I for taking this one trip, don't you!"

"Now, now Emma. Meg hasn't said that."

"Oh yes, she has. Just not in words. And I can't stand it. So I'm *not going*. There! Is everyone satisfied now!" Emma took to her room again.

They departed as planned on a modern ship out of Halifax harbour in August. But they returned together in October. A change of attitude had taken place in Emma. She had no desire to stay on in Yorkshire.

The voyage back to England had been such a contrast to the voyage to Canada thirty-some years earlier. The modern ship was enormous, luxurious, propelled by steam. It seemed to propel them smoothly over the ocean in no time at all. Whereas the earlier voyage she always remembered as one long vomit. That's what it was, one long vomit, during which she had thrown up everything but the baby within.

Then that first winter in the roughness and darkness of their log house. The frightening sound of wolves howling in the woods. The snow, bright and interesting at first, but then it piled up and stayed too long, making everything more difficult, the hauling of water, the clothing and washing and feeding of her babies and children. Everything more difficult and arduous than she had ever imagined life would be. When in domestic service at Squirrel Hall, her hours of work had been limited and paid.

Becoming a wife and mother, the mistress of Wolf Woods Farm, had seemed a bad deal, until she returned to England with Herbert and saw what had become of her sisters' grown-up lives. Her oldest sister, the one whose life had been ruined by getting with child, unmarried, had gone to Liverpool and never been heard from again. Her other sister, who was married and had the good fortune of few children, was wasting away of consumption. And no wonder! The small, damp, houses, smelling of the coal smoke that filled their lungs. Her third sister had married the lamplighter, who turned into a violent drinker and made their home a fearful misery. It was a mercy that he had died from the kick of a horse he had stumbled upon from behind. Her sister was better off as a widow who took in laundry and raised her three children herself, though one of them was sickly and would never be a help to her.

Emma came away from that trip home, feeling she had done very well in life, after all. She no longer saw herself as the lonely, fearful, weary, endlessly childbearing homesteader, but as the mistress of a prospering farm, with eight healthy children, and a husband who had become a respected politician. Her Yorkshire village now seemed diminished in size and prospects. She had choked on the coal fires, shivered in the dampness, found the buildings and the days dominated by the gloomy effect of grey and clouds.

Sailing back into Halifax harbour, Emma felt warmed by the sunshine and cheered by the colourful wooden houses. She had become a stranger in Yorkshire, but as they drove through the cobbled streets of Halifax, people waved and doffed their hats to her, the wife of Herbert Wilkinson. She smiled and nodded regally to them.

They spent a glamorous night in Halifax's biggest hotel, then next day purchased a gift they had agreed upon for Meg. Something she had wanted since she was a little girl. The others had gifts from England.

Meg and Alice had dinner prepared when Stew brought their parents from the stagecoach, down the lane of Wolf Woods Farm. Meg swung the gate open, welcoming them. Sitting in the buggy on Herbert's lap was a big black pup, which he lifted up to hand over to Meg. It looked like a small bear cub. "It's a Newfoundlander," said Herbert. "A rescue dog. You can swim in the ocean with it."

Meg called him Poley because of his roly-poly nature and bear-like appearance. She took him to the ocean where they swam long distances. He followed her everywhere he was allowed. Emma, in her newly acquired good humour, allowed him in the house but not up into the loft where he might sleep on beds. Alice objected to his being brought along to community social events such as the church picnic.

"No beaux will ever get near you," she said to Meg, "if you don't stop hauling that stupid bear around and hugging him in public."

"Love me, love my bear," said Meg, knowing that in fact young men would often approach the dog in order to gain introduction to her. And how they treated Poley was a good indication of their character. There were good characters around in the farming community, Meg concluded, but she was deeply dissatisfied within it. She felt trapped, caged, tied up. The more she thought about it, the more she longed to go to university and become a veterinarian.

"Why *not* become the first woman to do so?" Both Jean and Dr. Atkins had let that ring in her ears as a rhetorical question on the first visit she had paid to them while her parents were away. But longing is never enough. She came away with books to study. The challenge was getting the time to study.

The order of parents first at Wolf Woods Farm was stronger than ever after they returned from England. Emma put her new wardrobe to continued use in accompanying Herbert into Halifax for the opening of the new sitting of the legislature. Rather than obscuring the fact that she had been a servant at Squirrel Hall, Emma now spoke openly of it as part of the new opportunities she and her husband found in settling in the new world. Herbert would be seeking re-election in 1886. She gradually participated more in his campaigning, supporting as he did the building of the Canadian Pacific Railway that united the nation from the Atlantic to the Pacific Ocean. She took to reading newspapers as well as books. All this required time away from running the household. With Alice in school, the work was delegated to Meg.

"Your mother has come into her own," said Herbert to Meg one evening as they sat reading on the front porch. "She always admired my mother, and she reminds me of her more every day. There must be something in that old saying about the passing of one generation liberates another."

"I'm glad she's happy in her old age," said Meg.

Herbert looked at Meg then puffed at his pipe, gazing across the front garden where multicoloured hollyhocks grew at the rail fence, the creek meandered around rocks, and fat cows grazed in the meadow. "Your time too will come, Meggie," he said. "Don't think we don't know how unhappy you are putting your time in with the housework. But she did it for you, and me, for all of us, for far more years than you have lived."

Meg closed her book. She wanted to howl, howl like the wolves, her wolves who no longer howled in the woods. They had been exterminated.

"And don't think we don't know that all these books you're studying at every opportunity are for college entrance exams." Herbert avoided looking at her. "Sorry, Meg. I wish I had the money to send all eight of you there, but I don't. My own dream is to ride the new railroad from Halifax to Vancouver, with your mother, of course. But I don't have the money for that either."

5

RANDOLPH OLIPHANT IN HALIFAX

RANDOLPH OLIPHANT CUT QUITE A SWATH when he arrived in Halifax in 1886. He was the first passenger to alight from the first train to use the newly laid tracks coming eastwards from Vancouver to Halifax. Oliphant had such flair in dress and demeanour that reporters singled him out for interview. He did not disappoint them, with his readiness of comment and dramatic phrasing.

"Thrill of a lifetime," he said. "Absolute *thrill* of a lifetime to be so wonderfully transported across this wild young nation. Over the formidable Rocky Mountains, *flying* across the flat grasslands, *swerving* round great lakes, *racing* alongside the grand St. Lawrence, and finally coming to a halt in this *most* charming city. And do you know... it was all so smooth on that luxurious train, not a drop of champagne was spilled. Not a *drop*!" He gave pause for those who laughed or tittered then he pointed, with a swirl of his gold-tipped walking stick, to the harbour, the stone citadel on the hill, and the houses with their towers, porches, and trellises painted fanciful colours. "*Such* a pretty city! I plan to settle here. And you may quote me on that." Randolph Oliphant tipped his stylish hat.

The reporters stepped aside, some shaking their heads, some smirking, but all pleased with the colourful copy, as Oliphant made his way along the new station platform where a brass band was playing to the crowd that included the mayor, leading citizens, and politicians. Standing beside Joseph Howe, a Father of Confederation, was Herbert Wilkinson and family. Oliphant bowed to them in passing.

Meg noted everything visible about him. Light brown hair, blue eyes, unfashionably clean-shaven face. He wore a three-piece, fine wool suit with striped close-fitting trousers. His homburg hat was brushed to a shine, his shirt collar winged, his silk tie red paisley, a matching hanky protruding from his upper pocket. Porters followed him with not just one but two wagonloads of luggage.

When interviewed further by the press, Oliphant described himself as a man of many parts, a Continental who had a broom business in New York, which he had sold then moved to a gold-mining town in British Columbia where he had endured the tragic loss of his wife. She was *unparalleled* in womankind. He would mourn her to the end of his days.

What would he do in Halifax? Start another broom business and build himself a new house, with electric lights, telephone, and all. They would find him a sociable fellow. He liked to participate in theatrical productions and entertain at home on occasion.

"What rubbish they print in newspapers today!" Herbert turned noisily to another page. "Being the first off the train doesn't make him of endless interest."

When Emma read the article she put it down in distaste. "I'm sure it is of interest to every widow and spinster in the city. It sounds like an advertisement. Does the man have no shame?"

Meg and Alice sneaked the paper up to their bedroom. "He does sound rich," said Alice. "But if he acts on the stage, what lady would want him?"

"I'd like to meet him," said Meg. "He sounds interesting."

Halifax was a small city, dominated by British immigrants. Those who had grown rich in various businesses tended to socialize together, forming their own pack. But it was loosely ordered and open to newcomers of means who appeared similar to themselves. Randolph

Oliphant was welcomed, indeed lured into the social circle, but he proved to be a disappointment to eligible women, although he looked and behaved well enough.

He stayed at The Waverly, an inn of high repute on Barrington Street while he set about building a four-bedroom house on the outskirts of town and converting a warehouse on Upper Water Street into a broom factory. He said he was born into a family of broom makers in The Netherlands, then educated at Oxford. He kept a horse and covered buggy for use during the frequently inclement weather of Halifax, plus a handsome black steed for riding around town. He was a regular attendee and financial supporter of the theatres. He performed with great flourish in amateur theatre fundraising events. This decreased his attractiveness with a few ladies but so increased it with one spunky thirty-year-old widow of means that, after a lavish dinner party at her home, she contrived to detain Randolph after the others had departed and made a thinly veiled proposal to him.

A look of genuine sympathy and regret came over Randolph as he reached across the blue velvet chaise lounge and took her hand. "My dear Mrs. MacPherson, you are the loveliest of ladies. But everyone must understand, I simply cannot love again. My heart was taken by my Cecilia. It went with her. Do you understand? I simply cannot love again."

What tosh! thought Mrs. MacPherson. Pure melodrama.

When Randolph's house was built and furnished, he held a summer party, inviting a wide assortment of people, including the Honourable Member of the Legislature, Herbert Wilkinson and wife. Oliphant's housewarming party was the talk of the season. Surely he would entertain in the best style, having a house with such modern conveniences.

The house itself was wooden clapboard, gaily painted like other Maritime homes, though Oliphant's was more colourful than most, with red walls, corn yellow doors, and a wide wraparound verandah painted in two shades of sea blue. On the house top was a small "widow's walk" with a spectacular view of Halifax harbour, its small central island, and lighthouse. Fiddlers played merry tunes on the verandah. The many guests, greeted at the door by Randolph himself, were told to wander through the rooms as they wished. There was no staff to guide them, or indeed to serve the food and drink.

A keg of beer and bottles of wine were set out in the dining room where people were invited to serve themselves and construct their own sandwiches of freshly sliced warm roast beef and lettuce with pungent horseradish or sweet relishes. For dessert, there were raspberry tarts with dabs of soured cream.

This kind of party set the city circles talking with even greater perplexity about Randolph Oliphant. With such an expensive house, why didn't he employ more staff to entertain in finer style? Finger food was not the order of the day! Ladies with parasols and gloves simply couldn't cope with dripping beef in buns. They learned that he had only one servant, a housekeeper who lived out, in the Negro community. And there she was at the party, a Mrs. Rivers, spoken to by Oliphant as if she were a guest, though she was clearly more comfortable refurbishing the provisions and clearing away.

The exterior of the house was really too gaily painted, some decided. With people milling about, it looked like a circus carousel. The interior was also strikingly decorated, with dark green striped wallpaper in the entrance and dark red in the salon. But some ladies argued this was the height of Victorian fashion, as were the leather settee and armchairs. They had seen the like in Paris and London hotels. Then Randolph informed them that New York and Boston were his favourite haunts. His finer furnishings and large framed portraits of Mark Twain and Oscar Wilde had been brought from there. They were hung proudly in the entrance hall like family portraits. All the furnishings were arranged with such a good sense of comfort and décor that people were inclined to say the house had a woman's touch, but since it was Randolph's doing, they called it artistic.

Although there was no need for lighting on such a bright summer's day, everyone wanted to see the switching on of the light fixtures. There was electric lighting in some of the public buildings in

Halifax, but it was rare in private homes. As anticipated, Randolph called all to attention for the switching on of the lights. The ceremony was performed in the library where his impressive collection of books lined the walls and the chandelier of lights was brightest. Randolph raised his hand and turned the switch. "Let there be light!"

The light fixtures gave a brief flicker then expired.

"Ah well," said Randolph with a dramatic shrug. "Sometimes they work. And sometimes they don't. He giveth and He taketh away. Praise the Lord and pass the wine."

People could not decide if Oliphant was religious or sacrilegious.

"He certainly enjoys his drink," Emma observed to Herbert.

Guests followed Randolph upstairs where they found the eerie part of his home. One of the bedrooms was devoted entirely to his dead wife. It was painted a dusty pink with white trim. The velvet drapes were a darker shade of rose, with white lace hanging over the window panes. The single four-poster bed had a stack of white embroidered pillows propped up at the head and a soft high mound of covers topped with a pale green satin quilt. The white sheet with crocheted edging was drawn back over the quilt as though it were bedtime for the occupant.

"This is Cecilia's room." Randolph stood with his hand on the doorknob. "I had to part with my wife but I could not bear to part with her things. You may look in as you please. I must attend downstairs."

The gentlemen backed away but the women could not resist stepping in, looking curiously around at all the details. The dressing table with silver brush, comb, hand mirror, powder box, pearl necklace and earrings in a velvet box.

"This is like Miss Havisham's in *Great Expectations*," said Emma. "I can't quite believe it."

"These clothes are real enough," said another, opening the pine wardrobe, poking her nose amongst colourful silk evening gowns, cotton day dresses, a fine wool navy skirt with matching jacket and white blouse. "Wouldn't mind having these for myself."

Emma and others withdrew in distaste as the bolder and downright nosey pulled drawers open to see lace hankies, fine silk underclothes and nightgowns neatly preserved. In the dressing table drawer were lip colours, rouge, and eye powders.

"What kind of a woman wears rouge!"

"You'd be surprised. A lot do."

"I wouldn't want my husband to know all my beauty secrets."

"Ladies! We are speaking of the dead. Let us pay our respects. Cecilia was clearly beloved. Poor Randolph. I'm afraid he'll be in mourning for the rest of his life. He's a true Romantic."

"I find it all too extreme," said Mrs. MacPherson. "Honestly speaking, this room gives me the shivers."

But those who had not been rejected by Randolph felt sympathy for him in seeing the kind of shrine he had created in Cecilia's room. They wanted all the more to rescue him.

Appalled at the opening of drawers in another's household, and not inclined to gossip, Emma reported to her daughters only certain aspects of Mr. Oliphant's home and party. "I was most curious, "she said, "to see the workings of his telephone. But it was never put to use. I cannot imagine what it is like to speak to someone you can't see."

"I will have a telephone when I marry," said Alice. "I want a husband with a telephone and electric lights."

"Tell us more about Mr. Oliphant," said Meg. "His library. What kind of books does he have?"

"He's a well-read man," said Herbert. "I'll say that for him. He's a Liberal who keeps abreast of things. Quite a free thinker. He's actually much more serious minded than his manner suggests. There's more to him than meets the eye."

Although he was accepted into the pack at Halifax, Randolph remained a loner, wandering off a few times a year to New York and Boston, running his broom business, continuing to be a useful dinner guest, an affable host, and gentlemanly escort.

6

MEG MEETS MR. OLIPHANT

MEG WAS TOO YOUNG to be invited to city parties. But she found her own way of meeting the interesting newcomer.

"Dare me to sell some eggs to Mr. Oliphant?" she said to her brother Stew one Saturday after they finished delivering eggs in Halifax. "I've saved a dozen in this basket."

"You're joking. You wouldn't."

"Dare me."

"Done!" Stew struck the horse with the reins and soon they were bumping along up the road to Mr. Oliphant's. Poley, sitting in the back of the wagon, gave a woof at being so jostled then lay down to steady himself.

"And now I probably have half a dozen!" Meg held the basket of eggs as steady as she could on her lap while gripping the handrail of the wagon seat. She checked when they stopped at Oliphant's gate. "The top layer looks all right." She turned to Poley. "Poley, I want you to stay here with Stew. Stay!"

Poley sat up, looking sadly disappointed at this command, but stayed. As she walked along the stone path to the front steps, Meg looked up and saw someone quickly close the lace curtain across an upstairs bedroom. Whoever it was must have seen her. No chickening out now. She drew in her breath and proceeded to the front door knocker. She knocked once. No one came. Twice. Still no one. Meg looked back at Stew. He shook his head negatively and mouthed, "He doesn't want to see you."

Meg knocked a third and loudest time. Another wait. Meg turned to depart. She trudged down the steps. Then the front door opened.

"Hello there. You are quite a determined young miss, aren't you? I'm sorry but I do not take callers on Saturdays. I am busy with book-keeping."

"I sell eggs, sir." Meg was surprised at his appearance. He was known to be a dandy, a dapper Dan, with velvet jackets, brocade waistcoats, the works. But he stepped onto the verandah in his shirt-sleeves and trousers, not even a tie. There was interest in his eyes as he regarded Meg. She had dressed with meeting him in mind. Her dark blue school skirt and freshly washed white blouse, her Sunday jacket. She found hats a nuisance and had no money for a stylish one but she had tied her brown hair back with an expensive new red plaid ribbon. She hoped her face didn't look beet red as she felt herself blushing at her own boldness in disturbing this gentleman who was older than all her brothers, yet not the age of her father.

"Let us have a look at your eggs then, Miss ... ?" His eyebrows were raised and his smile welcoming as he invited her to introduce herself

"Wilkinson. Margaret, Meg Wilkinson, sir."

"Herbert Wilkinson's daughter? Well now, isn't this a pleasure! Perhaps you know I am Randolph Oliphant." He bowed. "I would take your hand but first you must be relieved of the burden of your egg basket. Won't you step inside? And your driver and his compan-ion? Would they too like to come in while we conduct our business?"

"That's my dog, Poley. And my brother Stew. Stewart. He has to stay with the wagon." She saw Stew's wide-eyed look as Randolph took the basket and gestured for her to come inside. "But he is dying to see your electricity, Mr. Oliphant."

"Well then, he had better tie up the horses and come inside. Would your dog, Poley, care to join us?"

"You don't mind? A dog in the house? He wouldn't damage anything. He's very well trained. He just likes to be near me."

"Perfectly understandable." Randolph beckoned Stew and Poley to join them inside.

They were invited into the salon, like guests, rather than vendors. Poley seated himself on the floor beside Meg's chair. Although three of the eggs had broken en route, Randolph insisted on paying for an entire dozen, scooping out the broken ones, gooey straw and all. He put them into a separate bowl, saying Mrs. Rivers, his housekeeper, would find use for them. He showed Meg and company round the ground floor, turning on the lights which worked better now that more houses in Halifax were hooked up to electricity. Meg was curious to see the dead wife's room but Randolph did not show them upstairs.

Meg was enthralled with his library. More books than they ever had at school. Leather wingback chairs. She was invited to sit in Randolph's desk chair which swivelled around. She put her hands on the edge of his large mahogany desk, looked at the open book of ledgers, the glass inkwell, the gold-trimmed ink pen, and informed him, "I'm good at arithmetic. My teacher said I should go to university."

"And will you?"

Meg looked away. "It's not affordable. Not even for my brothers. Right, Stew?"

Stew scowled at her. She was making their family sound poor. "Me and my brothers never wanted to go to any university. When I'm finished on the farm I'm going to be a fireman on the train. And then I might become the engineer."

"And what will you do, Miss Wilkinson?"

"I want to be a vet, a veterinarian."

"A horse doctor," said Stew with impatience, rolling his eyes to the ceiling.

"A doctor of animals," said Meg. "My mother calls it 'pie in the sky.' Completely impractical." She turned from Randolph to the ledgers on his desk. "But I could learn how to do these books."

"Meg!" Stew reprimanded her. "It's time to go."

"I keep the books for my egg business," said Meg. "In fact I can do all the farm accounts."

"I'm sure you can, with utmost competence." Randolph stood with one arm across his chest, the other reaching up to prop his chin as he scrutinized Meg. "When might you be delivering again?"

"Every Saturday, Mr. Oliphant. Do you want a dozen?"

"Plus conversation, please. I must learn more about this vet business."

"Please, sir. Do not encourage her." Stew pulled at Meg's arm. "Next she'll be on about the wolves."

Next Saturday afternoon. Randolph answered the door immediately, dressed nattily in pinstripe trousers, wine-coloured waistcoat, shirt and bow tie. But only Meg and Poley were at the door.

"My brother will be here soon," she spoke nervously. "He's having a pint at the Pig and Poke."

"Ah!" said Randolph. "Our conversation failed to interest him. And I have boned up on the subject of vets! And my good Mrs. Rivers has laid out a frothy lemon meringue pie plus quite a substantial pound cake, all concocted with your excellent eggs."

"He'll be here soon. He promised."

"Indeed he must, since a pretty young lady should not go about without a chaperone. And an old gentleman like myself must see that she is not compromised."

"You're not old, Mr. Oliphant, are you?"

"I've hit forty, my dear, forty!"

"Oh." Meg was surprised and thought, that *is* old. "I'm nearly seventeen. I'll be seventeen in August."

"I thought you were eighteen, ready for university entrance."

"My brother is eighteen. I'm ..." Meg looked down at her basket of eggs, feeling suddenly inadequate. "I'm still studying, on my own, for the entrance exams."

"Come in, Miss Wilkinson." He put his hand on her shoulder

encouragingly and led her into the salon. "I'll make a pot of tea. Come along. You put the eggs into a bowl in the kitchen while I put the kettle on. Yes. What we'll do is have our refreshments on the verandah, in plain view of all nosey people, while we await your brother. I want to hear *all* about your wolves. And where would you like to go to veterinary college? Toronto or Montreal? You see, I have done my homework. Oh yes I have. It's quite easy these days, with a telephone. I simply phoned the operator and had her find their locations for me. This is quite a new profession you have chosen. These vet colleges are almost as young as you are."

Meg began to smile, and laugh, and talk, as she had never done before. But she choked as she told Randolph what had happened to her wolves.

"After the death of Ma Wolf, the mother, I kept going to the rock pile, at least once a week, in the early evening when the wolves are on the prowl. I would howl, as much like them as I could, and they would answer. Yes they did! I kid you not."

Randolph who had looked mock sceptical, leaned across and put a wisp of her hair back in place. "I believe you, my dear. Believe me I do. I've read a bit about wolves myself, though I've never had the privilege of meeting one. Do carry on."

Seeing that he was genuinely interested, she continued. "The young wolves answered. I knew their sound. There was also the howl of the two older wolves. They often came to the edge of the woods and stared at me. When I walked away, they came out and ate the bit of food I left. I never left much because I wanted them to depend on their own hunting, not on me."

"Wise," said Randolph, pointing his finger approvingly. "Most considerate. And important. Wolves are not dogs."

Meg looked quizzically at him.

"The rest of your story," said Randolph, sitting up stiffly in anticipation. "Don't keep me in suspense."

"Then we got new neighbours. The MacDonald family. They bought the property on the other side of the woods. We visited them, brought them eggs, a chicken, welcoming gifts, and told them about our wolves in the woods. Mr. MacDonald scowled. Told us wolves will eat livestock, poultry, kill your dog, your children, everything that moves.

"Nothing my father or I said could convince him otherwise. My father is a forceful speaker and gets along with most people, but he ended up saying, 'Mr. MacDonald, I must warn you, sir, that the wolves live on our property. They are our property. It is against the law to do harm or damage to someone else's property.' Then..." Meg choked.

Randolph moved to sit beside her on the settee. He put his hand on her shoulder. Poley stirred then relaxed his head back down upon his front paws when he saw that Meg was not displeased with the hand upon her shoulder.

"You must tell me the rest," said Randolph.

"After that, sometime after that, when I called the wolves, they didn't answer. For two evenings they did not answer. Then my father agreed to get in the buggy and drive straight to the MacDonalds.

All the wolves were there, hauled into his barn, dead. He was skinning them.

He said they had come onto his property and were threatening his livestock, so he had the right to kill them. While he kept talking with my father, I examined their bodies. They each had only one bullet wound, perfectly placed. How could that happen? I know. I know he had poisoned them. Lured them onto his property with poisoned meat. They suffered a horrible death. And then he shot them, to make it look like he was defending his..."

Randolph put his arm fully around Meg and squeezed her shoulder.

"I know that's what he did. That's how he used my telling him how friendly they are and how I sometimes fed them." Meg wiped her eyes then folded her arms firmly across her chest. "I'll never trust," she said, "never again, in the goodness of people."

"A sensible conclusion," Randolph conceded, putting his finger to the corner of his eyes and began to discuss the issue with her. "One should believe in goodness. But as for people...ah, such complex creatures..."

When Stew came stumbling through the gate, Randolph was sitting with his arm around Meg. He stood up at Stew's approach. "Hello Master Stewart. You have come upon us in tears. I have just heard the sad story of Meg's wolves."

Stew hiccoughed.

Bumping along the dirt road back to the farm, Meg had much time to think. Stew had let her take the reins since there was no one around to see that he was not in the driver's seat. He was sprawled out on the wagon floor, snoring off the effects of pints of strong ale, while Poley was forced to sit up for lack of space amidst the empty egg baskets and town purchases. During the last hour of the ride, Stew woke and climbed over the seat to take the reins so that he would be seen driving up the lane in sober posture.

"You don't tell on me and I won't tell on you," he said.

"I have nothing to hide," said Meg.

"Oh, yeah? Practically sitting on old Oliphant's lap, on the front porch! What if that gets back to Mom and Dad?'

"He was just comforting me. He is the kindest man I've ever met. I've never found anyone so interesting and easy to talk to. We talked about everything. Animals, ideas, schooling, upbringing, ambition. He sees nothing wrong with girls having as much ambition as boys, women wanting to do jobs normally done by men. And he says that in the best of all possible worlds, everyone would have as much education as they want. He himself was educated at Oxford and he said it was the best time of his life. He thinks it truly unfortunate that everyone doesn't have similar opportunity..."

"Oh knock it off, Meg!" Stew snapped the reins. "That's all just easy talk from a rich man. Doesn't do a whit of good for me and thee, as our Mom would say."

"Mr. Oliphant wants to help me with my education. He says he could tutor me to pass the university entrance exams. And he will ask Mom and Dad's permission."

"Tutor you? What's that supposed to mean?"

"Lessons. If I had weekly lessons throughout the summer, I could probably pass the entrance exams, get into university and eventually vet college."

"As if our parents would let you do that! Even if there was money for it, which there ain't."

"I could pay for the lessons by keeping Mr. Oliphant's accounts for him. If I got into university, I could pay it all back once I started working."

"Meg, you are dreaming. You have no sense of practicalities. There are no women vets and there never will be."

Meg fell silent. What a difference between talking to a stranger like Oliphant and talking to her family. With Oliphant she could let her thoughts and hopes and plans soar. But her family was like an anchor, dragging her down, keeping her in the one position they were familiar with. If she wanted to get anywhere different, she'd have to break free.

"I'm not saying you're not good with animals, Meg," said Stew. "Your chickens come running to you like puppy dogs. And there's no denying you had those wolves dang well tamed. But horse doctoring is different. You have to be strong as a man to handle a horse. Or a cow. Or an old sow. That's what horse doctoring is all about. And I haven't even mentioned shooting horses. You have to, if they break a leg or anything. You know that. You wouldn't want to have to do that, would you?"

Meg refused to answer. She felt like crying. But damned if she would.

"I have an idea," said Stew as they turned into the lane of Wolf Woods Farm. "You know what you should do, being as you're so good with animals, taming them and all?" Stew turned to her, bright eyed with his own inventiveness.

"What?"

"Join the circus. Become an animal trainer. You'd be very good at that."

Meg pictured herself in the circus posters she had seen in Halifax, dressed like a ballerina, standing on the back of a pony, balancing on one toe, riding round and round the circus ring. She burst out laughing. "Good plan, Stew. Good backup plan."

She felt better, and better prepared to meet the opposition of her parents.

"What'd you bring me?" Alice called out as she ran to the gate, taking a ride on its cross-board as it swung open. "You're in trouble, you two. You're late! Mother is wringing her hands with worry. Father has had to help milk the cows. So guess how mad he is!"

Herbert came to the doorway. "Put the horses away and come to the table, straight away. You will explain yourselves after the meal."

In the imposed silence of the meal, Meg was summoning up arguments, feeling nothing but opposition within her family, whereas when she had talked with the Atkins and now Mr. Oliphant, she felt encouraged, stimulated, and more clarified about what she could do with her life. Invited to a Saturday lunch at the Atkins, she heard inspiring concepts. "To ease, to cure, to prevent suffering," Dr. Atkins had said. "That's the basic calling."

The first words permitted at this supper were her father's saying, "Meg and Alice, you may clear up."

"There's rhubarb pie for dessert," said Emma. "I'll bring it in."

"Dessert is for the deserving," said Herbert when Emma sat down with the pie and a pitcher of cream. "Meg and Stew, explain yourselves. Why were you so late?"

"Mr. Oliphant invited us to come in for tea," said Meg. "We talked a long time. He asked if I would accept the job of doing accounts for him on Saturdays throughout the summer. In exchange he will tutor me for college entrance exams."

Emma gasped and put her hands over her mouth.

"My other plan," said Meg, "would be to join the circus."

Emma put her hands over her entire face. There was a drawing in of breath around the table. Herbert slammed both hands onto the table. He stood up.

"Young lady!" He glared at Meg. "You will not make idle threats to your parents. And no daughter of mine will spend Saturdays, or any other day, or night, in the house of a man, un-chaperoned!" He leaned onto the table, lowering his head menacingly. "You will not accept Mr. Oliphant's indecent proposal. I have spoken!" He stood up rigidly.

Meg stood up. "Father, I am almost seventeen. Mr. Oliphant is an honourable man. It was I who made the ... the business proposal." Meg's face was red, her arms straight at her side, her fists clenched. "And I will honour it."

Herbert recognized in Meg his own rebellion, negotiating skill, and tenacity. But he found himself responding initially just as his father had. "You will honour *me*. Or not darken my door again."

There was nowhere to go in their small house in order to make a dramatic exit except to the bedroom. It was too early and undignified to go there. Herbert took his pipe and tobacco and stomped out onto the porch, yanking the door closed behind him. He sat on the squeaking rocking chair, hearing through the open window, lowered voices and the sound of dishes being done. He finished a pipeful of tobacco and batted at the insects beginning to swarm around him. He re-lit his pipe, wishing he could think of a way of retracting his ultimatum without losing face. He wished he had been able to visit his parents occasionally before they died. The prospect of not seeing his daughter again, the one he thought so like himself it was a wonder she hadn't turned out a boy ...

Emma opened the door and steered Meg onto the porch.

"Herbert, dear, Meg did not mean to appear disrespectful of you, or to be misleading in the recounting of events. She is sorry for that. And wants to ask something of you, as her father." Emma stood beside Meg. "Carry on, Meg. Ask your father."

"Father," said Meg tensely. "Would you please accompany mother and me to Mr. Oliphant's? He does want to discuss acceptable... arrangements."

Herbert emptied his pipe. "I will most certainly not allow the two of you to go alone."

In the privacy of their bedroom, Emma explained to Herbert. "It's the lesser of two evils. She would run off to the circus, or the theatre. It's what rebellious girls like Meg do these days. Better she should work for Mr. Oliphant. She's too headstrong, but not a foolish girl. No daughter of mine will let a man take advantage of her. Our Meg would run and hide in a haystack, if necessary."

Emma put her arm around Herbert as he lay beside her, something she would never do while she was young enough to get pregnant.

A wagonload of Wilkinsons arrived at Oliphant's gate the following Saturday. Stew and Dave were to go off to market. Alice, now fourteen, was not to be left behind. She had curled her golden-brown hair in rags for the occasion and wore her pink dress, the only one she had that was not a hand-me-down from Meg.

"It's not fair," Alice had argued when they were doing the dishes the night before, "that Meg gets everything she wants and I have to stay on the farm."

"*I'm* the one who's had to stay on the farm, for over *two years*," said Meg.

"And you've done nothing but study your stupid books!"

"If that were only true!" Meg gripped the dish pan.

"And now you're calling me a liar. Mother, please. I'm too old to be babysat by my brothers. Why can't I too meet Mr. Oliphant? I'll sit quietly out of the way while you and father talk to him. Please, Momma."

Meg cringed at what Mr. Oliphant would think when he saw the wagon full of her family arrive at his doorstep. But the boys quickly drove off with the goods for market and the door was not opened by Randolph Oliphant but by his housekeeper.

"Mr. Oliphant will see you in the library," said Mrs. Rivers.

But he came into the hall to greet them. "Mr. and Mrs. Wilkinson! How good of you to come. And what have we here? Two Miss Wilkinsons! This must be your little sister?"

"Yes," said Meg. "This is Alice."

Alice smiled sweetly and curtsied slightly, offering her hand.

Randolph took it briefly, then spoke indulgently yet disinterestedly, as to a child. "You must want to see the electrics," he said. "And perhaps the phone? Mrs. Rivers, would you kindly give this pretty child a tour of the house and whatever delights from the kitchen you have to offer, while we discuss our business in the library? Thank you, Mrs. Rivers. Oh, and morning coffee ... you will have some won't you, Mrs. Wilkinson, and Mr. and Miss Wilkinson?"

"Yes, please," said Meg, never having been served coffee before.

"Bring it to the library please, if you will, Mrs. Rivers."

Randolph sat in the chair behind his desk. He was very polite and very business-like, indicating this was a meeting for which he was well prepared but there were others he must get on to.

"I spoke with your daughter's former teacher, Mrs. Atkins," Randolph addressed the parents. "And her husband, Dr. Atkins, who is also my physician. They have, as you know, entertained your daughter occasionally and loaned her books for further study. I have been assured that Miss Wilkinson will be a most competent bookkeeper. And Mrs. Atkins is confident that with weekly coaching Miss Wilkinson could pass university entrance exams. Also, she's willing to fill in for me when I take a trip to New York or Boston, as I do from time to time. All of which makes this a mutually satisfactory arrangement. Do you agree?"

"Mr. Oliphant," said Herbert, "I am concerned about propriety."

"As indeed am I, sir. It is why I have asked Mrs. Rivers to be in attendance on Saturdays, for the duration. Fortunately, as you can see, she has agreed."

"Herbert," said Emma, too intimidated to address Randolph directly, "we are concerned about Meg's future. She must not be given false hopes. What is the good of passing university exams when she cannot afford to attend?"

"Mother . . . ," said Meg.

"Hush, Meg," Herbert interrupted her. "I guess we'll have to cross that bridge when we come to it, Emma dear. Passing the entrance exams can't help but be a feather in our daughter's cap."

"If I may say this," Randolph lapsed momentarily out of business mode. "My dear Mrs. Wilkinson, how can there be false hopes when the future is so unpredictable? One thing leads to another in surprising ways. And it is a fact that there are scholarships. Benefactors have been known to appear out of thin air." Randolph stood up. "I believe Mrs. Rivers has our coffee ready. I would like to say one thing in conclusion. You have here . . ." he looked at Meg, then at her parents. " . . . an exceptional daughter." Then he looked away. "Please excuse my sentimentality. But she is the daughter my Cecilia and I longed to have."

"I like his house," said Alice, as she closed the gate behind herself and her parents. "But I don't like him. Nor his fat darkie servant! Why'd you leave me stuck with her for so long?"

"Alice!" Herbert and Emma turned on her simultaneously.

"Your grandmother would have your mouth washed out with soap for speaking like that," said Herbert. "You apologize immediately and show respect for servants and Negroes henceforth, or . . . or else!"

Both Herbert and Emma stood their ground until Alice said, looking to the ground, "I'm sorry."

But that night when Alice recorded the day's events in her diary, she wrote: *What I'm really sorry about is that it's Meg who has all the luck and what's left for me?*

7

What Oliphant Was Hiding

Ike was not drawn to Randolph Oliphant, even though it was none other than Randolph who possessed the written story of Ike's life. No, Ike saw so little of the wolf in Randolph, he found it hard to give him due heed... until Meg was so clearly drawn to him. Practically chased him down. Modern females could be very aggressive. But then his own Piji was never one to cower. People are different yet not so different when you observe them through the centuries, Ike concluded, as he hovered over Meg. He began to see Randolph through her eyes and became alarmed at how blind she was to his hidden nature. If she would only get my story and run, thought Ike. If only...

OVER THAT SUMMER OF 1887, the territory of Meg's life expanded from Wolf Woods Farm to the city of Halifax, to the entire world. Thanks to the books, the conversations, and the outings Randolph Oliphant provided for her.

During the previous two years she had read and made notes on the books recommended by the Atkins to cover the secondary school studies she needed for university entrance, so that during the summer with Randolph, she had only to review notes and write tests and essays designed by him in concert with Jean Atkins.

European history, British literature, mathematics, some Latin and basic biology were all enlivened by Randolph's theatrics. He strutted round the library, struck amusing poses while balancing on the ladder reaching to the high shelves or reclining on the chaise, and changed his accent in imitation of various teachers he had had during schooling in Amsterdam and Oxford. Meg laughed most when he played the petulant, childish professor who pouted and stomped his foot in impatience. But it was his embellishments of the subjects themselves that expanded Meg's thinking.

He told her about what he called "The Subversives." Darwin, the scientific thinker who said humans evolved from animals and thereby provoked new interpretations of the Bible and questioning of purpose in creation; or political and economic theorist Karl Marx, who undermined capitalism with socialist concepts such as "from each according to his ability, to each according to his need"; the philosopher John Stuart Mill, who subverted hierarchies and was used to support democracy with his moral rule, "the greatest good for the greatest number."

Meg took hold of these ideas and gnawed on them hungrily. She wanted more than ever to go to university, where she expected unorthodoxy and open-mindedness would be part of everyone's conversation.

Randolph also often alluded to the unconventional life of artists, informing Meg of women writers like George Sand in France, who took on a male name and wore men's clothing in order to get about more easily in a man's world. He spoke of artists' communities in England, led by Rossetti and William Morris, where all kinds of art was produced, from poetry to paintings, furniture and fabrics. Randolph did not say so clearly, but Meg suspected the living arrangements in such communities were not of the normal order.

Randolph's personal favourite amongst The Subversives was the contemporary writer, actor and lecturer, Oscar Wilde. Randolph had

memorized many of Oscar Wilde's sayings and liked to impart them
to Meg. Only one stuck in Meg's mind: "Nothing is worth doing
except what the world says is impossible."

She was more intrigued by Randolph's fascination with Oscar
Wilde than she was with Wilde's sayings, which she found eventually
repetitious. When she analyzed them, most seemed to involve a simple reversal of conventional sayings. Yet she worried that there had
to be more to them than she was appreciating, since they so appealed
to Randolph. She noted the one he liked to say with the greatest flourish, raising his arm high into the air and pointing vigorously skyward
with his finger, "My *life* is a scandal."

He would shake his head emphatically as he spoke, then laugh and
explain that that was just how Oscar Wilde himself had said it. Randolph had seen him on stage in New York during Wilde's 1882 tour
of North America. "And now the man is married," Randolph said to
Meg. "Married in '84. Hard to believe of the man who said, 'bigamy
is one wife too many. As is monogamy.'"

Meg secretly hoped that one day she might accompany Randolph
on one of his trips to New York to see such famous performers and
theatre, opera, and ballet. But she also questioned what she was being
taught.

"It seems," she said to Randolph as she handed to him an essay
on the French Revolution, "that everything important happens in
Europe. Aren't there any books about our own history? I would like
to know more about life in Canada, in North America. We didn't
come from nothing! There were people here, and animals."

"Indeed!" said Randolph, his eyebrows raised in mock surprise.

"I'm serious." Meg frowned at him. "I don't want to be ignorant of
the world, or my parents' heritage. Or Oscar Wilde." She half smiled.
"But there must be books about my own country I can study."

"Ah! But they would not help you pass your entrance exams," said
Randolph. "When that is accomplished..." He stood up from his
desk, walked round to her and led her by the hand to sit her down
in his desk chair while he took his keys from his pocket and dramatically unlocked the bottom desk drawer from which he withdrew a

dog-eared, handwritten manuscript and placed it on the desk in front of her. "Then, and only then, I will consider giving you this ... this truly indigenous history to read."

It was entitled "Ike's Working Wolves."

Randolph could not be persuaded to show or discuss the manuscript again. "I obtained it from a dear, exceptional friend in unhappy circumstances," he said as he locked it away. "I have tried to get it published for her, but I am told it is unsuited to our times. 'Vulgar writing,' they say. It must wait until you're over eighteen, or have graduated from university."

Randolph could be infuriating at times, with his extreme sense of drama, but Meg was intrigued with him. And she missed him sorely when he went on a trip to Boston in August. She found her lesson with Mrs. Atkins dull and herself heavy-hearted, even though Jean Atkins was the most compatible and encouraging woman she knew. Randolph returned in time for Meg's birthday and insisted on taking her to the theatre in Halifax as her present.

"I'm afraid my parents ..." Meg began.

"Bring them along," said Randolph. "And your petulant sister, if we must. I'll put you all up in the Waverly Inn. There can be no objection to that."

But there was, from Herbert. "If my wife and daughters are going to the theatre," he said. "Then it is I who shall see to it. Randolph Oliphant will be our guest. I shall be no more beholden to him."

"As you wish," said Randolph

Meg had never had a birthday party, let alone such a sophisticated and cultured one. She was enthralled with the theatre and found the melodrama hilarious. Alice poked her, telling her to shush since no one else took it quite the way Meg did, except for Randolph, who seemed similarly amused. Emma thought the play foolish compared to a good novel but she couldn't help smiling with pleasure during the performance and clapping enthusiastically at the end. Herbert enjoyed being the host of this party for his daughter, who was whis-

pered to be the chosen protégé of Randolph Oliphant. Herbert nodded in recognition of the approving glances of prominent citizens
noting his presence with Oliphant, the popular supporter of Halifax
theatre.

Scrutinize as they did, no one found anything but proper behaviour on the part of Oliphant, though Herbert noted with a pang of
jealousy that his daughter shared more laughter and repartee with
Oliphant than she ever had with him.

"My accounts have never been in better order," Randolph said to
Herbert and Emma at dinner after the theatre. "I do owe your daughter more than a few tutorials."

Emma felt alarm. What would Meg be offered next? But Randolph
simply paid for the dinner, an offer Herbert was relieved to accept.

Randolph Oliphant was the well-groomed, well-behaved, perfectly
obliging gentleman and all went well until a couple of weeks before
the scheduled entrance exams. Then suddenly, midweek, a messenger came to Wolf Woods Farm saying that Mr. Oliphant was indisposed and Meg was to go to Mrs. Atkins for her final lesson before
the exams.

Indisposed. What could that mean? Anything from unwilling, to
flu, to heart attack. What had happened? What had come up?

Meg's lesson was set for mid-morning. She left Stew at the market
as early as he would agree to but still there was time only to drive by
Mr. Oliphant's house. All the drapes were drawn across the windows.
Meg drove on to Mrs. Atkins'. Poley lumbered up to the door with
her.

"Come in, Meg. And Poley." Jean Atkins smiled, trying not to look
anxious. "It's such a lovely sunny day, isn't it?"

"Please, may I ask," said Meg before sitting down at the table,
"do you know what is wrong with Mr. Oliphant? All his drapes are
drawn."

"We should do our work first, my dear. This is the last lesson before..." Mrs. Atkins saw Meg was so disturbed she concluded, "you won't be able to concentrate until you hear, will you?"

"No, ma'am."

"But then we will do the final review. You must put your mind to the task at hand. It is Mr. Oliphant's insistence as well as mine."

"I will."

"Well then, the good thing is, there is apparently nothing incurably wrong with Mr. Oliphant. Last Sunday afternoon, the neighbours say they saw his housekeeper call in on him, though normally she works only Tuesday through Saturday. He drew his drapes immediately after her departure and she hasn't returned since. The neighbours knocked on his door to see if he needed anything. There was no answer. They grew more worried and persisted, until he opened the door and told them in no uncertain terms to leave him in peace. But his appearance was so, shall we say, dishevelled, that they came to our door to ask Dr. Atkins to call in on him."

"When was that?"

"Wednesday. Wednesday morning. Mr. Oliphant opened the door when he knew it was Dr. Atkins. Mr. Oliphant was...in a sorry state...but clear-headed enough to make arrangements for your lesson today. Meg, he wants nothing to interfere with your exams." She looked kindly but firmly at Meg. "He wants no visitors. None at all."

"This doesn't make sense. What is 'in a sorry state'?"

"Meg, are you old enough to know about these things? A binge? Men who go on binges, of drink? It is an unfortunate weakness. All too common, particularly amongst people who live alone. Though we are quite surprised to find it in Mr. Oliphant. It is better not to speak of it. Just let it pass. You never know what brings it on. But women must steer clear of it. Do you understand that, Meg? My husband will keep a watch on the situation and let us know when Mr. Oliphant is...himself again. In a few days, I'm sure." Mrs. Atkins put her hand flatly on the table. "Now let us concentrate on our lesson."

When the lesson was finally over, Jean Atkins smiled ruefully as Meg rushed to the door. "Where are you off to now?" she asked.

"I have to pick up my brother Stew." Meg had her foot out the door.

"Then straight home?"

"Yes."

"Good girl. And good luck next week on the exam. Will your father take you there?"

"Probably," said Meg, but she was already determined that Randolph would be well enough to do so, if he wished.

She drove to the market and told Stew she wanted to spend a couple of hours in the library. He looked at her quizzically.

"Don't you want to go to the tavern?" she challenged him.

"So where do I meet you? Old Oliphant's library, or the public?"

"Don't call him that."

"You're not to visit if he's alone."

"I know that."

"So I'll see you at the public in a couple of hours."

Meg left the horses out of sight in Randolph's driving shed, instructing Poley to lie down in the wagon and wait for her. She walked up the back path, carrying a basket of eggs and thinking of the story of Little Red Riding Hood visiting her grandmother, who turned out to be a wolf in grandmother's clothing. I'm not afraid, she smiled determinedly, of Randolph Oliphant or of wolves. She approached the kitchen door. There was a nicely inscribed card pinned above the doorknob.

Illness. No callers, please.

Meg drew in her breath and tried to open the door. It was locked. She went to the back steps of the verandah and walked stealthily around to the library window. It was open. She put down the basket of eggs and put her head inside the window. She saw him, eyes closed, splayed out on the chaise lounge.

"Mr. Oliphant! Wake up. Please wake up!" Meg pushed the window farther up and climbed inside.

"My little Meg..." He stretched his hand out to her as he lay on the chaise, a crystal whisky decanter and emptied glass on the table beside him. "Aren't you the brave girl! Climbing in a window to visit the likes of me. You shall be rewarded. Yes you shall."

"Mr Oliphant, what is the matter with you? You have to tell me. I won't leave until you do."

"Ah, you shall hear soon enough. It's only a matter of time. Once I've been seen, it gets out. Goes aaalllll," he waved his arm floppily, "aaallll around town. I'm an embarrassment, a disgrace to mankind. My *life* is a scandal." He waved his other arm floppily into the air. "I have to leave town." He closed his eyes. "But I'm sick of it. Sick to death." He flopped his hand onto his head. "Oh God! My poor house-keepers. I've been careful, all my life. Never wanted them to see. But it's always they who find out. They come upon one so unexpectedly. Poor old Mrs. Rivers. What a shock for her. So now I must leave. Once and for all." He turned to Meg. "I have been happy here. Happy in Halifax." He laughed at the sound of that. "Happiest with you, my dear young Meg. Until my secret got out." He held her hand with both of his. "If I could have been a normal man, I would have taken a wife and had a daughter as delighting as you. Will you remember that about me, my dear girl, when I'm gone?"

"Mr. Oliphant," Meg had to laugh. "You are such a dramatist! Making a mountain out of a mole hill. You are not dying. You're just on a ... binge. You don't need to leave town. People don't mind that much. What you really need is some tea. Some very strong tea. You can't even remember that you had a wife. Your beloved Cecilia."

Randolph looked at her sadly. He let go of her hand.

"No, my dear Meg. I have never had a wife. Cecilia is my great fiction and my incorrigible truth. Cecilia is my other self. The strongest tea in the world will not rid me of the need to be her. Could you ever understand that? Every so often I need to dress like a woman." Randolph lay back and closed his eyes, exhausted by his confession and by being drunk for several days.

Meg backed away. She sat down in a chair to absorb what he had said.

"I'll make that tea," she said and disappeared into the kitchen.

When Randolph came to, Meg was trying to pull him up into a sitting position and offering him tea. "It seems so unfair," she said. "I have worn my brother's trousers and been called a tomboy. But I wouldn't get run out of town for it."

Randolph smiled. "There is more to it than that, I'm afraid."

Meg was thinking as hard as she could. "It's something you did as a child but never outgrew?"

"The desires do wane as one grows older, my dear. But unfortunately they still rear their ugly heads. I have tried to purge them. There are clubs for people like me. It's why I go to Boston. I come back thinking I can do without it for a long time. But ... I was dressed ... as Cecilia ... last Sunday when Mrs. Rivers came unexpectedly to retrieve her umbrella."

"How did she find you? Where?"

"I was in the kitchen," Randolph smiled weakly as he lifted his tea cup. "Making some of this."

Meg imagined the scene. "Why didn't you just say that you miss ... your wife, so much you sometimes put on her clothes? People do wear dead people's jackets and such."

"And wig and make-up, shoes, and ... underclothes?"

"You wear all *that*?"

"I do."

Meg swallowed. "But that's all you do? You don't ... inflict yourself on others, do you? Mrs. Rivers was just shocked. You didn't actually hurt her?"

"No, never. Mrs. Rivers was struck dumb, as I have come to expect. I asked her if she would return to work The answer was no. I gave her some extra wages. She said I could trust her to tell no one but I know I cannot. It will always come out. People just cannot manage to keep that kind of secret."

Meg stood up and paced like a man. "I beg to differ, Mr. Oliphant. Your secret is safe with me."

"My dear girl." Randolph held out his hand to her. "Come here. Are you not curious as to why I would tell you?"

"Because you are hopelessly drunk?"

"Because I am leaving you a trust fund so you will have all the education you want."

"You are not leaving anything!" Meg said. "Nor anyone! I shall be your housekeeper."

No. No. Randolph had protested, flailing both arms around in the air. She would never be able to stand it, being in the same house as a man like him, now that she knew what he did. It drove every normal person away. Even his own mother, who had never been cruel, rejected him when she found out. Of course it was stupid of him to let his parents know.

"No one wants to know anything but niceties in this age of ours." He flailed and tried to get up but fell back on the chaise, covering his eyes and forehead with his arms. "Everything interesting must be covered up. Cloths over piano legs. It's mad. Madness. Takes a man like Oscar Wilde to uncover the truths about human nature. But then he too must cloak it with something. Humour. Humour is his cloak. And a fine one too. He too went to Oxford. But after my time. Best time of my life I had there. Met men who understood. What a cocky young bunch we were. Brave as bulls let out of the pen. Raring to go. All too ignorant, all too ignorant of the spears and swords, spears and swords ..."

"Mr. Oliphant. That's enough. Please. You need sleep."

But he wanted to tell his story. It was in the cockiness of having graduated that Randolph let his parents discover his secret wardrobe and told them of his lifelong habit and need. His father said he knew of such perversities but certainly not within his honest and hard-working family. It was the stuff of the idle aristocracy. His mother refused to believe him, saying it was something unmentionable that he had picked up at school and she forbade him to mention it, let alone do it, ever again. The clothes they had found were burned. His mother could not bear to look him in the eye. Soon he was offered a financial incentive to take up work in another country. Randolph set sail for New York where he set up a broom business like his father's.

He eventually sniffed out men who understood or shared his secret habit in New York and at a club in Boston. But what he deeply wanted was a woman who could treat him as a man and tolerate the Cecilia side of him. In all his travels, pulling up stakes and setting up new businesses, Randolph had never found such a woman. In the old mining town in British Columbia, he had found a companion.

"'Crazy Annie' they called her." Randolph pulled himself up and pointed floppily to the desk drawer. "She's the one who wrote that story. Said it was true. Handed down through generations of her people, her Arctic ancestors, she called them. Who knows? Who knows where she really came from. Doesn't matter. She was my friend. She dressed like a man and had a handsome team of dogs. She delivered mail all winter long. Gone for weeks at a time. She shared my house. Wrote stories for days on end then took off again. Only woman I've known who could live with me knowing my... habit. But then..." Randolph laughed weakly. "Hers was similar." He closed his eyes tightly. "Some bastard attacked her on the trail one night. She came home with awful bruises. And... an unspeakable fear. A month later she left. Disappeared in the dark with her dogs. Left me that manuscript. The story of a couple such as Annie and I could never be." Randolph wiped tears from his cheeks with the back of his hands, then opened his eyes. "Leave me, please," he said, without looking at Meg. "Forgive and forget. I'm an embarrassment to the human race. And I will depart it. So weary, so weary of hiding and running..."

"Oh, don't be such a silly... sir," said Meg. She took his hand. "Let's make a deal. I can look after you, protect you and your ... 'habit.' That is the only way you'll get me to go to university and be ... 'the daughter you never had.' If you don't get your gumption back and stop drinking yourself to death, I will have nothing to do with you, or your money. Just think what people would say if you died now and left a sack of money to me. They would conclude that for sure I had acted very improperly with you, and my reputation would be ruined forever. Whereas if I work for you, it would be proper and fair. No matter what anyone thinks."

"You are a clever girl. And a hard bargainer." Randolph drifted off into sleep.

He snored loudly as Meg sat at his desk composing a letter to her parents. Then a note for Randolph, saying, "I will be back, very soon. Please leave the kitchen door unlocked."

She fetched Stew from the Pig and Poke, telling him to hurry up, they had to go to where the Negroes live and talk to Mrs. Rivers.

"I heard she quit," said Stew, steadying himself on the seat beside Meg who was hurrying the horses. "They say she found him on one hell of a bender and he's still on it. I told you he's an odd old bugger and you oughta steer clear of him."

"Shut your trap, Stew. The fumes coming out could light a forest fire."

"Ain't you in a mood!"

Mrs. Rivers stood up from her rocking chair on the porch when Meg drew up to her front yard. "Shoo! Shoo!" she said to children who were gawking at the strangers and chickens who were scratching in the earth and grass. "That you, Miss Meg?"

"Hello, Mrs. Rivers." Meg came up the path with Poley, leaving Stew to tend the horses. "May I speak with you?"

"Sure thing, child. Come sit down, here in the fresh air."

Mrs. Rivers' grownup daughter and young children came to the doorway. Mrs. Rivers settled back into the rocking chair as Meg settled onto the nearby chair.

"You all want somethin'," said the daughter, "somethin' cold-like to drink?"

"Some apple juice?" said Mrs. Rivers to Meg.

"That would be nice, thanks, but I mustn't stay long. My brother's chomping at the bit."

"Bring some juice for us and Miss Meg's brother, Sugar girl."

"Mr. Oliphant . . . ," Meg began.

"I hear he's poorly. I'm sorry to hear that. He weren't when I left."

"Would you come back?" Meg leaned forward. "Please. He would do you no harm."

Mrs. Rivers laughed. "I know that, child. Mr. Oliphant is a kind white man. And that's all I got to say about him. I'm retired now. Too old to be doin' for others. Mr. Oliphant gave me a tidy sum and I got nothin' bad to say about him. Though I'll say to you, since you come all this way and you got somethin' on your mind. You get on right well with him. I know that. But he ain't no husband material."

"What now?" said Stew, holding the reins.

"I'm going back to Mr. Oliphant's."

"Oh no you're not. Not till he's sobered up and found a new house-keeper."

Meg was quiet then said, "I left my satchel with all my books in it. I have to go back for that."

At Oliphant's gate, she jumped down from the wagon with Poley, smacked the letter to her parents onto Stew's lap. "Be a good brother, Stew. Read this. And go home."

"What the . . . !" He inadvertently snapped the reins. The horses began to take off. Before he got them under control, Meg and Poley had disappeared inside Oliphant's kitchen, locking the door behind them.

8

A Snake in the Outhouse

THE ROCKING CHAIR SQUEAKED as Emma and Herbert rocked back
and forth, back and forth on the front porch. Herbert sat smoking his
pipe in the chair beside Emma, his gouty foot resting on a stool. He
had gained much weight since the shock of that note from Meggie.
Terrible year that was, losing the election to a younger man and his
favourite daughter to a man who treated her like his own daughter.
He felt he was losing his place in the order of things.

These were perplexing times, when young women went on stage
or into the university. Well, better university than the stage. Emma
was right about that. Meg had much of his own mother in her, free-
thinking and wanting to do some good in the world. A lot like himself too. Once he got used to the idea, it seemed fair enough that a
daughter with his brains should want to go to a university if she had
the chance. He just wished that he had the means to provide for all
his children himself, instead of letting another man do it, particularly
when it came to his daughters. Though, when it got down to it, what
kind of sense did that make to be worrying about another man paying for his daughter's education when, as a father, he was prepared
to hand over his daughters as wives to other men for the rest of their
lives?

Perplexing times, indeed. His own parents must have felt similarly when he insisted on marrying their servant. He had to smile at that and look fondly upon Emma, touching her arm. His ever-so-serious, hard-working Emma. Married forty years now. And the last few had been the best of all, until this Oliphant stole his daughter. It gave him pains in his chest just thinking about it. Though Emma didn't think it so bad. She surprised him sometimes, the way she took things. Befuddled him. But he loved her, had loved her from the start. And she had served him well, she had. Herbert knocked the dead ashes out of his pipe and refilled it.

Rocking soothed the pain in Emma's lower back, though the effort of rocking was tiring. Such a beautiful evening, she thought. Early September was her favourite time of year. The heat of a Canadian summer was over and done with, the cold of winter not yet upon her. The air was pleasantly warm, plump red apples were ripening on the trees, yellow and purple plums had already been picked and preserved, as had the garden tomatoes. Thank the Lord that there was nothing to be done with the corn in the field except to pick, husk, and eat it, then throw the cobs to the animals.

She recalled how Meg liked to feed the animals, talked to them all as she did it, treated them like personal friends, tried to bandage their wounds, cure their ills. Tamed the wolves too. She'd weep over the death of any one of them, wild or farm animals. There was no curing her of this bent. Randolph Oliphant was another wounded wolf to her.

That note she wrote. So brief. Yet told all.

Dear Mother and Father,

I must stay with Mr. Oliphant. He is dangerously ill. He will recover, with proper feeding and watering. I will be his housekeeper. He wants to pay for my education. I know that you will not approve of this. It will look wrong in the eyes of others. But I must do it, because it seems right to me. Stew had no part in this. He is your obedient son. Please forgive me for ... whatever wrong you may think I am doing. I plan to make you proud of me, eventually.

I will miss you, and Alice, and Stew, all the animals, and the farm, so very much. Please will you visit? And let me visit? I am grateful for all you have done for me.

I am sorry for being ... your loving but disobedient daughter,
Meg

All the crossing out and writing over did not diminish the strong hand, the strength of voice and will behind it.

Emma had been struck with terror seeing Stew come down the lane without Meg. But it came as no great shock that Meg would do this. It was a parent's duty to keep children on the straight and narrow for as long as possible. They had done their best with Meg but she had taken off on her own.

Herbert had wanted to go and fetch her back that very night. He threw a fit. Raged at Oliphant. Raged at Meg. Gave Stew a kick on the rump for allowing Meg to get away. Threatened the lot of them with not darkening his door, or theirs, again. It was Alice who dared to utter what Emma hoped would be true. "I think she's lucky as can be. Meg can have everything she wants, living in that rich man's house."

Emma had felt strangely calm, as though the inevitable had happened at last, and once accepted, might be turned into a good thing. "It all depends on the outcome of her exams," Emma had said to Herbert in the privacy of their bedroom. "If she does well, she'll have proved herself. Then no one should stop her from going to a college, if that's what she wants, and we don't have to pay for it. We should just sit tight until the exams are over. Don't interfere. Let her go into them in peace."

"I can't sit by and have my daughter look like a whore!"

"Hush, Herbert! Don't let Alice hear such words!' Emma was angered. All the more so because she expected tongues would wag and say just that of her daughter. She bristled and sprang to Meg's defence. "The cost of college is certainly not more than one should pay for a good housekeeper! Mr. Oliphant is getting a good deal. He should have a staff of at least three to run that house properly. One for cooking, for laundry, for cleaning."

"If he were decent, he would propose marriage, not housekeeping," was Herbert's reply. "But I don't want my daughter marrying someone over twice her age."

Herbert would not sit tight. Midweek before the exams, he was banging on Oliphant's front door, Emma standing behind him, having packed up Meg's clothes and toiletries, and put them in the wagon in the likelihood that Meg would not return to Wolf Woods.

Meg opened the door, with Randolph standing stalwart behind her, Poley woofing and wagging his tail in welcome.

"Do come in," said Randolph. "We have been hoping you would visit ..."

"I'm not here for niceties," said Herbert. "I'm here for my daughter."

"Now, Herbert," said Emma. She stepped forward and held her arms out to Meg.

"Oh, Momma!" Meg hugged her and brought her into the house. "Thank you. Thank you for coming."

Randolph conducted all of them into the parlour. Sober and suitably attired, Emma assessed him. And he conducted himself well, but it was Meg who ran the meeting. She sat with a very stiff back and cut her father off at the pass when he charged in on the offensive with, "Sir, you are ruining my daughter's reputation by keeping her, unmarried as she is, in your household."

"Father, I'm here of my own free will. And Mr. Oliphant is my employer. He must not be insulted."

"Sir," said Oliphant, "I will do everything in my powers to protect the reputation of your daughter. Like you, I wish to see her married someday to a worthy young man of sufficient means. Indeed, I expect her to be wooed by several such candidates when she is at university and I will be the most diligent of chaperones. All that is required is that people see that I am her protector. It may take some time for people to realize this, and I would hope you and Mrs. Wilkinson would help by showing everyone your pleasure in your daughter's position here and at university."

"You'll be doing the work of a staff of three," Herbert thrust at Meg.

"What do you mean, Dad?"

"This house should have a cook, laundress, and cleaner. Ask your mother. She knows about these things."

Emma had to cough to prevent herself from smiling. Herbert stealing her words, plucking at straws. And the irony of it. All those years, she had done the work of a staff of Lord knows how many, and Herbert had not raised objections. Though he would have hired household help if they could have afforded it.

"Mr. Oliphant sends his laundry out," said Meg.

"I understand your concern," said Randolph. "In fact I share it. Your daughter must have full time for her classes and studies. We have discussed this and she has argued quite effectively that cooking for two is not more work than cooking for one. And I am quite a tidy person. I'm used to doing for myself. She thinks not, but there will be times when I will hire some extra household help."

"Settled," Emma had said decisively. "Meg, I have brought your clothes. I think we should thank you, Mr. Oliphant, for your generous treatment of our daughter."

"The animals miss you," Herbert had jumped in with his final plea. "Your chickens won't stop squawking. And this is no good for Poley. He's a farm dog."

"Poley is Meg's dog," Emma looked at him panting, sitting upright near Meg during the arguments. "He's happy enough at her side. But Meg, I want you to come home after your exams, for a visit at least. You'll do that, won't you? We all want to hear your results. The animals and hens in particular."

Meg had come home, driving Randolph's elegant black leather carriage with the collapsible hood to protect from wind and rain. Poley sat like a big black gentleman beside her. Then he leapt from the carriage and lumbered eagerly around in his old haunts. How much older Meg suddenly looked, thought Emma, as she watched her daughter arriving as a visitor in a fine carriage, sporting a new emerald green suit with black braid trim and a jaunty hat which Meg seemed embarrassed to wear. Alice quickly took it over.

"This outfit," Meg explained somewhat apologetically, "it's a kind of graduation gift, from Randol ... Mr. Oliphant."

"Randolph?!" exclaimed Alice.

"Graduation?" said the others.

"I passed the exams. Not with complete flying colours." She laughed. "They thought my answers 'unorthodox.' But I got on well with them in the interviews. I've been accepted into first year at Dalhousie University."

"University? What happened to vet college?" said Stew.

"I have to do a Bachelor of Science first, including a lot of medical courses. They let some young men directly into vet college from upper school, if they've had a lot of 'work experience.' But they won't let me. There's no actual law against women in vet college. But no woman has applied. I'm the first to try to get in, at least at McGill veterinary college in Montreal. There's another vet college in Toronto but that's too far away. They told me over the phone that they can't seriously consider me until I have proven myself academically with a Bachelor of Science, and then it's highly doubtful that I would have the 'strength of mind and body,' as they put it, to become a vet. So I'll have to show them that I do."

"We'll teach you to push horses around," Stew and Dave had offered. "Ain't much science to that."

"There is not." Emma had corrected her sons.

It was strange, Emma had mused, that last Christmas, to have her children all so grown up, gathered round the table at Wolf Woods. Joseph, Andrew, and Robert all had wives and children she was not familiar with because they lived so far away. George and his wife lived impossibly far away, on a farm near Winnipeg. Emma had resolved to enjoy such a rare family gathering, but she was not well. Pain in her lower back. And she felt so tired she could barely roll out pastry. Meg came home for a full two weeks of her holidays because

Mr. Oliphant, or Randolph, as she unabashedly called him, had gone to Boston for Christmas. Meg and Alice did everything from laundry and cleaning to cooking and clearing up. They made Emma sit back and observe.

I'm a lady, she had smiled to herself, Mistress of Wolf Woods Farm, being waited upon by a well-trained staff. How much easier her children's lives were, she thought: born into a new country and changing times. Her sons all with land of their own. But most remarkable was how opportunities had come to her oldest daughter.

Meg was doing well at Dalhousie University, if exams were the count. Passed her second year. There was an oddness about Randolph Oliphant that no one could quite put their finger on, but the arrangement was working well enough, had withstood the test of time in that Meg showed no signs of ruining her life. Most everyone had come to see and accept it as a peculiar benefactor-protege relationship. It was Herbert who had most trouble, feeling usurped as Meg's father. It was a sore point that was best swept under the carpet.

Alice was the one to worry about now. She had graduated from Lower School and was showing bitter resentment at having to stay on the farm to help out. Alice wanted to be in the city and have the "advantage" Meg had found. But who was to provide it? Alice was urging her and Herbert to give the farm over to Dave and Stew and buy a house in Halifax. But there was simply not the money for that. At best, they might hire a young girl to help with the housework. Emma could not manage it all on her own. The back pain had gotten so bad she relieved it by taking brandy openly in the evening and sometimes secretly during the day. Alice was pleading to be sent to Normal School to become a teacher. They might be able to come up with the money for that, but where was the fairness principle then, when none of the others had been given further education?

This worried Emma. She rocked with anxiety. It didn't bear more thinking about tonight. "I'll prepare now for bed," she said to Herbert. She rose unsteadily to go to the outhouse. She always filled the chamber pot with her many getting ups in the night. Best use the wretched outhouse before going in for the night.

"Do you need my arm, Emma dear?" said Herbert, seeing her unsteadiness.

"I'll manage, thank you, dear."

Emma opened the door of the outhouse, stepped in to remove the lid from the stinking hole. Something hissed and slithered into a coil near her hand. A snake. A thick, brown milk snake.

Emma gasped and screamed, tripped and fell backwards on the stone path. Herbert pushed himself out of his chair and ran as fast as his game foot and portly body allowed, to the aid of his wife.

"Perhaps it was a mercy," said the doctor, who declared Emma dead. "These growths in her abdomen would have caused severe pain for a long time."

"We'll take her to the Anglican Cathedral in Halifax for burial," said Herbert. "She was never comfortable in the local parish, amidst Scots Presbyterians. I'll see my wife out in grand style."

Thus Emma's body was lifted from the steps of the outhouse at Wolf Woods Farm and transported to the grand stone cathedral in Halifax via a black coach pulled by four black horses sporting black and red plumes on their heads. All the Wilkinsons were outfitted in new black mourning dress and followed the hearse in black carriages, including Randolph's, which he drove himself, conveying the young Wilkinson wives with him. The cathedral was filled with farm folk, city folk, politicians, and the mayor of Halifax, who had come to pay last respects to the wife of Herbert Wilkinson, longtime, highly regarded member of the provincial legislature. The eulogy praised Emma as the good and faithful wife of the Honourable Herbert Wilkinson and loving mother of their eight children.

Emma's body, laid to rest in a golden oak casket, was buried in the cathedral cemetery. Meg, weeping, put her arm around Alice as the casket was lowered into the ground.

Randolph had organized a reception at his house, catered by the Women's Guild of the Cathedral. Herbert stood for over an hour in the front hall of Randolph's house, receiving all the friends, acquaintances, and strangers who had come to pay their respects, show their presence, and have a look at Oliphant's house. Young men were interested in having a closer look at the Wilkinson daughters. Young women wished to give their condolences to the Wilkinson bachelor sons, so well turned out in black suits and felt-brimmed hats. Another wife would be needed at Wilkinson's farm, which was said to be well-maintained and prosperous. Women of the Guild fussed over Herbert, settled him in an armchair, and brought him a plate of sandwiches and strong tea or a mug of ale, whatever he wished.

"Mug of ale, if you will, please. And thank you, ladies." Herbert was used to being waited upon and suddenly felt particularly grateful for it, and the overabundance of it.

Alice moved from room to room like a diligent hostess, greeting all she could, receiving all the patronage offered. "My sister resides here," she said proudly to strangers, "while she attends university. Mr. Oliphant has in effect adopted her, as his protégé, if you know what I mean. Our mother thought highly of Mr. Oliphant."

Stew flirted openly and kept close to the ale keg. Dave, who was uncomfortable any distance from the farm, was so flustered by the attention and the city atmosphere he edged his way out onto the verandah and onto the lawn but was soon waylaid under the chestnut tree by a young woman, Isabel, who brought with her a tray of food and drink.

Meg wanted to get away from everyone. She retreated to the kitchen and offered to help with the clearing up but the Women's Guild wouldn't let her.

"It's our job," they said. "All proceeds go to the cathedral and Mr. Oliphant has paid handsomely." They eyed her and saw that she was grieving like no one else.

"We're sorry," one said, "about your mother."

"No one really knew her," said Meg, her brow wrinkling, her arms folded tensely across her chest. "including me. But there was more to her than ... 'wife of' and 'mother of' ..."

A silence reigned.

"It was a lovely service, dear."

"So many turned out. The mayor himself."

"Your mother would be … your mother *was* complimented."

"My *father* certainly was," said Meg wryly. Then her lips quivered. She turned to leave. "Excuse me, please. And thank you, for all the food and everything. It was lovely. My mother would have been … grateful." Though it was not a word Meg had ever heard her mother use in regard to herself.

That night, all had returned to their homes, except Herbert, who was snoring in the guest room, and Alice, who was sharing the downstairs "maid's quarters" with Meg and Poley.

The room was furnished with twin beds separated by a desk at the window overlooking the back lawn. There was a chest of drawers, a tall bookcase, and a leather reading chair. The walls were papered in teal blue stripes, blue velvet draped the window, white spreads covered the beds. Poley, who usually slept on his blanket on one bed, had been bumped to a place on the floor. Alice sat brushing her hair while Meg lay in bed staring at the ceiling.

"Doesn't it give you the creeps?" said Alice. "That dead woman's room right above your head? It's *way* beyond the mourning period and he still talks about his Cecilia. How can you stand it?"

"People do live on after death," said Meg. "We'll never forget our mother."

"We're not turning her bedroom into a shrine. And I wouldn't talk about her to others all the time. It's unseemly. If not crackers. Don't you think your Randolph is a bit crackers?"

"No!" Meg frowned at her. "I certainly do not. Randolph is interesting and he's a talker, period. In no way insane. And he *never* talks about her to me."

"Has he ever tried to … you know … take advantage of you? Mother is … was, always warning me about that. She said all men will, if you let them. Has he ever tried to get in here to your room, when you're sleeping?"

"Never! And he never would. All men are *not* the same, Alice. Randolph is an honourable man. And he's generous. He's extremely generous. He didn't *have* to provide a grand reception for our mother's funeral or buy us mourning dresses..."

"Or pay for *you* to go to university. It's not fair, you know. What's my future? Left on the farm? I'd like to be a teacher. Did you know that?"

Meg propped herself up on her elbow and looked at Alice. "Would you really? Then you must. You could get into the Normal School here in Halifax. Let's ask Mrs. Atkins how to proceed. She went there. And talk to Dad. Surely he could scrape up a loan." Meg sat up. "The boys get the farm. It's time you got something. You don't want to end up like our mom, marrying too young, having too many children, so unhappy all those years, and in the end, no real character of her own. At least not one that anyone could describe. That eulogy..." Meg fell back in dismay.

"I don't know what you're talking about." Alice put down her brush, having counted one hundred strokes, and got into bed. "I thought the funeral was perfectly grand. It did our mother proud. But what about me? I don't want to stay on the farm a minute longer. Could I live here with you?" Alice sat up. "I could help with the housekeeping."

"I'm afraid not," Meg said carefully. "Mr. Oliphant doesn't want any more housekeepers."

"Thanks a lot!" Alice lay down and turned her back to Meg, punching her pillow before setting her head upon it. "Thanks for nothing! I forgot. It's only you who counts."

"Don't be like that, Alice. We're sisters. I'm on your side. You and I will be more than just wife and mother. Where there's a will, there's a way."

9

To the Last Decade

"It's time to be movin' on," said Stew. "Time to seek my fortune as a fireman on the trains. I'll be off tomorrow if I can."

It was New Year's day of 1890. The Wilkinson family was gathered round Randolph Oliphant's dining table for a dinner of ham, baked beans and coleslaw, all prepared and served by Meg. Alice had brought maple walnut pies for dessert.

Randolph was in fine form, hosting the table with frequent toasts to the new year, the new decade—the grand finale of the nineteenth century. Herbert, given place of honour at the other end of the table, kept looking at Randolph but seeing Emma. Although her body was three months underground, her presence still stuck with him. It was she who belonged at the end of his table. Herbert struggled to raise his own good spirits up to the occasion. Whiskies and then wine had elevated him but now he was feeling disgruntled. That sense of being usurped was gnawing at him, again. All this talk of change. As though change were a new thing!

"Look at history," Herbert said to all at the table: Oliphant, Stew, his daughters, and quiet, hard-working Dave, now sitting beside his plucky fiancée, Isabel. Snatched him up, she did. And not a bad thing. Opposites attract and work out pretty well. As he and Emma had. He was no stranger to change. He had left his native land and taken up in this new country because it was so open to change. "History is the record of change. It's been going on since time began. The question is, is it for the good or not?"

Herbert took a sip from his glass and stood up. "I entered politics," he said, "because I believe in promoting change for the good. And so I salute you, son." He raised his glass to Stew. "Good fortune as a fireman on the railroads."

All raised their glasses to Stew. Then Alice looked across the table at Meg.

After their mother's funeral, Alice had pleaded with her father to move into a small house in town where she would keep house for him; in return, he would support her in getting a teaching certificate. Her father had refused, saying it was against her mother's wishes, unaffordable, and no more was to be said about it. So there she was, stuck on the farm, doing all the "women's work," resentfully, sulkily, sometimes at a go-slow pace, sometimes burning food and scorching clothes in anger. Her respite was to go into Halifax on Saturdays and stay overnight with Meg, where she was included in the various parties that Meg and Randolph hosted.

But Alice felt uncomfortable in their company and with the conversations at their parties. She was puzzled by the nature of Randolph's relationship with Meg and hers with him. They had a liking for each other that seemed abnormal, though Alice couldn't figure out the basis of it. But then she felt impatience at trying to figure out much in life. Things eluded her. She couldn't get interested, the way Meg did, in ideas and theories. Who really cared if we're descended from apes, or if there's no real proof that God exists? Not me, thought Alice. And the basis of morality ... why delve into it? The rules have to be obeyed or you'll get punished. That's all there is to it, as far as Alice could see. But Meg and Randolph would wrestle with topics like Utilitarianism until the cows came home. That seemed to be the real passion between them. It was strange.

It was not what Alice wanted from the company of men. Alice liked to be complimented, smiled upon, have her looks approved, her hand sought. She longed to go to a ball. There had been a New Year's

Ball just last night, at the Citadel, but Randolph did not attend. He hosted a dinner party at home, instead, for Meg and her university friends. Alice was included but the compliments were too few and the conversations too intense. Sometimes they laughed at things Alice couldn't see the humour of.

If she had the opportunity, she would create a salon that was more gay. There would be light-hearted conversations, a prettier table laid, flirtations encouraged. Meg had become all too serious, even strained, since attending university. Or was it since moving in with Randolph Oliphant? In any case, Alice did not want to go to university like Meg, but she did want life beyond the farm. And attending Normal School, becoming a teacher in Halifax could open doors in the city's high society, if only her father would set up house there. Now, with Stew's announcement of departure from the farm, and Dave and Isabel wanting to get married and live there, it was the perfect time for her father to move into Halifax with her.

Thus Alice looked across the table at Meg and found agreement in her eyes. All very well for their father to wish good fortune to Stew in getting off the farm. But ... "What about me?' said Alice, standing up "What kind of fortune is there for me stuck on the farm, waiting upon father and brother?" She left the table to bring in dessert.

"I suppose," said Meg standing up to clear the table and join forces with Alice, "I suppose what Alice might do is try to get a loan from the bank and board with a family while she attends Normal School."

"Banks don't give loans to women!" said Herbert angrily.

"Well then, elsewhere," said Meg jauntily over her shoulder. "I'm sure that mother would prefer her daughter not to have to go elsewhere for help, but if that's what a determined young woman must do ..." Meg trailed off into the kitchen.

Randolph cleared his throat and wiped the corners of his mouth with his napkin. Isabel gently nudged Dave.

"Isabel and I would like to get married, come spring," said Dave. "We was hoping that would suit you, Father, if we did."

"Were hoping, my lad. Just because your mother's not around to correct you ..." Herbert took a swill of wine. He looked forward to

Alice's pie. She was a good cook and pastry maker like her mother. She could look after him well. But it was clear he was going to lose her and end up an old nuisance on the farm if he didn't make the move sooner rather than later. The city had a lot to offer a retired popular politician like himself. Never was a farmer at heart. If he could find a little house he could afford ... "Spring is not very far away," said Herbert, noticing Alice and Meg hovering, ears perked, in the doorway. "If I were to be looking for a place in town, I should get started, right soon."

Alice sat down with two pies and a bowl of whipped cream in front of her. "How big a piece would you like, Father dear?" She smiled at him for the first time in three months.

Stew took the train to Toronto and found himself a job with the Canadian Pacific Railroad. Dave and Isabel married within two months, producing a fully formed "early" baby within six. Well before spring, Herbert moved with Alice into a small house near downtown Halifax. Alice busied herself sewing draperies, elegant table cloths, and as much of a new wardrobe as she could eke out of Herbert's income from the farm.

"Don't worry, Dad," she said. "I'll pay everything back with my teacher's salary. Just like Meg."

Alice was so happy with her new prospects she began to keep a journal, recording her new life in the city.

Strained? Oh yes, Meg had been strained at times since moving into Randolph's house. As was he. There was strain when they said good night. There was strain when he suggested it was time for her to spend a weekend at Wolf Woods or for a longer period while he went to Boston. *Why* he must be alone or go to Boston was a taboo topic. Randolph had insisted on that, ever since he regained his sobriety and agreed to have Meg takeover as his housekeeper.

The strain was highest during the first year when Meg would

let her hopes rise that he would not need to go away. Most of the time, he was attentive and interested in her, greeted her with such warmth each morning when he came downstairs, was so enthusiastic when she came home from classes, looked upon her with such affection when they talked over dinner or looked up from reading in the library. And when he retired at night, there was a strained reluctance in his demeanour. But then close his door on her he did, with firmness, sometimes with loudness that felt to her like a slam of rejection. Sometimes she heard him moving about in Cecilia's room. She tried not to picture what he was doing in there.

"Poley," she whispered to the dog lying on the other bed. "Let's turn on the light and read for a while, shall we?"

When the strain built up, Randolph would communicate through Poley. "Come here, my old bear." Randolph ruffled Poley's ears. "Need a little visit to the farm?"

"You want to go to Boston?" Meg said quietly.

"I'm afraid so." Randolph looked at his knees.

Meg put her face in her hands, then looked up resigned. "I understand."

She never could fully understand. But she learned to accept it, tried to make light of it, tried to overcome feelings she had to recognize as jealousy. "I'm the one who's crackers," she said to Poley. "Jealous of a woman who doesn't exist. But she's real enough to send us away. So off we go."

"You're a clever girl," said Randolph when Meg completed her second year. "These are very impressive results. Highest marks in the medical courses. If our Dr. Atkins is right, that is what will persuade them to let you into the college at McGill. He says the med school and vet college work hand in hand there. And if they don't let you in, I could vouch for you as the first woman accountant. My business accounts have never been in such good order. Thanks to you, Miss Wilkinson."

"It's thanks to *you*, Mr. Oliphant, that I have been able to pursue any studies at all."

Randolph raised his hand like a stop sign. "You have been unquestionably successful with your studies, Miss Wilkinson. But you have failed, my dear Meg, to acquire a beau!"

"Randolph, that is unfair!" Meg flushed and folded her arms tightly against her chest. "I have many friends. They come regularly to this house."

"For parties. Not for courting."

"I don't wish to be courted ..."

"You should." Randolph interrupted her. "You are of age now." He avoided her eyes and spoke in business-like tones. "I expect you to find a suitable young man in your final year at Dalhousie."

Meg bowed her head. I have tried, she thought. It would be nice to fall in love with a suitable young man who had no need of ... any other woman but me. But how do I know what other men are really like? What secrets does any man keep within? At least I know Randolph's. I don't like it but ... I just cannot get interested enough in anyone else. "You are right," She stood up and faced Randolph. "I have tried and I have failed, in that regard."

He stood up and embraced her. "I'm so sorry," he said, rocking her in his arms. "But you must keep trying."

In summer, Meg and Randolph often went to the seashore for picnics and swimming with Poley. Meg would have preferred to have kept it as a threesome but Randolph always made her invite friends along. Randolph had never learned to swim; in fact, he did not like cold, salty water, and maintained his place on shore as chaperone. In the autumn, when Meg entered her last year at Dalhousie, he threw a large party for her and her classmates, as though he was stepping up the pace of her socialization with young men. She was courted by a few but none of them captured her imagination, her sympathy, her intellect, her sense of adventure, or her heart, as Randolph did. She discouraged any suitor before he reached the point of proposing.

That Christmas, after the funeral of Emma, Randolph had not

told Poley it was time for him to visit Wolf Woods. He had not gone to Boston. Instead, he had invited Meg's family to his house for the holidays. Randolph was strained but determinedly cheerful. After New Year's, when the house was emptied of guests, Randolph sat beside Meg on the sofa in front of the fireplace. He began speculating about what the 1890s would bring and the future of his business, Clean Sweepers.

"Brooms will always be handy and useful," he said. "But they will not take us into the twentieth century. Typewriters are replacing pens, threshing machines replaced the scythe. They're inventing machines to replace horses and even to fly in the sky. They're bound to invent a machine to take up the dirt."

"To replace me?" Meg smiled. "Will I be thrown out with the brooms?"

Randolph sighed heavily and frowned. "What will I do without you?"

Meg put her hand on his knee. "Don't do without me."

"I am trying," said Randolph, "to do without Cecilia."

Meg took both his hands. "You needn't." She felt so sorry for him her eyes welled up. "I'm ... used to it."

He let go of her hands and sat back, putting his arm around her shoulder, drawing her close to his side. "You are so good to me," he said. "I'm afraid I'm not worthy."

"What utter nonsense!' Meg sat upright and faced him. "All you have done for me and my family! I owe you more than I can ever repay. And I love ...."

"Hush!" Randolph placed his hand on her mouth before she could finish. "Please don't." He took her hands gripping them in his. "It's not right. You're in my care. You will graduate in June. Let us say good night now, and speak no more of this."

Before he sat down to breakfast next morning, he took her by the hand, led her to his desk and proceeded to unlock the drawer containing Crazy Annie's manuscript.

"I think it is time to read this," he said. "You are old enough. It may give you direction in vet college and in marriage."

The temperature had dropped, puddles were freezing over and it was snowing heavily outside Meg's window, as she sat at her desk, a mug of hot chocolate in hand, beginning to read the manuscript. The handwriting was steady and legible, done by someone who wanted this story to be read. The style was indeed strange. Not eloquent English. Certainly not poetic. Not at all Victorian. It was of its own place and time. Like pictures drawn out of someone talking. There was a sort of rudeness about these characters that began to delight Meg.

Ike's spirit stopped hovering anxiously over Meg's shoulder. He sighed with relief as he threw back his parka hood and settled into himself.

10

Ike's Working Wolves

Ike in Ancient Times

IKE KNEW HE WAS NOT THE FIRST to tame wolves and breed them into dogs. He had no idea where it was first done and who did it. That would be like knowing who made the first harpoon. Various versions of harpoons turned up in many places around the same time in the Arctic. But he knew he was one of the first and that he was particularly good at this new venture. He took the wolf out of its natural den, but he never wanted to take the wolf out of the dog.

It had begun as play when Ike was a child. His mother had shown him and his young sister, Isa, a den of five wolf pups. They saw the pups venture out of the den in early morning when both parents had gone hunting. It was a new pack of only the mates and their pups, no pup sitters. Ike was not allowed to watch the pups for long on the first visit, lest the wolf parents return and find them there.

Ike and his sister pleaded to return daily, moving to a spot closer to the pups each day. The pups became used to the scent of the children and did not scurry back into the den when Ike slowly approached and let the friendliest pups mouth his hand. His sister did the same. They brought bones to entice and play with the pups, being careful to take the bones home again so the pups' parents would find no trace of them.

Ike asked many questions of his own parents about wolves. His father told him to stop visiting the wolf den, it was unmanly. He should be playing with other boys, wrestling and racing, building his muscles and speed in order to become good at the hunt. He was spending too much time with his sister and mother. He would become weak if he spent so much time watching baby animals. Wolves and other animals are to be respected and used when needed for food and clothes. "And do not feed the wolf pups," said his father, finally, firmly.

His mother kept silent. She was an observant woman but she made no report of missing meat to her husband after Ike stole some small morsels of hare to give to the pups in early summer.

The punishment for this came not from his father but from the wolves themselves: the next day, when Ike went to their den, they were gone. The den was completely abandoned. Ike and his sister said nothing about this to their mother and father. They were sure they had caused the young pack to flee.

Perhaps the parents had killed the pups for taking food from humans, his sister said, and would not pursue wolves any more.

When his father went on a long fishing trip with the other men, Ike spent several mornings searching for the wolves. He spotted them in a clearing near the forest by a small lake. Both parents and all five pups were there, chasing each other, wrestling each other to the ground, leaping over each other, doing all the things his father said he should be doing with the other boys.

When his village moved to another location in the autumn, Ike resolved that if he found another den of pups, he'd take one for his own and raise it to be his friend. He liked wolves better than boys. But as long as Ike was a boy living in his father's house, he was not allowed to keep a wolf pup.

When Ike grew up and took a wife, his father was not surprised that they bore no children. But he was grieved. His son had never been normal.

Ike's wife, Piji, was deeply disappointed and depressed that she did not bear children. She mated often with Ike, before they slept and when they awoke. He was good to mate with. They mated in the forest. On the river bank. In the full and in the waning moon. Nothing worked. Then Piji secretly bargained to mate with another married man who had produced three babies. Nothing. No babies came of this affair.

Piji cried. Ike comforted her. In her distress she confessed to him about the affair and its fruitless outcome. Ike took his arms from around her and was quiet for a long time. Only the noise of his sharpening knife was heard in their summer hut.

Then he turned to Piji and said, "Will you raise wolves with me?"

They started by stealing just one pup from any litter they found of more than four pups.

They justified their theft by pointing out that an entire litter seldom survives into adulthood and that one less mouth to feed could mean the remaining pups would get more and grow stronger. They stole a pup only when it was more than one moon old and could live on chewed-up meat.

The first pup Ike stole was from a new pairing of lone wolves who had no nanny to tend their litter of six hungry pups. Ike had watched as the mother growled and herded the pups to stay in the den while she went with the father to bring down some caribou. When the parents were far from sight, Ike lured the pups out of the den with well-chewed pieces of meat. He observed their behaviour ... the ones most aggressive, least cautious, most trusting of a human hand. Ike played with those willing to play, turning them over to see which were female. He chose the female most willing to nuzzle his hand for food. She may not be the smartest, he thought, but she's strong and should be the most trainable. Yuki, they had decided to name her. She had a dark coat, with a white face and underbelly. Ike picked her up, threw meat to divert the others and ran off with Yuki as fast as he could.

He was a thief with a mission and a conscience. As he ran, he assured himself he had done well, for no pups had been harmed and all had good chance of survival. But what stayed in his mind was the memory of the most cautious, or thinking, pup in the litter, the one who would not take food from his hand, though she would fight for food dropped to the ground, and she would not allow him to touch her. She dodged and ran to a spot where she could sit and observe him. That's a lead wolf, he thought. Some day I'll have a pack with one like that in the lead.

He carried Yuki in a sack so she couldn't see or smell the trail. It was a long day's run through the dwindling forest then along the frozen river, back to the spring campsite of his village. Piji was waiting with a bone bowl of fresh caribou near the fire. Ike set the hide sack on the bed of furs, pulling the opening wide for Yuki to come out. She would not. She was so terrified she had not made a sound during the journey, and the sack was soaked with saliva from her mouth and sweat from her paws. Piji pulled her out of the sack and lifted her up by the pit of her forepaws.

"Beautiful face!" Piji nuzzled Yuki's snout, then held her close to her body.

"She's not a baby!" Ike grabbed Yuki by the scruff of the neck. "Pick her up the way a wolf would. Like this!" He handed her back to Piji.

Carrying Yuki close to her body, Piji frowned at Ike, took Yuki outside and set her down on a patch of lichen where she squatted for a long piss, her ears back. Yuki trembled as the village children and adults formed a circle around her. The children were noisy with exclamations until Ike silenced them and promised that soon they would be able to play with her. Indeed, they would be asked to help keep Yuki within the confines of the village, but first she needed time to get used to her new family. Piji picked up Yuki and carried her back to their hut where she greedily devoured chewed meat while keeping a wary eye on Piji and Ike.

During darkness, Yuki lay still on the bed of moss Piji had made, with her back up against the poles and hides of the summer hut. Every time Ike or Piji stirred, Yuki would look up, sometimes sit up, staring intensely beyond the glow of the oil pot flame.

With firm instructions from Ike, Piji was left to look after Yuki while he went in search of a mate for her. "Don't forget you're a wolf mother," Ike said. "Keep picking her up by the scruff of the neck. Chew her meat and spew it out for her to swallow. Lead her outside to piss. But keep her away from the village brats who want to tease or maul her. Keep her away from everyone as much as you can until I get back. And don't let her out of your sight. From now on you are her mother and I am her father." Ike howled like a wolf then laughed and departed.

Piji smiled and said to herself: my husband has his own wisdom and I have mine. This wolf pup is my baby. She picked Yuki up, lifting under the shoulders, as she would a baby. She set her on her lap and put her finger in Yuki's mouth, letting her sniff and then mouth her fingers and hand. Then Piji put meat on her hand and Yuki ate from her hand. Piji used food to lure Yuki around and to have her sleep on a caribou skin up against Piji's feet

Finding an unguarded litter of more than four pups was not quick or easy. Ike grew weary and impatient as he tracked and searched upriver, night and day. The moon waned from full to a sliver. Then Ike found a litter of three, out of their den, sporting and mousing in a clearing, guarded by an old wolf. They were handsome pups, like Yuki.

In a flash of desperate covetousness, Ike abandoned his principles and speared the slow moving old wolf as she rose up in alarm. Seeing their nanny speared, fallen, bleeding on the ground, the pups yelped frantically and scattered in fear, circling in confused directions. Ike pursued the largest one, which did turn out to be a male. The pup yelped and growled on being grabbed but went silent and still once the sack was over his head. Ike then speared the fallen wolf in the heart. Her body stopped writhing and lay dead. He wanted to touch her, apologize, explain. But the pack might return at any moment. Ike fled.

Back downriver he ran, carrying his pup, and haunted by the scene of the old guard wolf, speared, encircled by the frantic pups.

"She's fat!" said Ike upon seeing Yuki. "Working animals can't be fat!"

"You've been gone a full moon," said Piji. "Yuki is still here and healthy. I have done a good job. What have you brought me?"

Ike set the sack on the earth floor. They watched in silence while Yuki sniffed the air and stared at the loose opening of the sack. Nothing moved within it until Yuki whimpered at the scent of another pup and then sniffed all around the sack. The pup then emerged, slowly, cautiously.

"I have brought you a mate for Yuki," announced Ike.

"Yukitu!" Piji clapped her hands and smiled as the pups sniffed at each other, circled each other. Then Yuki lay down and rolled over onto her fat back, in submission. Yukitu wagged his tail, then stood stiff in alarm at his surroundings. His coat was darker than Yuki's. He had a similar white underbelly, chest and face, but with dark marking around the eyes.

"Looks like he's wearing sun goggles!" Piji laughed. "But he's handsome. This is a good looking pair. Like you and me." She smiled and reached out to pet Yukitu.

"Water," said Ike. "He needs to drink and eat. Me too."

Ike sat down in front of the doorway so the pups could not escape while Piji assembled a bowl of water and meat for Ike. Yukitu had run to the far wall and sat watching while Yuki deliberated between following him and following the food. Piji filled her hand with unchewed meat which the pups were now old enough to eat. She made the mistake of setting a portion down in front of Yukitu first. With unusual alacrity, Yuki pounced on the food then Yukitu pounced on her and a vicious fight ensued. Ike and Piji dove in to separate the pups. Yuki got the worst of it but both were bleeding from bites on ears, neck, snout and back.

"Never do that again!" Ike shouted at Piji as he held Yukitu and she held Yuki.

"What!" said Piji. "What did I do wrong? Food must be shared. It was right to feed him first. He hadn't eaten in a long time. Yuki has to learn to share. She did wrong, not me. Do you understand, Yuki? Share!"

"Wolves don't share."

"They do. They eat from the same caribou. Pups suck from the same mother. Don't think I don't know how to raise these babies."

"They are *wolves*!" Ike shouted.

The pups' ears flattened at the shouting. They struggled to get free.

The neighbours' ears perked up. They smiled knowingly at the sound of parents quarrelling over how to raise their young.

"You feed Yukitu," said Piji more calmly. "I'll feed Yuki."

"No!" Ike stomped his foot firmly. "Yuki is not for you and Yukitu for me. That is no way to raise our wolves. There must be order. Order in the home as in the pack. They must eat together and work together."

"Peace and order," said Piji. "You speak like an elder. There is no need. There is peace and order in our home." Especially when you're away, she thought. Though I do not like it when you are away. "I will clean the pups. And then I will feed them. You bring home the meat and I will prepare it. I give you food and then I will give to Yuki in that place." She pointed to one end of the hut. "And then to Yukitu in that place." She pointed to the opposite end. "That will be the order in our home."

She wet a thin piece of hide in the water pot and proceeded to wipe the blood spots off Yuki and Yukitu. Ike settled them into separate corners where they lay down eyeing each other. Ike took his seat near the fire while Piji chopped pieces of caribou and fresh fish. Yuki rose to sit near the food source.

"Stay!" Ike said and pointed firmly to where she should stay.

Yuki looked at Piji, who carefully kept her back to her as if in perfect solidarity with Ike's command, though she was saying to herself: you have to learn, Yuki, that there is a new order now that you have a mate. Yuki lay down.

"The village has kept me well supplied while you were away." Pigi handed Ike a bowl of fish and water.

"I'll go fishing at sunrise," said Ike.

"We're not owing," said Piji. "I have made leggings and parkas and traded well."

"Good wife." Ike picked his teeth and smiled at her. "We need much time to train these wolves. Two summers from now we should have the first litter. May it be large. Then Yuki and Yukitu will pull sleds for our village. We will be able to move faster and further than any village. We will be the greatest traders on the greatest river. Our wolves will be known as the great sled pullers of the Malamutes. They will be famous up and down the Yukon."

"Now?" Piji smiled as she held up two long-handled bone ladles of meat.

Ike nodded. He picked up Yukitu, holding him above his feeding place.

"Yuki, come!" Piji dumped one ladle on a flat stone in her place.

While Yuki was busy eating, Piji put the food on Yukitu's stone plate and Ike set him down. Yukitu hesitated, looking cautiously at Ike and at Yuki, who looked up momentarily from her food, growled threateningly, then dug in again. Yukitu gobbled his meat in two swallows.

The pups were led outside, each in a leather harness with leather rope attached, designed and sewn together by Piji. Yuki was used to hers. Yukitu, still traumatized by fear of all that had happened to him, had to be nudged into his harness; once in it, he did not want to move until he saw Yuki assuringly at ease. He followed her, the only familiar creature in sight. After Yuki had squatted to pee, Yukitu followed suit, lifted his leg and pissed on the same spot.

Ike and Piji then led their pups through the village towards the chief's hut. Yukitu stopped frequently to sniff, in extreme wariness of everything around him. Ike did not yank or force him on his first walk but he would not let him turn off in any direction.

The chief stood at his doorway, having donned his best jacket. He was amused at the presentation of the fat and thin wolf pups in harness. He was familiar with Yuki, now the pet of the village and fed by too many. She leapt up in friendliness at others but she was taught to sit respectfully in front of the chief, who leaned over to scratch behind her ears.

"Sit down," said the chief, pointing authoritatively to Yukitu.

Yukitu sat down.

"Very good!" The chief clapped his hands together and laughed.

Yukitu jumped back. Ike attempted to make him sit again. Yuki put up her paw, demanding more attention.

"Now you have competition, fat wolf," said the chief. "This will be good for you."

"Welcome," he said to Yukitu. "Our village is honoured to have two wolves."

Piji had felt the chief's blessing. In walking back through the village with their wolf pups, Piji felt a new sense of pride in her husband and in herself. Ike was not a normal man. He had never really proven himself as a man. No great hunter. No great carver or maker of weapons. And no children. He was a dreamer. But now that they had a male and a female pup behaving like tamed wolves in harness, the harness she had invented, and it was she who had taught Yuki to sit and offer a paw, like a respectful child. Now Ike's dream of turning wolves into co-operative, working members of the community, seemed like a practical plan. The villagers had begun to look upon their peculiar family with respect and hope.

Of course there were the scoffers. Those who joked about her "suckling pups" and "sleeping with wolves." But always there are scoffers. Piji had a clear new role in life. She would raise wolves who would be as good as, if not better than children. She would raise them with affection and discipline. They would have good manners, be kept clean and healthy. They would grow up into strong working adults. And when her own body perished, she knew where her spirit would reside. It would be in all the wolves she would raise. Yes. She would make a perfect job of this. Beginning with admitting her first mistake and proceeding to correct it, with the help of her practical partner and mate.

"Yuki," Piji said to her when they were out of earshot of the villagers, "you are too fat. Ike is right about that."

Cut off from constant snacking, Yuki put her mind to raiding the food sources. When Piji and Ike had their backs turned, absorbed in piling stones all around the foundation of their summer hut because Yukitu had taken to digging his way out of the confines, Yuki tore open the sack of dried fish and managed to fill her stomach to bursting before she was caught. Ike was so angry and disgusted, he raised his foot to kick Yuki.

"Don't!" Piji stopped Ike by kicking his foot.

A fight ensued, Ike and Piji grappling with each other.

"Don't raise your foot to me, woman!" Ike held her at a distance by the shoulders.

"Order!" Piji cried. "Order!"

Ike released her as he saw Yukitu, head lowered, slinking away from such human behaviour. Yuki tried to run away but staggered to the ground.

"She's going to die!" Piji bent over the pup, feeling her taut stomach.

"Stealing food," said Ike, justifying his violent reaction. "It's the worst thing. She might be killed if caught doing that to someone else's supply."

"She has killed herself." Piji began to weep. "Her stomach will burst open."

"That never happens," scoffed Ike. "Give her water. Flush it out." Ike proceeded to get the water bowl.

Piji considered. "No!" She held up her hand to Ike. "Water will make the dried fish bigger."

Ike put the bowl back in its place. My wife is smart, he thought.

Sometimes a mother knows best. He put his hand on Piji's shoulder. They sat together, watching over their pups. Yukitu moved a little closer, watching intently, with his head resting on his front paws.

"It's my fault," said Piji. "I spoiled her with food and now she'll die from it."

"No." Ike sank back into a comfortable position to see this situation through. "I chose Yuki because she will do things for food. You have taught her much and Yukitu learns from her."

"She has taught me never to leave food where she can get it. We must ask the neighbours to keep their food away from her ... if she survives."

"They would kick her. They might beat her to death." Ike thought it over. "It was good you stopped me from kicking her. My father kicked me. He hit my mother. I hated him for that. I never wanted to be like him. It's good you stopped me."

"My mother never let anyone strike my brother or me." Piji reflected. "What would a wolf do if it was attacked?"

"Fight to the death."

As they imagined that, Yuki got up onto her paws. She walked carefully, as a human might walk with hand on a painful stomach. She found her way to tufts of grass outside and took a few large bites of it. She lay down. Yukitu lay down several lengths away. Villagers gathered around.

"Yuki looks sick."

"Is she dying?"

They listened to what had happened. They were worried. They felt Yuki and Yukitu belonged to all of them. Everyone had joined in the protection and training of the pups. They had joined in the chase and rescue when Yukitu had escaped the village boundaries, Yuki following after him in pursuit of rabbits or squirrels, geese or freedom. Yuki they had known and played with the longest. She was more affectionate and was more attached to them than Yukitu was, as yet. But in the life and offspring of both was their growing hope to have working dogs that would transport their goods easily and quickly, making for better hunting and trading. With such dogs, their village could become rich and famous in the land of long darkness and long light.

Yuki stood up. She arched her back and lowered her head. She barfed up a pile of grassy, sodden chunks of fish. A large pile. Piji, Ike and others dove in to pull her away from re-eating the pile.

The pups were taught early to work. They started small, dragging a few sticks of firewood in a sack. Yuki took to this quickly, enjoying the applause and the morsel of meat at the end. Seeing Yuki's example, Yukitu wanted to do it too, and do it harder, faster. When harnessed together by a slack hide tie between them, Yuki would try to lean into Yukitu, perhaps to nudge him aside, but Yukitu would then pull ahead and Yuki would do her best to keep up with him.

Yukitu had quickly become dependent on Yuki's company and stimulation, but he took longer to become relaxed and comfortable in the hut. Early one morning, Piji and Ike were enjoying a roll and hump in the furs, when they were stopped by the sight of Yukitu pissing at intervals around the hut. Piji began to rebuke him. Ike put his hand over her mouth. "He's marking his territory," Ike whispered into Piji's ear. "Yukitu has accepted us."

"A roll and a hump in the furs!" Meg exclaimed out loud and laughed. *"That's* barnyard *talk, such as my brothers were never allowed to speak in front of Alice and me.* Giddyup! *Let's go!"* She turned the page onto the next chapter.

Turning Wolves into Dogs

WHEN THE WINDS TURNED COLD and geese formed flocks to fly south, Ike's village prepared to move north with the caribou. The ground froze as snow arrived in windy gusts, blizzards or dense, steady falls during the increasing darkness.

The pups were nearing their full size and had grown thick fur coats. They were big and practised enough to pull a light sled but their legs were still too young and pliable to cope safely with deep snow. So the villagers, pulling their own sleds, went first, breaking trail, packing a path for Piji and Ike who had hitched themselves behind Yuki and Yukitu, guiding and helping them to pull a heavily loaded sled. They travelled beyond the forests to a place where they could build igloos of snow and be close to the water too deep and wide to freeze.

All went well enough, except for the haunting howls. Ike had taken the pups as far as he could from their packs' territories. With constant attention, feeding, activities and affection, Ike and Piji had become the pups' replacement parents, the villagers their extended pack. Pulling and carrying heavier and heavier loads further and further became the only work and challenge that the young wolves knew, life within the village the world they had become familiar with. But sometimes as darkness descended, or the moon and stars lit up the sky, when the winds were quiet, the plaintive call of wolves came from afar.

Piji and Ike tensed as they lay pressed together in their bed. This was why Yuki and Yukitu were locked into their home at night. Their ears perked straight up at the sound of a distant wolf pack. Yukitu sat up, then Yuki. They began to howl in harmony. Piji got up and sat in front of the secured doorway. She joined in the howl.

Ike covered his ears. He would have covered his eyes if it would have blocked out the vision of Yuki's shocked and bewildered siblings, of Yukitu's dying nanny, his panic stricken siblings. And along with that, Ike had the acute imagining of what it might feel like to have these pups taken from him now. How badly did they want to return to their own, to their natural life? He couldn't bear these imaginings. He lay paralyzed with guilt and fear.

Meanwhile, Piji howled with the wolves. Yuki was excited. She turned from one direction to another, sometimes yelping in the howl. Yukitu sat still, his head raised high in howling sonorous lament, a beckoning appeal. When the howling subsided, Piji clapped in encouragement, not reprimand. She reached out to the pups, petted them, scratched their ears, stroked their backs. Yuki rolled over to let

Piji rub her chest and belly, but Yukitu remained alert. He looked for exits, tried to escape, but the exits were blocked. Sometimes neighbours would join with Piji in howling or chanting from within their own dwellings. Yukitu eventually settled down, keeping his eyes open with a look of not full resignation.

Yukitu had a charcoal-coloured coat, which sharply defined the white fur of his face, chest, underbelly and legs. His black "goggles" became more prominent. Yuki was sable–coloured, with black guard hairs on her winter coat. The whiteness of her underbelly, legs and chest also sharply defined her face. Both wolves had ginger-coloured eyes, almond shaped and narrowly rimmed with black skin that intensified their shape and glow. With all the pulling they were trained to do, they developed bigger chest muscles, though Yukitu was naturally larger and could pull ahead just a little harder than Yuki. No one could tell which of them was clearly dominant, for they pulled together so closely and behaved as though they were more afraid to be separated and left alone than concerned with dominating. No one saw them growl or snarl at each other, except in warning over a favourite stick, a bone or food.

As they became yearlings, everyone noticed greater displays of affection between them. They leapt and rolled over each other. They put their chins over each other's neck, let themselves be mounted, briefly, playfully, in turns. They licked each other's snouts. But they were too young to mate in their first spring. They shed their winter fur in clumps as Piji combed them smooth with her own comb.

Word of this handsome pair of tamed wolves spread from village to village, along the river routes and around the coastal settlements. But no serious attention would be paid to the pair until pups were born. Then a new generation of dogs might be declared.

It happened at the end of the following winter.

"Eeewww!" said Piji to Yukitu. "You stink!"

The smell within the igloo was always pungent: the burning seal oil, the dead fish and raw meat, the hide underwear, the dampening fur outerwear. The farts that Ike enjoyed but Piji did not, the smell of wet wolves when they came in covered with snow. But now Yukitu had a different odour.

"Eeewww!" Piji repeated.

Ike sniffed. "This is good," he said. "Yukitu is ready to mate."

"No!" Piji yelled at Yukitu as he lifted his leg to leave his mark on the igloo wall. "That is not allowed inside."

Yukitu did not lower his ears. He looked around, cockily. Yuki looked unconcerned, but she was restless that day and kept cleaning her private parts. At night, Yukitu slept very close to her. Early next day, still in darkness, Yukitu began scratching at the ice block door to be let out. Yuki stood quietly.

"No! It's too early. You can wait," Ike told him, eyes still closed.

But Yukitu scratched and moaned until, drowsy and grumpily, Ike got up and pulled back the ice block. The wolves rushed out. Ike was taken aback, not quite awake.

"What's going on?" said Piji.

Then they both remembered that Yukitu was in male heat and perhaps Yuki was receptive. They ran out into the cold dark morning. Yukitu and Yuki were already out of sight.

The village was alerted. Ike and Piji began to give chase, following the tracks of their wolves. But after a while, Ike, who was far in the lead, stopped. He saw ahead of him the forested area of spindly evergreens. This is not right, he said to himself. We should let them mate on their own. And pray they will return to us. He turned around and went back to meet the villagers, telling them to turn back, to respect the privacy of mating wolves.

"I can't bear it,' said Piji. "I can't just stand here and wait. They could join another pack."

"Another pack won't accept a mating pair."

"Then they will be killed by another pack as a threat to it. They'll be attacked for being on another pack's territory."

"Wolves want to bring down caribou, not each other.'

"You don't know everything about wolves!"

"I think they'll come back on their own."

Piji frowned. Her husband could be such a dreamer. "I'm going after them. Our wolves are known upriver and down. They could be stolen. I'm going to go and call them back."

Ike turned his back on her. He returned to the igloo, which was beginning to melt, and lay down on the furs. He lay down with his guilt and his fervent hope and his resignation. The guilt of killing and stealing the creatures he admired most of all in nature might be assuaged, if he simply left it up to them to return or not to return.

Led by the chief, most of the villagers accompanied Piji into the woods, following the tracks of Yuki and Yukitu. They carried satchels of fresh and dried meat. The tracks of the wolves ran side by side, then scrambled together in some kind of tumble and sport, then moved on again side by side. The short span of daylight was being obscured by clouds. Winds were gathering in force. Piji stopped. She called Yuki and Yukitu. She broke into a sorrowful howl punctuated by urgency. It was the best imitation of a wolf she had ever achieved. The chief and villagers supported her, the chief slightly annoyed that his howl was not quite as good as Piji's. They waited for a response.

There was only the ominous sound of wind whistling through evergreens, the gathering of a late winter blizzard. The chief pulled his fur parka closer round his face and bent into the wind, leading Piji and the others in the tracks of the wolves. He stopped and held up his hand.

Yes. Far off in the opposite direction, Piji could hear it too, the sound of numerous wolves, a large pack.

"We must be quiet," he said. "No more howling. That pack will think their territory is invaded."

They trudged on, following the tracks to an open expanse along the river. Then the blizzard was upon them. They moved back into the small forest and huddled together, making seats of their snowshoes under the shelter of tree branches. The storm did not end until long after nightfall. Stars appeared illuminating the fresh deep layer of snow that covered all tracks.

For two more days and nights, they searched for fresh tracks of Yuki and Yukitu, but people on snowshoes, expert as they were, could not catch up to runaway wolves. The chief ordered a return to the village to regroup and consider a new plan. The consensus was that Piji must not be allowed to continue the search on her own. At that pronouncement, Piji lifted her head in a most desperate howl. No one joined in with her. She put her head down and wept as she trudged along in the footsteps of the chief. No one looked back. Consensus ruled. That was the order in the village.

It was a peculiar sight, one Ike would never forget. The tired and grim troupe of the chief and villagers, including his wife, Piji, who looked grimmest and yet still defiant.

"We have to leave," she blurted out as she rushed to Ike. "We have to leave this village and search for our wolves on our own. I won't give up until I die."

As she said this, also in sight, though very far behind the village troupe, were Yukitu and Yuki, bounding out of the forest, heading in no uncertain terms towards the village, their igloo, their food.

There was much speculation as to what had induced the wolves to return. Piji believed it was because of her search and call. Ike liked to think it was the wolves' own choice, that they had taken the turn away from forming their own wolf pack and preferred to stay with the village, be fed, loved and work for their keep. But no one could be certain. Ike and Piji were all the more determined to be vigilant and rewarding to Yuki and Yukitu, who paraded themselves now as mates rather than pals. They acquired an air, subtle but noticeable, of regality.

When Piji announced that she had felt some formation of pups in Yuki's belly, the villagers cheered. They agreed to move immediately to find a good location for hunting and fishing on the greatest river, where commerce for their new breed of dogs would be better. It took more than the full turning of the moon to reach the Yukon River, which was still frozen. They found a clearing where they could build sturdy shelters of wood like the ones built by the clans who lived this far south year round. Ike and Piji built their hut near a small cave-like piling of rocks, which they cordoned off and linked to their hut by a fence of tough branches, as tall as Ike. They secured the base of it with stones. Yuki and Yukitu were kept within this wide area of fencing when not in harness.

"Good wolf! Good Yuki!" Ike and Piji applauded when Yuki began to dig a tunnel near a fallen tree within the fencing.

Villagers gathered outside the fence to watch as Yuki dug deeper and deeper. Earth and small stones flew with a force no one wanted to get in the way of. At the end of the tunnel would be the den where Yuki would have her pups. She was busily occupied, digging hard and gnawing at roots that got in the way. But Yukitu was restless, pawed at the fence to get out.

They tried to keep him busy, or tired, by having him haul loads for everyone in the village. When Ike trusted a neighbour to handle Yukitu, he got away. Ran into the woods. Ike and villagers pursued but could not catch him until they found him coming back with a rabbit in his jaws. Yukitu would not let go of it, growled and snarled threateningly, until he dropped it in front of Yuki.

One time Ike caught a villager hitting Yukitu with a stick to keep him in line. Yukitu yelped in shock then snarled menacingly.

"Never, never strike my wolves!" Ike took Yukitu away from him. "They will strike back."

"You have to teach them who's boss," the villager shouted. "They should be taught to obey, like children."

"Not my wolves," said Ike. "They're smarter than children. You have to respect them and gain their co-operation."

"You're not doing very well then," the villager retorted. "Your wolves are always running off."

Piji stepped in to back up her husband. "All a stick teaches," she said, "is fear and retaliation. Our wolves must never be beaten. Yukitu could leap up and kill the next man who tries. We want to tame these wolves, not make them vicious."

The villager turned his back on her. "I don't argue with women," he muttered as he walked away.

When Ike was off hunting and Piji was busy brushing the beds in the hut, Yukitu took a run and leapt over the fence to catch a passing squirrel. Piji and others ran after him and he returned willingly enough but it was decided that the fence had to be built twice as tall as Yukitu could reach when standing on his hind legs.

"You should just tie that wolf up," a villager advised. "Keep him tied up."

"Would you do that to your children?" said Piji. "Think about it. What would it do to the spirit of your children to be tied up night and day?"

"Ours?" The villager's wife laughed. "They'd cut loose and run like the wind."

"So would our wolves," said Piji. "And never come back."

The chief observed the situation. He noted the bleary-eyed, overworked condition of Ike and Piji, managing their project at this crucial stage, guarding, working, feeding their wolves to ensure a safe and healthy litter. He heard the voices of criticism. The chief then called a meeting of the village and made a brief speech commending the villagers for co-operating in the project of taming wolves so successfully that they were about to produce the first litter in their village. He spoke of the fame and fortune that that could bring to their village. He then asked for consensus in helping Ike and Piji make this project a success. He received a unanimity of nods, no one wanted to be a saboteur at this stage. The villagers agreed to follow Ike and Piji's rules of wolf taming, and they organized night and day volunteers, since in this new, warmer territory, there was the added danger of lynx and cougars on the prowl for unguarded wolves and pups.

Snow remained on the mountain tops and the ice had not yet broken up on the Yukon River, but the land along the river valley had absorbed the melted snow and was sprouting various shades of green, as moss, shrubs, flowers and spindly trees came to life. Evergreens had fresh tinges of blue or green. Bears had come out of hibernation. Hawks and eagles soared and swooped down upon scurrying mice. Porcupines lumbered along the river bank, twitching their small ears at the sounds of ice beginning to break up.

Yuki's belly sagged with the weight of her unborn pups. Then, for the first time in her life, Yuki ceased to eat every morsel of food.

"Look!" said Piji to Ike. "She has left half a fish."

Yuki lay down near her tunnel. Yukitu kept an eye on her while he finished his fish. Then he decided to go for her leftovers. She let him.

"Either she's very sick," said Piji, "or her time has come."

Yukitu lay down near her, licked his chops, but did not relax or rest his head on his paws. Yuki rested hers for a while, then got up to take a drink of water. She lay down beside Yukitu but looked uncomfortable. She whined very briefly then crawled into her tunnel. Yukitu paced at the entrance. Piji wanted to go and calm Yukitu. Ike held her back.

"Is it happening?" said the villager on guard outside the fence.

"Probably," said Ike. "But keep back. Keep quiet. We must leave them alone."

The villager considered this command, then ran to inform the chief and everyone else. The chief led the procession to Ike and Piji's hut. He took his place beside Ike and Piji in their doorway looking onto the wolves' pen. Villagers gathered round outside, peering through the fence, whispering and conversing in hushed tones. Yukitu paced and lay down, paced and lay down. If Piji or Ike made any move in the direction of the tunnel, Yukitu curled his lips. The chief, well-practised at sitting regally still, couldn't help but smile at Piji and Ike looking offended at being so fiercely turned away by Yukitu.

"A wolf is a wolf," he said. "How many generations will it take to make these wolves into what are called dogs."

Ike looked at the height of fencing all around and shrugged. "I don't know, Chief."

Eventually the villagers went home for their supper. The chief dined with Ike and Piji. Then they heard excited whining from Yukitu. They stood up in the hut and went to the doorway holding pieces of raw moose in their hands. They saw Yukitu dancing about on all fours. When Yukitu halted his excited dance and began to howl, the villagers came running.

The humans howled as much like Yukitu as they could. It was so loud that it carried to a wolf pack on the other side of the Yukon. All joined in on what they hoped was the birth of a large litter of healthy pups.

Next morning Yuki emerged from the tunnel for food and water and a long pee. Then she went back into the tunnel to attend her pups. Piji noticed that all eight of her teats were swollen and in use. The second day, Yuki came out for longer periods and allowed Yukitu to crawl in for a look. The villagers brought the best meat and fish to feed Yuki and Yukitu.

On the third day, Yuki emerged from the tunnel carrying in her mouth a dead pup, its eyes not yet opened. She carried it to the furthest corner of the compound. There she lay it on the ground while she dug a hole, then lifted the pup into it and buried it. All the while, Yukitu stood watch at the entrance of the tunnel. Piji stood weeping. Ike put his hand on her arm. Yuki took a drink, accepted some meat, then crawled back into the tunnel.

After that, everyone watched with fear. The great smashing sounds and loud cracks and blasts as the Yukon River's ice broke up held little interest to Piji and Ike compared to their vigil at the wolves' den. They watched through a full turning of the moon. No more dead pups were brought out.

They could hear the sounds of baby pups whimpering as they nudged and nuzzled against each other, coming closer to the opening of the tunnel in their increasing explorations. Yukitu's watch at the tunnel entrance began to change in manner. At first he growled, telling the unseen pups to stay back. Then he became more lax, sometimes coaxing with the pups, sometimes scaring them back quickly.

"He's teaching them and warning them of dangers outside," said Ike.

"It's been a full moon," said Piji. "Yukitu should let the pups come out."

"The pups come out when they are ready. Yukitu won't stop them. I have seen it before," said Ike.

"Yes," said Piji. "That makes sense. Children walk when they are ready. A father doesn't stop them. Look!" She nudged Ike in the direction of Yukitu. "See how proud Yukitu looks. I think he wants us to see his pups. Maybe they will come out now."

"I'll send for the chief," said Ike.

The chief was standing with Ike and Piji at the doorway of their hut. Yuki and Yukitu stood outside the tunnel entrance. Yuki lay down calmly. The sounds of several pups increased at the entrance. Everyone watched intently, the villagers peering through the fence, as a snub-nosed grey pup put its head out, squinted at the bright sunlight and quickly withdrew. Soon it emerged again and ventured wholly out, staggering and tottering its way towards Yuki. A second and third, a fourth, fifth, sixth and finally a seventh, tumbled out and converged on Yuki.

Yukitu lowered his head and growled, drawing attention to himself. The pups' ears went back. Some cringed. Yukitu looked at Ike, Piji, the chief, then lay down regally beside Yuki and all the pups, his paws straight out in front, his head held high.

Piji clapped her hands together and jumped in excitement. "Look at that!" she exclaimed. "He's grinning. Positively grinning!"

"Wolves don't grin," said Ike.

The chief looked at Piji and Ike. They could bicker over their interpretations of wolves' behaviour all day. "Yukitu is proud," he declared. "He has done well."

"Yuki," Piji said quietly, feeling a watering in her own eyes, "delivered the pups."

The chief nodded, turning to Ike and to Piji. "You have done well."

He turned to the villagers cheering outside the fence. "Our village has done well."

There was a feast. There was drumming, dancing, chanting, well into the night.

The Hard Part

THE PUPS LOOKED BASICALLY ALIKE. They all had white faces, chests, legs, and underbelly, though some had darker coats than others or more markings around their eyes. They were of varying temperaments and strengths. Ike and Piji studied the character of each pup and experimented to determine the most orderly arrangement of them in a team.

It was expected that the first pup to come out of the den would be named in honour of the chief because the first to come out was male and presumably the most brave and aggressive. He was a handsome pup with a shining dark coat and white face. But he turned out to be so un-cautious that he could not be trusted to be in the lead and avoid thin ice. He was so avaricious and daring, or arrogant, that he attempted to steal a piece of fish Yukitu had inadvertently dropped. Yukitu tore into him, grabbed him by the neck, shook him and threw him down. After that, he kept a respectful distance from Yukitu but he did not get along well with his siblings, always trying to lord it over his brother and five sisters, rather than play or work with them.

The chief laughed ruefully at his behaviour. "He reminds me of a comrade I once had," he said. "Don't name him after me. That comrade was eventually banished for stealing from his hunting partners. This young comrade has trouble sharing even water."

And so, that male pup was named Comrad and the other male was called Chiefdog. Comrad was given a position of strength on the team, the one closest to the sled, but he kept trying to over-ride the others and had to be constantly reigned in.

The leader of the pups proved to be Icebarb, a female who was sharp as a barb of ice, impressive and aggressive as Comrad, but wary of dangers and deferential when necessary. Icebarb was placed in training behind Yuki and Yukitu. Chiefdog was harnessed beside her because she would tolerate no females in that position.

Piji frowned at Icebarb's behaviour. "She treats her sisters as though they were simply 'the others,'" said Piji, "as though she has no dependence on them at all."

"She had better learn," said Ike, "that seven or nine pulling together are much stronger than one."

During that summer and autumn, kayaks and canoes, traders and adventurers travelled up and down the Yukon River, stopping to see the tamed wolf pups. Trades were made and stories exchanged in a mixture of sign language and sounds and words common to Malamute and other languages of the north. Some marvelled at the Malamutes' wolves, declaring them better natured and better trained than any other tamed wolves they had seen. Others pointed out that you couldn't tell much from first-generation pups. They had yet to prove themselves as working dogs. Who knows ... they might run off and revert to the wild at any time.

As winter set in, some strange looking teams came along the frozen river. Or so they were judged by Ike and Piji. They were sled dogs of various descendants of various wolves. They came in various colours and markings. Some teams had an all black or all white dog. Some dogs were different shades of brown. There was a distinctive silver-coat dog. Not many had white faces like Yuki and Yukitu. Their eyes were ginger to dark brown. They all had the body shape, sharp ears and bushy tail of wolves. They were strong and made to pull hard. Some sleds were pulled by only two or three dogs.

Ike judged those sleds overloaded. And the way some of the mushers treated their team, using a whip, angered him and Piji.

"You'll see," one musher with a whip told Ike. "It's the only way to keep a big team in line."

Piji thought some of the dogs exceptionally beautiful. "Imagine a whole team of that silver one," she said.

"Never!" said Ike. "I will always honour Yuki and Yukitu, and their packs. Our teams must look like them."

"It takes all kinds," another trader argued with Ike, "to make a strong team. You should have your pups mate with my team when yours are old enough. I could give you a good deal on that. Want me to bring my team back here, end of next winter?"

Ike stood up in silent disgust and walked away.

"We must go away from here," he said to Piji, after relating the trader's proposal.

"Yes!" Piji cringed in alarm. She had lived in dread of Yuki and Yukitu running off, or being taken by a pack of wolves. Now she imagined their precious pups being seduced, or attacked by a team of "all kinds," all at once. It was an indecent proposal. "Let us speak with the chief," she said.

It was agreed they would go back up north but not so far as they had been before, since they had seven young pups to transport, their legs not yet strong enough to go a long distance. It was a peculiar sight, the village of Malamutes on the move over early winter landscape, the people pulling sleds with their belongings, and one sled full of wolf pups, bound together, sitting up, looking attentively ahead, as their wolf parents pulled them onward.

When they came to a clearing near a river where they could ice-fish and where caribou had been sighted, the villagers camped and built their igloos. They helped Ike and Piji construct a kind of double igloo where their wolves could have adjoining quarters, though access was only through Ike and Piji's. Thus they raised their pups in isolation from "all kinds," treating them like their own children. It was a good-looking team that coursed around the village, carrying people and products. Ike had succeeded in creating a team, not just a pair, of working wolves.

The following spring, when Yuki and Yukitu had produced another litter, five healthy pups, Ike and Piji faced the fact that they must eventually let go of some of their progeny and allow outside influence. A team of more than nine was unwieldy. A team of five could work, but who could be trusted to train it as well as they did? Several villagers offered much meat and furs if Ike would give them pups from the next litter. There were just a few in the village Ike could bear to let handle pups when they were separable from Yuki. It worried him to do so, but he knew that it was inevitable, if his line of wolves was to go on.

"Icebarb won't always defer," said Piji. "She tests Yuki's authority sometimes. Yuki puts her in her place but Icebarb may be driven off in time."

"She wants her own litter," said Ike.

"But daughter must not mate with father, nor sister with brother," said Piji. "We need new wolves."

"I'm not stealing any more wolves!" Ike shouted. Then he spoke calmly. "You must prepare Yuki and Yukitu to accept other litters in the village, litters of their own descent."

"I?" said Piji. "I?"

"Yes. You talk with them best. It is you who brings them back. And I must bring in new blood. I'm going to find some dogs for Icebarb and her sisters when they come into heat next year."

"What's the difference?" said Piji. "Tell me again the difference between a wolf and a dog. You said wolves are dogs when they stay with you for food and work for you. To me, Yuki and Yukitu will always be wolves. I still fear they will take off. Though their pups work hard and aren't always trying to escape."

"They try to go after any animal they see on the move," said Ike. "Rabbits, mice, martens. Even birds and geese. It's just that we can hold them back now, in harness. And look how many men it takes to hold them when we go on a caribou hunt! They're always trying to break loose and show us how to bring down a caribou."

"How many generations will it take to get that out of them?"

"Never!" Ike declared. "Never! "Our dogs will always be wolves."

Next winter, when Comrad, Chiefdog, Icebarb and the four other females were in their second year, Ike set off with them pulling the sled towards the Yukon River. Piji stayed in the village with Yuki, Yukitu and their new pups. The plan was for Ike to find mates for the females, then, well before birthing time in late spring, he would bring them back to join Piji and the villagers at the old summer camp grounds. Ike's sled was laden with a month's supply of dried fish and meat for the trail, plus furs and clothes sewn by Piji to be traded for dogs or stud services.

They had travelled over frozen open spaces of flat and rolling landscape, through mountain passes and dense forest, following the same route Ike had travelled so much more slowly with his village. Alone with his team, Ike rode on the sled when going on the level or downhill. He ran beside it when going uphill. He fed his dogs as much or more than he ate himself. He slept with them curled up around him, his sled as his shelter. He talked to them and chanted under starlight, setting them to howl in harmony.

First thing upon reaching the Yukon, Ike used his biggest spear to make a hole in the ice to fish. He camped for several days. No one and no dogs had come into view. Then he stopped peering up and downriver and just got on with the business of fishing, hoping that not looking would bring someone along.

Suddenly Icebarb sat up on the alert. Ike narrowed his eyes, trying to see through snow being blown sideways by strong winds. He could see nothing coming but reached to secure his wolves in any case. Too late! Icebarb took off and there was no holding any of them back. The brake on the sled served only to tip it on its side, dumping the cargo of furs, weapons, utensils. Ike ran upriver on the rough ice, chasing the sled track through swirling snow.

He heard several sharp barks, brief silence, then the voice of a man shouting commands angrily. Panting, Ike came into view of Icebarb prancing provocatively in front of the lead dog of a team of five. Both teams were straining to engage in play or combat.

"Keep your dogs in control!" the musher was shouting at Ike. He was wielding a whip.

Ike yanked his sled upright and stood on it. Comrad snarled at the lead dog, who was responding to Icebarb. The lead dog snarled at Comrad then turned his attention back to Icebarb. With a frantic jerk, Comrad broke his harness and ran to attack the lead dog. The musher lashed Comrad repeatedly and expertly, driving Comrad back in shock and pain. Ike drew his knife and threatened to throw it into the musher's chest. The musher gave a lash to his dogs and took off in the direction Ike had come from.

Comrad lay down on the snow, blood seeping from the lash marks under his belly near his vitals. He would not let Ike touch him, let alone put him onto the sled to return to camp. The few hours of light were fading into darkness. Ike settled his wolves around him, preparing to wait until Comrad could recover enough to stand on his own. The wind had calmed, letting snow fall lightly. Ike prayed that it would cover his scattered belongings from the sight of the musher, whom he pictured scooping up all his furs, weapons, tools, utensils. Would he also find his camp and steal his food stores? One who would whip his dogs, thought Ike, would steal anything.

His wolves' ears suddenly quivered. They raised their heads sniffing in the direction of their camp. Some sat up, but all stayed silent when Ike heard the familiar shout of the musher, then saw him appearing, on foot, through darkness and snow.

"I left my team back there," he spoke with gestures and a language similar enough to Malamute for Ike to understand. "Don't want to fight with yours. I picked up your furs and stuff. They're on my sled, back there."

He went over and looked at Comrad who snarled as he bent over to look closely.

"You've got bad manners," he said to Comrad. "I could have whipped your balls off for trying to attack my dogs." He turned to Ike. "He'll be all right in a day or two. Come on." He looked at Ike's sled. "Let's get him onto the sled and back to your camp."

"Can't," Ike shook his head. "He won't move."

"Then move him!" he shouted. "You're the musher, ain't you!" Impatiently, he pulled a large hide he had draped over his shoulders and stretched it out beside Comrad. "Bring the sled close. Stuff something into his mouth so he doesn't bite me. We'll lift him onto the sled."

Ike put the sled beside the hide and took off his inner mitt to stuff into Comrad's mouth. But Comrad lifted himself onto his legs and moved himself onto the sled.

The musher laughed. "You're workin' with a pack of wolves here, ain't you, pal. I saw that right away. They could destroy my dogs in a fight."

The musher set up camp with Ike for several days so they could hunt together, stocking up a store of meat. As they skinned a caribou, Ike listened to the man's advice.

"Keep them tied up so's when you want them to run, they go like the wind. And never let them get the upper hand. Use a whip. It's just like a woman. Words are never enough."

"Do you whip your wife?" asked Ike.

"No." He laughed. "I wouldn't have a wife and none would have me. My dogs are enough for me. I'm always on the run. Been to the source of this river and to its mouth. Plenty of women along the way. And I've got the best dog team, right here with me."

He looked over at his dogs who were tied to a tree within sight, but not within reach, of Ike's team. Ike's dogs were similarly tied to a tree, as the only way of controlling them while on the hunt or in range of other dogs.

"Lie down!" shouted the musher.

His dogs lay down. Ike's remained in their various positions.

"And stay!" The musher's dogs stayed still.

"There, see!" he said. "That's the hardest to teach them, to lie down and stay, on command. Wolves won't do that."

"How long did it take you to get them to obey like that?"

"Five generations," he said. "I started with two wolves, just like you. Then I did some trading, took whatever behaved liked dogs, up and down the Yukon. That's what you'll have to do. And if you want to start soon, I'll trade you that Comrad, plus a parka, for one of mine."

Ike had already considered trades. Decided he did not want any smaller dogs or ones without white markings similar to Yuki and Yukitu. He wanted to keep his line distinct, with big, heavy-weight pullers, as much like the wolves he had started with as possible, without having to live in fear that they would run off and re-join the wild at the first opportunity. The way to do this, he had concluded, was not by whips and constant tying. He would continue as he had begun, by gaining their co-operation, and arguing it out with them when necessary, as he did with Piji. Domination on his part and obedience on theirs, was not how he would proceed. For in the end, he realized, in travelling over ice, he had to depend on their instinct and intelligence to say when it was safe or not. They were in the lead. He wanted to respect and develop their intelligence, not beat it out of them.

The only dog of the musher's mixed bunch that Ike wanted was the one that attracted Icebarb, the lead dog who was big, mostly black, with white mask and light brown eyes.

"Comrad is my biggest male," Ike began to bargain. "And he was first out of the den."

"Ah," said the musher, pleased but not saying so. It was what he was looking for, an aggressive dog, new aggressive blood for his team which was fast, but becoming too timid. He was impressed by Comrad for breaking tether to attack his dogs. And first out of the den makes a good lead dog. His own lead dog was getting old at six winters. "Maybe I'll take Comrad, without the parka."

"Maybe," said Ike.

"Why isn't he your lead dog?"

"Too headstrong," said Ike. "Like a bad wife."

The musher laughed. "You like my dogs? Which one you want?"

"Your lead dog."

"Can't trade my lead dog," said the musher, but thought, yes I could. I need a new stud dog, young, aggressive.

"How old is your lead dog?" said Ike.

"Four winters," he said readily, feeling virtuous for having lied by only two winters. This Ike couldn't tell the difference.

"Must be six or more," said Ike.

"I'm tired of talking." The musher threw down his knife. "My lead dog for Comrad. Take it or leave it.'

"Comrad plus a promise."

"What's the promise?"

"No whip. No whip on Comrad ever again."

The musher shrugged.

"Speak," said Ike. "I want your word."

"You have my word. If he's smart, he's learned his lesson already."

"Comrad is smart."

This is the hard part, thought Ike as he parted from Comrad, leading him over to the musher who gave Comrad a hunk of meat then patted him on the head and scratched his ears.

Ike tried not to think or feel. Raising dogs felt good, but putting one's dog into the hands of another man and never seeing him again, losing all control over what happened to him . . . .it didn't bear thinking about.

The musher was used to this. He was ready with food and pats and encouraging words as he led Comrad to the front of his team. He shouted at the rest of them to lie down while he tethered Comrad to the front. The musher gave him one more piece of meat, then ran to the sled, put one foot on the runner and yelled, "Hike!", cracking his whip on either side of the team.

Ike flinched. He could not see the startled look in Comrad's eyes as he was forced to speed ahead with the others on his tail. But Ike could hear his startled yelps as he disentangled himself again and again until he took the lead, running faster than he had ever run.

All the while there was the intermittent, frantic howling and yelping of the deposed lead dog, Snowface, whom the musher had tied to a tree.

"Keep him there until I'm long out of sight," the musher had said. "But feed him and all your dogs right away. Get their attention away from us. Put that one you call Chiefdog back where Comrad was and put Snowface up with your Icebarb. Let her and Snowface race it out for lead. I bet your Icebarb will want to show him her furry rear end."

The musher proved to be right. Ike headed up the frozen Yukon River with Icebarb in the lead, Snowface keeping close to her with a new excitement in his eyes. But Ike had a new disquiet. It was the trust with which Comrad had accepted being put on a lead and taken by Ike and then the look of being betrayed and sudden resistance Comrad had shown when being handed over to the musher. Ike could not forget that look, hard as he tried to counter it with imagining Comrad enjoying mating and being lead dog. Nor could he put much trust in the word of the musher. It would be up to Comrad to avoid the whip through obedience.

Ike also felt a new tension in his team with the replacement of Comrad. He tried to squelch this feeling and ease the tension with rational assurances. Snowface was a good acquisition, Ike assured himself and said so to all the dogs, in calming, confident words. When breeding time comes, Ike said to himself, this dog's white face and black coat should combine well with Icebarb's and some of the other females' markings. And he should be an old hand at mating: well-practised, no young fumbler. But Ike needed more than one new male to take back to his village in order to create new strong lines.

Chiefdog was his favourite male: smart, quick to act, greedy for food but more interested in sporting than dominating. Chiefdog had a way of insinuating himself into a position he wanted, rather than demanding it. He habitually sought affection, nuzzled up to his mother and leaned up against his father, until they snarled at him, telling him he was too old for that. Then he leaned up against his sisters and Ike and Piji. Ike also liked his sense of humour, the way he liked to tease his sisters, and how, when Icebarb got annoyed at him, he would take a running leap over her back. Ike planned to keep Chiefdog, acquire a female for him and another male for his sisters. He travelled far upriver encountering various dog teams and mushers.

I'm certainly not the first and only to come up with this idea, thought Ike as he sat near his fire, his dogs sleeping around him. But I am doing it differently. Most mushers don't mind what their dogs look like. They trade and breed for speed, strength and obedience. They were more or less like the first musher he had traded with. And they criticized him for having such an unruly team.

It was true. Since acquiring Snowface, there was a new disorder in the pack. Snowface got along with the females. Icebarb confirmed her position as lead and the chosen of Snowface by strutting imperiously around her sisters and snarling fiercely if they approached Snowface. Sometimes they curled their lips in return but they did back off. The fights that broke out were between Snowface and Chiefdog. Snowface started it and Chiefdog would not back away.

Ike had seen that Snowface was obedient, whereas his wolves were at best co-operative. If Ike raised his hand when he called an order, Snowface would cringe and immediately obey. This helped when they were in harness. Snowface's immediate obedience and Icebarb's siding with him, made the rest of the team follow in reasonably quick succession.

Ike knew that Snowface's obedience was the result of years of training with the whip. He knew he could never bring himself to whip his wolves and certainly didn't want to, when he saw in Snowface its side effects. When Snowface was out of harness, he wanted to fight with the nearest male and beat him to the ground. That had happened the first time Ike released the team to feed and rest at the end of the day. After his supper and brief rest, Chiefdog had gotten up to sport with his sisters. Snowface then attacked Chiefdog in the midst of a prance. Icebarb leapt on side with Snowface and the others leapt into the fray.

Ike had yelled to no avail. He saw blood spouting from Chiefdog's snout. Ike grabbed his spear by the spearhead and tried to whack Snowface on the rump. He got Chiefdog on the back. Chiefdog kept on fighting. Ike jabbed and whacked, dispersing the others. Snowface was well practised at evading whips, but when Ike did crack him on the back, he stopped, snarled, threatened to begin again but slunk away. Icebarb then went for Chiefdog's ear and came away with a piece of it, halting when Ike rapped her on the snout.

All had small injuries, including Ike, with blood on his hands and arm. Snowface came out of it with a bleeding neck, though it was not in a crucial place and it soon healed. Chiefdog had reacted so smartly that he couldn't be pinned to the ground and he protected his neck. The bite marks round his head soon healed but his inner ear remained more exposed, and vulnerable as it was to piercing winds from behind, his hearing became impaired. But it was the shock to his psyche that affected him most.

Chiefdog ceased to sport. He wanted to get away from further attack but was also ready to fend it off at the slightest suggestion of its coming his way. He began to growl more readily and fiercely. Ike bestowed more affection on him. He responded as of old, leaning up against him, but a new distance and wariness grew between him and his siblings and the male intruder.

Ike's heart felt heavy. He did not like the work of a trader.

When he reached the junction where the Klondike flowed into the Yukon, Ike knew that this was where he had to finish the job of trading for new blood lines, in order to get back to his village in time for the mating season. This junction was the centre of northern trade routes. The flatland made a convenient winter campsite. The large rounded snow-covered mountains rising up on both sides of the rivers served as barriers against the worst weather. Owners of dog teams from distant regions converged and stayed here for days at a time to trade and talk. It was here that Ike saw his dream team of dogs, driven by a couple who shared his ideals.

They had come from another large river which flowed further north, into the Arctic, a river to be called the Mackenzie. They had eight big dogs, all with dark coats and white markings, wolf-like in appearance, though broad in the chest. They were at ease in the harness and confident and friendly with people. The dogs were as harmonious and orderly as a well-led wolf pack, except when vying for attention from people greeting them. They did not cower.

After observing them, Ike approached the couple, a strong old man and his wife who smiled approvingly and knowingly at him and his team. He found himself choking with emotion as he said, "No whips?"

"No whips." They invited him to share their campfire.

Ike returned to his village like one who had travelled to the sun and rubbed noses with the Great Spirit. They had exchanged gifts. Ike returned with proof positive of the existence of the ideal.

"This is Tarak Amorak," said Ike, introducing to Piji a big, handsome, wolf-like creature, whose name meant Shadow of the Wolf. "He is so like Chiefdog and he is most certainly a dog. His head is maybe a bit too big but look how he behaves!"

Tarak was leaping up and putting his paws on Piji's shoulders.

"You won't see a wolf do that!" said Ike, folding his arms over his chest triumphantly.

Chiefdog would do that, thought Piji, if he were here. But she didn't want to say anything to spoil the joy of Ike's safe return.

Ike told Piji all about his exchange with his ideal traders.

"The couple is old but strong," said Ike. "Their dogs keep them fit, they said. Like us, they have no children. They started with stolen wolf pups then mated the first generation with two different families' third-generation tamed wolves. So we're doing the right thing, Piji, just like I thought. With our two new males and our five females, we can make many dogs. Smart, friendly working dogs, like Tarak. The couple said it took six generations to produce such a broad-chested heavy-weight puller.

"They observed me and our wolves for several days before they would even consider doing business with me. Mushers will hide their whips and lie to get one of their dogs, they said. They won't take a man's word for it when he promises not to beat or tie up a dog." Ike looked away from Piji as he said this, thinking of what might have happened to Comrad.

"That couple was smart as wolves." Ike continued. "They saw that Chiefdog had lost his place in the pack and needed a new pack. That's what they said to me. 'You better trade him, quick, before the mating season, or he and Snowface will fight to the death.'"

In the end, they rescued Chiefdog. And they'll mate him with one of their best females. They understand him and they like his temperament. Chiefdog will create another strong line for them." Ike coughed to disguise the lump in his throat. He missed Chiefdog so much he had to surreptitiously rub his eyes.

"How many pelts?" said Piji. "How many pelts did they take, along with Chiefdog, for this wonder dog, Tarak Amorak?"

"Five."

"Hmmm," said Piji. "Hmmm." She looked into the flaming oil. "And for this cowering, bad-tempered Snowface, who is always trying to hump Icebarb?"

"Comrad," said Ike. He did not mention the promise, for since conversing with the couple, he realized how unlikely it was to be kept. He bowed his head, dared not look up with watery eyes.

Piji moved closer to Ike. She was silent as she tried not to picture the handing over of Comrad and Chiefdog.

"You're a strong man," she said to Ike. "I couldn't have done what you did, all on your own." She put her hand on his hand and then on his vitals. "Now we can get on with the best part of this dog vision ... raising more pups."

What Happened to Yuki and Yukitu

THIRTY WINTERS PASSED. Ike and Piji had become elders in the village grown famous for its dog population. Through careful but basically experimental breeding, and diligent training, they had produced their dream line of dogs. Big dogs, with broad chests and brown eyes like Tarak, dark coats, white underbelly, chest, legs, and white around the eyes and snout like Yuki and Yukitu They were well-fed and treated with respect and affection so their tempers were generally even, their nature friendly and their tails often raised and held plumelike over their rump. They pulled sleds to and from hunting grounds. They transported people and possessions from winter to summer campgrounds, grounds even better and further than the village had been able to reach before the invention of these malamute dogs.

The fame of Ike's dogs spread up and down the great river trade routes of the Yukon and Klondike. Through lucrative barter for their coveted dogs, Ike and Piji obtained good meat and fish supplies, the warmest bear skins for their bed, tools, weapons, pots, even a fine collection of carvings. When they obtained more than they needed or could easily transport, they passed it on to others in the village.

"Our dogs have no use for this," Piji would say in handing over the item.

Piji was regarded as somewhat mad after the death of Yuki and Yukitu, though no one doubted her continued competence with dogs. She could train and drive them as well as Ike. Ike always had been regarded as a bit mad because of his obsession with wolves, but it had paid off. Ike and Piji achieved worldly success in their own life time. They enjoyed the admiration of villagers and traders from distant places. The envy, jealousy, rivalry and pirating of their vision and invention was another matter. It was their dogs that gave them deep satisfaction.

And Ike would never forget the good feeling he had, the sense of approval and blessing he felt, when he and Piji encountered again the couple who had traded Tarak for Chiefdog. Chiefdog recognized him and Piji, leapt up and licked their faces, as Tarak did with the couple. Chiefdog had sired many healthy litters, as had Tarak. Both dogs were well-treated, well-trained and well-fed, never beaten or overworked. Ike received a broad smile of approval from the couple that meant more to him than the congratulations of the chief and all the lucrative trades put together; for the rest of the business too often depressed or infuriated him, worried or wracked him with guilt.

It began with what he learned had happened to Comrad. He heard the story from other traders. Comrad's musher had genuinely admired Comrad enough to use him to sire all his females in one season. But Comrad reacted to being tied up and kicked by attacking the musher's leg, for which Comrad was bludgeoned to death.

It was a long time before that story found its way back to Ike. It gave him nightmares and nagging fears about the fate of other dogs he had traded in good faith. He tried his best to vet his traders. But who knew what a man would do once the deal was done and he was out of sight.

People like to entertain each other with stories, lonely traders all the more so. Ike practised listening and soliciting stories so that he might the better glean the character of others. He reported stories of cruelty to Piji.

"A musher went mad with snow blindness," he told her. "He hacked a hole in the ice and tried to drive his dogs into it. They balked and pulled him around the hole but he tipped his sled and fell into the hole himself. He scrambled out by grabbing onto the sled which the dogs held for him and then pulled him to a village where he recovered."

"That's a good story," said Piji. "I believe it. He'd be good to his dogs from then on."

"How can you believe that?" Ike frowned and raised his voice. "If he could do that once, he would do it again."

Piji sat in silence. She couldn't bear to imagine terrible things happening to her pups, as Ike did.

"This story even I won't believe," Ike began another. "A musher was a poor hunter. He was without food for several days in a blizzard." Ike looked at Piji forcing her to imagine the scene. "He killed and ate one of his dogs."

Piji stood up. "I don't want to hear any more stories."

She picked up the carefully preserved, whole fur-hide of Yuki. It included the head which she fitted onto her own head. Sitting down, cloaked in the hide of Yuki, she took up her sewing.

"I would never eat my dogs," Ike spoke with solemn conviction. "It is like eating your own child. I would die with my dogs and hope that I go before them."

"Put on Yukitu's hide." Piji nodded to where it lay flattened out on the floor but was never walked upon. "It will give you his strength and comfort."

Ike looked at her in angry silence. Even his wife could not be trusted to act the way he wanted her to. He would go and talk with his friend Pakak.

"It is known," said Piji with her new calm that so irritated Ike, "that by eating the heart of a wolf and wearing its clothing, you take on its spirit."

Ike shook his head. It was better than shaking her, which he had done when he found her in the woods, lying with the corpses of Yuki and Yukitu.

Yuki and Yukitu were monogamous mates all their lives. They were always "the wolves" to Ike and Piji and everyone in the village. Their litters, from the generation of Icebarb onwards were called "the dogs" within the village, and eventually "the Malamutes' dogs" in the world beyond.

Yuki and Yukitu continued to be the leads in Ike's dog team for six years. Stronger dogs were bred but Ike and Piji would not demote their original wolves. Yuki and Yukitu were given special privileges. They were allowed to run off with each other during the mating season. They would return in a few days and a good sized litter would be produced two months later.

The others, beginning with Icebarb and Snowface, then Tarak and selected females, were penned for mating, according to the method recommended by Tarak's first owners. A female in heat would be put in a high walled snow pen, then Tarak would be allowed in. He would romp and nuzzle, courting her for a long while, until he received her solicitation to mate. Afterwards, they wanted to stay with each other but Ike and Piji had to separate them and get on with the business of others mating in the pen. Ike was told by other breeders and traders that penning was a waste of time.

"Just tie the bitch up," one said, "and let him ram her."

But Ike and Piji would have none of that. They saw the devotion between Yuki and Yukitu and felt guilty about not letting Tarak mate for life. He was an affectionate dog whom Piji thought trusted each time that he would be allowed to stay with the female and help raise the pups.

"He's not so stupid as to keep trusting, when it never happens," said Ike. "He's learned to enjoy just the mating well enough. He's good at it. There's not a female yet who has turned him away."

Piji hated taking pups after they were weaned, to be given away in trade. She suffered most in taking pups from Yuki and Yukitu, imagining that Yuki would feel as she would in having to sell her babies.

Ike rationalized it. "It would happen wherever they were," he said, "whether with us or in the wild. Pups grow up and leave their pack. Sometimes they're forced out. Yuki and Yukitu couldn't manage to keep six or seven pups every year."

At the end of their sixth winter, Yuki and Yukitu ran off for only a day. Ike took this as a further sign of their voluntary dependence on him and Piji. Why scrounge in the wild when you have ready food and shelter at home.

"Look!" he said to Piji. "They are wagging their tails like dogs. They will always come back to us."

Piji welcomed them with words and big chunks of meat. It will always feel like a knife twisting in my stomach while they're gone, she thought.

Over the next two months, Piji kept stroking Yuki but could feel no sizable litter growing inside. Yuki was less energetic but that seemed natural at her age. She dug her usual den and stayed inside it for three days. No kind of enticing would draw her out. When she did crawl out, she carried a dead pup in her mouth. Yukitu sat in silence, watching her bury it. She would not look at him as she returned and crawled back into the den. She brought out another dead pup and buried it. Then she lay down flat, with her head between her two outstretched paws, looking at no one, particularly not at Yukitu, who lay down near to her.

When Icebarb who was about to produce her fifth litter nosed her way into the vicinity, Yuki roused herself and snarled, then lay back down while Ike led Icebarb away. At the end of the day, Yuki got up and accepted some food and water. But she remained listless and melancholy.

"She's ill," said Piji.

"She'll recover," said Ike. "She needs to get back to work with the team."

He brought hers and Yukitu's harness. Neither of them would arise to receive it.

"I'll put other dogs in their place," said Ike, "until Yuki recovers."

While Ike and Piji were busy inside, Yuki got up, followed by Yukitu and headed towards the forest.

Villagers quickly informed Ike and Piji. They ran to the village edge where they could see Yuki, followed by Yukitu, proceeding slowly into the forest.

"Let them be," said Ike. "They want to be alone. Give them a day or two."

While Ike was sleeping, Piji stole out with a sack of food in pursuit of Yuki and Yukitu.

The next day, Piji was found lying in the snow with the bodies of Yuki and Yukitu. There was much blood in the snow, and the tracks of a battle with a large wolf pack.

"I saw them kill Yukitu," Piji reported when she could speak. "He died protecting Yuki. The wolf pack left when they saw me coming at them, wielding my knife and spear."

11

A Proper Pioneer

Randolph came into Meg's room when he heard her push back her desk chair and fall upon Poley, weeping.

"It is so sad!" Meg clung to Poley, then complained to Randolph, "What a terrible ending! I don't want to believe it. How could anyone write that? And just leave it at that!"

"Annie was a plain-speaking woman," said Randolph, sitting down with Meg and Poley. "An indelicate woman, one might say. If she's alive, I expect she has written more, but this is all Annie left with me."

"I like her," said Meg. "I'm grateful she gave us this much. I'm afraid it's the truest story I'll ever have about the origins of dogs. I must see these dogs that are so like wolves. Will you come with me, Randolph? Someday?"

Randolph gave an exaggerated shiver and nodded towards the snow gathered round the window panes. "Isn't it cold enough for you here?"

Ike came out of his own story feeling more tortured. To live it all again! And yet those good times were very good. He missed Piji.

Missed her as much as he missed the wolves. They were all of a family. It was a pity his spirit couldn't find rest where hers did.

But I won't give up, he told himself. I've never been one to do that. And if this Meg can follow through ... If my story can keep her on track ...

Meg received a letter from the Faculty of Comparative Medicine and Veterinary Science at McGill University asking her to come for an interview in mid-March. She wanted Randolph to go with her but travelling alone with him was out of the question.

"Completely improper," Randolph declared. "It is your father's happy duty to accompany you to Montreal and conduct you through the college. Take every opportunity you can, my dear, to appear proper, conventional, and normal, when embarking on something so unconventional as becoming their first woman graduate. Offer them no grounds but your God-given sex to dismiss you."

"Proper, conventional, and normal?" Meg smiled at Randolph. "How unattractive."

"Oh no it isn't!" he responded sharply. "Though I thought as you do when I was your age. Now I would do anything, *anything* to turn myself into a normal, proper man." He turned away from her. "For you."

"Randolph," Meg said quietly. "I heard that."

"You should not have. You must forget it. It is an impossibility. And I must say good night to you now." He turned his back to her and walked to the doorway. "Good night, my dearest."

"It's very rude," said Meg running to take him by the elbow and turn him around, "not to face the lady you are addressing."

He put one arm and then the other around her, hugging her tightly. "I have been so good. *We* have been so good. You are about to graduate. Let us not spoil it now. My darling girl." He hugged her silently then took her by the waist and steered her into the hallway pointing her in the direction of her bedroom. "Go! Quickly. Please."

Herbert was pleased to be asked to accompany Meg for her interview and tour of the college. He hoped she would be accepted and find there a husband who would set up the vet practice that so interested her, let her dabble in it, but mainly provide for her to be a good wife and mother. "You do want to have a family some day, don't you?" he asked when they were settled into the plush velvet seats on the train.

"Oh yes!" she answered firmly. "Not quite so many children as you and Mom, but at least four."

It was Meg's first train trip and she was thrilled by it. "Such speed!" she said, "The view of our nation literally flying past the window! You can't even see what's propelling us. Doesn't it feel like we're flying right into the future!"

"That's my little Meggie," Herbert patted her knee. "Still looking for tomorrow, aren't you? Ever the optimist."

"Not entirely, Dad." She patted his knee. "I have my doubts at times. But I certainly am curious about what tomorrow will bring."

It's right to call this machine "the iron horse," she thought to herself. It has replaced horses for long distances. Next will be machines for short distances. And then what will the horses do? And horse doctors? Maybe there is no great future for horse doctors.

She thought of *Black Beauty*, the novel she had been given by Mrs. Atkins, two summers ago, about a horse who experienced every miserable, as well as every comfortable job, horses were ever put to. It hadn't moved her the way "Ike's Working Wolves" had, but it did make those who read it empathize with horses and more knowledgeable about how to treat them. It used the word veterinary and veterinary surgeon, as opposed to the common term: "horse doctor."

In going for an interview at McGill's vet college, Meg would have her first look at what a veterinary surgeon does. She had never seen an animal operated on. If their farm animals got sick and did not recover through rest and the application of a poultice, liniment, or mash, the animal would be put out of its misery with a bullet in the head. Meg didn't ever want to have to do that. She focused on becoming a surgeon of animals, learning how to relieve, cure, prevent their suffering. She looked forward to seeing the surgical facilities and practices at the college. She expected that the hard part for her would be the interview, being interrogated about her abilities with big animals, the issue of handling and shooting horses.

I was raised with horses, she would tell them. I can ride, drive, and handle them. Shoot them, if necessary. Though she told herself, I could always get a man to do that part.

But it was the tour of the surgical facilities, not the interview, that shocked and threw her into doubt at the veterinary college.

There was little overt derision of her applying to become a veterinarian. Everyone she met was male, beginning with the registrar, who looked at her with curiosity when she showed up for her appointment accompanied by her father. "Ah, Miss Wilkinson," he said. "The applicant, I presume. And Mr. Wilkinson?"

"Yes," said Herbert, pulling his shoulders back, "the father." He extended his hand.

"Pleased to meet you," The registrar shook hands. "Parents do not usually accompany the applicants but this is an unusual case from the start, isn't it?"

"Pleased to meet you," Meg held out her hand.

The registrar shook it. "Indeed. May I congratulate you on your marks at Dalhousie, so far." He stepped back and nodded, holding his hand out in the direction of the door leading back onto campus. "Shall we begin our tour with a look at the lecture hall?"

Back home with Randolph, in the calm and privacy of his library, Meg still felt her stomach cramp at what she had seen that day in the college.

"Of course the lecture hall was fine," she said. "Not much different from what I'm used to at Dalhousie. McGill's campus is just bigger and more imposing. Some very grand, new, grey stone buildings. The grounds slope down to a good view of Montreal. Male students and male staff everywhere, except for the odd woman student passing amongst them, giving me a look of appraisal and solidarity. But absolutely no women to be seen in the veterinary college, apart from me.

"The faculty and students were clearly prepared for my arrival that afternoon. I think my case had been well discussed in the common rooms and whispered about in the classes. You know how universities pride themselves on being open–minded, and students are on the lookout for what's new and maybe ground breaking. I felt like a welcome curiosity. And I had a distinct impression that the authorities at the vet college had concluded that if women were allowed into medical school, it was logical they should not be refused application to vet college. Vets not to be outdone by meds. But ..." Meg had to take in her breath. "It's as if they wanted to show me that animal doctoring is ever so much harder than human doctoring. The books, the lectures, the diagrams on the chalkboards in the lecture halls, I had no trouble with. But the labs ... oh Randolph!" Meg hugged her stomach. "They were *gruesome*."

Randolph sat closer, pried his arm through hers and took hold of her hand. "Tell me."

"It was like a slaughterhouse. Dogs and cats strung up by their hind legs, like pigs at the slaughter. And of course, there were pigs. And rabbits. Strung up to be operated on. Dissected for study. It was nothing like dissecting frogs in biology. We don't string up frogs. They're laid out mercifully, like humans, on an operating table. It was so gruesome!"

Randolph paused, then said carefully. "They were dead, weren't they? Cadavers?"

"Some were. And some weren't. There was a lab where they were neutering, and performing intestinal operations on dogs and ..." Meg winced. "Thank God, Ike and Piji didn't live to see that done to their dogs!"

"Strung up live, by the hind quarters?"

"Yes. From hooks on a wall."

"Good Christ! Why?"

"They're easier to keep still that way."

"Do they pour some brandy or something into them first?"

"No." Meg had to smile at that but in the lab she had been so upset she couldn't speak and had to put all her fortitude into not shrieking and pleading to cut the animals down. She had watched in silence. "It was like a torture chamber," she said to Randolph. "Or so I thought. But the surgeons and students had become used to it. I guess the way soldiers get used to what they see on the battlefield. That lab was the last place they showed me.

"'This is not for the faint hearted,' they had warned me. I think they were prepared for me to faint. But apparently I surprised them, from the start.

"At the end of the day, the principal invited me into his office. He was a good-humoured man who complimented me on my looks."

"Did he!" interrupted Randolph. "Of course it's warranted. You are surely the prettiest thing he has seen come into his office. But I'm not sure I like it that he did."

"He said he had expected their first female applicant to be a bit of a Calamity Jane."

"Calamity Jane!"

"Yes. You know. She was big and tough. Talked and dressed like a man. Rode around out west with Wild Bill Hickock. Dad was quite incensed that I should be compared to her. But I was complimented. I told the principal I was prepared to dress like a man if that would make my presence more acceptable. At which point, Dad rose from his seat in anger. But the principal calmed him with saying that would not be necessary, or desirable."

"I would do it." Meg looked Randolph in the eye. "I don't see anything wrong with it. I have thought seriously about it, you know."

Randolph squeezed Meg's shoulder. "On with your story, my girl."

"Not much more to report. A Dr. Osler from the medical faculty came in and explained that McGill has exceptionally high standards, that I would be taking some of the same classes as the medical students and if I changed my mind on becoming a veterinarian, I could, with further studies, become a medical doctor.

"I think he expects that I will end up doing that, even though I said, 'Thank you but I prefer to work with animals.'

"The principal smiled at that and asked if there were any questions arising from my tour, any conclusions reached. I complimented him on the college, said it was a far cry from the days when an animal with an ailment was just shot. The research being done on worming and inoculations is going to lead to big changes in animal medicine. Great progress has been made. But we still have a long way to go in treating animals as well as we do human beings."

"You mean the *same* as human beings?" said Randolph.

"That's exactly how Dr. Osler responded. And Dad was twitching to correct me, starting to mumble that I didn't mean quite that, when Dr. Osler stated, slightly tongue in cheek I think, 'The argument is that animals are "dumb beasts" created to serve, not rival human beings.'

"I said I don't think of them like that. I knew I was getting on shaky ground intellectually but I ended up blurting out, what about wolves? Or skunks? They don't serve human beings. Not in any direct way. But I think they should have a place in the world."

"'I couldn't agree with you more,' the principal piped in. 'But we're not clear as to what you might mean by treating animals as well as human beings.'

"Give them some gas or chloroform and lay them down on a table for operations," I said.

"Oh my!" Randolph drew in his breath in exaggerated askance. "Were you shown the door?"

"The principal and Dr. Osler looked at each other. Dr. Osler gave the nod as if to say, this is your office, not mine. The principal wrapped his fingers on the edge of his desk. Pondered. Then turned to Dad. 'Mr. Wilkinson, sir. Do we have a trouble maker here before us? Or a proper pioneer?'"

Randolph clapped his hands high in the air. "That is good. That is very good. And your father's response?"

"Dad grinned and slapped his knee. 'A proper pioneer, sir,' he said. 'Like her parents before her.'"

"I'm proud of you." Randolph picked her up and swung her around. "Even more so than your father."

She clasped him tightly. "But it's three years. Another three years. Far away from you. I don't think I can bear it. There's another way." She stood back and faced him squarely. "After graduation in June, I could apprentice myself to a vet, one of the horse doctors in Halifax. Learn all there is to learn from him, except surgery. I'll be like the doctors who prescribe but do not perform surgery."

"No, you will not. Not under my tutelage." Randolph pointed his finger at her. "You will be a proper pioneer."

Ike landed firmly on Randolph's shoulder, folding his arms tightly across the front of his parka. "Yes!" he said to Meg, loudly as his spirit could. "You must!"

12

THE YOUNGER MALE

JACQUES BENOIT WAS TWENTY, the same age as Meg, when he thumbed his way to Halifax in the spring of 1890, arriving on the roof of a stage-coach carrying nuns from Antigonish. He had left his home in Sydney Mines, Cape Breton Island, at age fourteen. There, he had worked underground in the coal mines ever since age ten, when his father, also a coal miner, had died. His mother then married another miner, who got belligerent when he was drunk. His mother learned to keep silent or out of his way when he came home drunk, but Jacques took offence at his insults and eventually muttered one back. His mother rose to Jacques's defence and would have herself been slugged, had not Jacques's stepbrothers stood in the way and persuaded their father to back off and go to bed. Next morning, Jacques's mother gave him a small stash of money and, tears in her eyes, ordered him to go and find work away from the mines.

Jacques spent a few years working on farms and boats, keeping in touch with his mother by letters, until he was summoned back to Sydney by a letter from his older sister. His mother and stepfather had "died in their sleep." After the funeral, his sister gave him more details. They had each died from suffocation. "No one knows for certain," said his sister, "But I sure as shootin' hope it was our mama who put the pillow over him before she did it to herself, and not him

who done it to her. She was a changed person after you left, Jacques.
She missed you terrible."

Jacques had thoughts of digging up his stepfather's grave, grabbing him by the heels, and swinging his body round and round until
it flew off the ends of the earth. But he got himself very drunk instead
and left town feeling worse than he had when he left as a fourteen-
year-old.

He crossed onto the mainland of Nova Scotia and found work in
a tavern at Antigonish. It was a high-class tavern frequented by student priests, professors, graduate students, the mayor, and policemen.
Jacques was befriended by all of them, including the proprietor and
his spinster niece who was called Winnie. She was born with a pretty
face and curvaceous figure but she walked with a limp. "And I can't
have babies," she readily told Jacques. "You can 'practise' on me."

Jacques took advantage of this offer and was not required to pay
every time, as were the frequenters of the tavern. Winnie taught him
how to give, as well as take, pleasure. She told him he was handsome
and "wholesome," which Jacques didn't quite understand but knew it
had to do with comparison to other men who practised on her.

"You will make a good husband if you do what you have learned
with me," she told him, with a sad look in her eyes. "Other women
want what I have taught you. They don't only want babies."

Jacques comforted her and enjoyed giving her pleasure so much
that he practised giving it before taking it himself. He felt the best
pride and satisfaction when he peaked with her. But her basic sadness
he did not want to share for the rest of his life. He wanted to have a
family who would love him as he had loved his father, his kind and
hard-working father who had been crushed to death in the mine. He
wanted to find and please a woman who was blessed with good health
and had sparkle, not sadness in her eyes. The pickings were good in a
big city like Halifax, he was told.

"Dress smart and don't say 'yous'," he was advised by the tavern's
frequenters. "Get a job in a good business. Marry the boss's daughter." They laughed and raised their pints to Jacques the night before
he left Antigonish.

Halifax was such a futuristic, huge, and rich-looking city compared to Sydney, Louisburg, and Antigonish, all the big towns he had
ever seen. From the top of the stagecoach, Jacques could almost reach
up and touch the maze of telegraph, electricity, and telephone wires
that lined and crossed the main streets. On the streets he saw women
in suits with form-fitting jackets and slim-fitting skirts that showed
the shape and movement of their legs as they walked briskly along.
The hats were small and jaunty on these busy modern city women.
Jacques raised his cap to them. Some were bold enough to give him a
smile or a backward glance. The pickings looked very good indeed.

As his coach passed along the bottom of the Citadel, he saw a small
crowd gathered round a loud-talking man on the street corner. He
was demonstrating the use of something Jacques had not seen or even
heard of. He grabbed his bag and jumped down from the stage coach.
He thanked the driver and the nuns who were leaning out the window
to see the strange-looking vehicle. It had two thin wheels, one in front
of the other, with handle bars at the front and a tiny rude-looking seat
in the middle. It was unbelievable that a man could sit on that and not
injure his private parts. But the man sat himself upon it, took hold of
the handle bars and cranked the pedals around under his feet. It was
incredible, but that vehicle kept upright and sped ahead, fast as could
be, scattering people out of its way. Without the help of a horse, wires,
or steam engine.

Jacques believed he was seeing the vehicle of the future. It wouldn't
have to be fuelled, fed, watered, or stored in a big place. It wouldn't
stink up the streets with horse farts or shit. Jacques envisioned the
streets of Halifax teeming with bicycles. Bicycles on their own, bicycles in pairs and teams, pulling carts and wagons and carriages.

The man riding the bicycle was demonstrating its use as a sport.
He acted like an entertainer rather than an entrepreneur. Along with
a few others, Jacques followed the man on the bicycle to a shop where
there were rows of these vehicles lined up for rental at a dollar an hour.
Jesus, Mary and Mother of God, that was steep! But Jacques eventually drew the money out of his wallet and said before all, including a
couple of pretty young ladies, that he wanted to try his hand at one of

them new-fangled things. With bravado and a good sense of balance, Jacques was able to keep the bicycle upright though it wavered like a spinning coin until he got up some speed.

Shouting "Make way! Please, folks. Coming through!" he cycled round and round the Citadel's base road. Some cursed him for frightening the horses or making themselves scatter, but others cheered him on his way. Ladies smiled and clapped. When he returned the bicycle to the shop, Jacques asked the owner if he could give him a job.

Not making enough yet to support myself, thought the owner, Jos Andersen, but this young man is a good advertiser. "Tell you what," he said to Jacques. "I'll give you a start. You work Sundays for me and I'll give you free rental on Saturday afternoons."

"Good enough." Jacques shook his hand. "For a start."

Jacques found a cheap boarding house and immediate work in the dockyards. Then he read newspaper ads looking for a job with prospects. He was sure he had found that at Clean Sweepers. The owner, Oliphant, was quite the gentleman. An outstanding dresser. But not a really hard-driving businessman. After a couple of weeks as Oliphant's delivery man, Jacques could see there was room for improvement at Clean Sweepers. Too many slackers. He could see himself replacing any one of them.

Then Jacques was introduced to Oliphant's "accountant." That's what he called her, his accountant. The sparky-eyed Miss Wilkinson, whom he treated like both a business partner and a daughter. Strange relationship there. But then strange things were to be found in a big city. A comely young woman business accountant, keeping house for the boss and attending the university.

Jacques lay awake at nights imagining giving pleasure to her and indeed to any of the pretty young women whom he saw in church, in the library, and along the street, as he cycled past on a Saturday, showing how he could ride with his hands on his waist when the way was clear and smooth.

He could hardly believe his luck when he saw Oliphant and Miss Wilkinson walking their dog in the park one Saturday and they flagged him down on his bicycle.

"That looks like fun," said Miss Wilkinson. "Is it very hard to learn?"

"It's a might difficult in skirts," said Jacques, "But..."

"Then I'll wear trousers," she said, "like you."

Jacques laughed. "You wouldn't dare."

"I'm afraid she would," said Oliphant, smiling indulgently at her. "But the question is, can you teach us? Miss Wilkinson is very keen to ride a bicycle and I might give it a try myself. Could you get hold of a pair of bicycles from that shop where you work and give us a lesson or two?"

"I'm sure that could be arranged, sir." said Jacques. "Would next Saturday suit you?"

Oliphant consulted with Miss Wilkinson then said, "Two o'clock next Saturday?"

What luck! he thought as he cycled away. And with a bit more of it, I might just get that Miss Wilkinson on a bicycle and ride off into the sunset with her.

But it sure didn't turn out that way. He arrived at Oliphant's gate, two o'clock sharp, pushing two bicycles by the handle bars on either side of him. Oliphant and Miss Wilkinson had been watching out for him and came down the front steps in tandem. It was shocking. They were dressed like twins. Both were wearing tweed jacket and trousers, plus-fours with red knee socks, and flat shoes. Smart outfit for cycling. It was what Jacques himself wore. But a woman shouldn't dress like that.

"You don't mind, do you?' said Meg, smiling happily. "Randolph, Mr. Oliphant, thinks I'm making trouble for myself, but really, men's clothes are so much easier, aren't they, for riding bicycles? And other activities as well. It's not fair, women having to wear skirts all the time."

It put Jacques off, seeing Meg in that outfit. He couldn't imagine giving pleasure to a woman in trousers. Skirts were made for that very activity, surely. What does a man do with a woman in trousers? He was flummoxed by Meg. It was easy teaching her how to cycle, once he took her and Oliphant to a smooth clear lane. But she treated

him like a kid brother. He tried to make her see him differently, see
him as a man. When he was helping to steady her on the bicycle seat,
he drew his hand lightly over her buttocks. Winnie would have cooed.
Miss Wilkinson got promptly off the seat and glared at him. He pretended not to know why.

"Randolph," she said, "Could you please help me adjust to the seat?
It seems to be awkward for Mr. Benoit."

Jacques stood back while they had a whispered conference. It was
apparent that Oliphant thought she was being too sensitive, probably
misinterpreting, and Jacques was to be given another chance. Whew!
thought Jacques. Any other man would have taken her word for it,
boxed my ears and sent me packing. That was a close call. He had
better tread more cautiously in future. Maybe Winnie did not know
all women. Modern city women might be very different. Especially
those in trousers. Jacques proceeded more cautiously. Kept his distance. Gave spoken instructions, touched only the bicycle parts.

Meg quickly caught on to cycling, acquiring speed and leaning
gleefully over the handlebars like a good horse rider. Oliphant was
nervous and unsteady. Wouldn't get up enough speed to balance comfortably. After the second fall, he said good-naturedly, "I give up. I'll
stick to horse and carriage. Jacques, take this wretched invention and
accompany Miss Wilkinson into the countryside. Make sure she gets
home safely."

She had offered to give up along with Oliphant, but he would have
none of that. Jacques took her cycling on the outskirts of the city,
embarrassed as he was to be seen with a young woman dressed like a
man. In fact, he wished she'd put her hair up under a cap so's people
would think she was a man. Dressed like that, she was a bad advertisement for the bicycle trade. Normal young women wouldn't consider riding a bicycle if they had to dress like that. He cringed at the
startled looks on people who saw them pass and had no trouble at all
in keeping his distance from her, no trouble at all. He led her back to
Oliphant's on the least-travelled route. Once he had become formal
and distant with her, she relaxed and was friendly with him. She was

exhilarated by the cycling and not at all embarrassed by the stares of onlookers.

When Oliphant drew Jacques aside to say he wanted to purchase a bicycle for Miss Wilkinson, Jacques decided to talk to him, man to man, even though Oliphant was his employer. "Sir," he said, "at the risk of losing your custom and even my job, I must say, with all due respect, and you know I believe in the future of bicycles and I want ladies to be encouraged to ride them but ..."

"Not in trousers?" said Oliphant.

"You object to my dressing like a man!" said Meg.

"It's all right for you," Jacques said. "But other ladies ..."

"Would be driven away," Oliphant interjected in a tone of dismay. "They would be put off the sport. Thank you for your frankness. Miss Wilkinson and I will discuss the matter."

In the end, both were more understanding than Jacques had expected. Oliphant bought a bicycle, saying it would be a graduation present for Miss Wilkinson and they invited him to Sunday dinner. It would be a family affair. He was to meet Meg's father and sister.

"I look forward to that, thank you Miss Wilkinson, Mr. Oliphant." Jacques doffed his cap to them and wondered as he shut the gate, what the sister might be like. Maybe normal, he hoped. That Miss Wilkinson and Oliphant weren't. There was no getting between them. They were a pair, of some peculiar sort. Yet he couldn't help liking them and feeling more lonely himself. He hated being alone, night after night in his cheap rooming house bunk, alone amidst the snores, farts, horking, and spitting of other men. But things were looking up. If he could just move up in Oliphant's business, maybe become a salesman. Then he'd have enough money to buy his own bicycle and then some. If he could stick with it another couple of years or so, he might have enough to open his dream sports store.

It was not an impractical dream. City people were crazy about sports. Unlike coal miners, they had enough time and money for it. He could sell sports equipment year round, not just bicycles in summer. That was the problem with Andersen's shop. Too limited in scope.

Jacques would have tennis and lacrosse rackets, baseball bats, hockey sticks, skates, toboggans, canoes, and another new thing: skis. Yes, he, Jacques Benoit, had his eye on the future as he walked away from Oliphant's gate. Then he glanced back at Oliphant's fancy house. Electric light shining through the windows. Imagine living in such a place! What luxury. What peace and harmony and fresh clean smells within. With a wife and family to keep you company ... Jacques shook himself. Back to reality. Back to working his way up to such a future.

"He's a suitable young man," Randolph had pointed out to Meg. "Handsome, industrious, not without ambition. He should be given a chance to prove himself."

"But not with me," Meg had replied. "I think Alice should be given the opportunity of meeting him."

Alice and Herbert arrived early for the Sunday roast beef dinner. Randolph was on the phone to friends in Boston. Herbert settled himself in the salon with a sherry and yesterday's newspaper. Alice interrogated Meg in the kitchen.

"What are you up to Meg? You have been seen bicycling around town in the company of some young man. Your own age, for a change! And what's this about trousers? You shouldn't be cycling period. It's unladylike. But to do it in trousers! Have you no concern for *any* kind of propriety?"

"Rules that I believe in," said Meg. "I try to follow them. I think every woman should feel free to cycle around in trousers, if she wants to. You should try it. Cycling is all the rage in big cities like New York and London. Haven't you seen that in the newspapers?"

"I would never do it in trousers," said Alice, reconsidering, if it really were the new fashion. "But you haven't said who this young man is you've been cycling with."

"Jacques Benoit. He works for Randolph. And you're about to meet him, Alice. He's coming to dinner."

"Why didn't you tell me? I'm not wearing my best..." Alice

stopped smoothing her skirt and looked sharply at Meg. "Is he courting you?"

"Definitely not. Like you, he finds me improper." Meg continued to
scurry round the kitchen, mashing potatoes, simmering gravy. "Will
you answer the door when he arrives? You'll find him very presentable, I'm sure."

It was mutual. They were attracted to each other at first sight.

Jacques had bought himself a jaunty dark red bow tie for the
occasion, polished his shoes, wondered if he should change his style,
abandon the knee high socks and over the knee trousers for the sleek
perfectly pressed trousers other men wore. No. He didn't want to
look common. He wanted to look like someone who rode about town
on a bicycle and would own a sports shop someday. Alice smiled at
him approvingly. Batted her eyelashes. Put her hands on her cinched-
in waist, made him notice the shapely curves beneath her lacy bod-
ice. He saw her as pleasingly different from her sister. Alice was very
feminine, seemed to have a softness and coquettishness, and was not
dumb. She had opinions and a striving nature that he thought matched
his own. She wanted to be a school teacher.

"I plan to go to Normal School in the autumn and get a teaching
position here in the city," she said when they were seated at table.

"Holy Moly!" Jacques reacted. "Are all you Wilkinsons so brainy?
I've never met girls who go so far in school. Why do you do it?" Then
he blushed and felt stupid for talking like the country boy he had
been.

Meg laughed. "Because we can, Jacques." She passed the bowl of
potatoes on to him. "And because someone generous like Mr. Oliphant has helped me."

"I shall have to do it somehow on my own," said Alice with a sigh
that touched something in Jacques.

"Now Alice, you know you're going to get help from me." said
Herbert. "Though none of my sons went beyond Lower School and
they're doing just fine. I was an adventurous man myself. But then I
was raised in a time when there were new continents to be explored,

new nations to be settled. Now that we have Canada and the United States settled, it seems young people have nowhere new to go. They think sitting in a classroom is an adventure."

"Father!" Alice exclaimed, putting both hands down hard on her lap.

Meg laughed. "It *is* an adventure, Dad. It can take you more places than any ship. It can even take you back in time. But I see what you mean. Now that we're heading into the twentieth century, people are adventurous in different ways. Look at all that's been invented in Alice's and my time. Telephones, electricity, photographers in every city, trains across the country."

"And bicycles," said Jacques. "I can see everyone riding into the next century on a bicycle."

There was a moment of silence as they all pictured that. Again, Jacques felt embarrassed when Meg clapped and laughed, with too much heartiness, as did Mr. Wilkinson and Oliphant. But Alice responded with an earnestness which reached Jacques's heart.

"I think then, Mr. Benoit, that I should learn to ride a bicycle, like Meg. Though I wouldn't want to have to wear men's apparel. Do you think you could teach me?"

Yes indeed he would. Here at last was the woman of his dreams, who would believe in him and share his ambitions. She would help him and he would help her. He would be proud to court and marry a teacher. That was an impressive ambition on her part, not unrealistic and strange, like wanting to be a woman horse doctor. Teacher training for a year, then a couple of years of teaching ... that was about as long as he needed to establish himself with a sports store. Then they could marry and have a family. That would be most satisfying: to provide for a wife and children, with a good safe job, above ground. He hoped to live a long time to enjoy it all. Jacques was full of good food, hope, and plans when he cycled back to his smelly boarding house.

"He's so good looking," said Alice to Meg after Jacques had left. "And so smartly dressed. Very manly, without being boorish. He will be promoted at Clean Sweepers, won't he? Couldn't he become foreman?"

13

THE CALL TO BOSTON

"YOU WON'T DO IT, WILL YOU?" Randolph had said to Meg after the dinner with Jacques. "You stubbornly refuse to engage with a suitable young man. You fend them off, cut them off, even foist them onto your sister." Randolph stood up from his desk and approached her where she sat curled up on the chaise. "I've a good mind to withdraw your graduation present."

"Randolph, I'm tired," she appealed to him. "Tired of pretending. You know what I want for graduation." She couldn't look him in the eye but she could manage to say, at last. "I want to be engaged to you."

Randolph sat down on the chaise in silence. He straightened out her legs and edged up to lay beside her, his head propped on his hand. Still she couldn't look at him. She felt reduced to tears, to complete submission. She felt him take her in his arms, guide her face to his, and kiss her on the lips with more than tenderness.

"Your wish is my command," he said, then stood up at military attention. "I am a man of my word. The bicycle you may have now. But there will be no proposal on my part until after your exams."

Meg leapt up and wrapped her arms around him kissing his face.

"Ah! Ah! my dear girl!" He unwrapped her arms and held her at bay. "Discipline and propriety until you have graduated."

During the weeks that followed, Randolph sometimes looked strained and worried, but mainly he was relaxed, playful, and openly affectionate in the house with Meg. She studied and began writing her exams with more happiness and concentration than she'd had since entering university. Come summer, it would be a year since Randolph had had a trip to Boston. He had friends there, such as Geoffrey, whom he telephoned occasionally, just to see how he was, Randolph explained to Meg. Geoffrey had a conventional marriage but also a secret life. Randolph would explain no more. "You must keep your mind on higher things," he told her, tapping his temple.

The night before her last exam, Meg heard Randolph rummaging in the room above. Cecilia's cupboard and drawers were being opened and closed, a trunk moved. Then Randolph called to Meg from the top of the stairs, as he had been doing of late. "Good night, my love. See you in the morning."

Next morning Randolph was cheerful and more than affectionate with her.

"Off you go to the final of finals. I know you'll do well, my darling." He embraced and kissed her behind the closed door, then opened it onto the foggy morning. "Ah, more rain in store. You'll need your umbrella. I have much to do today. And must call my friends in Boston. But I'd like to fetch you after classes, if I may."

"Oh Randolph!" Meg reached up to kiss him.

"Ah! Ah! Ah!" He held her back. "Let us not be improper before the world. I have a serious question to put to you this evening."

Meg started to whistle a merry tune as she walked along the street, though she was out of practice. She used to whistle better than her brothers when she was on the farm. She hadn't whistled much in the city. It made people stare, some frown, at a young woman whistling. But this morning Meg whistled determinedly, in defiance of people and the inclement weather.

At the end of the afternoon she stood at the big stone campus gate, watching for Randolph to arrive in his carriage. She thought she had done well on the exam. She was whistling in good tune. Until she saw, not Randolph but Jacques, drive up in Randolph's carriage. She was intensely disappointed and then worried.

"I was expecting Mr. Oliphant," she said. "Has something come up to detain him?"

"He's gone to Boston," said Jacques. "Had to catch the afternoon train."

"What!" Meg burst out. "Why? Why today?"

"An old friend of his suddenly passed away. He wanted to attend the funeral."

Meg gripped the carriage seat. A likely story. Perfect explanation for strangers. For those who don't know why he goes to Boston. I cannot believe it. Has he fled? Fled from proposing to me? Or just gone for a fling? A last fling? Or forever… Why am I still afraid of this? That he won't come back? Or won't want to?

Jacques noticed tears sliding down her cheeks. "My sympathies to you, Miss Wilkinson. I guess you knew the fellow too."

Meg scowled at him. Jacques was so ignorant, so ignorant of all that was in her mind.

But Jacques kept his eyes on the horse so as not to embarrass her in her tearful state and continued talking. "Mr. Oliphant was very upset at the news of his death. It was so sudden, he said. Completely out of the blue. Mr. Oliphant said he'd get through to you by phone as soon as he can."

Meg wiped her cheeks. Maybe it was true. People do die unexpectedly.

"Thank you for fetching me, Jacques," said Meg after getting out of the carriage. "And do call me Meg. You are courting my sister."

"My pleasure, Meg." Jacques tipped his hat to her. "Mr. Oliphant asked me to keep an eye on things in his absence. Phone me at the office if you need anything."

"At the office?"

"Yes. I said I'd bunk down there until he gets back. There's the couch, phone and all."

Meg was eating scrambled eggs at the kitchen table. It was odd, even eerie, being in the house without Randolph. The floors creaked. The silence was ominous. Poley kept close to her but when she talked to him, her voice cracked and Poley woofed at her in sympathetic anxiety.

"Good old Poley," she hugged him, thinking, there's no better friend. Or relative. Dogs are ever so much more reliable, predictable, compliant, and comforting than human beings. If you were good to a dog, he would never, never leave you. Certainly not to go off and dress as a female. Meg tried to laugh at that but could not.

She got up from the table, went into the hall, and turned on the upstairs light. She ascended the stairs guiltily. Upstairs was the domain of Randolph and Cecilia. Only the bathroom was open to her. But she wanted to see what clothes Randolph had taken to Boston. His normal clothes? Or ... She yanked on the doorknob of Cecilia's room. It was locked. Infernally locked! "Damn!" she shouted, and went into Randolph's room and tried the door adjoining Cecilia's. Also locked. "Double damn!" She stomped her foot, then retreated downstairs, where Poley looked up at her, questioningly.

"Right, Poley," she said to him. "Good question. What is the matter with me? How normal am I?"

The phone rang early next morning.

"Hello, my darling girl! Have I wakened you? Did you have a sleepless night? It was very bad of me to leave you so suddenly."

"You haven't left me, have you?"

"Oh dear. You are distraught. I am so sorry, Meg, I had to catch the noon train. My dear friend Geoffrey ... are you prepared? It is tragic ..."

"Jacques told me someone had died."

"In the most awful manner ..." Randolph choked. "He took his own life."

"Randolph? Are you there?"

"Yes." He cleared his throat. "I'm sorry. I'm finding it hard. But his wife ... his poor wife and son. They didn't know. And they *cannot* understand. I must help them. I'm sorry, my darling. The telephone is not right for this. I'll be home just as soon as I can. A few days. I'll let you know when." He cleared his throat again. "How was your exam? You did well I trust?"

"Yes, I think so. But ... Randolph, I was so afraid you had left to ... that you had fled ..."

"Silly girl. Have you had your breakfast?"

"No."

"You must have your breakfast, then go off for a good walk in the fresh air. Take Poley. Or your bicycle. I can tell you have had a bad night. We'll talk about this when I come home. The telephone is not the place ... Goodbye, my darling."

"Goodbye, my love." Meg hesitated before hanging up. She could hear the operator and others hang up. Meg smiled, suddenly felt cheerful and in tune with the sunny day. "How about some breakfast," she said to Poley, "then a walk to the seashore?"

People nodded pleasantly to her as she walked by in her long skirt, Poley ambling beside her. After an early supper, Meg left Poley dozing on the verandah while she went for a cycle ride. The evening was warm with lily of the valley and lilacs coming into bloom. Meg wanted to cycle out of town where she could smell the lilacs along laneways. She had put on her plus-fours and tweed jacket, but no hat, wanting to feel the wind in her hair. Most people who saw her in passing stared, smiled, or shook their heads at her apparel. But one man spat at her. She cycled on, deciding to take a different route home. On the last street of houses, a group of boys had to interrupt their game of street hockey to let her by.

"Thanks boys!" she called over her shoulder to them.

"That's that woman who dresses like a man," she heard one say. "Let's see if she can take it like a man."

Meg sped up but as she rounded the curve, a twig they threw caught in her spokes. She swerved and fell onto the cobblestone roadway. By the time she got herself up and extricated, the boys had run into hiding. She walked the bicycle back along that street, her knee scraped but not seriously hurt. She looked left and right, planning to speak her mind, tell those boys she could summon the police. But no

one appeared except at windows. Cowards! she thought. Who taught
them such behaviour? No kids of mine will be like that. She got back
up on her bicycle and took a different route home.

Randolph phoned late that night. "How are you, Meg? Can you
manage another day or so on your own? I need to help this poor wife
sort things out. Perhaps you should have Alice and your father come
stay with you."

"Oh no. You know what Alice is like ... reprimands and complaints.
No thank you! I'm perfectly fine with Poley." She did not mention the
cycling incidents. "When do you think you will come home?"

"Sunday. You can manage till then?"

"Of course. Though I miss you ... more than I can say."

"And I you, my dear girl. We can talk on Sunday."

My dear girl. What happened to "my darling," Meg wondered.

Randolph returned punctually on the Sunday evening train but he
looked haggard, weakened, as though the wind had been knocked of
him and he was struggling to be strong. He hugged Meg, kissed her
on the forehead, and whispered, "We'll talk at home."

Meg stirred the fire pensively in the library while Randolph poured
himself another very large scotch.

"Was it very bad?" she said, sitting on the sofa, noting that he chose
to sit apart, sinking into his arm chair.

"It was dreadful. Perfectly dreadful." He took a big swallow of
scotch. "Geoffrey's wife in such shock. She'll never recover. Not
properly. And his son, Jason ... just seven years old ... completely
bewildered. Crying for his father to come home. Heartbroken and
confused ... probably for the rest of his life. God knows what he'll
do."

"Please come sit by me." Meg tapped the place beside her on the
sofa.

"I'm sorry," Randolph shook his head. "But I must speak. Try to
have you understand. It's no good. Trying to make your life with
an abnormal man like me. Geoffrey tried to have a normal life. But

he couldn't. Couldn't kick the habit, the wretched *need*," Randolph slapped his own leg, "to get dressed and go to the club ... to seduce men." Randolph hung his head.

"I don't understand. I don't know what you mean."

"It's not me. I don't do that. I only want to dress ... But Geoffrey had a lover ..."

"Randolph, my love. I think you need some food. And sleep. Let me get you a roast beef sandwich."

"Let me finish, Meg. Dammit, *make* me finish!" He finished his scotch. "Geoffrey's lover threatened to tell his wife. And so Geoffrey killed himself, shot himself in the head. Tried to make it look like a robbery-murder, his wallet missing, evidence of struggle. His wife wouldn't just leave it to the police, who have seen such things before and would have let it remain as an 'unsolved.' She hired private investigators who ended up telling her the damned truth. She couldn't accept it. Then she heard it straight from the lover ... who is the scum of the earth. The absolute scum of the earth. There's always scum. Oozes out, to ruin people's happy illusions. Now she lives in fear her son will turn out like his father. And she'll ruin him ... scrutinizing him as she does, an innocent little kid." He stood up to pour himself another drink. With his back to her, he said, "Meg, my dear girl, I love you more than I can say. And so I will not ruin your life by marrying you and I must never run the risk of having children who might turn out like me."

Meg stood up. "Come Poley. We'll make him a sandwich."

"Dammit, Meg! Is that all you have to say?"

"Yes!" She said angrily. "Apart from, 'stop swearing and stop calling me Meg, your dear girl.' I am a woman. And I'm going to make you a sandwich and tea. I will talk to you in the morning."

"You think what I say isn't true because I'm drunk?!"

"How could all that happen in such a short time? How come you get the call to this Geoffrey's funeral the very day you're about to propose to me?"

"You clever girl." He smiled wanly at her. "You clever, thinking girl. I called Geoffrey that morning after you left for classes because

I wanted his advice on ... men like us ... marrying. I thought he had a good marriage. But it was his wife who answered. Geoffrey killed himself just over a month ago. She was still so distraught, I went to try to help her to understand and sort things out. I helped her with some business arrangements, but not very much with ... the rest, I'm afraid."

"That can't be true." Meg put her arms around him. "You're the kindest person in the world. And she wouldn't have kept you for so long if you weren't a great, a *great* comfort, to her. Now I'll make your sandwich and we'll talk in the morning."

"I won't relent. I know what is best for you."

"Oh no you don't." Meg fairly sang over her shoulder. "And you forget the important difference. I have no illusions about you."

Meg brought him tea and a sandwich. Told him to eat and go to bed. She went to her bedroom. Tossed and turned, thinking things over all night. She imagined how Piji might handle the situation. Just before dawn, she crept up the stairs, quietly opened his door, and slid into bed with him. He was snoring. Gradually he stopped as she gently rubbed his shoulders and stroked his back, his chest and ...

"My darling." Randolph turned over with a pleased groan and began to kiss her, taking every interest in her female body. He was careful not to, as they said in those days, 'plant a seed.' They dozed, entwined. When they awoke and sat up, Randolph dramatically pulled back the sheet revealing a small dark red stain. "The dye is cast!" He spoke like a Roman warrior. "Now we *must* marry! And quickly." Then he held her closely and spoke into her ear. "Will you marry me, knowing all that you know about me?"

"I will."

"I will try not to do it. I would never do it in your presence."

"Perhaps you should." Meg held on to him with her eyes closed, for she didn't know if she could actually endure seeing him as anyone but her Randolph.

"No," he said. "Now that I have you, surely I can do without ... her. And for your sake, no one must know. Ever. You would be mocked and humiliated. We need not even speak of it again. Do you agree?"

"I'm not sure."

"Ah!" Randolph's entire body sank. "You want out. You want to flee. Already."

"Randolph! That's not what I meant. I just can't be so sure of what to do, as you are."

"I know. Believe me, I know. Humiliation is just the first step. It can lead to suicide. Even murder."

"Really, Randolph, you talk in such extremes! Can we please return to us and our marriage?"

Randolph stood up. "You are right, my darling, as usual. I will speak with your father this morning and the priest this afternoon. Now come. I have something to show you."

He unlocked the door into Cecilia's room. All the toiletries had been removed. Her clothes and hats and shoes put away in trunks.

"For you," he said. "I could do this. This is no longer Cecilia's room, but yours."

Meg considered that. "Thank you, my love, but I don't want a room apart from yours."

They decided to marry the following weekend, in the cathedral, with dinner and dance party afterwards at a large hotel.

Herbert was surprised when they appeared hand in hand before him, but Oliphant had proved himself to be an honourable man for over three years and Herbert took what they told him at face value: "We are in love. We have waited a long time. We don't want to wait any longer."

Herbert resolved to lead his daughter up the aisle in his most dignified and proud manner—which wouldn't be easy since he suffered from increasingly severe gout, walked with a limp, and used a cane. He wished they hadn't left him to convey the news to Alice. She was shocked, disgusted, and furious. She began to harangue her father.

"Father, how could you just let them do that!"

"My dear Alice, they have made their decision and their announcement. There is no stopping them. I am grateful they did not decide to elope. I look forward to taking my first daughter up the aisle, as I look forward to taking you."

"I would *never* do it like that. It is shameful. Look at Dave and Isabel. Their sudden wedding plans and then Isabel having an 'early' baby. Everybody knows. And now Meg, has to get married within a *week*! How can I hold my head up in public! This family has become ... disgusting! Mother will be rolling over in her grave."

"I think not. My beloved Emma will know from her place on high that our Meg has kept her virtue. I am sure of that. You should know that too. Therefore, what is so shameful? The plans are well thought out. They said the cathedral is available. Randolph has generously offered to pay for the party, a cost I could ill afford. All the more left for you, someday, my dear."

"Father, you are letting them live alone together before they are married!"

"Oh." Herbert drew on his pipe. Sipped more port. "I see. I was so taken aback by their announcement..."

"We have to go and stay with them. Or Meg has to come and stay with us, until they are married. Meg is behaving like a common ... whore!"

"Alice! How could you ever say such a thing! Leave my sight immediately!"

But that evening they stood together on Oliphant's doorstep.

"Randolph, if I may," said Herbert, "since you are to be my son-in-law."

"You may indeed, sir."

"In the interests of propriety, I must ask that Meg not stay in this house alone with you, while you are betrothed."

Randolph looked at Meg. "That's unreasonable," said Meg. "I have been living 'alone' in this house for years. Another week can't make a difference. Besides, I need to be here with Randolph to sort out all the arrangements."

"What rubbish!" scoffed Alice. "What selfish rot! You're the unreasonable ones in being engaged for only a week. Do you realize what people are *saying?*"

"We have no interest in that," said Meg.

"Oh no? You're the complete cause of the scandal."

"Scandal, Alice?" Meg folded her arms and smiled.

Alice stomped her foot. "How dare you take a superior tone with me!"

"It is time," said Randolph, "to end this discussion. Mr. Wilkinson, I invite you to act as chaperone in my home until we are married."

Alice drew Meg aside. "Are you with child?"

"I will not answer such an impertinent question." Meg bristled and turned her back on Alice. "Time will tell you and everyone else, soon enough."

"Good!" said Alice. "That tells me you're not."

It was a grand wedding for the times. Alice approved and stood proudly by the bride, who wore a cream silk gown and a hat concocted of her mother's veil and fresh red roses. The groom cut his usual swath in top hat and tails. He and the father of the bride made eloquent speeches at the sit-down dinner, where champagne was unstintingly poured. As bride and groom led off the dancing there was much animated, whispered commentary in the crowd.

"All very lavish, isn't it ... for a shotgun wedding."

"You'd think they'd be ashamed to do it like this. So sudden. Makes it clear what they've been up to all along."

"The biggest waste is all that university education. A Bachelor of Science isn't required to change diapers."

"Randolph Oliphant has proved himself to be more common than we thought," said Mrs. MacPherson. "Aging man marries young housekeeper."

"Isn't this a splendid celebration!" Jean Atkins stepped deliberately into the circle of gossip. "Have you ever seen a happier bride and groom! And I'm so looking forward to seeing the new Mrs. Oliphant as our new veterinarian, aren't you?"

14

HERBERT'S LAST COMMAND

MEG GRADUATED FROM DALHOUSIE with First Class Honours and the top marks in anatomy and biology. She was accepted into the veterinary college at McGill University with a personal note from the principal saying, since there is no written law prohibiting women from studying veterinary science, they welcomed her into their college but felt obliged to warn her that were she to succeed in obtaining a degree they could not assure her of obtaining work in the profession, as they could with male graduates.

"Forewarned is forearmed," was Randolph's reaction.

Meg smiled and hugged him. "Where would I be without you? But I am worried, Randolph. It's three more years of paying for my education and if I don't get work, how could I ever ... how could it be worthwhile?"

"My dear wife! You are living the kind of courageous and progressive, *absolutely* worthwhile life that I would *love* to live. So thank you, and let us not create barriers before we come to them."

"If we have a child ..." said Meg

"Hush!" Randolph snuggled her face against his shoulder. "We'll cross that bridge ... if we come to it."

"The expression is, *when* we come to it," said Meg.

"I know, my darling, I know." He rocked her in perturbed silence.

It was noted amongst all those who had attended their wedding, indeed amongst all their city acquaintances, that Meg showed no evidence of bearing a child within the first months of their marriage. In fact, no baby came within a year, two, three, four ... the entire five years of their marriage.

That first summer, Randolph did not go to Boston. They worked together running Clean Sweepers, Meg going into the office each morning with Randolph, Poley settling by her desk while she did the books. Randolph also taught Meg more of the actual workings of the factory. The employees got used to seeing Meg as the boss's right-hand person. Not all of them liked it, but they knew they'd be fired if they showed any sign of disrespect. Jacques was made foreman at the end of the summer when Meg started vet college and work ran out at the bicycle shop.

Prepared to postpone her plans if she became pregnant, Meg was relieved that she was not, when it came time to leave for vet college. But then as the years rolled by, she felt a growing undercurrent of fear and doubt as to why. She had studied human anatomy but there was still widespread ignorance about male and female reproductive systems and genetics. It was a common belief that the human female was fertile just when menstruation began, similar to animals who are "in heat" when the genitals swell and drops of blood appear. So, the "safe" time for a woman not wanting to conceive would be the rest of the month, *if* she had a regular cycle.

Meg, with her natural affinity for animals, too readily subscribed to that theory. Victorian morality inhibited women from revealing anything at all about their cycles or sexual activity to male doctors. Hence doctors dealt with births, not birth control or fertility. Even "free thinking" women like Meg were reluctant to discuss sexual matters. The unproved theories, myths and "old wives' tales" prevailed:

"All men carry the seeds."

"Females determine the sex of babies."

"Some women are barren but men aren't."

"You'll conceive during a full moon."

"Bad women never 'get caught,' Good women always do."

"It's all a matter of luck."

"It's all a matter of virtue ... restraint and abstinence."

Randolph never imposed upon or tried to lure Meg. When she showed interest, he complied. She felt he didn't completely enjoy "the act," but she was too inexperienced to know for sure. Randolph was visibly pleased that Meg could enter vet college without *that* worry. He was in such high spirits when he took her to Montreal a week ahead to find an apartment and have a holiday together, that she couldn't help wondering if he was planning a trip to Boston afterwards. But she refused to probe.

They found an apartment that allowed her to keep Poley as her companion and bodyguard. Outside of classes, she was dependent on Poley for companionship. As the only woman, and a married one at that, there were no social circles she fitted into. Her classmates grew generally friendly with her. They thought her pretty, wasp-waisted, and well-groomed, but not alluring in the usual feminine manner. She was interesting to talk to but not comfortably so, since she was not a man, like them. And she was always questioning the way of doing things. Kept asserting that animals had feelings much like people. This was not entirely new thinking. Particularly since the publication of *Black Beauty*, many people, women especially, had been harping about kindness to horses.

"But a veterinarian has to be strong of mind, as well as body, in handling horses and any other animals," colleagues argued with Meg. "Animals have to be shot when there's no cure. And a surgeon can't keep thinking to himself ... this animal I'm operating on has feelings. It has to be held down and kept still. That's why tying them down, or stringing them up by the hind legs if they're small enough, is a necessary thing."

They could see Meg was squeamish about all this. And she kept arguing that the animal should be laid out on a table, like a human. "Give it some gas, chloroform, smelling salts, whisky," she pleaded, wanting to yell. "Whatever helps to ease the pain."

"She should be in med school, not vet college," some concluded. "Or at home with her husband. She'll have to give this up when she has babies. Meanwhile she's wasting our class time with all these questions."

Others wondered and thought she might be right, but then who would pay for such new methods for their animals? Or the installation of new facilities, equipment, and supplies? The vet college had trouble enough starting up, as is.

Yes, the young Mrs. Oliphant was altogether a might too interesting for her own good. But they tipped their hats to her and opened doors for her. She was their pet woman, not unlike a colourful parrot that often squawked out of turn.

The principal and Dr. Osler kept interested watch on Meg's progress. Several years before they had co-operated in establishing the high standards of McGill's veterinary college. Osler was satisfied as long as Meg continued to do well in the courses which were part of his med school. Principal McEachran tried not to become personally involved. But he was a Scot who had managed to set up this fine veterinary college in Canada and he kept his eye on the big picture. There was a woman attending the vet college in Ireland. If she got through, he hoped this Meg Oliphant would do so as well. His college was not to be outdone by the Irish. Looking down from his office window, he couldn't help but smile upon the young woman walking across campus with that big black dog lumbering along beside her.

Meg often thought of "Ike's Working Wolves," wished she could interest her colleagues in that story and what might be learned from it. But no students wanted more papers to read, particularly not an unpublished, probably unpublishable, manuscript. "The origins of dogs in their own far north?" No. They were not interested in that. Horses and farm animals were the focus of their job prospects. But not for me, Meg gradually concluded, with Poley at her side. She wanted to work on dogs and other small animals.

"Horses aren't the only working animals," Meg pointed out when she came home at Christmas. "Think of all the work that dogs do. Newfoundlanders like Poley do rescue at sea, German Shepherds do police work, and there are all the various breeds of guard dogs, the collie herding dogs, the hunting hounds, Labrador retrievers, St. Bernards for mountain rescue. And up in the Arctic, dogs are the only means of transportation."

"They ride dogs?" said Alice.

"No," Meg laughed. "They have them pull sleds over the snow, like horses pulling sleds in winter."

"Why don't they use horses?"

"It's too cold. And there's no hay. And the horse's legs would break on the terrain."

"All right. All right," said Alice. "Become a dog doctor if you want."

"I intend to," said Meg, "right here in Halifax. This city is full of dogs that need help. And cats. I think I could build a good business here, doing everything from worming right through to neutering."

"Ouch!" Randolph made a face. "Don't like the sound of that. But anything to keep you close to home."

Alice completed her basic teaching qualifications. But the only position she could get was in a one-room school four hours away from Halifax. She was accommodated in a local farmhouse where she had a small room of her own, but she had to have her meals with the family, including two of the children she taught.

"It's horrible," she wailed to Meg. "There's no escape. A schoolhouse full of brats and whiners by day, then two pouters staring across the table at me at breakfast and dinner."

"That does sound uncomfortable. But don't you like any of the kids? And isn't it nice to be on a farm, when you don't have to do the chores? Pleasant places to walk, animals to pat and talk to? I often miss our farm, don't you?"

"Not in the least. I want the city life, just like you. And quit trying to make me feel good about where I am. It's dull and stupid and horrid. You have a fabulous time in Montreal and when you want, you take the train back to Halifax. You have no idea what it's like to cry yourself to sleep every night. You've always gotten just what you wanted And you've never had to worry about being separated from ..."

"Oh Alice." Meg reached out to her. "Jacques will wait for you. He's so proud of you."

"I know that." Alice stepped away from Meg. "He writes to me every day. You're not the only one with someone who's completely devoted to you. It's just that yours already has his own business. Mine will too."

Completely devoted, thought Meg. If you only knew ...

While she was at vet college, Randolph took occasional trips to Boston. First it was because he wanted to visit and tend to something or other with the widow and her son. But he was so tense and guilty sounding when he told Meg he felt he had to go: he didn't want to worry her, but also didn't want to just go, without her knowing where he was, in case something happened ...

"It's all right," Meg said over the phone, knowing operators and others listened in. "Do what you must, Randolph. My love goes with you."

Then he went regularly once each term, for a week. Meg suffered jealousy and disappointment, some anger and resentment when he went, but became resigned to it. She made herself think of all the possible faults a husband might have and concluded that Randolph's habit was not so bad. Some husbands have mistresses, or gambling habits, are drunks, or violent. And some are crippled or diseased or injured, she told herself. Some are stupid, or cold, or arrogant, miserly, or poor providers. Some just plain mean to their wife and kids.

Randolph was like a husband with a mistress about whom he was utterly discreet, but whom he could not do without. Meg could not see or understand it clearly. She knew she hated his absence and the tension that built up and yanked him away. She tried not to think about it. The hard part was not being able to talk about it with anyone, to have even her sister think she had a perfect life.

In the second year, Alice again failed to get a teaching position within the city, but she did get one in a village school, a two-hour stage coach ride from Halifax. She took a room weekdays at the village inn and travelled back to Halifax each weekend. In fall and spring, the road became so muddy and pot-holed the coach wheels got stuck and she was delayed for hours. In winter, storms sometimes prevented the coach from leaving the station or reaching its destination. Alice arrived at either end jostled and so cold she vowed not to do it again, but did. She finished the school year but neither she nor the school board wanted her to do another year. With the low salary and the cost of accommodation and transportation, Alice came out of two years teaching having accumulated nothing more than new clothes.

Again Alice applied for teaching positions in Halifax but none were as yet forthcoming. She began the summer discouraged and depressed, reverting to looking after Herbert, who was now chair-ridden with gout and other ailments. Herbert's savings afforded him a housekeeper while Alice was away teaching, but it was her duty and payback to take over as housekeeper during the summers.

"How come I'm the only child with the duty?" she grumbled to Meg. "There are seven others."

"It is unfair," said Meg. "But I do have a duty to my husband."

"You're lucky. You can afford to be married. With my luck, Jacques and I will never be able to afford it."

"He has proposed?"

"As much as he can without the income he needs to support us." Alice raised her chin. "I could have other suitors, you know."

"I'm sure you could. But Jacques is the one, am I right?"

"Unfortunately."

Meg laughed. "You're an incorrigible pessimist, Alice."

Alice looked tearful and turned away. Meg tried to take her hand.

"Alice, I'm sorry. I wish I could help. But there's a bit of a down-turn in the business this year and I have no money of my own ..."

"Oh don't tell me your troubles," Alice pulled away from her. "You have no idea what trouble is."

✦

Just after Meg and Randolph's second anniversary, Jacques got an offer from the bicycle shop owner. Jos Andersen decided to sell his business and move to Toronto, where he said all the money and enterprising people were. Besides, Toronto was flat, more like his native Copenhagen, easier to cycle around. He did not tell Jacques he suspected a general downturn in the economy was beginning. He wanted to sell out, right away, and get his new business going in Toronto, but because he liked Jacques, thought him an industrious, loyal lad, he gave Jacques a lease of the business for the summer which would give Jacques more time to find the money to buy it.

"Sounds like as a good a deal for Andersen as it is for Jacques," said Meg to Randolph.

"But it's the opportunity Jacques has been looking for," said Randolph. "And, unlike me, Jacques has no good reason to hesitate when he's offered what he wants."

Randolph accepted Jacques's resignation at Clean Sweepers with all best wishes. Then Jacques asked Herbert for Alice's hand in marriage.

"With my blessings, lad. With my blessings. Hope the wedding isn't too far off. I want to live to see it."

"I can't marry right away," said Alice. "What would people think! We can't afford a big wedding, but I do want a very nice one."

They decided on a ceremony in the cathedral at the end of the summer with a garden party afterwards. They accepted Meg and Randolph's offer to use their house and garden.

"I want an exquisite menu," said Alice. "No farmer's food."

"Farmers' food?" said Meg.

"You know ... roasts and mashed potatoes and help yourself to the pies. I shall have an exquisite buffet of salmon mousse, scalloped potatoes, glazed string beans, with corn soufflé to start. I want to have a harpist for music and a man in tails to serve the wine. Is it all right with you if I decorate the verandah with white gauze ribbons and roses?"

"Sounds gorgeous. Where did you get the ideas?"

"I keep myself informed," said Alice. "Don't you read *Ladies Home Journal*?"

Invitations were sent out. Preparations were begun. The plan was for Alice and Jacques to live with Herbert.

"It's *so* unfair!" said Meg, dropping in on Alice and Herbert.

"What!" said Alice. "Are you stealing my lines?"

Meg laughed. "I mean about women not being allowed to teach if they're married. It's stupid and unfair. You should be allowed to teach as long as you want to. Think how ideal it would be if you had a job here in the city. I think women should challenge that law. Why don't you? I'd support you. So would a lot of other women, Jean Atkins for one."

"Jean?"

"Yes. We've become friends. She says I've become the teacher to her, with all my new ideas, which is nonsense of course, but . . ."

Herbert banged his cane on the floor as he sat in the chair listening to their chatter. He had become very irritable of late. Feeling useless and a burden. He was afraid he wouldn't be able to even hobble up the aisle with his daughter. It made him doubly irritable when people around him talked as if he weren't there. "Marriage is for the pro-creation of the species!" he shouted. "You can't have teachers quitting part way through the year because they suddenly find themselves with child. Alice has done her stint with teaching. Never much liked it anyway, did you, Alice? Hardly worth the cost of the training. You're better off married to a good man like Jacques."

He banged his cane again. It was the only way of getting attention, an old man, in his own household. "And you needn't look so disheartened, Meggie. I'm right. If you want to go campaigning, campaign for the vote. Women like you should have the vote."

"What do you mean, like her? What about me, father?"

"You too. All you smart young women should have the vote. That's what I've come to think. And don't you forget it."

"Why Dad ..." Meg ran to him. "Thank you!"

"Father!" Alice also put her arms around him. "You surprise us!"

He reached to put his arms around them. Suddenly he grimaced and gasped for air. His body slumped, dead, crashing with the chair onto the floor, his daughters tumbling on top.

Herbert had willed the house to Alice which she and Jacques could then use as collateral for the loan to buy the cycling business. Herbert's savings and the value of the farm were divided amongst his sons. Meg received his pocket watch.

"Along with his good wishes, I trust," she said to Randolph. "I must remember that."

The wedding lunch was an exquisite mess. The day was so hot the salmon mousse melted and oozed over the serving plate. The corn soufflé sank in the middle before it was presented. But the idea was impressive. Alice tried not to be tearful over its unfortunate execution. She was sustained by the compliments on her beautiful white silk dress, her ever so stylish hat, adorned with veil, flowers, birds, and all. And the heavenly notes of the harpist while the wine server floated around the garden. Yes, it was a beautiful, an elegant wedding. She just wished Meg didn't have to spoil the atmosphere by being so obviously tearful over the absence of their parents. The harp wasn't *meant* to be such a reminder of those in heaven!

And Jacques was superb. So handsome and manly in his tailored suit. He never ever said "yous" any more. He was popular with everyone. More down to earth and easier to talk to than Randolph. And his prospects now were so good! Everyone wished him well and surely would support him in the new business he now owned, The Sport Shop.

But in the privacy of their bedroom that wedding night, Alice was surprised and confused. The way that Jacques adored her body made her respond in a way she had never heard about. Her body went out of control! Jacques assured her that was good and normal. He was loving, affectionate, pleased with her and with himself. Alice felt duly adored, at last. And the future looked so full of promise. But she wondered why other women, especially her sister, hadn't intimated that the man and wife act was ... surprising. It felt so different from the "duty" she had understood it to be. When she discovered she was pregnant, probably from that very first night, she felt embarrassed, worried, not at all proud. She feared she would be burdened, like her mother with eight children.

15

THE DOG DOCTOR OF HALIFAX

ALICE GAVE BIRTH to a healthy baby boy, George. She had screamed in terror and pain at the second stage of birthing and felt humiliated by having Dr. Atkins see her so exposed, with total loss of decorum. "I kept thinking of your Ma Wolf," Alice said to Meg. "Wishing I could do it alone as she did. Human beings have it much worse."

Meg smiled and felt tears well up at seeing Alice adeptly nursing her first baby. "You're a good mother, my little sister."

"Any woman can do this." said Alice, stroking her baby's head. "You're the exceptional one." She looked up at Meg and held her hand out to her, trying to smile.

Meg was called into the principal's office before her final exams. Fearing the worst, but not knowing what it might be, she entered the office and stood her ground with as much fortitude as she could muster. Both McEachran and Dr. Osler presided at the meeting. They stood side by side behind the desk, inviting her to take a chair, as a lady should, before they did.

"I prefer to stand, if I may, sirs." Meg wanted to be treated like the male students.

"As you wish." They sat down. Osler nodded to McEachran to begin.

"Your marks and your conduct have been outstanding," said Principal McEachran. "Your conduct a little *too* outstanding." He smiled wryly. "Your concern that animals be treated and laid out on tables, more like human patients ..." He paused and turned to his colleague. "Dr. Osler, would you care to make your remarks at this point?"

Oh, oh, thought Meg. Here it comes. I'm about to be tossed out of here.

"Mrs. Oliphant," said Dr. Osler, "I and other members of the Faculty of Medicine recommend that you continue your studies with us for two more years and become a doctor of medicine. You are clearly capable. Would you?"

Meg's heart sank. She drew in her breath. "I thank you for the ... compliment, Dr. Osler. I realize that being a doctor of medicine is ... a high calling." She refused to say a higher calling. "But I want to work with animals."

Osler and McEachran exchanged glances as though they had anticipated this answer.

"You want to work with small animals," said McEachran, his elbows on his desk, chin on his clasped hands, "specializing in pets? Such as your dog, which, I must say, is the size of a small horse. Is that what you want to do?"

"It is."

"And you have practical plans for opening such a practice in the city of Halifax?"

"Yes, sir."

"Seems a pity, doesn't it, Dr. Osler," McEachran turned to him, "that our college would stand in the way of such a pioneering venture?"

"It does." Dr. Osler nodded.

"The Faculty of Comparative Medicine and Veterinary Science of McGill University," said Principal McEachran, "is independent, yet subject to certain edicts of the Royal Veterinary College in Edinburgh, Scotland. They have never allowed a woman to sit the final exams. We have word that one Aline Cust, the first woman in the British Isles about to complete her studies in veterinary medicine, will not be granted her degree because of her sex. What do you think of that, Mrs. Oliphant?"

It made her angry. Am I being played with, she thought. Tested, or teased? She stood her ground. "The more relevant thing," she said, "is what you, Principal McEachran and Dr. Osler, think of it."

They smiled, broke into approving laughter. They had plans to turn the tide of veterinary history in Meg's favour, with a clever invisible twist.

"We think we must find a way around unprogressive authority, enable it to do what it would wish to have done, had it the benefit of historical hindsight," said McEachran. "We think, Mrs Oliphant, that you might be the first of many female veterinarians who will make their way into the twentieth century. And thus we must ask you another question. Your first name is Margaret, hence the initial 'M,' is that correct?"

"Yes."

"Thus so far, the name we must submit to the authorities, that you might be granted a degree, would read M. Oliphant. If your second name were to begin with an 'R' ... and if there were perchance a third initial to throw in ..."

"Randolph," said Meg, beginning to smile. "I am legitimately called Mrs. Randolph Oliphant. And my other name is Anne."

A "Mr. A. Oliphant" was recorded at the Royal Veterinary College in Scotland. The degree which the Principal of McGill's veterinary college bestowed upon Meg in Montreal in 1893 read: Dr. M.A. Oliphant.

The launch of Meg's new veterinary business required significant money and other help from Randolph. They converted a ground floor section of the broom factory building into Meg's premises, with a reception area, an operating room, and space for six kennels.

Randolph and Poley accompanied Meg in the carriage when she

drove around the streets of Halifax delivering her brochure, adver-
tising:

THE HUMANE WAY
Veterinary Services for Small Animals.

Worm Treatment, Rabies Prevention. Flea, Lice and Tick Removal.
Disease and Injury Medical Care. Neutering. Grooming.
Modern Animal Hospital Methods.

M. Oliphant, Doctor of Veterinary Medicine
Upper Water Street, Halifax. Telephone: 667

Wearing a trim navy blue skirt, white blouse and jacket, Meg
knocked on doors and introduced herself. There were some joke and
crank responses, men saying they knew a bitch they wanted to bring
in for neutering or grooming. But Meg was greeted with more curiosity than anything else.

Her first customer was Jean Atkins, and then other well-off friends
and acquaintances, with dogs or cats to be de-wormed or de-fleaed.
The word spread that her premises were indeed like a clean hospital for pets, with an operating table, instruments, and medicines that
worked. People began to think in terms of curing pets with ailments,
instead of having them shot, drowned, or poisoned.

Meg had dreaded her first surgical procedure, working on her own
without the backup of experienced teachers and the facilities she'd
had at college. But then she had dreaded much more the first time
she'd had to dig a knife into a live pig, strung up by the hooves at vet
college. And she had managed to do that.

"Do what you must to cure the ailment. You're not inflicting,
you're helping. Hesitation hurts. Be sharp, incisive." Meg kept all the
instructions and mottos from vet college running through her head
to force herself to do what had to be done. And she practised until
she could perform well, without undue qualms. She found it easier in
her own premises, first putting a heavily chloroformed cloth over the

animal's muzzle, then laying it on the table, drawing the cutting lines, performing the incision, extracting, snipping, suturing, draining bile, and closing up, stitching with cat gut.

Randolph was her assistant until she found a reliable woman to hire and train. He kept a white lab coat in Meg's office and donned it whenever summoned to help restrain an animal or to stand with instruments in hand while Meg performed surgery. Queasy though he was naturally, Randolph summoned his acting talent to appear confident, experienced, and adept. He made Meg laugh when he imitated those surgeon's qualities in her. He comforted her when the patient died in spite of her efforts or when she had to administer a lethal dose of chloroform because there was no cure for the animal's intense pain.

Meg worried about the future and profitability of her practice when it took so long to build up clientele in a society used to seeing dogs suffer or shot, beaten, have their tails and ears clipped. Then, in her second year of work, a book came out that seemed made for the promotion of her practice. It was the international best seller *Beautiful Joe*, a very didactic novel about a beaten, clipped, long suffering, and very courageous dog, whose story made people more aware of dogs' needs and the proper care of them. The author was Margaret Marshall Saunders, a Nova Scotia woman who wrote about the plight of a dog she had actually met up with in Meaford, Ontario, but she set the story in Maine, USA, to interest the larger market.

"I met this Margaret," said Meg, holding up the book at Sunday dinner where Alice and Jacques were gathered with her and Randolph. "She was taking some courses that winter in my last year at Dalhousie. She called herself Margaret then, was planning to become a teacher. But she's turned into this famous Marshall Saunders instead. Glad she did! This book is going to do for dogs what *Black Beauty* did for horses and *Uncle Tom's Cabin* did for slaves."

"Set them free?" said Alice. "There are already too many dogs running wild in Halifax."

Meg started to laugh then saw that Alice was in no mood to be joking. "The popularity of *Beautiful Joe* will be good for my dog doctoring business," she explained. "In the book, Joe the dog, definitely a poor Joe, tells the story, speaks like a human being. It's full of injuries, malnutrition, and diseases that cry out for the services of a good vet. And it begs for them to be treated more like human beings. All the readers should be beating a path to my door. And just think, the book has sold over a million copies." Meg took more wine and raised her glass. "Here's to *Beautiful Joe*!"

"Alice, my beautiful wife," said Jacques, "why don't you write a book? You like to write in your journal. Maybe you could do a book about cycling women?"

"When?" said Alice sarcastically. "Between babies? Though I do agree your business needs some kind of boost."

"Your" business, Meg noted, and exchanged glances with Randolph. Alice, already in her second pregnancy, glowered at Jacques.

"Most businesses are having to tighten their belts," said Randolph. "People are talking about worldwide recession. But it's talk that creates it, particularly in the world of investments. And it's careful optimism that gets us through it. Bicycles are an excellent investment."

"In winter?" said Alice.

"The Sports Shop will pick up again in spring," said Jacques.

"You were going to ask something," said Alice firmly, staring at Jacques.

He cleared his throat. "I was wondering, if there's any spare-time work at Sweepers." He made himself face Randolph squarely. "Just through the winter, like. I was thinking of opening The Sports Shop afternoons and weekends only, until spring."

"Certainly," said Randolph and Meg almost in unison.

They were eager to help Jacques out of the discomfort he was being made to feel at their table and in his life. Randolph had, for economy's sake, not replaced Jacques at Clean Sweepers. But they would be glad to re-hire him and make adjustments elsewhere.

"How come it works for you?" said Alice to Meg when they were in the kitchen. "That 'method' you described. But it doesn't for me? You've had perfect luck with it for *years*. And look at me ..."

"It doesn't work for most people," said Meg pensively. "Maybe

Randolph and I are the unlucky ones. Maybe we won't be able to have children when we really want them."

"What would be wrong with that?" said Alice. "Honestly ... who *really* likes changing and washing diapers? And I don't know why you want to be looking after mangy dogs, either. Why don't you just relax and enjoy being a rich man's wife?"

Meg laughed. "Because I couldn't? And Randolph isn't all that rich?"

"Oh don't give me that!"

Meg shrugged. There was no changing Alice's thinking.

Business was going well enough for Meg to hire a full-time assistant, Ardiss Arpin. Ardiss, a tall, strikingly pretty young farm girl, was so thin Meg doubted her abilities when she came for an interview.

"Are you sure ... ?" Meg began to question.

"I'm strong enough?" Ardiss rolled up her sleeves revealing muscular forearms and pointed to Poley who lay near the operating table. "Want me to get that bear up onto your table? What's his name?"

"Poley."

"Poley," said Ardiss, patting him on the head. "Time to get up and ... sit! Good boy! Now I'm going to help you put your front paws up on this table and then I'm going to hoist you up by your hindquarters. Ready? Let's heave ho!"

Poley was up on the table and Ardiss was hired.

The following summer, when Poley was nearing ten years old, he accompanied Meg and Ardiss on their Saturday swim. He had become slow-moving and he was happiest in the water. As he lumbered up onto the beach behind Meg, he began to falter. She turned and caught him round the neck, falling with him on the pebbles. Ardiss helped to shift him into a more comfortable position with his head on Meg's lap.

"Must have been his heart," Meg tried to speak clinically when she saw he breathed no more. Then tears streamed down her face while Ardiss fetched the wagon to carry him home for burial.

My longtime, lumbering, absolutely faithful pal, Meg kept saying to herself as she stood over his grave in the ravine behind their house.

Randolph comforted her as best he could.

"I want to have a child," Meg said as they lay in bed.

"I know, my darling." Randolph said in the darkness. "Let's try."

Summers brought good business to The Sports Shop. The rest of the year it was open part time with Alice helping to run it while tending young George and toddling Victoria. A third baby was on the way for Alice and Jacques. Meg and Randolph had none.

"You can have this one," said Alice, tapping her stomach.

"You don't mean that." Meg felt sick at heart to hear her even say it.

"She's joking," said Jacques, frowning.

Meg looked at Alice who shrugged non-committally

Meg was deeply disappointed each month that they didn't conceive. Randolph attempted to revive her optimism but couldn't conceal his own complexity of attitude.

"You should have children," he said. "But I'm not the husband I wanted to be for you and what kind of a father would I make, if I could be one? Perhaps this is divine retribution, or at least a good thing."

"Randolph, please, please don't talk like that. You would be the kindest of fathers. And with your good looks and intelligence, you could produce..."

"Hush, hush." He pulled the bed covers more tightly around her and held her body as close to his as he possibly could. "Enough about me."

"Don't be so mopey," Alice rebuked Meg when she visited. "You don't know how lucky you are."

"Knock it off, Alice. Just *knock it off*. You're the one who doesn't realize how lucky you are, you and Jacques."

"Jacques has turned into a drinker. Gets drunk every night. How lucky is that?"

"I find that hard to believe."

"Of course you do. You have a perfect husband and have no idea..."

It was too wearing being around Alice. Meg resolved to keep a distance. Jean, Ardiss, and the women who volunteered in rounding up stray animals and other charity work were the women she felt comfortable with. With their help she started a kind of Humane Society in Halifax, bringing in as many stray dogs and cats as she could accommodate, finding homes for them if she could, neutering them if she thought it right.

The silence and evasion that had come into her marriage gathered up Meg in invisible waves of loneliness and sometimes indefinable fear about what lay ahead. Her loneliness subsided when she was at work with her animals: greeting them, soothing them, easing their discomfort and pain, making them well, or just clean and groomed, getting to know their individual characters, which were generally a reflection of their owners'.

Maybe I'm another Piji, she half smiled to herself, and these must be my wolves.

But don't you think for a moment, Ike's spirit bounced up and down, wanting to yell in her ear, that I'm like Randolph! In all my centuries, I've never seen such un-wolf-like behaviour.

Meg did not question Randolph on his activities in Boston, except to ask what became of the widow and her son.

"She has married a normal man," said Randolph. "She'd now like to erase the memory of her first husband. She asked me, as nicely as she could, to leave them alone now to make a new life. But her son, Jason, is suffering. He followed me out the door, telling me how he can't get along in the new regime. He's resentful of his stepfather because his mother is trying to foist him upon him, make him the replacement and superior role model for Jason. He doesn't understand why his mother has become so watchful, harsh, and critical of his every gesture that reminds her of his father. She did let Jason know that his father committed suicide but won't discuss why, just speaks of it as a 'sin.'

"God only knows how he'd handle the truth if he were told it. In any case, my lips are sealed, by his mother. Last I heard, Jason was sent to boarding school."

16

On Boston Common

The late night ringing of the telephone startled Meg and Randolph as they lay in bed. Randolph got up and hurried down the stairs to answer it.

"Jason's mother," said Randolph returning to Meg. "Jason jumped from his school dormitory window. He has broken bones and a serious neck injury but is expected to recover. She wants me to come and talk to him. Poor kid. He's only thirteen."

Randolph called from Boston.

"His body is recovering, but his mind ... is struggling. His mother is beside herself with fear that he's like his father in every way, and will ... find another window, so to speak."

"Do you think that's likely?"

"Not if I can help it. But I need more time with him. Seems I'm the one he will talk to."

"What does he tell you ..." Meg paused, "that you can tell me over the phone?"

"Ah yes." Randolph paused until they heard the muffled click of at least two receivers. "He was devastated by his father's death but then bewildered and hurt by the way his way his mother has treated him since. He just couldn't understand her behaviour, or the mystery and condemnation surrounding his father. Then he learned things in the upper grades of boarding school that made it easier for me to try to explain about his father and ask about his own inclinations."

"Which are?"

"Girls, my darling. He's adamant about his interest in girls, but he developed deep fears about ever being loved or approved by them. And he has lost trust, serious loss of trust in everything important, from people to life itself. But he's begun to make sense of things."

"When do you think you can come home?"

"After the weekend. I miss you, my darling. I'll keep in touch with our Jason. He's made me feel I might be a good father, after all. And I want to get back to you, my wife."

The next call was on Sunday evening when Alice and Jacques had come over. Meg was upstairs in the bathroom, bathing young George and Victoria, who loved to splash in Auntie Meg's big porcelain tub. They had only a small tin tub at home. Alice was feeding the new baby, Herbie.

The children screeched with delight and held their ears. The phone sounded to them like the sudden passing of the fire wagon. Meg laughed at them.

"Would you please get the phone?" She called down to Jacques. "It's probably Randolph. Tell him I'll be right down."

Jacques picked up the hearing piece of the phone and faced into the speaker on the wall. "Hello. Hello."

"Hello, sir. This is Inspector Mick O'Mara, Boston Police, calling. I'm trying to locate the next of kin of one Randolph Oliphant. To whom am I speaking?"

"Jacques Benoit, sir. I am the brother-in-law of Randolph Oliphant."

"Is there a closer relative in the house?"

"His wife."

"His wife? Oh Jesus…" There was the sound of a hand going over the phone then Inspector O'Mara's voice again. "Pardon me, sir. I do not have good news to convey. Is Mrs. Oliphant of strong mind?"

"She is. But maybe you should tell me first."

"Do you have a chair at hand?"

"I'm good on my feet, sir. What has happened to Mr. Oliphant?"

"He has been found dead. Murdered. On Boston Common. Are you all right, sir?"

"As well as can be expected." Jacques put his hand over the phone to gain his bearings.

Alice came into the hall carrying Herbie.

"What is it? Who is it?" Meg called from the top of the stairs.

Jacques signalled for Alice to go up to Meg.

"Inspector O'Mara," he spoke into the phone, trying not to let Meg hear his words.

"Inspector! Is that the police?" Meg came running down the stairs. "Watch the kids," she said to Alice and grabbed the phone from Jacques.

"This is Mrs. Oliphant. To whom am I speaking? What has happened to my husband?"

"Inspector O'Mara, ma'am, Boston Police."

"Has he been apprehended?"

"Ma'am, I must ask you to sit down and take assistance from your brother-in-law."

"He has brought me a chair. Now please tell me frankly what has happened. It is your job, is it not?" She made Jacques step away.

"Mrs. Oliphant I regret to inform you that the body of your husband was found on Boston Common. I'm sorry to say, he was the victim of foul play ..."

Meg absorbed the news, gripping the phone speaker for support.

"Mrs. Oliphant ... are you there? You have my deepest sympathy. Shall I speak to your brother-in-law now? We must make arrangements for the body to be identified and brought home. Perhaps he, or another man in the family, could ..."

"I will come myself," said Meg. "Please," she began to choke, "let me handle this on my own."

Inspector O'Mara waited on the platform for Meg's train. It was the worst part of his job, he thought, informing the next of kin. He had been surprised to find a wife in this case. The victim had been dressed as a woman. Did the wife know anything about that? Probably not. In his several years of experience in the police force, Mick O'Mara had found that the wives were generally the last to know and it wasn't necessary to tell them everything. He liked the protect and defend part of his job, not the discovery of repugnant crimes and cruelly strange human behaviour. Behaviour he had no idea existed before he joined the police forces.

Human beings were in fact so much stranger than the general populace realized. It made it hard for him to have a real friendship outside the police force. He had good friends on the force because they shared a knowledge of the dark and hidden side of human nature. But the general populace, and women in particular, were too innocent or ignorant for him to be comfortable with. Yet the chief landed him with jobs like this because he was known to be good with the public, the bereaved in particular.

Such a complicated and ugly case, this one. The strangled and mutilated body. Identification and money left in the purse thrown into the bushes nearby. Woman's dress and unusual undergarments had been ripped from the man's body with a knife. The body now under a sheet in the morgue, the torn clothes put in a holding box. All details had to be put in the reports. Apparel, wig, female cosmetics applied on the face. Stab wounds to private parts. Facts not fit for a wife's ears. Nor anyone's. It looked like the work of the Boston Stabber. The victims were all women, until this case. None mutilated like this one.

The Stabber must have acted out of rage. Did he think he had discovered an undercover policeman? It was a strategy they had thought of employing to catch him. Clearly very risky. But then this victim was so like a normal woman he carried no weapon. Professional women carried some kind of defensive weapon. What was in the mind of this man who dressed as a woman and walked across Boston Common at midnight? If the general populace only knew how strange and foolhardy humans beings are.

O'Mara watched the passengers alighting from the train. He was to look for a woman with a red umbrella. Mrs. Oliphant. She sounded brusque and efficient, maybe a bit of an old battle axe who browbeat her husband so much he escaped to Boston and got into the weirdo clubs.

Ah! There was a red umbrella being held up. By a pretty young woman! Looking brave and troubled. Jesus, Mary and Joseph, this is going to be tough! And delicate.

She looked anxious as he approached her in his uniform. He took off his cap and bowed slightly. People stared.

"Mrs. Randolph Oliphant?"

"Yes."

"Inspector O'Mara at your service. May I take your arm?"

"Please do," said Meg. "People are staring as though I'm about to be handcuffed."

O'Mara smiled. Some sense of humour. That could help. Indeed it could. He led her through the crowd to the black police coach and horses. Once inside, he asked gravely, "Would you like to repair to the hotel where we have kept Mr. Oliphant's room for you?"

"Where is he?"

"In the morgue, I'm sorry to say."

"Take me there first, please." Meg looked out the window to hide her tearful eyes.

Mick O'Mara steadied Meg by the elbow while the mortician pulled the sheet back from over Randolph's face. He was relieved that the mortician had done a thorough job of cleaning the victim's face. But there was no wiping away the knife wound in his cheek. And Meg saw the gash at the base of his neck as the sheet was lifted back over his face. She put both hands to her own face as her body began to sink. O'Mara caught her by both elbows and led her to a private room.

"Smelling salts." He handed them to her as she sat down.

Meg said to him in a quiet voice, "Where are his clothes?"

"I'm afraid they were damaged. Beyond repair."

"Was he murdered for his wallet?"

"Not apparently. It was found, with money and identity intact, nearby."

"This will be reported in the papers?"

"Yes. All murder cases."

"Then you must tell me now. What was he wearing?"

"Since the body has been identified, it is not necessary to report on apparel. What do you expect he was wearing?"

"He had a need to dress as a woman. Is that why he was murdered?" Meg's eyes filled with tears.

O'Mara handed her his own clean hanky. "You are an unusual woman, Mrs. Oliphant," he said in a tone which made Meg feel it as a compliment. "I will tell you in confidence, because we have as yet no proof. But we conjecture that your husband was the victim of mistaken identity. Have you heard of the Boston Stabber? He stalks and kills 'women of the night.'"

O'Mara lingered with the young widow. Felt more than comfortable with her. Wanted to do even more than his duty for her. Wanted to embrace her. But he maintained his professionalism. Accompanied her to Oliphant's hotel, where she could take care of his effects. He had already packed up the women's things and stored them at the station. Meg asked him to give them to the poor along with Randolph's other clothes, except for a suit to attire the body when it was placed in a casket for the return train to Halifax.

O'Mara conferred with the chief who then dealt with the press.

It was reported that the man's body found murdered on the Common in the early hours of Sunday, was a Mr. Randolph Oliphant, of Halifax, Canada. The murder had the mark of the Boston Stabber ... the face wound, the neck slit. It was not necessary to detail other wounds. This was Boston after all, not New York. Discretion prevailed.

Reporters and the general public speculated as to the circumstances. Possibly the victim, Mr. Oliphant, had surprised the strangler, perhaps interfered with his attack upon a woman, perhaps rescued her. Witnesses were invited to report to the authorities. In any case, the hunt for the Boston Stabber was now intensified.

O'Mara arranged for the transport of Randolph's casket on the same train that Meg had booked a seat on, and took her to the station, giving her a copy of the newspaper with its speculated story of Randolph's demise, as a rescuer.

"I hope we meet again, under happier circumstances," he said, standing to attention, cap under arm.

"I do, too." She gave him her hand.

He took it and kissed it. Damn! he thought as she boarded the train, shouldn't have done that. Out of line. She'll think me a common fool.

Meg looked out the window, wanting to signal her thanks to him, but she saw only the back of his uniform. How unusual is he, she wondered.

The cathedral was overflowing for Randolph's funeral.

Jacques gave a touching, plain-spoken eulogy describing Randolph's generosity with his employees, with his extended family, the theatre, and the city's cultural life in general. He was a popular man about town, always good-humoured, eloquent, and well turned-out. A gentleman of the highest order. Clearly a successful business man. But most outstanding was his love and dedication to his wife, Meg, and hers to him.

Meg remained stoically composed throughout the service but reached out and squeezed Jacques's hand when he came down from the pulpit to sit beside her and Alice. People found Meg stiff but grateful when they approached to offer her condolences and memories of

Randolph's private acts of kindness or witty entertainments. They noted the red rims of her eyes when she lifted her black veil and concluded she was more soft-hearted and feminine than they had given her credit for.

Alice had been strangely quiet since the news of Randolph's death. Mercifully quiet, thought Meg, and she was grateful for Alice's good management of the reception in the cathedral basement and her ease in handling people with small talk.

Meg refused all company when she went home after the funeral. She locked herself in and lay on the lounge in the library with a large glass of dry sherry. It is over and done with, she thought. His grand final appearance. Randolph would have wanted a funeral like that, his secret kept. Whereas she had an almost overwhelming urge to suddenly tell everyone. Make an announcement from the pulpit. Randolph was murdered because he had a need to dress like a woman. She hated it, but it was part of him, part of his gentility and finesse. He didn't hurt anyone, except her, in his need to leave her and go to ...

Meg got up and poured herself another large drink. If she were to keep her promise to Randolph, she would have to keep this wretched secret for the rest of her life.

"I hate it!" she said out loud, flinging her arm as Randolph would. But the more she ruminated, the more sense it made to maintain the image he wanted maintained in the society around her. "Polite society!" she mocked, and enjoyed feeling drunk. "With such people in it! And what about the human monster who murdered him in such a horrible way and for what horrible reasons?" She wanted to get away from this society. Live with dogs. Go into the woods with wolves. Animals were much easier to understand and live with. Or were they? She wanted to find out. On the other hand, she wished she could be with people who knew and tolerated the complexity of human beings. She knew so little herself. She wished she had asked O'Mara more about what he knew. She downed her glass and grabbed her way up the stair railing to go to bed alone.

Alone, but for the spirit of Ike, hovering closer and more anxious than ever.

17

THE LONE FEMALE

An undeserved fate, thought Ike of Randolph's. Ike had witnessed such before, had himself been the perpetrator in one. It was he who had put the spear into the wolf nanny. Ike shuddered at the memory, then turned his thoughts again to Randolph, trying to make sense of him. Even in ancient times, in his own village, there was odd behaviour between the sexes. Though he hadn't seen quite the like of Randolph's. Maybe that was only because in Ike's community there was not much noticeable difference in men and women's clothing. Was it the city influence? No, Ike concluded. In his centuries of observation, cities were basically the same as villages, but with far too many people.

Ike had thought Randolph so un-wolf-like. But then European wolves did have a different image. Ike didn't care to mix with them, but he knew their legends. Wolves there were known for their ferocity. There were a couple of stories of wolves raising human babies, one of whom went on to found the city of Rome. But the story children grew up on, was of a wolf who would eat children and grannies, even dressed as a woman to do so. Must

*have been that European influence in Randolph, Ike conjectured.
Who really knew? I do know, Ike concluded, that wolves have
odd ones too. But as long as they obey the order of the pack,
they are tolerated. Otherwise, they are killed or driven away.
Ike worried about what would happen to Meg now. She was a
lead female without the protection of a mate. The pack she was
in could bring her down.*

MEG LEARNED THAT RANDOLPH had willed the house and business,
everything he owned, to her. People regarded her as a rich young
widow. And I am, thought Meg as she sat in the library, at what was
now her desk, going over the accounts as she had done, for nearly a
decade. Twenty-four is young, as widows go. Though had I not married, I'd be regarded as an old spinster now. Eighteen is considered
a mature bride. And I would have a lot of money if I sold the house,
horses and carriage, the broom business, and my "pet vet" business,
as Randolph affectionately called it. She smiled thinking about the
delightful spin he put on things.

She missed his conversation. Missed him in bed, at the table, in
their library, at work, going about town. And yet his presence, his
company, was so much with her in the time after his death. Every-
day she could remember what they were doing on that day, when
he was still alive. The first year, every day is going to be a poignant
anniversary, she warned herself. And she worried it could become a
devouring quagmire of self-pitying nostalgia. A sinking backwards
into sourness.

Not for me, she resolved. Every day is a new day. And there *is* a
tomorrow. Randolph has enriched me in every way...except children. She twisted the pen in her hand. I do want to have children,
she thought, determined not to dwell on the hard part of their marriage, but not wanting to endure that again. So many nights being left
alone, being not desired. And was it normal to feel, after making love,
so...un-spent? Not for the first time, Meg wondered what it would

be like to make love with a man who was simply a man and had no qualms about having children with her. "*That's* what I want to find in my tomorrow," she said, pointing her pen into space, "along with some adventure."

But this is today, she reminded herself. And when all the bills and salaries are paid, I have very little to play with. No, I cannot afford to take off on any adventure now, much as I want to, would love to travel across this country by train, see the West Coast, make my way up north to see the sled dogs that look like wolves. Ike and Piji's working wolves; she smiled at the image of them in her mind. "And I *will*, as soon as I can," she spoke out in resolve as she stood up from the desk.

She put on her plus-fours and set out for a cycle in the fresh spring air. She decided to wear trousers whenever she felt like it. And carry a big stick. Always travel in the company of one of her Humane Society dogs. She would make Jacques general manager and give him as much of a raise as she could afford. Yes! she thought, in fact, why not drop in on Alice, please her with the news, have a comforting chat with my sister.

It took a few moments for Alice to answer the door.

"Oh it's just you! I needn't have grabbed a clean apron. I was in the midst of baking." She shifted Herbie onto her other hip and brushed strands of hair off her forehead. "What are you doing in that outfit?'

"Hi Herbie." Meg kissed him and followed Alice inside. "Just cycling around."

"Must be nice. I guess you can afford to, now that you own everything."

Oh, oh, thought Meg. Guess I'm in for it. "I'm busier than ever, actually. Up at 6 a.m. Couldn't sleep. Going over everything. It's suddenly a lot of responsibility."

"If you had kids you'd know what sleepless nights really are. And let me tell you, I'd take every penny of your 'responsibility' any day."

Meg sank down onto the kitchen chair. George and Victoria started to clamber over her.

"Auntie Meg, you look funny in those trousers," said George glee-fully.

"Auntie Meg *is* funny!' Victoria hugged her and tried to hang between her knees.

"You really should get rid of those plus-fours," said Alice. "They don't suit a rich widow. Do you want some tea? It's all I have."

"I'd love some tea. And cookies! Look at all those cookies. Aren't *you* the lucky kids to have a mommy who makes all these good cook-ies! Can we have some, Mommy?" She got up to take Herbie while Alice made tea.

"You're not sad any more?" said George. "Are you the merry widow now?"

Meg felt stabbed. Bowed her head.

"George!" Alice shouted. and stomped her foot. "Kids come out with the darnedest things. I don't know *where* he got that."

"Auntie Meg! Don't cry!" Victoria looked frightened and grabbed a cookie. "Here, have one."

"See what you've done, George," said Alice severely. "Apolo-gize. Apologize to Aunt Meg. I don't know *why* you would say such things."

"Auntie Meg!" George began to cry. "I didn't mean to make you cry. I hate you sad. Everybody sad. Or mad. All the time." He began to cry miserably.

"Here! Here!" Meg swooped up the children. "I'm the one who has to apologize. I wasn't crying. Just got tearful for a second. I miss Uncle Randolph. You do too, don't you?"

They nodded. Alice busied herself at the stove.

"It's all right: it's right, to be sad at times. But we don't stay that way, do we? We remember how Uncle Randolph loved to make us laugh and play. So that's what we should do." Meg heard Alice click her tongue and saw the slight toss of her head as she raised her eyes to the ceiling. "Come on, kids, let's go out and play while the kettle boils."

Meg didn't look at Alice. Didn't want to see her again. Ever. When

Alice brought out tea and cookies on a tray, she drank up and departed as quickly as she could.

"What's the sudden rush?" said Alice at the door.

"I just ... can't talk ..." to you, Meg thought, but said, "yet."

"Don't you think you're laying it on a bit thick?"

Meg cycled away from her sister.

Jacques looked pleased and relieved when Meg told him she would like him to be general manager. "But I'm afraid I can't give you a very big pay hike," she said. "We have to tighten up the business. I'm having a hard time balancing the books."

"I can understand that, Meg," he said. "There's a general recession. It's hitting all the businesses."

"I know," said Meg. "I hear the talk. And I read the papers. But I don't like to bandy that word around. It can have a snowball effect. People start putting their cash under their mattresses. It's bad for the economy, that gloom-and-doom talk."

"Right hard on the soul too."

Meg eyed Jacques. "How are things with you? Alice and the kids? I dropped in yesterday but couldn't stay long."

"Yes, I know." He looked uncomfortable. "Alice should be happy to hear about my promotion."

Next morning, Meg observed that Jacques made effort to be good-humoured and brisk about his work but, unguarded, he looked hang dog, if not hung over. Meg wondered what really went on in their household. What basis was there in Alice's complaint about Jacques's drinking? George's little outburst about people sad or mad all the time? Maybe she, Meg, was the unsympathetic, unhelpful sister. At the end of the day, Meg asked Jacques if they would like to come over for a meal on Sunday.

"It's good of you, Meg. The kids love going to your place. But it shouldn't always be you entertaining us ..."

"Oh who cares about *that*! Come for lunch. After church. I feel a

need for church. We'll roast a chicken. Let the kids play in the tub."
She stopped, thinking of the phone call, the previous time the kids
were in the tub.

"Are you sure? Maybe it's too soon," said Jacques empathetically.

"You are family, Jacques. It will be fine. I'm not attempting to entertain strangers." She smiled. "And if the phone rings, we'll refuse to
answer."

Alice was tense when she arrived. But that was not unusual. Meg
was determined to have a pleasant time, if not a jolly one, for the
kids. They had sherry on the verandah while the kids played in the
leaves piled up under the trees. Then Jacques lit a fire in the library
where Alice sat feeding Herbie while Meg bathed George and Victoria. They decided to eat round the kitchen table because it was easier
to maintain the kids there. Herbie slept in a big drawer brought from
the dresser and laid upon the floor.

"You and Jacques can sit at each end," said Meg. "I'll sit in the middle here, with one cute kid on either side of me. George? Vicky?" She
patted the spots on the bench where they were to sit.

"Yaaaay!" they shouted.

"Mind your manners," said Alice.

Meg set a pitcher of ale on the table.

"What's this?' said Alice. "No wine? Part of the tightening up?"

Jacques looked at her in alarm and dismay.

"Partly," said Meg. "But it's early in the day and I thought you
said a glass of ale was better for nursing." She raised her glass. "Well,
cheers! Here's to the future."

"Jacques says you don't believe in the recession."

"Alice!" Jacques put his glass down hard. "That's *not* what I said."

"All very easy not to believe in the recession when it doesn't affect
your business. People always need brooms. They can do without bicycles. Did you know we're closing up the shop? For good."

"Alice! Not in front of the children!" Jacques clenched his fist on
the table. "That is not a fit subject for this occasion."

"Let's pass the vegetables around, shall we?" Meg gave George and Vicky a squeeze. "What did you think of the sermon today, Jacques?"

"Go on, Jacques," said Alice. "Give us your opinion of the sermon. I don't have one. Since I was home feeding Herbie."

Jacques proceeded to give a very strained opinion. He finished his meal as quickly as the children finished theirs. "Why don't I take the kids out to play?" He reached to finish off his mug of ale.

"Might as well take a mug with you," said Alice sarcastically.

"Why not?" said Meg. "Go ahead, Jacques. I think Alice and I are going to have a talk."

Jacques took the children out into the yard.

"You always have to act like the queen bee, don't you!" Alice stood up and shoved her chair into the table as Meg started to clear up.

"Alice that is completely unfair. I try to help..."

"What help is that meagre raise you gave to Jacques!"

"It wasn't *meagre*! And it was the best I could do in the circumstances."

"*Your* circumstances! What could be better? You have no one to look after but yourself. You're rich. You'll probably marry someone richer. And look at us. We're bankrupt."

"You're not!"

"We are. And Jacques is too damn proud to tell you."

"Alice! You *never* swear." Meg half-smiled.

"Oh shut up! I'm sorry I told you. I knew you wouldn't understand. You have no idea what it means."

"Of course I do. I run a business. I know what bankruptcy is. But is it true? Look Alice, I'm sorry. You've taken me totally by surprise. Come on." Meg put her hands on Alice's shoulders. "Let's make some coffee and talk this over. How bankrupt are you?"

"We have to sell the business. Which no one is likely to buy. Not if they see our winter sales. No one has any use for bicycles in winter. They're completely impractical and a stupid idea for this hilly city. And we can't make a living off sleds and skates. Everyone already has them or can't afford to buy them. Not now in a recession. The Sports

Shop is a lemon. A white elephant. Who but a dreamer would want it. And Jacques took a huge loan on the house to invest in the store and stock. We can't possibly pay it back now. So we'll lose the house. And what does Jacques do about this? Cry in his beer. I had no idea he was such a weakling."

"Jacques is not a weakling!" Meg stopped in her tracks. "And you're not actually bankrupt."

Herbie began to cry. Meg went to pick him up.

"Oh sure. Spoil him. Pick him up the moment he cries. Then hand him over to me. Must be nice to be an aunt."

"Alice, you have to *stop* this. This *horrible* ... what is it? It feels like hatred. You hate everything I do."

"You know I don't hate you. I just hate my life compared to yours. And I hate most of all having to be the begging sister."

"It's not a question of begging ..." Meg turned to Herbie who was howling.

"Oh, for heaven sake, pick him up, if you want. I'll wash the damn dishes. And then feed him."

"I'll help you, Alice, as best I can, with the debts, and the damn dishes."

Alice washed the dishes while Meg carried and calmed Herbie.

"Don't you get lonely in this big house alone?"

"Sure," said Meg. "But I'll get used to it."

Alice was feeding Herbie and Meg was drying the dishes when they heard Jacques come up onto the verandah with the kids.

"There is an obvious solution," said Alice. "Not Jacques's idea. Mine."

"What is that?"

"Rent out our house. And move in with you. Just long enough to pay off the debt. It shouldn't take long. You like the kids so much. I'll look after the house and meals. Keep the kids out of your hair when you want peace and quiet. You really shouldn't be in this house all alone. Just think about it."

"Auntie, Auntie Meg. We have *beautiful* red tulips for you." They banged eagerly on the screen door.

It wasn't long before Alice moved her family into Meg's house. Meg had fought it mightily in her mind. The only person she could discuss it with was Jean Atkins.

"Alice is my sister and I have a deep natural feeling for her," Meg moaned to Jean. "But right now, she's not the sort of person I would choose to sit beside at a dinner table, let alone live with. She's in some awful state of looking upon others with jealousy and envy rather than genuine interest. She sees only what they have and she lacks. It makes her miserable. She can't enjoy any of the good she has. Particularly husband and children."

"That must be very hard for you to see," said Jean. "Though I've seen it myself. Alice and you have never been very alike. But you're her big sister and she admires you tremendously. Maybe she admires everyone too much. Thinks the grass is always greener on the other side of the fence. But I think she is in a trying stage of life, with three young ones born so quickly. I know it's against popular belief, but I don't think every woman is well-suited to motherhood. The early years can be very hard. Alice may be much happier when the children are at school and she can get involved in more adult activities, charitable works, and such. Look how we women enjoy working with all your new veterinary ideas. You're like the alpha female you talk about in wolf packs. And you do run ahead of the times. Alice is more of a follower. But she certainly has her strengths."

Jean looked discerningly at Meg's troubled brow and concluded. "You won't refuse her request for help, will you?"

"No, I won't. Refusing would be against every good moral principle."

Meg gave over the upper bedrooms to Alice and family and moved herself back into her old single bed in the room near the kitchen.

"Oh, thank you," said Alice. Actually gave Meg a kiss. "This master bedroom with small bedroom attached . . . it's perfect! The only sure way for me with Jacques. Separate beds. There's no 'safe time' for me. They say you're not likely to get caught while still nursing. And look what happened to me! But now I won't have to send him downstairs to the sofa. And to have this big bathroom with flush toilet, right next door. Oh Meg, remember how *far* it was to the outhouse on the farm? This house is *bliss*!"

Meg drew the line at being drawn into Alice's sense of social life. She retreated to the library when Alice held afternoon teas. Alice begrudgingly accepted that big dinner parties were unaffordable. Her mood changed to high excitement when Meg got tickets for them to attend a performance of Pauline Johnson reciting her poetry at the theatre.

Pauline was a poet born on the Six Nations Reserve near Toronto, the daughter of a Mohawk chief and his English wife. She was the most famous of the new Canadian poets and managed to make her living touring across Canada and in England, giving dramatic recitations of her poems, lively narratives and lyrics reflecting her closeness with nature, the heroics of her people, and her own champion canoeing skills. Meg read her poems as soon as they came out in magazines. Randolph had liked to recite them at parties. Meg was at the front of the line when tickets for her performance went on sale.

"Wouldn't mind seeing her myself," Jacques had said, "but I'll tend the kids, Alice, so you can go."

"Such good seats!" said Alice at the theatre, done up in her best dress, looking round at all the people behind her.

"I can't *wait* to see her!" said Meg. "And I'm dying to hear her do 'The Song My Paddle Sings.' Wouldn't you love to paddle a canoe!"

During the first half of her performance, Pauline Johnson appeared in an elegant white silk and lace gown. She recited her more lyric poems, dramatizing with graceful gestures, great poise and eloquence. Alice was enthralled. "Isn't she beautiful! Such a perfect lady. You'd never know she's part Indian. She makes stage acting look perfectly acceptable. I'd love to be able to do that. What a life, travelling the country, having people clap and admire you where ever you go. Wouldn't you love that!"

"I'd like to be able to write poetry the way she does," said Meg. "And to recite. She's very talented. And beautiful. It's a wonder she isn't married."

"You can't be married and have a life like that!" Alice whispered harshly. "Husband and kids following you around the country? Not likely! I'll bet she's happy, with a hundred suitors in every city. And when she settles down, she can choose amongst them."

The curtain was raised for the second half. Pauline appeared with her hair let down, wearing a doeskin dress with colourful beaded wampum belts hanging at the waist, a bear claw necklace, feathered and fringed decorations on her sleeves. Meg burst into applause and others quickly joined in. Alice looked around uncertainly. Pauline Johnson gave a dignified smile and slight bow. Then she launched into recitations of her more narrative and dramatic poems. She moved and gestured like a powerful actor, speaking with rising crescendos, fiery peaks and lulling, sad ebbs and flows. Meg leapt to her feet in applause, calling for encores as did the whole house, though other women didn't yell and whistle like Meg and the men. Alice clapped properly and frowned at Meg.

"Isn't she fabulous!" said Meg. "Absolutely bewitching!"

"I preferred the first act," said Alice.

Meg was invited to a reception afterwards for Pauline Johnson. She took Alice with her, missing Randolph, who would have thoroughly enjoyed Pauline's performance and had charming things to say to her. Pauline had changed into a grand red velvet dress for the reception.

"I think you are truly great," Meg found herself saying, meaning every word but knowing it sounded dull-witted. "I liked every thing about your performance. And I find your poems wonderful to read aloud and think about. But you must be exhausted, travelling all the way from Montreal today and giving such a performance tonight."

"Why thank you!" Pauline smiled warmly. "This kind of life *is* exhausting but I'm never too tired to hear a word of praise. Have you written poems?"

"Oh no. I have absolutely no talent for that. I'm a veterinarian. Better known as the dog doctor."

Pauline laughed and clapped her hands in the air. "I've never heard of such a thing. You must tell me more."

"There are a lot of people here who want to talk to you," said Meg, feeling Alice's impatience at her side. "This is my sister, Alice Benoit."

"Hello Miss Benoit..."

"Mrs.," said Alice. "I also admired your performance. Such a beautiful dress you had in the first act! Of course, the second was very interesting. And this striking red velvet..."

Pauline's brow furrowed.

"Excuse me," Alice continued, "I didn't mean to talk only of your dress. But you are truly glamorous. What I really wanted to ask is how you become a famous poetess."

"How does one become a poet? And famous? Is that what you're asking?"

"Yes."

"By spending a lot of time alone, writing. And re-writing poems. And writing to publishers. Travelling in uncomfortable coaches. Staying in hotel rooms that are not nice, or too expensive. And performing on stage whether you feel like it or not. I'm sorry, that's not what you wanted to hear, is it? Are you thinking of becoming a poetess?"

"Not now, I'm not," said Alice, thinking nor will I tell you I keep a lowly journal about ordinary life.

"It isn't the life you think it is." Pauline smiled and looked round the room full of people wanting to meet her. "But it is a wonderful life. And I'm honoured to be a voice for my people. It's nice to meet you." She turned to Meg. "May I give you my postal address? I would like to learn more about dog doctoring."

Meg laughed. "I would like to learn how to paddle a canoe."

"I don't think I like her at all," Alice whispered to Meg when

Pauline was taken up by other people. "But I love this party. Come on, introduce me to all these theatre people. Jacques and I never get out to things like this."

"Thank you," said Alice when they got home from the party. She gave Meg a quick hug. "Thanks for everything. You're my favourite sister."

The Sports Shop remained on the market through summer and winter. When it finally sold in March, it was a fire sale, selling for less than Jacques had paid for it. The merchandise went for less than half price. Jacques kept five bicycles and stored them in the driving shed.

"One for each of the kids, when they're big enough," said Jacques. "And one for me and you, Alice."

"I hate bicycles," said Alice. "Keep them out of my sight."

The broom business and the pet vet business were just treading water in terms of profit, but that was good considering the economic climate.

"This is a recession," Meg conceded. "But it can't last forever."

"With my luck, it will." said Alice.

"Your luck?!" Meg laughed. "Alice, this is everyone's bad luck."

"You could kick us out, now that the shop has sold," she said. "And we could kick out our tenants, move back into that little house with the mud patch for a yard. As long as you can keep paying Jacques' salary, we can live on that. Just. But we could get ahead maybe, if we could stay here longer. Through the summer. You know how the kids love your big yard, the swing and all. Would you mind?"

Yes, I would, thought Meg, I mind very much. I can't bear your complaining nature and the way you treat Jacques, making him miserable when he walks in the door happy to see his kids. No wonder he's depressed and takes as many swigs as he can before he gets home. "Of course you can stay through the summer," is what she answered. "And don't worry. Jacques earns his salary. He's managing Sweepers very well."

"I bet I could learn to do the books," said Alice, "if I had time."

✿

It was shortly after the anniversary of Randolph's death that Meg
received a letter from Mick O'Mara, Deputy Chief of Police, Boston,
USA.

Dear Mrs. Oliphant,

*I'm not sure if you are at this address or how else your circumstances
may have changed. Perhaps you are engaged, even remarried. Mine have
changed only in that I was made Deputy Chief of Police, in charge of the
case which so unfortunately involved your late husband. I have hesitated
to write this letter, being awkward as I am with the written word, but it is
my duty to convey to you the news that the Boston Stabber has been found.
I should say, in fact, found out, although he was deceased. There was no
trial and conviction since the person in question was deceased but the cir-
cumstantial evidence was proof positive.*

*This is what transpired after your return to Halifax. Given the pecu-
liar circumstances of your husband's unfortunate death, I began to think
of a different way in which the forces of peace and order might track down
or indeed trap, the Boston Stabber. My men were exceedingly reluctant
to assume the disguise of, you understand the expression, "ladies of the
night." There was also the practical problem of the men on my force being
too tall and broad of shoulder to be taken for women. But I was convinced
that that was how we would catch the Stabber.*

*Therefore I recruited four civilian men last summer to work in pairs
for this special patrol. They were acquainted with your husband from
his visits to a certain Boston club and glad to aid in the capture of his
murderer. However, the Stabber did not strike again, not until after New
Year's, which further substantiated my view that he had been surprised and
averted by his discovery of the identity of Mr. Oliphant. But strike again,
he did. The victim was another most unfortunate young woman, mother
of a young child, plying her trade near Boston Common.*

*I recalled our special recruits. They worked the night shift in pairs, pre-
tending to operate from a house of ill repute. They would leave the house
in the small hours of the morning, escorting each other across the Common,*

then separate near the entrance of two boarding houses. After one month and three days of this routine, one of them was approached from behind by a man wielding a knife. My recruit reacted quickly with the gun in his purse. The Stabber was fatally wounded but he did not die before my recruits managed to extract from him a full confession to seven murders, including that of your husband. The true identity of the Boston Stabber is that of Jerome Hebb, aged 26, expelled from medical school for disrespect to cadavers. In his rooming house quarters were found torn and stained ladies' undergarments, including a pair identified as being from his latest victim.

My dear Mrs. Oliphant, or Meg, if I may, I am sorry to evoke painful memories by the contents of this letter. My hope is that it will also bring you some consolation in that the murderer was brought to justice.

I wish to add that I was moved by your case and impressed by your person. This is an uncommon kind of letter for me to compose. I never married. The nature of my work is so indelicate that I did not think a normal lady could ever understand my dedication to it. But I think perhaps you could. If you are not committed to another and would like to meet again with serious purpose in mind, if you would be willing to move to Boston . . . please let me know, in your own good time.

In any case, I wish you well and will always think of you as a lady of great composure and understanding.

Yours sincerely,
Mick O'Mara

Meg read and re-read the letter. Kept it locked in her desk drawer and running free in her mind. Did not want to answer it immediately because that would give conclusion to it. It was a peculiar kind of company for her. Mick O'Mara was the only person she knew who shared her memory of Randolph's secret life and sordid death. He was someone she could open up to. And he had opened up to her in such an unusual but natural manner, leaving himself vulnerable, like a wolf making its presence known in the night forest by its lonesome howl. Meg felt the dead weight in her heart begin to lighten. The loneliness alleviate.

She wanted to simply run to him, embrace him, nuzzle into his broad shoulders and neck. She recalled how good looking he was in his officer's uniform. Much taller than her but not much older. Serious blue eyes and reddish hair. Ears a bit big but good bone structure face. Altogether a good anatomy, she smiled, in studying him in retrospect, from the outside. Ah, but behind the uniform ... what secret habits? I must be cautious. And yet, how open and frank he seems. How altogether unusual, this letter and this man, she concluded, and how very, very nice! I must think carefully and answer with the same openness of heart.

Dear Deputy Chief O'Mara, ... Mick, if I may,

How very kind of you to send the, let us be frank ... ugly information ... to me. And yet, as you say, it also brings a sense of justice, which has given me a peculiar satisfaction. When I think about it, the satisfaction comes more from knowing that no more loved ones will be murdered by that man. I do not derive much, if any satisfaction at all, out of vengeance. I keep thinking of the other victim's young daughter growing up without her mother and with the knowledge of how she was killed. But perhaps she will not be informed of the worst. Not if you are handling it. For I remember how deeply considerate you were with me, prepared to spare me information that might have shocked and disturbed me.

I want to say I find it a surprising comfort and relief to know that you share the secret I'm bound to keep about my late husband, Randolph. It is a secret I promised him I would keep. It created a peculiar loneliness in my life and I feel burdened by it at times. There is so much I don't know or understand about the behaviour of men, or perhaps I should say, of human beings. It would be enlightening to talk to you. I regret that I was in such a state when I met you that I could not converse with you and I am grateful to be able to correspond with you now. More than grateful.

But first I must say, I think you are not just clever, but original, in your pursuit of justice. Randolph said there were "clubs." I remain ignorant of that side of his life. He wanted to keep it completely separate from the normal life we shared. I would like you to convey to your "recruits" my admiration for their courage and resourcefulness in capturing the murderer. Though, the resourcefulness was more yours.

You are an unusual and most admirable man whom I would like to know better and better ... fully, to be honest. Your seriousness of purpose in regard to me is a great compliment and has stirred my heart and mind. I would indeed like to meet again and have proper, intimate correspondence. But, as for my willingness to move to Boston ... that is a more complex and difficult question. I have thought very seriously about it.

I'll admit I am not always happy in my own home since I have, of necessity, given it over to my sister and her little family, whom I love, but there are tensions which sadden me deeply. I do, however, get great satisfaction from my veterinary work. It is something I cannot abandon. I think I must not.

As for Boston ... I am somewhat afraid of the city itself. To put it dramatically, it lured my husband to his death. On the other hand, it is a city of great intellectual and cultural reputation and history. And you are the Deputy Chief of Police. You should know that I am not generally regarded as a "normal lady" since I run a business and have a habit of cycling around town in breeches because they are more practical for that purpose than a skirt. Not fit material for a wife of the Deputy Chief of Police ... IF ... seriousness of purpose led to that! I'm sure all Boston would agree. And I'm afraid I can't change my habit, or give up my love of being a dog doctor. If I did not change my habit, or give up my vet practice, I would be an unsuitable wife and if I did, I would be an unhappy one. I have seen that an unhappy wife can make a husband miserable. I wouldn't want to do that to you.

Yet I already feel deeply unhappy in having to say this, the honest truth, to you now.

I thank you for your letter, your good work and the great compliment of your proposal to meet again, with seriousness of purpose. Can we please continue to correspond?

Yours most sincerely,

Meg

18

LEAVING THE PACK

MEG DID NOT EXPECT A REPLY by return of post, though she hoped for it and came home from work each day looking first to the hall table where her letters would be placed. She had told Alice and Jacques that Deputy Chief O'Mara had informed her of finding Randolph's murderer but disguised from them her hope of receiving more letters from him. The days gathered into weeks and Meg's hope turned into disappointment then depressing resignation. She concluded that Mick wanted all or nothing. He was not a man who had time or inclination for intimate correspondence.

Ike's spirit drooped as he worried over Meg. Observing the behaviour of the pack surrounding her, Ike's disgust with people was renewed. "A strong male will go to the female," he muttered and muttered, inaudibly, in her ear.

Through the dark winter nights and cold spring rains of that long year, Meg locked herself in the library, after reading bedtime stories to her niece and nephews. She did the business accounts and read to herself. She re-read "Ike's Working Wolves" and old novels. Anything to distract her from loneliness and the scenes with Alice and Jacques.

Alice feared she was pregnant again. "Just my luck," she complained when Meg came into the drawing room after bathing the children. Jacques was slumped in the corner of the couch, trying to keep his eyelids up. Alice was hemming children's clothes. "Other wives have years between children," she said. "I never get a break. I get caught every time."

Meg hated being brought into matters which should have been private between Alice and Jacques, particularly when both parties were present. But Alice relished it, counting on Meg to back her up. Meg tried to deflect her this time with humour. "No rest for the wicked, I guess."

"Not funny, Meg! All very well for you, who have nothing to worry about."

"Hold it," said Jacques. "Meg's a businesswoman. She's got plenty to worry about these days. Same as me."

"Yes, well at least Meg doesn't come home drunk every day."

"Alice!" said Meg. "What good does it do to say something like that!"

"It's the truth," said Alice. "He drinks so much before he gets in the door, he's lurching and tumbling about like a clown with the children. It's a wonder he doesn't topple over onto them."

"Alice! Jacques is here in front of us. You talk as though ..."

"I'm gone," Jacques stood up, wavering slightly as he stepped towards the door. "Absent," he said, "just the way you like me."

Alice laughed. "See what I mean? Lurching."

Jacques turned around. "What do you want, woman? *This?*" He got down on the floor, lay on his back, put his hands and feet in the air and said, "Dead dog. Is that what you want? Want me to roll over now?"

Meg was too appalled to speak. Herbie, upstairs in his crib, began to cry.

"Oh get up, Jacques," said Alice. "You're being pathetic. I'll be dead long before you. I'm the one who has to keep bearing children."

"Stop it!" Meg shouted as she went over to help Jacques to his feet. "I won't have this. Not in my house."

Little George and Victoria could be seen through the doorway with their heads poking through the stair railing.

"Now we have it," said Alice rising to her feet, children's clothes bundled in her arms. "We are about to be evicted. From my *sister's* house."

Victoria began to wail. George ran into the room and clung to his father's leg.

"No one is being evicted," said Meg, going to pick up Victoria and bring her into the room, soothing her. "I'm just asking for civilized behaviour. Jacques would you please put the children in their beds while I talk to Alice?"

Meg closed the drawing room door while Jacques led the children upstairs to the nursery. Now it was Alice who slumped into the corner of the couch, her arms folded across her chest. Meg sat down beside her.

"Well?" said Alice.

"I don't know, Alice. What more can I do? Can't you just be glad of your children? Mother wasn't miserable with eight."

"Oh yes she was."

"She was not. Well, not all the time. And she was nice to Dad. She didn't blame him. You blame Jacques for being a normal man."

"And a poor provider."

"Oh stop it. You live more comfortably than most."

"Thanks to you, I'm supposed to say."

"I never ask you to say that. It's Jacques who pays for all the food and necessities."

"And what am I? The household servant?"

"You're a normal woman doing normal things."

"And you think you're the Queen of Sheba."

Meg stood up. "Apologize. Apologize for saying that."

Alice stood up. "I *won't*! Why should I! I'm leaving. I'm leaving, right now." She stalked out of the room towards the front door.

Jacques came running down the stairs. "Alice, don't. Come back. You are needed ..."

Alice hesitated, then opened and slammed the door behind her. Jacques looked appealingly at Meg, then followed Alice out onto the front path. Meg watched Jacques pursue Alice, pull her back, put his arm around her, lead her back up onto the verandah, sit with her on the wicker love seat. Meg went upstairs to comfort and reassure George and Victoria, who were whimpering at the top of the stairs, and Herbie, who was crying as he grabbed the rails of his crib.

When Alice came back into the house, she assumed the air of the victimized, not speaking to Meg for several days, then finally speaking with remote politeness, until she felt it was sufficiently established that Meg was in the wrong. A couple of weeks later, Alice discovered that she was not pregnant, which made her happier for a while but not less pessimistic about her prospects in life, compared to certain others. Jacques stopped coming home from work lurching, but took to spending some late nights at a tavern where he could pay for the use of a woman and drown his dreams in drink, for a while.

Meg gave up on trying to be comfortable in her own home and took to her bicycle and evening walks on the cliff side, overlooking the ocean.

Meg sat near the edge of the cliff, watching the waves lap upon the beach below and the sun sink into the ocean. Cuesey, a mournful-looking hound from her kennels, lay beside her. Here I am, driven out of my own home, Meg said to herself. And Jean thinks *I'm* the Alpha female! Meg tried to find that funny but could not. She was heavily depressed. She seriously considered her situation. Would they all be better off without me? If I just jumped off this cliff into the waves ... Would Alice be happy if I left her and Jacques the house and business? The children ...

Meg pictured it happening. Her not coming home. The search for her. Finding her bicycle. Police searching for her drowned corpse. The fear and terror in the minds of the little children. They would miss her. They would have to grow up imagining her death and why she did it ...

"*No!* What am I thinking!" Meg spoke out, clasping both sides of her head.

Cuesey sat up, yapped in alarm. *Ike's spirit fluttered and bounced about in panic. He shouted and yanked at Meg's shoulders, grabbed her with his insubstantial hands.*

"Stop this!" Meg rebuked herself out loud. "I've got to get away. *Away* from these terrible thoughts. *Away!*" She got herself up and moved back from the cliff's edge. She turned and grabbed her bicycle. Cuesey barked decisively and fled home with her, long ears flapping in the wind. *Ike rode upon her shoulders.*

Meg made herself a hot milk with rum and went straight to bed to reckon with herself.

It's my job to alleviate suffering, not to add to it, she reprimanded herself. There is no way of killing myself that would not leave a horrible scene, a corpse to be identified, unanswered questions, guilt, suffering for my family, a terrible example for all.

She thought again of how helpful Mick had been when she had to cope with the corpse of Randolph. Mick was a kind man. Was she misinterpreting his not responding to her letter? Perhaps he had not received it. It was not just loneliness she was suffering, but a sense of unspoken rejection. And the awful unhappiness in this house ...

"I do need to get away," she concluded quietly, out loud. "But in a civilized and kind manner. Prepare for it properly."

She would send another letter to Mick, asking if he had received the first, hoping that he did want friendship, at least, also hoping he did want to see her again. And she would take that train trip she had wanted to take for so long. Travel across the country, from one coast to the other. See it all. Carry on up to the north, the land of ice and snow, where there were no horses, only dogs. Dogs that looked like wolves. Ike and Piji's dogs, pulling sleds. Working dogs that could use a good vet. Dogs for company. And dogs would be her children if she couldn't find a suitable man to have a family with.

Meg began thinking of who might take over The Humane Way and who might do the books for Clean Sweepers. She would write letters of her adventures to her niece and nephews. She would become the interesting, adventurous aunt who inspired and entertained the children. Not the one who threw herself off the cliff in a time of despair.

Meg felt some lightness of being, some of her old strength and determination return. A distance developed between her and the complaints of Alice now that she had a secret resolution to the situation. She confided it to Jean Atkins.

"Oh dear," said Jean. "I will miss you awfully. And so will all the dogs and cats and pet birds of Halifax. You will return, won't you?"

"Maybe with a whole new breed of dogs." Meg smiled. "But while I'm gone, I need someone to do the accounts at Clean Sweepers. I trust Jacques to manage the business but I need someone, a trusted friend, someone who taught me how to add and subtract, someone who has kept the books for a medical doctor and so could handle mine. She would be well-paid ..."

"To keep an eye on the assets, in your absence." Jean laughed. "Someone outside the family, eh? Hmmmm ..."

Meg telephoned the principal at her vet college in Montreal, asking if he would advertise the lease of her veterinary clinic amongst the graduating class.

"Mrs. Oliphant, your business is already the talk of the college," he said. "And your 'Humane Way' has corrupted our teaching practices ever since you were here. We have, as yet, no other female graduates but I'm sure we will, now that you have opened the gates and even have an established business for lease. I expect you will have many applicants for it. Will you accept them if they are male?" Principal McEachran could not repress a small chuckle.

Meg interviewed several candidates who wanted her business. She chose the one who was willing to maintain the name and employ her assistant, Ardiss Arpin, whom Meg said had taught her a thing or two about handling difficult animals and people.

When the deal was completed, with rent in advance, Meg told

Jacques and Alice of her plan. "I want to have everything in order," she said in conclusion, "so I can leave in July."

"I knew something was up," said Alice, who had stared intently at Meg while she spoke.

"You've sure caught *me* by surprise" said Jacques pushing back his hair. "But whoa, Meg! I don't think you should do this. It's not safe for a woman to travel across the country on her own. I'm not sure I can run the business without you ..."

"Of course you can!" Alice interjected. "And why hire an accountant? I could learn to do the books. Just as you did. How about hiring some household help instead?"

"Jean Atkins will see to the books," said Meg, firmly.

"The kids will miss you so much ..." said Jacques.

With her plans in place, Meg felt she had the dignity and strength to write again to Mick.

> *Dear Deputy Chief of Police, ... Mick, if I may,*
>
> *That is how I began my letter, in response to yours, of May 5th. Can you please let me know if you received my letter, for I have received no reply.*
>
> *Perhaps you are now chief of police, or married. Perhaps both, in which case I wish you very well and understand why you would not want to continue any correspondence and friendship with me. I am finding it very awkward to write this letter, and so I will make it short, sparing you and myself further embarrassment. In mid-July I shall take the train west to Vancouver and make my way north to the Yukon, where I hope to practice for a while with the sled dogs which I have long taken interest in. This is an adventure which I feel I must embark upon now, or never.*
>
> *If you wish to meet again or correspond I would be very glad of that and send you my particulars when I know them.*
>
> *Yours very sincerely,*
>
> *Meg*

Again Meg hoped for a quick reply, but nothing came by return of post. She began to worry that Mick had come to harm and she would have her letter returned "deceased." She occupied herself with final preparations for departure. She would take a load of brooms, whisks, and clothes brushes to be shown as samples from Clean Sweepers.

"Why not drum up business across the nation?" she said to Jacques. "With the ease and speed of train travel we could ship anywhere."

"Good idea," said Jacques. "But I worry about all this. And the kiddies are all upset at your leaving."

"I know. But I've told them I'll be back and there'll be letters, a phone call whenever possible, and I have a plan for the day I leave."

"What's that?" said Alice, whose spirits had improved since she was going to be mistress of Meg's house and have the income from their rented home for an extended period. She had already hired cleaning help and bought a new dress. But she remained resentful of the fact that Meg had hired Jean Atkins to manage the business accounts.

"I've found a Labrador retriever pup to give to the kids on the morning of my departure," Meg replied. "That should cheer them up. I'll suggest they call it Meggs"

Jacques smiled. "They'll love it. You think of everything, Meg."

"And couldn't be more generous," said Alice as though she were reciting a line. They looked at her. "I mean it," said Alice. "What makes you think I don't?"

"Nothing," said Meg. "Thanks for the ... compliment."

Jacques looked perturbed.

"Jacques thinks you're being nudged out of your own home," said Alice. "Thinks it's because of my complaining. But I think you're just doing what you've always wanted to do. Travel. Go to theatres across the country, just like Pauline Johnson, whom you admire so much. Except you don't have to perform. You've got enough money to just travel. Wish I could ..."

"Alice!" Jacques shouted then closed the salon door so the children couldn't hear.

"What?" Meg bristled. "You wish you could be like me, Alice?

Would you really, would you really want to be alone, without your children and your husband?"

Alice smiled tight-lipped, eyebrows raised.

"Don't say it!" Meg leapt to her feet. "No one wants to hear it."

"I don't intend to." Alice folded her arms over her chest and leaned back on the sofa. "I'm not half as stupid, or complaining, as you think I am."

"I don't..." Meg started, but decided to give it up. "I'm going to say good night to the kids."

"The perfect aunt," said Alice when Meg was in the hall. "Easier than perfect mother."

The week before she was to leave, Meg heard the phone ring late in the night. She felt paralyzed as she heard Jacques rush downstairs to answer it, then say, "Yes, sir. I'll bring her to the phone." The dreadful silence until Jacques knocked on her door and said, "Meg, Deputy Chief O'Mara wants to talk to you. No bad news, he said."

Jacques went back upstairs and closed Alice's door then his own, behind him.

"I'm sorry to call so late," said Mick. "It's the only time I have some privacy here. Just got back today from some bad business I had to tend to in New York. I have your letter in front of me. Meg, I must see you. If only to apologize."

"For what?" Words tumbled out before Meg could get hold of them. "Oh Mick, I've been so *worried*. I can't believe I'm hearing your voice!"

"You should have heard it all those months ago. I should have written. But every time I tried, I didn't know how to begin. Never felt so stumped in all my life. Couldn't see a solution. You with your work there, me with mine here. The cases keep coming in and I bury myself in them until they're solved. That's what I did. Buried myself like a coward. Felt so bad. Didn't know what to say to you. Hopelessly stumped. And listen to me blatherin' on about it now. Over the phone! Can I come to see you, Meg?"

"How soon?"

"I can get away Wednesday. Have to be back for the weekend, when people do their worst. Nothing like the weekend to bring out human nature."

Wednesday, Meg hovered near the door.

"Expecting someone?" said Alice.

"You know I am," Meg snapped, in no mood to be drawn in by Alice.

"Mick O'Mara, Deputy Chief of Police in Boston," said Alice. "Sounds like a good catch to me. And deputy usually becomes chief, doesn't he?"

"Alice!"

"Meg!" Alice put her hands on her hips, imitating Meg. "You never *will* take advice from your 'little sister,' will you?"

"What is your advice?"

"Deputy Chief O'Mara doesn't come all this way for chit chat. You will have to choose between him and your 'adventure.' Which will you choose?"

"Your advice is ... ?"

"Well, I'm sure there are dogs to be doctored in Boston. They have working police dogs, don't they? And if you're in love with this stranger, and you're certainly acting like you are ... I have never seen you so ... agitated."

"Alice, what is your advice?"

"Have your adventure first, or you'll regret it the rest of your life. Have your family later. Mother had me when she was over forty." Alice turned away then faced Meg again. "There! And you don't think I really care about you. I'll keep the kids out of the way when he arrives."

Mick O'Mara arrived at the door in civilian clothes. Meg opened it.

"Mr. O'Mara!" said Meg, knowing Alice was hovering in the background. "I'm very pleased to see you. Do come in." She extended her hand. Mick took her hand and held on for more than a handshake. "This is my sister, Alice Benoit, and ..." Meg extended her other hand towards them, "children."

Mick let go of Meg's hand. "Mrs. Benoit." He bowed to her then reached out to the children. "Lads." He shook each small hand. "And Lass." They stood dumbfounded.

"You are highly regarded in this household, Deputy Chief O'Mara," said Alice, smiling. "Welcome! Now, if you'll excuse me, the children and I have things to do." As she backed them into the kitchen, Herbie could be heard saying, "He doesn't look like a policeman."

"Shall we go into the library?" said Meg, walking towards it.

Once inside, with the door closed, Mick stood before her.

"I've come all this way, rehearsing lines, and now I don't know what to say, other than ... we have so little time before ..." He looked at the floor. He put his hat on the table and looked at her seriously. "I won't, I couldn't, hold you back. You're more, even more, unusual and desirable than ever. May I ..." He stepped towards her. "... just hold you?"

Meg held her arms out to him. He caught her up in an embrace, hesitated, then kissed her. And she him. They sat down together.

"What can we do?" he asked, practically. "I have my job in Boston and you have this ... mission ... way the hell up on the other side of the continent."

Meg could hear Alice chasing after the children who had escaped into the hall and were running towards the library.

"We are about to be invaded." She stood up. "How about a ride into the countryside? Do you know how to cycle? Or shall we take the horse and buggy?"

"Sure an' I can cycle. But horse and buggy would be more comfortable."

"I'll make a picnic."

The children clamoured around as they made their way to the kitchen.

"Ever had a ride on a policeman's shoulders?" said Mick.

They drove out into the countryside, Mick taking the reins, letting the horse know they were eager to get away from onlookers. Outside of town he relaxed and put his hand on Meg's.

"What can you tell me about those clubs in Boston?" asked Meg.

"Not much." He looked at her. "I don't frequent them voluntarily."

"What do you like to do, when you're not working? When you're on your own?"

"I go fishing when I want to get away from people." He inched closer to her. "I have my own little boat. And I like to read. Do you?"

"Oh yes. Who's your favourite author?"

"Can't say, off the bat." Mick paused to consider. "I've always enjoyed Dickens. And you can't beat Mark Twain for humour, with a point to it."

"What about Oscar Wilde?"

"Too wisecracking. Not my way of thinking." He turned to Meg. "How am I doing in this interrogation?"

"Just fine." She smiled. "What do you do for company?"

"I fiddle." He smiled at Meg. "I'm the great Uncle Fiddler. Play at all the family gatherings. Play in my favourite Irish pub. Get a lot of drinks for free."

"Tell me what's wrong with you?" Meg took the crook of his arm with her two hands and yanked gently. "I need to know."

"I had a misspent youth." He slowed the horse and spoke seriously. "I got my young girlfriend in trouble. Her mother took her away for a time. And somewhere in Ireland a baby was put into an orphanage because of me. No one would tell me where. It's an 'unsolved' that will always bother me. Maybe I should go back and try to solve it, but I'm not sure of the good it would do. And I'm always working on some big case in Boston. Sure an' I couldn't leave your case unsolved." He smiled grimly at Meg. "They say that about me. I'm a man who can't leave a case unsolved."

"What a terrible fault!" Meg entwined her arm with his. "But you took two days away from a case to visit me?"

"That I did."

"Then we mustn't waste a moment."

They picnicked in the evening on Meg's favourite cliff overlooking the ocean. Watched the sun set. Talked and embraced in an unVictorian manner. They went down to the beach and built a fire. Cooled themselves off with a swim in the ocean. The picnic cloth was their towel. Picnic and horse blankets their bed, as they watched the summer moon rise over them and heard the calm ocean lapping onto the land. Meg learned what it was like to make love with a man who was only a man, was careful not to get her in trouble, and left her feeling... "Spent!" said Meg, smiling. "I feel completely spent."

"Will you be condemned for spending the night out with me?" Mick stroked her.

"Undoubtedly," said Meg, "But I can't imagine ever regretting this night."

They awoke with the rising of the sun and lingered until it was time to go back to the city for breakfast at the train station café. Meg didn't mind that the waitress was obviously speculating as to why Mrs. Oliphant was breakfasting at the station with this stranger. Meg smiled with her secret pleasure at everyone she encountered. But as they stood together on the train platform, the pain of parting gripped and twisted inside her.

"I would try to change your mind about this dog business," said Mick. "But I've got too much respect for your mind. And your person."

"Thank you," said Meg, refraining from exhibiting her natural feelings publicly. "I feel the same about you and your police business." She tried to smile. "This parting is very hard to bear. But, you are a man who must serve justice and I, the animals."

He could not refrain from pulling her tightly to him. "I love you." His lips touched her ear. "You'd be amazed at what a man will do for the woman he wants."

"I plan to be at Hotel Vancouver in August," said Meg. "You could reach me there by letter. You will let me know when your current case is solved, won't you?"

PART TWO

DAWSON CITY

1

THE BEGINNING OF DAWSON CITY

Ike's spirit was soaring as he rode with Meg across the country to the West Coast. He fairly bounced on her shoulders in excitement. It was like the good old days of being alive and mushing with his malamutes. He was on his way back home with a good healer for his dogs. It had been a close call with that Mick. A man with good wolf instincts, thought Ike. No wonder Meg got on so well with him. But her own instincts were leading her just where Ike wanted her to go. It's a wondrous thing when that kind of harmony is found. Ike remembered it well ... the perfect synchronizing between musher and team, when no words need be spoken. Just place your feet on the back of the sled, hang on and the dogs take off knowing exactly where you want them to go.

IKE WAS FAMILIAR with a very extensive past, but the future is unknown to the living and the dead. While Ike was concentrating on the life of Meg, a great change was taking place in his home territory. It began in the 1870s with white men making their way over the northern Rocky Mountains and down the Yukon River towards the

junction of the Klondike. Some came through Alaska, up the Yukon
River, as Ike had done when he first met the couple who had traded
Tarak Amorak for Chiefdog. Few in number, these men were loners,
adventurers, and eccentrics, most of them prospectors, hoping to find
gold. They were the losers and ever hopefuls who had failed, or had
arrived too late, to make the earlier gold discoveries in California or
British Columbia.

They got on quite well with the native people, who were composed of various clans. The newcomers called all of the natives Indians, just as the natives called all the migrants from various countries,
white men. Some of these migrants considered themselves superior to
natives, refused to respect or learn from them, and remained ignorant
outsiders. But others had the sense to know they were outnumbered,
that they were treading on foreign territory, and were dependent on
the goodwill of the native people. Several prospectors showed such
respect that they were allowed to mate and marry native women and
benefit from membership within a clan.

In the 1890s, there was general peace and quiet along the trade
routes of the Yukon and Klondike Rivers…until the discovery of
great veins of gold in the creeks feeding the Klondike. It happened
in August of 1896, while Meg's train was making its way towards
Vancouver.

It was a typically warm, sunny summer day in the Yukon territory,
but a day of ill-boding for Silent Kate of the Wolf Clan, even though
it was she who first saw that big chunk of gold. She was a Tagish
woman whose name was Shaaw Tl'áa, born of a mother from the
Wolf Clan and a Tlingit father of the Crow Clan, a woman whose
American husband called her Kate. She was gathering blueberries and
then washing up in a stream called Rabbit Creek. As she shook the
water off her hands, she noticed something gleaming in the stream.
She was used to keeping a sharp eye out for telling signs in water or
on the land, for she was an experienced hunter and fisher, as well as
a cook, home keeper, berry picker, wife, mother, and gold seeker. It

was her husband, George Washington Carmack, who had taught her how to look for gold.

George Carmack was a second-generation gold seeker who had made his way across the southern states and up the west coast of America to the far northwest of the Rocky Mountains. By the time he got to the Chilkoot Trail, which is an arduous four and more days' hike over the Rockies from the Alaskan to the Yukon side of the mountains, George was fed up with prospecting. He took up with a couple of professional packers whose ancestors had been guarding and working the Chilkoot Trail ever since it had been used by human beings. The one packer was called Skookum, because he was about as tall as a tree and strong as a rock. His clan name was Keish; he was the brother of Shaaw Tl'áa, but Carmack called him Skookum Jim. The other fellow was Kaa Goox, cousin of Shaaw Tl'áa, and Carmack called him Tagish Charlie. Charlie was short, strong, and, according to Carmack, fast as a weasel.

Skookum Jim held the record for weight, speed, and earnings as a packer on the Chilkoot. Carmack would never come close to him in that, but they became friends. Skookum Jim introduced Carmack to his village, his family, and their way of life. Carmack took to all of these enthusiastically, learning the language, wearing Tagish clothing, adopting their culture and skills, and marrying one of Skookum Jim's sisters. But she, like several in the family, and many in the village, died of influenza, the disease which white men carried. The custom was, that if a wife died, her sister would then marry the widower. Shaaw Tl'áa was in line for this since she herself was a widower, having lost her husband and daughter to influenza.

There was serious grief to be submerged and family complications to be set aside, but Carmack married Shaaw Tl'áa, his Kate, in a Tagish ceremony in 1886. She was a young beauty, about eighteen, with extraordinary strength and skills. The first summer of her marriage, she spent hiking up and down the Chilkoot Trail, packing alongside her husband, brother, and cousin, carrying loads for the Dominion Land Surveyor, William Ogilvie. She carried lighter loads, but also did the cooking, washing, some hunting, and berry picking.

George and Kate got on well in their early years. He had so much respect for her and her culture that he was called by some from his culture, Squawman George. The only thing he apparently disliked about her culture was the habit of living and sleeping in communal family housing. He insisted on building a separate log house for Kate and himself. They built their first one in the small community of Dyea, on the inlet at the foot of the Chilkoot Trail.

As time went on, Carmack also acquired the name Lyin' George. This was because his lust for gold had returned. He moved into the Yukon territory, prospecting for gold in summer, hunting and trapping in winter, with Kate at his side, sometimes also Skookum Jim and Tagish Charlie. George staked a claim near the small mining community at Fortymile on the Yukon River in 1890, when he had found a little gold. George's enthusiasm for his ventures and the worth of his claims was so over the top that he was called Lyin' George.

His interest in his own culture also showed signs of returning when they had a baby girl in 1893. Kate was at that time running a trading post they had started near Five Finger Rapids on the Yukon, while George worked on the construction of a Christian church, called St. Andrew's. He had their baby baptized there. Nick-named Graphie Grace, she was taught English by her father.

Kate missed her own parents and village as she moved amongst these miners' settlements. She was always busy, helping George to dig or sift for gold, tending Graphie, and doing the domestic work. She lacked the time and facility to mix with the few other women in the settlements. Some of those women did nothing but dance and sing and lay with men. They spoke English. Kate understood English well enough to get the gist of things but she did not like to speak the language since she was sometimes laughed at or not understood.

The language was tricky because it had several names for one thing. Prospectors, miners, gold seekers, all the same kind of man. Some tried to come up the Chilkoot Trail with a strange animal that looked like a giant dog. Mule, donkey, ass, they called it. Three words for the same animal that could not get up the trail, was too big to feed, too stupid to hunt for its own food, and too weak to withstand the winter storms. And then that same word, ass, was applied to humans and human parts. Sometimes both at once. When George got angry at Charlie, he called him a stubborn ass. He would say, "Get your ass on out of here," and "Asshole!" Then there was the "ass end of the tea kettle." Except water came out of a tea kettle and only from the one end, that looked like a man's front piece. It was all too confusing, and funny in a way people who spoke this English didn't realize.

Kate enjoyed telling native wives these funny things that a white husband said. It made them wonder and think and laugh. It made them enjoy her. It took away the loneliness she felt in the long periods away from her people, alone with her child, awaiting the return of George and Jim and Charlie from their long hunting trips. It was so much better than the feeling she had in the company of white people. White people didn't hurt her. George saw to that. But she couldn't bear the way they laughed at her, from inside their faces. That's where they tried to keep their laughter when she failed to speak the way they did. She stopped trying. Then she got the name Silent Kate. Fine. It suited her well, when she was amongst them.

In the summer of 1896, George took her and Grace to the native fishing camp at the junction of the Klondike and Yukon Rivers. She could communicate well enough with the Han women there, and she had the company of Skookum Jim and Charlie and his young brother Koolseen, whom George called Patsy. Kate was in a good mood as she collected berries in her cedar bark basket that morning of August 16th. George and Charlie were still sleeping. Jim had gone farther up Rabbit Creek. There was an unnatural tension in the air, the kind of tension that comes when men stir things up. George was always stirring the fire, couldn't sit still or silent for long like her people. That used to interest her about him, but it could be tiresome. He had stirred things up many dawns ago by telling everyone about his dream.

"It was a dream full of fish," he said. "Teeming with fish. Ordinary greylings, but so many the river couldn't contain them. They were leaping into the air. Then suddenly, two giant, golden, gleaming salmon swam upstream in the midst of all the small greylings. These two salmon stopped, right in front of me. I was at the river's edge.

The eyes of these two salmon were pure gold, round like twenty-dollar gold pieces. Their scales were golden nuggets. They stared at me like messengers. They were summoning me."

"What for?" asked Jim.

"Don't know for sure. Must be there's gold. Or one hell of a fishing spot that I'm supposed to find."

He has many dreams, thought Kate. Treats them like visions. One man cannot have so many visions as George does. Not ones that lead nowhere or have no useful story. He's more like a dream catcher than a good storyteller. But that dream of his did lead us to the fish camp this summer and there are many big salmon stopping in our nets. Enough to feed ourselves and throw to the dogs through winter. It was a good summer all around. Lots of fish in the Klondike, moose in the pasture at the junction of the Yukon, not too many bear to get in the way of berry picking. It was the best time for George, Jim, and Charlie to cut the trees on shore and float the logs down to Ladue's mill for a good price. The wolf pack that roamed the ridge over Moosehide Gulch and howled from the smooth top of the Dome Mountain was a big one and sounded well fed. Jim said it was a pack of nine.

Then came the day in mid-August when that tall skinny white man with the frowning face and eyes of a crow, Bob Henderson, crashed in on their lunch. Kate had prepared fresh salmon baked in hot ashes. Graphie and Patsy were sitting on a log at the river's edge above where someone had tied a small rowboat with a much-patched bottom. A shallow layer of river water rested in it. George was sitting round the fire with Jim and Charlie, having a smoke before getting back to work. Kate was checking the sourdough bread she was making in the men's gold-sifting pans. From the evergreens and white-barked trees at the base of the Dome, a man emerged. They watched him flailing his gold pan at mosquitoes as he made his way through wild raspberry and salmon berry bushes, then tramped across the grass and dirt trails of the fishing bank.

"Well, if it ain't!" said George, standing up. "Bob Henderson. Haven't seen him in a coon's age. Still lookin'. And still not findin', I'll bet ya."

Jim and Charlie rose to their feet. Graphie ran to hang onto Kate's skirt. Patsy went to stand by Charlie. They all stared at the approaching dark-haired, moustached man loaded down with prospector's equipment, shovel and pick over his left shoulder.

"Hey, Bob," said George. "What the hell you doin' in this neck of the woods?"

Bob nodded in greeting only to George. George the Squawman, Bob was thinking. Siwash George. Lyin' George, some call him, the way he builds mountains out of mole hills. Sold out completely, he has. Wearing moccasins just like the rest of these Siwashes. That looks like his half-breed daughter over there. Can't restrain himself, George can't. Like a lot of the boys, takes up with whatever's handy. What happens to the squaw and kid if he strikes it rich? Dropped as soon as picked up, I'll wager. It's a cruelty to take up with the natives. God meant like to breed with like. Even grizzly bears know that.

"Bob? You bushwhacked or what? I just asked you, what's up?"

"Just making my way, George. From Fort Ogilvie. Up the Klondike."

"What for, Bob? Any good prospects?"

"May be. Found something in a small creek that heads up against the Dome."

They all noticed an unusual gleam in Bob's eye, a holding back with his words. It was prospectors' honour to tell other prospectors of a find, of any good prospects. George waited for Bob to come forth.

"I figure," said Bob carefully, "that creek empties into the Klondike about fifteen miles up from here and I'm looking for a better way to get at it than going over the mountains from Indian River."

George glanced at Jim and Charlie. Bob kept his eyes averted from them.

"Is it any good of a prospect, Bob?"

"We don't know yet. We can get a prospect on the surface. When I left, the boys were running up an open cut to get to bedrock."

"What are the chances to locate up there? Everything staked?"

Bob then glanced at Skookum Jim and Tagish Charlie, studiously ignoring Kate and the children. Then he addressed George. "There's a chance for you, George, but I don't want any damn Siwashes staking on that creek." He lifted his pick and shovel up onto his shoulder, tramped off to the river bank, and slid down into the boat.

"What's the matter with that white man!" Skookum Jim jammed his empty pipe into his pocket. "He kill Indian moose, Indian caribou. Dig at gold in Indian country. No like it Indian stake claim? We show him!" Jim spat on the ground. "He no share prospect. No share tobacco. No good, that white man! Damn fool, him!" Jim spat again.

"Never mind, Jim," said George. "This is a big country. We'll find our own creek."

"You go now," said Kate.

They looked at her but she would not say more. She would never run off at the mouth like her brother, speaking in that pidgin English which made men like Bob Henderson smirk. Kate wished Jim would stick to Tagish words, and habits.

"You're right," said George. "Henderson wouldn't act like that unless he was onto something big. I've seen a few men look like that in my day. A good prospect can change a man in no time. We'll go follow his trail tomorrow. Or next day. We got a lot of fish to deal with now."

"Go now," said Jim.

"Tomorrow's soon enough."

"Charlie?" said Jim.

Charlie shrugged his shoulders. He didn't care when.

"Let's all go now," said Kate in Tagish.

"Where?" said George. "Sounds like Henderson came from Gold Bottom Creek. Where else would be good?"

"Rabbit Creek," said Jim and explained in Tagish. "It comes down from the mountain close by here. It's a good trail for gold. Better than the one Henderson came from."

"You figure Rabbit Creek?" said George to Kate and Charlie. "We could follow Henderson on Gold Bottom."

"Rabbit Creek," said Charlie.

Kate nodded in agreement.

"Rabbit it is, then." George removed his brimmed hat and wiped his forehead with the back of his hand. "But I'm not setting off until tomorrow."

"Go now," said Jim. "Lots of time before dark."

"Indians are supposed to be lazy," said George. "How come I wind up with ones like you."

Kate then packed up food and some fur-hide bedding from their shelter in the fish camp. It was good to get away from the strong smell of fish being smoked and laid out to dry. Though she knew that the farther from the smoke and the parched banks of the Klondike they moved, the closer they would be to damp ground and mosquitoes. George poled her and the children in a small boat, two miles upstream to the mouth of Rabbit Creek. Jim and Charlie walked along the banks, moccasins squishing in the bogs. When it became too shallow for the boat, they got out to find a place to set up camp.

They trudged along the creek's bed of silt and mushy earth. Sharp spiked plants, thorny scrub bushes, and mossy tufts grew up from the oozing black earth. Slippery rock lay beneath. Grace had to be carried. Kate had to lift her skirts like a saloon girl. Their moccasins were soaked through. Mosquitoes swarmed around, biting their hands as they fended them off their faces. Everyone but Jim decided to head for higher ground. He trudged on upstream.

Jim had been fascinated by the prospectors he met, fascinated by their belief in hidden stashes of gold beneath rocks, in creek beds. He understood the power of money that was paid to him for packing on the trails and he understood that gold was its source. He liked to buy things, like white men's clothing for himself and his relatives. He liked a good hunting gun and tools. He liked to buy drinks at a bar. He wanted to find gold, but he didn't have the patience to sift through water, sand, and pebbles for long.

The others set up camp in the woods on drier ground. Kate put mud packs on Grace's face, her more tender skin swollen with mosquito bites. Rain was not likely at this time of year and the sun would set for only a few hours. Kate made strong tea and another meal of salmon and sourdough bread.

"Wouldn't mind some fresh berries with this," said George. "You get us some tomorrow, Kate? I'm going to get some shut-eye now."

She nodded that she would. She took the children into the bushes to relieve themselves, making them chatter on route to ward off bears. She settled them onto their fur hides and tidied up the camp. Jim returned, waking everyone with his excitement. He had found a sprinkling of gold dust.

"Fool's gold," said George. "That bit of dust won't buy you a chew of tobacco. Find any veins? Chunks? Pieces?"

"Where there's smoke, there's fire," said Jim. "After a sleep I'll find more. Rabbit Creek, it's good."

"Good place to run logs," said George. "It would be dead easy to cut them down right here. Roll them into the creek. Float them down to the Klondike. Ladue will give me twenty-five dollars a thousand feet. Now that's smart gold!"

Jim finished off the salmon and tea and went to sleep. Kate tidied up then lay down to sleep beside George.

Jim got up at first light. "I'll find us a moose, if I don't find more gold," he said. "I'm fed up with fish."

George, Charlie, and the children slept on. Kate took her cedar basket and a gun to go find a berry patch. Likely to meet bears amongst the berries at dawn. But she did not. Probably, she surmised, because of the pack of nine wolves she saw running through the foliage towards the woods. They ran single file in orderly formation. An impressive looking pack. Strong, no stragglers. She put her gun behind her back. It was an honour and a good omen to see wolves. The lead wolf slowed down, stopped briefly and eyed her, then carried on, all of them keeping pace with the leader but also keeping an eye on her until they were out of sight.

Kate filled her basket then went to a slippery rock part of the creek to take a drink, and wash her hands and face. That was when she spotted the gleam in the water. She waded in to it. Dug under the surface with her knife and dislodged a piece of gold. Not gold dust, but a chunk of gold, big as a stone in the palm of her hand. More gleamed beneath the water amongst the rocks.

She ran back to their camp. Stepped quietly over to her husband

George. Touched his shoulder. He awoke. She smiled and placed in his hand the chunk of gold.

That was the morning of August 16, 1896. Kate would remember it as the day when her husband, her family, and the land itself began to change. With her husband, she couldn't tell if it was more like him putting on a mask or taking it off.

It began with the dance of joy. George and Charlie whooping it up as they dug and chiselled away at the vein of gold she had found. Soon Jim joined in with more gold he had found farther up. The children jumped up and down with them. And then the deliberations. Claims must be staked. How many could they? In whose names?

"A woman can't stake a claim," said George, looking at Jim and Charlie. "And I'm not sure about you boys."

"I am your wife," said Kate in clear English.

"Wife. Woman. It doesn't matter." He was so intent on the gold nuggets in his hand, he didn't look at her. "I'll stake a claim for you. And for you boys." He looked at them. "Just in case they give us an argument about being Indians. I'll make sure you get your share. You know that, eh Jim? Charlie?"

They nodded solemnly.

"And Kate." George looked at her. "You're my wife."

Graphie ran to him. He picked her up and swung her around. "And my little girl."

He set her down. "Better get going, boys. I'll take Kate and Graphie and Patsy. Leave them at the fish camp. Then paddle on down to Fortymile and get as many stakes as I can for us on this creek. You guard the claims? Deal?"

"Deal," said Charlie.

Jim pondered. "Two can paddle faster than one to Fortymile. You take Charlie with you. Me, I stay and guard the claims."

"All right, Jim. You come with me, Charlie?"

"Deal," said Charlie. "Better deal."

"And whoooppeee!" George slapped his knee with his hat, grabbed Kate and tilted her up and down trying to get her to dance a jig with him.

When they were poling back down Rabbit Creek George was bursting with realizations and plans. "We are *rich*! Unbelievably rich!"

"What's rich mean, Daddy?" said Graphie.

"It means, my little girl," George mused, "it means that you will see the Outside. I will take you and your mother to San Francisco. We will land with suitcases full of gold. You will have silk dresses. Your mother ball gowns. We'll buy books. And a piano! You'll learn to play the piano. You can go to boarding school and learn fine manners."

"Patsy too?" said Graphie. "And Uncle Charlie?"

"If they want." George lingered over the pole. "We'll drink champagne, Kate. You've never had champagne."

"Me too," said Charlie. "I drink that too."

Kate stood on the bank of the Klondike River at the fish camp watching George and Charlie get into the canoe to go downriver to Fortymile. They started to paddle, then George, looking across the river to an old prospector's camp, suddenly shouted, "Whoa, Charlie! Let's go across to the other side first." He yelled over his shoulder to Kate. "Got to tell my old friend Eli, about the prospect."

It was the easiest time of year to paddle across the Klondike, with the water at its lowest level, the currents weak. But it would cut into the time getting to stake their claim. Kate approved. He's a good man, she thought. Better than that old crow, Henderson, who won't share and has no respect for us. But George was acting like a wolf about to move on, to a new territory. He said he would take her with him. She did want to see this place called San Francisco. She would follow him anywhere. She was his wife. But the Outside was beyond the mountains. It floated on the endless ocean leading away from the Chilkoot Trail, where white men went when they left their native wives and never came back. That is why the spirit of fear had landed on her shoulder like a sharp-clawed hawk.

George and Charlie paddled into Eli's landing. Eli slid down the bank to grab the front of the canoe.

"Hello Carmack. Charlie." Eli nodded to him. "There's a lot of commotion over on your side of the river. What's up? You look as though you found something."

"Well now, Eli," said George. "That I did." Once he had both feet on the ground, George put his hand in his pocket and waited for Eli to speak.

"You follow Henderson?" said Eli. "I heard talk of something over near the Dome. But you and your Indians come down a different direction. Henderson was talking of something on a creek he's named Gold Bottom. Anything in that? I don't think my legs can take me up another dead end this summer."

"Would you call this a dead end?" George produced the large gold nugget from his pocket.

Eli squinted, looked George in the eyes, then held out his hand. "You mind if I feel the weight of that?"

George placed it in his hand.

"Where did you find this, George, my friend?"

"Up Rabbit Creek, Eli. You have to see it to believe it. There're great slabs of gold in the bedrock of that creek. Great slabs, I tell you. I've staked all I can by law. Two for myself as discoverer and one each for Skookum Jim and Tagish Charlie here." He nodded to Charlie who nodded to Eli. "We're off to Fortymile now to register them. You get yourself up there and see for yourself. Jim's there. He's guarding our claims."

"You're a good fellow, George, to come across the river to tell me this."

"One old prospector to another," said George.

Eli began to gather up his equipment. George and Charlie got back into the canoe and paddled fast towards the junction of the Klondike and the Yukon River which would take them to Fortymile.

They could still be seen from the fish camp side. Graphie and Patsy ran along the bank following the sight of the canoe until they ran out of breath.

"When they get to the bend," said Graphie to Patsy, "my dad will lift his paddle into the air and wave to us. He always does that."

But this time George did not. He was concentrating on speed. Charlie at the rear had to make his J-stroke extra strong to keep them on course.

Fortymile had two main log buildings. One was McPhee's Saloon. The other was The Northwest Mounted Police Headquarters, where claims could be registered, mail picked up, and disputes settled. George went there first with Charlie in tow. Charlie did not correct George in claiming to be the discoverer of the gold because he believed that Kate could not register a claim and he trusted George and the authorities in these unfamiliar matters. The police inspector had no reason to question George and thought justice was served in granting Skookum Jim and Tagish Charlie claims. That done, George and Charlie went straight to the saloon.

Charlie enjoyed a saloon. Liked to have a shot or two. Show the white men he could handle it. Just like he could handle more weight on the trail than they could. He could move faster too. But he didn't go into saloons much, because George didn't. George was their guide in a saloon just as he and Skookum were George's on the trail. When George had become one of their Wolf Clan, he didn't go into saloons much. Most of the time they didn't have the money for it anyway. Today they did. They sure did.

George led the way. Pushed open the saloon swing doors and strode over to the bar, plunked his closed fist upon it. He ordered two whiskies for himself and one for Charlie. He swallowed both of his then turned his back to the bar and leaned against it. He held up his hand to get the attention of the downhearted miners leaning over their tables, over the backs of chairs, up against the rough-hewn plank of the bar. Charlie pushed his shot glass towards the bartender for a refill. The bartender ignored him while George spoke.

"Boys," said George Washington Carmack, "I've got some good news to tell you. There's a big strike up the river."

"Strike, hell!" somebody shouted. "That ain't no news. That's just a scheme of Ladue and Harper to start a stampede upriver."

"You're dead wrong, you big rabbit-eating malamute!" George shouted back at him. "Neither Ladue nor Harper knows anything about this." He pulled out his pouch full of gold and dumped it on the gold scales placed near the bartender. "How does that look to you, eh?" George leaned back against the bar, his chest out, his thumbs in his pockets.

"Me, I got claim too," said Charlie to the bartender.

"Is that so, Carmack?"

"Ever heard Tagish Charlie tell a lie?"

"We've heard *you,* Lyin' George!"

"Yeah, Squawman! Is that some of that Miller Creek gold that Ladue gave you? Ain't worth nothin'."

"Weigh it up," George shouted. "And give my partner another drink. Hell, give everyone of these washed-up miners a drink. Give 'em two! Come on McPhee, weigh it up. We'll see who's lyin' and who ain't."

Bill McPhee checked and double checked the measure on the scales.

"Never seen gold this heavy and yellow before. Not in my lifetime. Nowhere around here. Boys, maybe you'd better be givin' Carmack the benefit of the doubt."

"Naw. Been fooled too many times. Carmack's never been a serious prospector."

"Never bought drinks on the house before, neither."

"Where exactly did you find this, Carmack?"

Kate and others from the fish camp gathered on the river bank. They saw a swarm of boats coming up from Fortymile. Mostly flat-bottom boats, being rowed at a racing pace. All those white miners with squashed hats and dirty clothes, shirts that were wet under the arms and smelled worse than pungent meat that could make you retch. Miners without wives to look after them and keep their male piece satisfied. They looked like mangy dogs, some with beards such as only white men can have.

They were racing against each other. Hollering from boat to boat. Laughter. A good-natured race. They were after some prize. They could be so like children, these white men, when they were excited and drunk. They shouted, yee-hawed, slapped themselves, and stomped their feet. You had to be careful when they were drunk. Best hide. Or they'd take you. Rough as they could. Hurt young girls and not care. No animals mated with cruelty as they did. Or so Kate heard from the stories passed around. It was not her experience with George. He touched her face and stroked her hair in the affectionate way that mated wolves licked each other on the snout and pawed each other's ears. And he put his arms around her when he came home from days away. It was a white man's particular way of greeting that had frightened her at first. But now she looked forward to it.

The swarm of miners rowed on up the Yukon to the Klondike River, shouting comments to one another as they passed the fishing bank.

"What are they saying?" an older Han woman asked Kate.

Kate laughed. "The usual. They don't like the smell of our dead fish. They think it comes from us."

"They don't like the smell of *our* camp? They should smell their own village. We don't build small houses with a hole in the floor and fill it full of piss and shit. Nothing but piss and shit. How do they think that smells?"

George neglected to embrace Kate when he landed. But he handed her a blue satin ribbon for her hair and he had a small bag of peppermint candies for Graphie which she shared with Patsy. The rest of his purchases were mining equipment. Three shovels, two new pickaxes, a large tin tub, and a pair of thigh-high, hard-soled rubber boots.

"They won't fit Skookum Jim," said George. "He's too big. But Charlie and me can take turns with these in the creek."

"No," said Charlie. "Me, I don't need them."

"We're going to need a lot more than this, once we get going," said George. "A lot of logs to jack up the banks. Wood boxes. Sluices.

Have to build a cabin on the claim before winter sets in. Have to get all that stuff from Ladue's store. Right now, this is all we can afford until we get more gold out. So let's get goin', Charlie. Would you believe how all those dumb farts sneaked off in their boats, hot footin' it up to Rabbit Creek after calling me a liar! Lyin' George. They'll never call me that again.

"Funniest thing you ever saw. Once it dawned on them that I had the best gold they had ever seen and I tell them, 'Rabbit Creek,' and suddenly, McPhee's is empty and the boats are full. Those too drunk to sit tight got tied up on the bottom until they snored it off. Wasn't that something, Charlie! We sure put them on the run. Kate, be a good woman and hurry up with the grub. Gold awaits us. Every minute counts."

Gold awaits us. Every minute counts. Strange talk, thought Kate as she dried more fish, laying in food supplies to take to the men who had gone up Rabbit Creek. As the word spread throughout the valley of the Yukon and Klondike, more boats, canoes and men on foot with pack dogs came travelling past, heading for Rabbit, Gold Bottom, and every other creek in the area.

Kate saw Ladue arrive on the flat swampy land just down from their fish camp. It was a bad site for a camp. Although it was the meeting place of both rivers, the land itself was too wet during the spring when the snow turned into rain and in the autumn before the rain turned into snow. Now, in the season of sun, the ground was hard under moccasins. But soon they would squish and sink in the mud. That land is good for nothing but moose pasture and wolves on the hunt. Ladue had tramped over it as a prospector, a hunter, and a trader. Now he was a trader all the time, had his post just upriver. Kate wondered what he was doing, tramping around on the moose pasture now.

He camped there overnight. In the morning she saw him take down his tent. Load up his boat. He got into it and began rowing upstream towards Rabbit and Gold Bottom creeks, just like all the other prospectors who had suddenly come out of the woods. But then Ladue stopped. He turned around. Landed again on the flat land and pounded a stake into the centre of it. He stood looking at that stake as though it were a very smart thing. Then he set up his tent again. Kate pretended she had not been watching him when he came over to their fish camp.

"Hey, ma'am," he called to her.

She put her head down, looking onto the twig shelf of smoking fish.

"Kate. Carmack's woman. Remember me? Ladue. Joe Ladue. From the trading post. You understand English, eh? You trade fresh fish?"

His French accent was difficult for Kate to understand. She called Graphie to her side. Men behaved better when children were at your side and Graphie spoke correct English. Kate beckoned Ladue to follow them to the campfire. Other women gathered and sat down with them. Kate poured tea from the big kettle hanging over the fire.

"I 'ave staked claim," said Ladue. "Gonna build big lumber mill. Tell your man he come dere, for logs. Soon." Ladue's eyes were fired up like her men's were when they saw gold. "All miners get supplies from me, eh? Ladue. Over dere." He pointed to Moose Pasture, the home of mosquitoes, moose, and wolves on the hunt. "Dat dere, my land. First ting, big sawmill. Den city. Big city. Dawson City. My land. Me, I gonna call it Dawson City, after my famous government friend, George M. Dawson."

2

Hotel Vancouver

MEG REACHED THE CITY OF VANCOUVER in September of 1896.

Now I have seen them all, she wrote to Alice and Jacques. *All the big cities united by the railroad across our country. I trust you will receive the picture cards I sent from each city. I could not write a proper letter while on the train. Smooth and fast as it is compared to any horse and buggy, the train cars do jerk and sway. Besides, I didn't want to miss a moment of the landscape rushing by!*

My strongest feeling after seeing our country from coast to coast is one of gratitude, to men like our own father and all the Fathers of Confederation who believed in the concept and fought so hard to make it all one nation. But then I think of the people it was taken from and what can we do for them? It is a question that gnaws at me, like remembering what happened to the wolves in the woods at our farm. Not that I think native people are animals! But we are all interconnected. Dependent on one another. The water, the land, the animals, the people. Oh dear. Too complicated for a letter. And way off topic!

You'll be glad to know, Jacques and Alice, that I found a way of protecting myself as a woman travelling alone. It occurred to me in Montreal while I was staying in the hotel where Randolph and I had dined when he visited me while I was at college. The maitre d'hotel was particularly kind and protective towards me when he learned that Randolph died. That made me think of purchasing a mourning arm band to see what difference it made. It works!

With the mourning band on my coat sleeve, suddenly gentlemen treat me with a grave respect, rather than, shall we say, curiosity, as to whether I'm a lady with a destination or a courtesan on the run. Women look at me with a concerned sympathy, rather than the suspicion and outright contempt that I was sometimes receiving. It became very handy when I stopped over in a city and took a cab to look at the sights. Cab drivers were very kind indeed. In hotels and on the train, it was assumed that I did not want to be pestered. If a gentleman got too solicitous or invited me to dine with him when I did not wish his company, I would assume a demeanour of deep grieving. They would tip their hat and pass on their way. On the other hand, if I liked the looks of someone and wanted to converse, I could assume a more friendly expression. I could withdraw into grieving at any point I wished. And yes, I'll admit to you, I altered the recentness of my husband's demise according to my needs.

I had wonderful conversations with some very nice and interesting people.

As for the landscape ... marvellous! You already know about the trip from Halifax to Montreal: the solid grey stone farmhouses and inns that dot the route along the St. Lawrence River. Ottawa is also beautifully situated with the parliament buildings overlooking the river and forested hills to the north. But it's still rather new and small, with grand brick houses only in the centre. The route to Toronto passes through cleared farmland with log houses like our own on Wolf Woods Farm and then it goes along the shore of Lake Ontario. It and the other Great Lakes on the route away from Toronto are like small calm seas. Much building and modernity in Toronto. More electric street cars and lights and wide flat streets than we have in Halifax. But of course it's not half so charming and historic. The bigger houses throughout Ontario are generally red brick, with yellow brick highlighting their contours and some fancy woodcarving, like lace hanging, along the front porches.

Guess who drove the train from Toronto to Winnipeg? Yes! Our very own brother Stew. He had it all planned as a surprise after I telegraphed to him my arrival date in Toronto. He's duly proud of having become an engineer. I stopped over in Winnipeg so we could visit with George and family on their enormous farm. He wouldn't say so, but I think it has been hard for them, having no sons to help out. But our nieces are married now and two of the husbands have nearby farms and share in planting and harvesting.

Winnipeg is the place for bicycles, Jacques. The widest, flattest main streets in the country! And it is booming with new businesses. The Gateway to the West, they call it. They're building grand clapboard houses, not colourfully painted as ours in Halifax, but they are grand.

Regina is not half so big and bustling but it has its own character as a prairie town with those tall distinctive grain elevators you can see for miles. I noticed very modern threshing machines, such as Dave would love to have on the farm. But the fields of grain are so endlessly large, it would take weeks and weeks to harvest without the new machines. I tried to imagine the prairies with herds of buffalo still roaming across. And got sad, of course!

You must, you and the children, see the rolling ranch land around Calgary and then the absolutely awesome and majestic Rocky Mountains! Seeing mountains from a distance is truly wonderful. But to ride on a train climbing up into, around and over them is a thrill that takes you into the terrifying. The tracks run on some very narrow ledges so high up the edges of those dark rock mountains, I could not look out the window. I was rigid with fear. Then the train tracks became so steep, the poor engine could barely pull us. We were going so slowly that passengers who wished to, were invited to get out and walk along the mountain side. Not the cliff side! It was the men who chose to do so. Plus me. Then a couple of other lady travellers. I actually felt much better, safer, relying on my own two feet for that steepest part. Then we got aboard again and began the descent into the remarkably flat area around Vancouver on the Pacific Ocean.

Aren't I lucky to have experienced all that? Alice, I know I am.

Much love to you both. And the most affectionate hugs and kisses to my dear little George, Victoria and Herbie.

She'll hate that letter, thought Meg. But so be it. If I didn't write she'd be mad at that, would call me selfish. If I wrote about my loneliness, my longing to share every adventure and sight with ... Meg sighed and smiled wryly at herself ... with one who is dead and another who lives in Boston and I may never see again! There was no letter awaiting from Mick when she arrived at the Hotel Vancouver.

Oh, the disappointment of that! And all along the journey, what an ache in the heart it was to get into a hotel bed or climb into the train berth, alone, hearing the sounds of couples laughing, whispering, embracing in their own happiness.

Get going, Meg, she told herself. Get over the disappointment of there being no letter from Mick. He's a sincere man. Not one who trifles. Surely. Have faith. And press on. Up to the Yukon you go. You're a lone wolf in need of a new territory. But she lingered several days. Perhaps a letter would come by the next train, or the next.

There was talk of the Yukon in the hotel lounge. Meg approached the concierge, asking how to get to the Yukon.

"Pardon me, ma'am," he said, "but I've heard it's rough and tough going up there. No place for a lady."

"But how do they do it, the gentlemen?"

"It's not gentlemen who go there. It's prospectors. A hardy bunch of roughnecks. They never stay long in this hotel. Come here for drinks and a good meal, mostly."

"But I want to know, how do they get there, to the Yukon?"

"They take a boat. There's a steamer goes up the coast, all the way to some port in Alaska. The furthest is St. Michaels in Alaska. Then they take a riverboat up the Yukon River to the interior. That's the long and expensive way. Operates only in summer. Prospectors take the cheap and rough route. They get dumped into a bay at a place called Moore's Landing then take one of two routes over the mountains into the Yukon. One route, a couple of days longer, is over the White Pass from Moore's Landing. The other is steeper but quicker, the Chilkoot Trail going up from a place called Dyea, not far from Moore's Landing."

Meg put on her black arm band and sat in the lounge ordering tea in the afternoon. Other ladies were sitting at tables by the window. She sat close to the bar where she might listen in on the conversation of men at the bar. She heard mention of the Yukon as a dead end and the coldest place on earth. She heard mention of it as the last frontier for gold, a sportsman's paradise where the natives were friendly and their daughters free for the asking.

"Gentlemen," Meg got up her courage to approach the men. "Please excuse me for interrupting ..."

They looked at her, her armband, the ring she now wore on her right hand.

"Ma'am." They tipped their hats to her.

She nodded. "I am a veterinarian. I wanted to ask about the dogs in the Yukon. Are any of you gentleman prospectors?"

"Cursed that I am."

"Me too."

"Used to be. Given it up. For sure this time."

"I am, when I can afford to be. Ain't right now."

"Ma'am," said the youngest looking one, perhaps twenty, big-bodied, blue eyes, bushy, dirty-blond hair. "My name is Finn. Mind my askin' ... what's a vetarian?"

All the men looked interested in the answer to this.

"A veterinarian" Meg laughed. "A doctor of animals. I'm most interested in dogs, sled dogs. Do you know anything about them?"

"Holy Liftin!" said Finn, banging his fist on the bar. "I can't believe this! We was wonderin' what you're all about, hangin' around the bar but not lookin' like a ..." He cleared his throat. "This calls for another round of drinks, eh men? And one for this good lookin' dog lady. Go ahead, men. Tell her. Do I know about sled dogs! Ma'am ..." Finn performed a deep bow to her. "I'm a musher."

"A musher!" Meg exclaimed.

"He drives the dogs."

"Does the mail run."

"Messenger boy is our Finn." They gave him a friendly punch in the arm. "'Cause he can't find no gold. He's a failed prospector like the rest of us. Just a bit younger, that's all, eh, Finn?"

Finn was staying in a tent down by the docks. Couldn't afford a hotel room. Spent what he could on drinks. He was on a bender in Vancouver. A couple of weeks of big city life before he went back up to his dogs, left behind with friends in a camp on the Yukon River.

"Summer's hard on the dogs," said Finn over dinner that evening, which Meg insisted on treating him to. "Mine are big malamutes. They can pull heavy loads a long way in winter. Summer they sleep a lot. Ned, he's the swimmer. First one into the lake on a warm day. Maybe because he's got the thickest fur. Though it was Yukon Jane who taught them all as pups. She's the teacher and leader. Always has been. She's a throwback. More wolf-like than any of them. Too narrow in the chest and long in the legs to be sold for as much as Ned would get. Not that I'm about to sell them, mind you. They're my bread and butter, as they say down here. Though you don't find no butter in a miner's cabin. I sure appreciate this fine dinner, ma'am."

"Meg, please." She smiled with huge satisfaction, felt she had found a gold mine of information in the city of Vancouver. "Tell me," she said, "how might a woman get over the mountains and along the Yukon, with her baggage? I have vet supplies and brooms."

"Brooms!" Finn laughed. "Unless you can fly them, witch-like, you'll have to hire a bunch of Chilkoot packers. Haul all your stuff for you. But it don't come cheap. They charge by the pound. A man like myself carries everything he needs on his back. A woman has to have strong legs and money for packers. Either that or a husband like Clarence Berry. He hauled his wife over the pass in '94 on a sleigh. Wait for winter and I could get my dogs to pull you over the White Pass and downriver on the ice. But with brooms and all, you're going to need packers. Packers and a river guide. I could do that. I could get you through the rapids."

"Rapids!"

"Yes, ma'am, there's a couple of stretches of rapids. Miles Canyon and Five Fingers. You'll want an expert like me or the Indians to get you through those. I'm for hire." Finn grinned.

Meg gave him a warm handshake and said good night, then went to send a telegram to Jean Atkins asking her to forward money from Clean Sweepers. She lay awake in her hotel room, devising lists in her mind. I won't just outfit myself, she decided. I'll take things to sell, to keep me going while I build a business. It'll be the same old struggle to get started I had in Halifax. People not wanting to or unable to pay for my services. I'll take other things that they need and don't question having to pay for.

Candles, toothbrushes, bolts of cloth, matches. Why not a book or two? Shampoo, soaps. Things I would want if stuck in the wilderness in winter. Must be easy to pack.

Jean telegraphed back.

CONFERRED WITH JACQUES STOP YOU SHOULD RECEIVE FUNDS IN FORTNIGHT STOP MISS YOU STOP BE SAFE
JEAN

How safe would it be, Meg asked herself, to hike over mountains and paddle downriver with Finn and an Indian or two? It was not the treachery of the mountains and river rapids that bothered her so much as travelling alone with men, strangers, at that. Can I do this, she thought? Should I?

"Do you know of any other women who might want to go to the Yukon with me?" she said to Finn.

"None of your sort." He grinned

"Anyone," said Meg.

"You can trust me," said Finn. "I'll make sure you're safe. It's the timing I worry about. Last boat up the coast is early October. Can't miss that. You don't want to do the Chilkoot just as winter sets in. And then the Yukon starts freezing up ..."

Meg was sitting at the writing desk in the grand entrance of the hotel when a swashbuckling woman came in the front door. Swashbuckling is how Mad Mitzi Bonaparte struck Meg from start to finish. She was dressed in swishing dark red taffeta, with a velvet cloak and a hat animated with swaying plumes and birds that looked as though they might sing. She swirled a parasol like a sword and plunged it into the floor demanding attention. She was imperious with the valet and loudly flirtatious with the well-dressed gentleman who paused to tip his hat to her.

"You must come to my dance hall, monsieur," she said so that others could hear. "You'll find Mad Mitzi *more* than entertaining. You will fall *madly* in love. *Au revoir, mon cher.*" She spoke in an accent meant to be French, laughed gaily, and blew a kiss to someone across the room. She approached the front desk and declared, "I am looking for the notorious widow Oliphant."

"Mrs. Oliphant is occupied, Miss Bonaparte," said the desk clerk very formally, then turned back to his work.

"Occupied with what?" she demanded, raising her chin and looking around her, away from the clerk as though he were unworthy of her attention. "She will want to see *moi*, Ma'mselle Madeleine Mitzi Bonaparte."

"Mrs. Oliphant is at the writing desk."

"Ah!"

Meg stood up as Mitzi swept across the room to her.

"Mrs. Oliphant!" Mitzi smiled hugely, held out both hands, took Meg's. "*Charmante! Charmante*! Come, let us have a drink, get acquainted, *immediatement*. I have heard about you."

They sat in the lounge. Mitzi ordered champagne.

"Oh no," said Meg, "That's much too expensive ..."

Mitzi flung her hand in the air as though flinging away petty concerns. "I am a *danceure*," she said. "My *grandmotheure* danced for Napolean Bonaparte. My *motheure* was his love child. And of course, I am hers." She laughed. "Mad Mitzi, love child of Napoleon. What a life!" She laughed heartily and finished her glass of champagne, then signalled the waiter to attend to them with more champagne, raising her glass like a snap of the fingers.

Meg was embarrassed at Mitzi's treatment of the staff, tried to compensate by smiling at them apologetically, but she was intrigued with this woman who apparently ran a dance hall, was warm and generous to her, and could afford champagne before dinner.

"I have heard you are a doctor," said Mitzi, "and you own factories on the other side of this colony that calls itself a nation."

Meg laughed. "I'm an animal doctor and I own a little broom factory. Who told you about me?"

Mitzi narrowed her eyes, considering Meg's information. "I hear everything, *chérie*." Mitzi swept her hand in the air. "Men flock to my dance hall. They all wish to be intimate with me. I don't have time for everyone. I pick and choose. I do not listen to everyone. Not everyone can have my … attention." She leaned close to Meg. "You may tell me, *chérie* … what do you know about this rumour of gold in the Klondike? That is why you are going there, isn't it?"

"I'm going to the Yukon." Meg smiled. "To tend to the dogs."

"That's what Finn said." Mitzi laughed. "He is … *naïve*. You know what I mean? Young and *naïve*. He has no money. Do you know that?" Mitzi leaned in as though she were revealing something very essential.

"I don't know him well at all."

"Do you know about the Klondike?"

"It's the other big river, flows into the Yukon. That's all I know."

Mitzi leaned closer. They were each on their third glass of champagne. The bottle was turned upside down in the silver bucket. "I heard that some struck it rich on the Klondike. Very rich. Very recently." Mitzi touched her blonde upswept hair, looked around the lounge, then back at Meg. "Is that not why you are going there, *chérie*, by the fast route?"

"No." Meg smiled. "But if what you've heard is true, then you should come with me. You for the gold. Me for the dogs."

They both laughed and laughed again.

"I will think about it," said Mitzi, her French accent fallen by the wayside. "Rumours are a dime a dozen." She looked around the room. "Now, who is going to take us to dinner and pay for this champagne?"

"What!' said Meg.

"I have to dance tonight, *chérie*." Mitzi stood up. "Must have a *petite* meal now, *d'accord?*" She turned and went to the bar where she began to talk to an expensively dressed man.

Meg told the waiter she would pay for the champagne and would he please tell Miss Bonaparte that she was going out for the evening. She waved and mouthed "*au revoir*" to Mitzi, who was accepting a drink from the gentleman at the bar. Meg went up to her room and decided to make good on her word. I had better find a good, cheap place for a meal, she calculated, to try to make up for the cost of that champagne. She put on her arm band and went to a place the concierge had recommended as inexpensive but not well-suited to a lady of her standing.

"But is it safe?" was all that concerned Meg.

"Oh yes. That it is."

It was a small inn run by Herr and Frau Bauer. The evening meal was served at 6 p.m. and 6 p.m. only. It was a set meal of meat, potatoes, another vegetable, fresh bread roll and butter. Pie for dessert. Guests sat on benches along two large tables.

Dinner back on the farm, thought Meg as she sat at a table, completely outnumbered by men. There were only two other women. Frau Bauer had seated Meg between them, a seamstress and a "typist," a woman who wrote on cultural topics for the newspaper. She was short, fashionably dressed, unintimidated, quick to interrogate, and quick to turn away from a conversation that bored her. She took a sharp interest in Meg and Meg in her. But Meg kept locking glances with a man seated at the other table who also wore a black arm band. He was exceptionally handsome, like the hero in a Marie Corelli novel. Black hair ruffling into curls, neatly trimmed moustache, dark eyebrows, and intensely blue eyes. Tall and slim with strong cheek bones.

"Anton Stander," he introduced himself to Meg when the meal was over. "I see we have something in common." He indicated his arm band. "My condolences."

"And to you," said Meg.

"Perhaps I'll see you here again?"

"Yes. It's very good food."

He bowed and backed away. As she stepped onto the boardwalk leading back to her hotel, she looked up at the inn and saw him watching from the window. Soon she heard someone running up behind her. She stopped and faced him.

"You didn't tell me your name.," said Anton.

"Meg... Oliphant. Mrs.... formerly ..." Meg stopped, flustered.

"Mrs. Formerly." He smiled and removed his hat. "May I walk you home?"

Meg laughed. "My name is actually Margaret, Meg, Oliphant. I am a widow."

"I have made you laugh. Is it all right to make you laugh?"

"Oh yes." Meg was annoyed with herself for blushing. "My husband died some time ago. May I ask about you?"

"If you let me walk you home." He smiled.

"I don't live here. I'm staying at Hotel Vancouver."

"Another coincidence. I don't live here either. May I?" He motioned to walk along side her.

She smiled and nodded. They proceeded together.

"I'm here only a few days," said Anton. "Heading up to the Klondike on Friday."

Meg stopped in her tracks. No. Not another coincidence, she thought. It's too much. He'll think I'm lying. She laughed. Or following him there!

"What is so funny?" said Anton. "Going to the Klondike may be foolish. May be another dead end. But why does it strike you as worthy of laughter?"

"I'm sorry," she said. "I was thinking of something else. I'm not laughing at you. I'm sorry. May I ask? Who have you lost? Who are you mourning?"

"My mother." Anton heaved a sigh. "In Austria. I haven't seen her since I left. Nine years ago. I didn't get the news... until long after ... I always thought ... I planned ... to see her again."

Meg took his hand in both of hers. "I'm so sorry."

He put his other arm around her, hugging her, then took her arm. Meg didn't care that people stared at them, embracing in a public place.

"I must have a drink," said Anton. "Will you join me in a drink at this hotel of yours?"

Why not, thought Meg. It's a safe place.

Anton downed several whiskys while she had coffee and a brandy and extracted his life story from him. Raised in a mountain village in Austria, landed in New York at age twenty with only a few words of English and precisely one dollar and seventy-five cents in his pocket.

"Worked my way across the continent," he said. "Been everything from coal miner to sheep herder to cowboy. Cowboy suited me best because I worked on a ranch close to the mountains. Guess mountains are in my blood. Like my mother. Rest her soul." He looked into his glass then across at Meg. "What's in the blood stays there. But life moves on. I've got a good paycheque in my pocket and I hear there's good prospects up in the Klondike. Let's drink to that."

They clinked glasses, hearing music starting up in the ballroom. Meg felt exhilaration and a lightness of being that she hadn't felt in months.

"Would you like to dance?" said Anton. "I'm aching to waltz with a lady, like you."

Meg thought of Mick. Would he mind? Would he approve? Would she disapprove if he danced with someone? No, of course not! It would be good for him. This would be good for her. He had not sent her a word in three months. She was free to dance.

Meg considered her outfit. High neck blouse, navy blue wool skirt and jacket. Anton was in a three-piece tweed suit with white shirt and tie, a man who liked to dress well in the city. "I'm not suitably attired," she said. "But I do have a dress in my room."

"I'll wait for you," said Anton.

Meg reappeared in her turquoise silk gown, her hair done up with combs and a blue velvet ribbon. No black arm band.

"Ah!" Anton kissed her hand. "My lady, Margaret." He put his arm band in his pocket.

He waltzed like an Austrian, having heard the music from birth, trained as a child. He swirled her around the ballroom. He did the polka with vigour.

"You're not too tired?" said Anton, with his arm around her waist, another waltz about to begin.

"Oh, no. Not at all!" She tried to catch her breath, knew she was smiling from ear to ear. "I haven't danced in *years*. I love it!"

"Bravo!" He swept her up in the waltz. "I like to put the orchestra to bed."

They danced the last waltz, then Anton in silence walked her to the door of her room.

"Thank you," said Meg. "I had such a wonderful time..."

He put his finger tip on her lips. "No need to say. You know what I'm thinking."

"No," she said with a slow movement of her head, "I don't."

"It is you I would like to put to bed." He kissed her, lingered in embrace, then stood back abruptly and bowed. "Good night, my lady."

"Good night, sir." Meg smiled.

In her room she laughed and waltzed, humming the music, wondering could I become "the merry widow"?

Next day was Thursday. She hoped to encounter Anton in the hotel, on the street. But he was not to be seen. She arranged for a bath in her room before going to dinner at the Bauer Inn. The portable tin tub was placed in the centre of the room. The Chinese maid, who was too shy or discreet to speak or look at Meg, brought buckets of hot water. Meg got into the tub. The maid was to return with a final warm-up bucket.

"Ah the luxury of a fresh bath," said Meg to herself, remembering sharing them with Alice, once a week, when they were growing up, and then when they were too big to share the tub, fighting over who got the water first.

There was a knock on the door and a key inserted.

"Wu Ling?" said Meg. "Come in."

Anton opened the door, carrying a bucket of water. He put his finger to his lips and advanced with the pail. "I encountered your maid. I bribed her. Please don't raise the alarm. I couldn't help myself. I'll do you no harm. I had come just to see you and walk you to the Inn. But what man could resist ... Will you allow me to pour the water?"

Meg thought better of standing up naked in front of him. She held her knees up to her chest. "Anton, I ... don't do this!"

He poured the water in. He took off his jacket and rolled up his sleeves. "Let me be your servant. Let me bathe you ..."

What woman could resist, Meg thought afterwards. The way he lapped the water over her, touching ... She had stood up dripping wet, intending to call a halt. But she let him, let him proceed in silence. The towel on the bed. Laying her on it. His undressing. That's when she should have gotten up. But she said instead. "I could get ..."

"I'll see that you don't," he said, reassuringly.

And she let him continue. He withdrew at the crucial moment. She put her arms around him, in gratitude and pleasure. It felt good to embrace a handsome, healthy man. But it was not with the love and shared understanding and mutual instinct she had felt with Mick. She was perturbed. Anton is expert, she thought. And I enjoyed that. But what kind of woman am I? What am I becoming? On the other hand ... what am I discovering? That the world has many men I could enjoy? Maybe so. But I want just one, one who wants to marry and have children and do some good in the world, together.

"I'm hungry," Anton had said, kissing her cheek, then getting up to wash himself and quickly dress. "We can't be late for Frau Bauer or she won't feed us."

Meg tried not to look guilty as she left the hotel with Anton. She worried that she did not feel very guilty.

Anton spoke in German to Frau Bauer with the result that they were allowed to sit beside each other at the table. They waltzed again at the hotel until the orchestra quit. Anton came into her room and put her to bed, getting in with her.

"I would like to postpone my trip," said Anton. "But it is urgent to get going as soon as possible. I don't have money to spare or time to waste. This rumour of gold on the Klondike is gathering momentum. The first to find are the first to claim. There may not be much or there may be a lot. You understand, Margaret, why I can't linger?"

"There's something I haven't told you Anton."

He sat up. "Tell me," he said, rather harshly.

"I am going to the Yukon, leaving in about a week's time."

"Why? Why didn't you tell me?"

"Because I've said very little about myself and you haven't asked. And you might have thought I was following you."

"It's a very bad idea, Margaret. You are not the type. I know mountains and mining camps. I know their dangers. You could be killed in an avalanche, mauled by grizzly bears, starve or freeze to death, be ravaged by men. And never even see a bathtub!" He got out from the covers and sat on the edge of the bed. "I thought you were wintering in Vancouver. As you should! I could send for you, if I strike it rich. You must not follow me now."

Meg sat up with the cover over her. "I'm not following you!"

"I can't take you with me. It's impossible. Far too dangerous. You must *stay here!*"

"I will do what I want. And I will *not* be shouted at!"

He put on his clothes and stood with his hand on the doorknob. "I apologize. I have a very bad temper. I will go now. And trust that you will not follow me."

What arrogance! thought Meg. What conceit! He thinks he knows me and he never even asked what I am besides a widow who took the train across the country. She sank down under the sheets. He's not seriously interested in me. Only himself and his prospects. But he made love with such interest. And to dance with him is to forget oneself, to be caught up in a cosmos of music and rhythm and oblivious romance. Still, I'm not one to simply dance through life. And "hand-some is as handsome does." Someone who shouts at me, orders me to stay where I am, turns his back, stomps off … Forget him!

But next morning she couldn't resist going to the docks to see his departure. She kept back out of sight while she saw him go up the gangplank, carrying a big pack on his back, with a pickaxe sticking out of it. He wore breeches and sturdy boots, a winter jacket, and his black brimmed hat. As the boat left shore, he joined the passengers at the stern, leaning over the railing. Meg raised her arm and waved at him, smiling.

He saw her, stood up straight and waved with a pleased expression on his face. He blew her a kiss, then pointed his finger in a manner that said, "Stay there!"

It was late in the afternoon when a telegram was brought to her room.

NO TIME FOR LETTER STOP SEND NEXT ADDRESS
STOP YOU'LL BE AMAZED MY LOVE
MICK O'MARA

Meg read and re-read it, held it in her hands like gold. Tucked it into her camisole, close as she could get to her heart.

3

Going for the Dogs

Ike's spirit was in turmoil, again. Meg was too human, after all. That wasn't proper mating, what she did with Anton! Lead wolves don't do that. It was what he had made his dogs do. Mate then separate and mate with many. Ike groaned with guilt, again. If only he could blame the city influence. Too many people. Too many choices. Ike hated cities. He wanted Meg to get out of Vancouver. Get on up north to tend his dogs. He worried. Would Meg make a habit of that? He remembered Piji using another man, to try to have a baby. Though after that, she loved only Ike and their pups. Ike missed Piji now. He wanted to be with her spirit again. And find out what was truly happening in his home territory… to the wolves and the dogs. Rumours. Piff! He had never had time for them.

He watched over Meg for another few days as she consorted with Finn by day, going to the outfitters stores, ordering dry goods and a six months supply of food. She had consulted members of the North West Mounted Police as to what was requisite for getting through the winter in the far north. She spent the nights in her hotel room, alone.

When a telegram arrived from her bookkeeper in Halifax, Meg cheered out loud and went straight to the bank. Then to find Finn in his tent by the docks. They went to a saloon where they did much toasting, clinking their glasses of beer. They went round to the outfitters and paid a large bill. They pre-booked tickets on a steamship called the City of Topeka, *which would make its last voyage of the season up the Pacific coast, in two days time.*

Ike then smiled again upon Meg. The steamship would take her straight to Moore's Landing, where she would find his highest standard malamutes. They were bred by Amy Moore. And there, resting with Amy, Ike would find the spirit of Piji. He couldn't wait.

"Bon voyage!" Ike patted Meg affectionately on the head. "We will welcome you at Moore's Landing. Piji and I, with the dogs. You'll love them."

NEXT AFTERNOON, Mad Mitzi swept into the Hotel Vancouver and demanded to see the merry widow Oliphant. She was directed to Meg's room.

"I'm in the midst of packing," said Meg cheerfully. "But do come in."

"You must take a break, *chérie*. Come, let's have some champagne. I want to hear all about this venture of yours."

"Can't afford champagne." Meg smiled at the remembrance of who paid for it the last time. "I have some cider in here. I'll get another glass."

"I don't drink cider." Mitzi turned up her nose and came in, closing the door behind her. She shifted books off the chair and sat down.

"But I have this, for emergencies." She pulled out a silver flask from her velvet purse, took a swig. "It's very good brandy. Have some."

"Cider's fine for me." Meg poured some from the jug and made a spot for herself amidst the clothes on the bed.

"What's all *this* for?" Mitzi pointed to the beaver parka, flannel underwear, thick wool trousers, boots, tweed jacket, and rubberized poncho piled amongst other things.

"Climbing mountains in all kinds of weather."

"You truly are going to the Klondike. Are you following Anton Stander?"

"No!"

"Ooh la la, *chérie*! The lady doth protest too much." Mitzi laughed. "He is a handsome man and if he strikes it rich ..."

"I'm a veterinarian. I'm going for the dogs."

Mitzi laughed loudly. "So you said. *Mais* ... I have been thinking ... with this much smoke, there must be fire. Meaning gold, of course. *Bien sure.* And if there's a rush, *danceures* will be in high demand. *Peut-être*, I will go with you, *mon amie*."

"Do! Finn said the Chilkoot is a tough hike, but if you have strong legs ..."

"Does a dancer have strong legs!" Mitzi pulled up her skirt and raised her leg in the air. She began to sing and dance the cancan.

Meg laughed and clapped. "And you're not afraid of mountains?"

"I don't get stage fright. Why should I have mountain fright?" Mitzi took another swig.

"What about your dance hall? You can't just leave it suddenly, can you?"

"*Chérie*, it is not *my* dance hall. I am just the best one in it. I come and go as I wish." Another swig. "And I have become *trés* bored with this city of Vancouver."

"But if the rumours are false and there is no gold rush ..." Meg took a big swallow.

"*Merde!*" said Mitzi. "I am not *stupide*! I have counted the numbers heading to the Klondike this autumn. If there is no gold, there are still men. Men are as good as gold." Mitzi laughed loudly. "Are they not? Good as gold. With their ever ready... instruments."

"'Instruments'!" Meg hooted and took another swig of cider. "Not the kind I use in my work."

"To each his own, *chérie*!" Mitzi raised her flask to Meg.

"Maybe you should get packing," said Meg.

"Oh it won't take me long." Mitzi brushed the thought away with her hand. "I know how to get out of town fast. But tell me where you got those boots. They look useful."

"At Johnston and Kerfoot Outfitters on Cordova."

"*Bien*. I must open an account there."

There was a cold rain pelting down when Meg and Finn were loading their packs onto the *City of Topeka*. Finn, like other prospectors, travelled light, with one pack. Meg had brought a wagonload of stuff. Four large packs, of one hundred pounds each, plus a much lighter pack for her own back, and a whack of brooms bound up in her canvas tent. Finn carried the big packs one by one up the gangplank and stored them in the hold. Meg dragged the brooms behind her with a rope. Finn hoisted them easily up on top of her pile of packs. They and every other passenger were being scrutinized by the steward, whom Meg noted with surprise was a woman. She was not tall and her jacket was a couple of sizes too big but she had no trouble fitting her role.

"That's a lot of baggage for two people," she said sharply.

"It's actually just mine," said Meg. "But there's still a lot of space here, for the other passengers' stuff."

"I'll be the judge of that! Belinda Mulroney's my name. Chief Steward. Only steward. I'll settle with you later."

Meg took her pack to a small cabin of four bunks, designated women only, then returned to the deck to watch for the arrival of Mitzi. She stood with Finn under the shelter of the small upper deck where the captain stood.

"Want some?" said Finn, offering her his flask.

"Too early for me, thanks." It wasn't quite nine in the morning.

"Time is no matter now," said Finn. "We're on our way to the land of the midnight sun and soon no sun. Winter is coming on. And we're floatin', just floatin', before the big climb. I'll drink to that." He nudged her with his elbow. He leaned into her ear. "You're quite a woman, Meg. Proud to be your guide."

"I'm glad to have you, Finn. But where's our Mad Mitzi?"

The captain rang the bell in warning of gathering up the gangplank.

"She'll come late," said Finn. "She likes to keep people waiting."

Three men came running towards the gangplank. They were prospectors Meg had conversed with at the Bauer Inn. All three had warned her against going to the Klondike this late in the season and staunchly declared they'd had it with prospecting.

"Well, if it isn't!" Meg stuck her arm out of her poncho and waved to them. Pete the Dutchman, Jethro the Negro, and Leo the oldest. "Changed your minds, I see," said Meg, stepping forward to shake their hands as they came on board.

"Reckon there's no fool like an old fool," said Leo, tipping his hat.

"Curiosity's gonna kill this cat," said Jethro smiling.

"Come to keep an eye on you," said Pete.

"Hey men." Finn stomped forward in his high lace-up boots, leather jodhpurs, red plaid shirt, long waxed coat and cowboy hat. "That's my job."

The captain rang the second warning bell.

"There she is!" Finn waved towards the shore.

Mad Mitzi arrived at the dock in a black coach, the horses whinnying at the sudden halt to their galloping and the last call of the ship's bell. Mitzi emerged from the cab in a red fitted coat with black fur trim and matching hat. She wielded an umbrella, ordering the coachman to bring down her trunk and carpet bag, immediately.

"Time!" shouted Belinda Mulroney. "Gangplank coming up!"

Mitzi swept to the gangplank, laughing and pointing her umbrella in the air, she stomped her foot on the gangplank and shouted up to them, "Tell the captain Madeleine Mitzi Bonaparte *est arrivé*!"

"Stay the gangplank," shouted the captain.

Belinda growled but obeyed.

"I need porters," shouted Mitzi as she advanced up the plank. "Where are the porters?"

"Let's go, men," said Finn.

Only Pete would go help him haul Mitzi's trunk and bag up onto the ship. Jethro and Leo didn't like Mitzi. She had snubbed them on the street after gladly receiving drinks from them in the dance hall. The captain did not know Mitzi but he was keen to make her acquaintance. She was invited to dine at his table and visit his cabin. Mitzi never did sleep in the ladies bunk room with Meg. And therefore she refused to pay Belinda anything for it. The captain told Belinda he would take care of the matter.

The *City of Topeka* pushed its way through the cold blue waters and coastal fogs up the coast north of Vancouver Island, north of the Queen Charlotte Islands and amongst the islands off the southern thumb coast of Alaska. The coastline was forested with evergreens and deciduous trees, now charcoal skeletons, their leaves shrivelled and dead on the ground. The highest peaks of the Rocky Mountains were snow covered, the others were dark purple rock, forming an insurmountable barrier to the interior. Or so it seemed to Meg, on a clear and chilling evening from the ship's deck. She was sitting on a pile of cargo with Belinda Mulroney. The men were drinking and playing cards in their bunk room. Mitzi was lounging in the captain's cabin. They were to reach Moore's Landing the next day.

Meg had been seasick when the waters got rough.

"You're not with child, are you?" Belinda had asked, looking in on her in her cabin.

"No!"

"No call for offence. Women heading away from civilization often are. If you're just seasick, lie back. Rock with the waves, not against them. It's a lesson in life, wouldn't you say?" Belinda closed the door. Checked in on Meg later and found her no longer leaning over the chamber pot.

"I'm fine," Meg waved to her, smiling weakly from her bunk bed. "As long as I just rock here in my cradle."

Belinda worked long hours throughout the voyage. She got things done and would take guff from no one, particularly Mitzi. When Mitzi had put her high-heeled boots outside the captain's cabin to be shined, as one might in a hotel, Belinda had picked them up and banged on the cabin door.

"Are these your boots? They're in my way."

"Yes they are. I want them cleaned and polished, steward-*ess*."

"You want I should throw them into the ocean? That's the only way they're going to get cleaned and polished by *this* steward-*ess*!"

Only on this, the last night of the voyage, did Belinda relax and converse with Meg on the cargo pile, under a sky exploding stars.

"Never met a woman more conniving and less 'mad' than that one," said Belinda of Mad Mitzi. "Treats people like rags. We're to wipe her you-know-what and be thrown away."

"Whoa!" said Meg. "That's pretty strong. She's just a goodtime girl, isn't she? Lives by her wits, as they say."

Belinda laughed. "Wits and tits, I'd say. She's not the only one of those. And not the first or last the captain has kept in his cabin. But better watch out when the going gets tough. I wouldn't want to do the Chilkoot with her.

"At least she's gotten rid of the trunk. Very clever of her to leave it with the captain to have it delivered by riverboat next summer. Of course she's taken the dire necessities out of it to be packed up in canvas. Dire necessities like silk dresses, jewellery, high-heeled shoes, rouge, powder, and bottle of brandy."

"Hey," Meg laughed. "You sure know the passengers' luggage."

"I'd like to know what's in yours. Those are mighty big packs. And tightly bound."

"Practical goods."

"What sort of practical goods?"

"Just supplies ... food, clothes, a few things to sell."

"Such as ..."

"You want a detailed list?"

"I ain't beggin'. Just asking." Belinda turned to Meg, digging her fists into her waist. "Jeez, you're hard to get things out of."

Meg laughed. "You're the hard bargainer. But all right. Here goes: sun goggles, fur-lined mitts. Hats with flaps. Mosquito netting. Writing paper and pencils. Needles, thread, scissors, and cloth. Matches, candles, cocoa, coffee, and candy. Many tooth brushes and combs. Shampoo and soap. Plus some books. But I'll rent those out. Oh yes … swamp boots and lots of wool socks. Then I have the usual stuff in my own rucksacks: bedroll, clothes, towel, toiletries, and food. Bacon, beans, sugar, flour, yeast, and tea."

"And brooms," said Belinda.

"And vet supplies. You want a detailed list of those?"

"What the frig is vet supplies?"

Meg explained.

"Dog doctor!" Belinda slapped her knee. "That beats all. I thought I'd been just about everything. But I never thought of being a dog doctor. Want a drink?"

"Sure."

"Seventy-five cents a swig." She produced a flask from her pocket.

"I can't afford that! That's highway robbery."

"This is a boat, ma'am. Way up north. Things are very expensive. But tell you what … how about some tea with rum in exchange for some shampoo? Can't remember when I last shampooed my hair."

They went down to the galley to make tea in a pot, into which Belinda carefully measured six shots of rum. They took it with mugs back up on deck. The moon was nearly full. With the stars, it cast silver light on the swaying ocean and made the mountainous coast look like a formidable fortress. Meg did up the buttons of her parka.

"You're taking a big risk at this time of year," said Belinda. "You know that, don't you? It could snow any day now."

"That's why I have this beaver parka."

"You're right determined, aren't you?"

"You're not the type who gives up easily either."

"You got a lady's education, didn't you?"

"Not really. I never learned to paint flowers or play hymns."

Belinda laughed and slapped her thigh again. "Nor did I. But I could run a ship or a restaurant and deliver babies. I've done that right here on this ship. Funniest thing you ever saw. The captain and me. No doctor on board and no women but me and that poor passenger screaming in her cabin. The captain read from a manual, shouting instructions as he stood outside the cabin, me inside, doing the job. Healthy baby girl I brought into this world. They named her after me. Though I may never see her again in this life. They disembarked in San Francisco." Belinda poured more from the pot.

"Are you from Ireland? Do I detect an Irish lilt?"

"That I am," said Belinda. "Got left there by my parents when they went to America to try to make a go of it. Took my sisters but not me. I was raised with me brother and cousins. Taught me how to fight and work for what you get. I was pretty well grown up when they sent for me. My dad was a coal miner then, on the East Coast. I didn't settle in. Worked my way clear across the United Sates of America. East Coast miners to West Coast cowboys. And everything in between. Before I was twenty years old, I opened a restaurant where they had that big exhibition in Chicago. Made myself a good eight thousand dollars. Travelled in style to California, on a railroad train that served chilled champagne with oysters and caviar. I had more silk dresses than I could have worn in a month of Sundays. I bought a house in California that had all the latest inventions. Telephone, electrical lights, kitchen and bathroom with water piped in and out. Then I got foolish with one of my suitors and was swindled out of my entire fortune. But I'll build it again. You just watch me." She offered Meg a refill from the pot. "I have a suspicion you are going where the last great fortunes are to be made. This continent is just about used up, except for where you're headed. Don't be surprised if you see me there, come summer."

"Let's drink to that," said Meg.

"To us!" Belinda raised her mug.

"None better!" Meg laughed.

"Good business women," said Belinda. "Never give anything away for free. Don't depend on a man. And charge as much as the market will bear."

"My customers," said Meg, "the dogs. They don't understand such principles."

When she went to her cabin, she saw Finn sitting on the deck, propped up against the railing outside her door.

"Meg!" He stood up, swaying, hung onto the railing to steady himself. "I've been waiting so long. Aren't you ever going to invite me into your bunk?"

"No, Finn. The answer is no. And you'd better remember that tomorrow. And all along the trail. You're my guide and my friend. Nothing more. Is that understood?"

"Right, ma'am!" he saluted. "Don't worry. I'll be a good boy. You won't fire me for bein' in love, though, will you?"

"Good night, Finn. Let's not speak of this again." Meg went in and locked the door.

Next morning they entered the Lynn Canal, a narrow inlet with a rickety wharf at the end that looked a mile long. The inlet was walled by steep, jagged and rocky mountains whose tops were hidden in clouds of fog.

The *City of Topeka* stopped part way up the canal. All passengers assembled on deck watching a man in a large rowboat being rowed from the wharf towards them by six native men. An empty scow was towed behind the rowboat. Meg leaned on the ship's railing, noting a long rope ladder that had been lowered over the side. Packs and sacks of provisions were piled nearby.

Mad Mitzi looked at the wall of mountains and fog, the rope ladder, the approaching rowboat. "Captain John!" she called to him on the upper deck. There was panic in her command. "Take us to the wharf.

Why are we stopped here?" She turned to Finn. "And where are the horses on the landing? Where is the road through the mountains?"

"Far as she goes without running aground," the captain called down, keeping watch on the approaching boat.

"No horses," said Finn. "No road. Where'd you get the idea there was?"

"There has to be!" Mitzi screamed, looking around in fright. "I can't go down a *rope*." She spun around. "I'm going back. Captain John, take me back to Vancouver!"

Captain John called out instead to the approaching boat. "Captain Moore. Ain't it time you retired if that's all the boat and crew you can manage?"

Moore was a white-haired, bearded man, his face weather-worn and animated. "Enough of the wisecracks, son," he shouted as they approached the ladder. "It's clear you haven't heard the news or you'd come up with more passengers than this!" He sprang to the ladder and climbed up it expertly.

"Bill Moore," Finn explained to Meg. "Been in these parts long as anyone remembers. Had a fleet of steamboats running into Alaska. Now he owns this landing and is the best musher I ever seen."

Captain John came down to the lower deck to greet him. "What news, Moore?"

Moore looked around impatiently. "I ran the news to Juneau. Thought it would have reached Vancouver before you left. There's gold struck on the creeks running into the Klondike. George Carmack found it first. Then Henderson and God knows how many more, now. Already renamed the creeks. Bonanza and Eldorado. Prospectors been coming out of the woods thick as blackflies. Ladue's got a town springing up around his sawmill, faster than he can saw logs. Calls it Dawson City. No fool, him. He thinks big. They need supplies, John. How much did you bring?

"Only what you ordered," said Belinda.

"Make another trip!" shouted Moore. "God Almighty! I've been telling everyone about this for over ten years. I knew it would come.

Had Ogilvie do the White Pass so we could get pack animals over the mountains. And here you've come, last ship of the season and nothing on board. What the *hell's* the matter with people on the Outside? Will they *never* believe me!"

"I believe you." Mad Mitzi stepped forward. "Will you take me to this Dawson City? I'll make it worth your while."

"Madam." He looked her up and down. "I have more important things to do."

Mitzi turned her back on him and flounced off, swirling her skirts behind her.

"You look ready for the voyage," said Moore to Meg, dressed in plus-fours and boots.

"I hope I am," said Meg, thinking, if I get down that ladder, the rest should be a piece of cake.

"Let's go!" said Finn, "Time's a wastin'."

The other prospectors stood ready with gold pans and pickaxes attached to their packs. Belinda ordered the crew to begin throwing all the packs over the side into the scow.

"Hey, stop that!" shouted Moore. "Those pickaxes are going to put holes in my scow. You want holes in the side of your ship?"

"Talk is cheap." Belinda faced him. "Where's the money for the supplies you ordered?"

"Show me the supplies," said Moore.

Belinda went over to the pile of sacks. "Sugar, flour, dried soup, bacon, yeast..." She kicked the various sacks with her boot. "Now show me your money. We got to get back down to Vancouver. See if we can make another trip. Right, Captain John?"

"You see who runs my ship," said John to Moore.

Mad reappeared in a pair of boots like Meg's and a serviceable dark wool skirt that had been shortened to well above ankle length and had no cumbersome underskirts. She laughed at the sudden stares, flicked up her skirt, showing her white frilled bloomers. "I'm ready," she declared, "for anything. *Toutes choses!* Captain, you *will* lower the lifeboat, for the ladies, won't you?"

Two crew rowed Mitzi, Meg, and some of the prospectors to the wharf. Meg sat, alternately watching the *City of Topeka* recede behind her, and the flat muddy beach of Moore's Landing come closer and closer in front. A forest of evergreens lined the shore. She could not see, dancing excitedly on the shore, applauding her arrival, the welcoming spirits of Ike and Piji, stomping their mukluks in the mud, fur parkas open and flapping.

The fog evaporated from the mountains, revealing snow on the highest summits.

"That's come early, that there snow," said one of the rowers.

"You reckon? I seen snow many a week earlier than this."

Mitzi and Meg looked at each other, then Mitzi looked away as though a conversation between crew members could have no relevance for her.

"What's the word on the Pass?" Jethro asked the crew.

"Which Pass? The White or Chilkoot?"

"Chilkoot. Only a fool would do the White Pass this late in the year."

"What's the difference," Mitzi intervened sharply, "between the two?"

"About a week."

"I'd say life and death if winter sets in early and you ain't prepared for it."

"Not that either of us have done it." They laughed.

"We just pick up the remains of them that made it. Never see them that don't."

"A lot of hearsay, though. We get a lot of hearsay."

"I asked," Mitzi spoke precisely, "what is the actual difference between the passes?"

"The White is long and slow. The Chilkoot is short and steep."

"They say a woman can't do the Chilkoot," said the other. "Unless she's a squaw. Yous don't look like no squaws, ladies." He smiled and tipped his hat pointedly at Meg.

"Sir," said Meg. "I do not understand that as a compliment."

The men eyed each other. Eyebrows were raised, a hat adjusted, spit sent into the water.

"Squaws are native ladies, aren't they?" said Meg. "And if they're strong enough to climb the Chilkoot then I would like to be like them. And I shall certainly try."

"*Moi, aussi.*" Mitzi turned her glance haughtily away from the men.

As soon as all the sacks and packs were loaded onto the wharf, the bargaining began.

"Captain Moore," said Meg. "Are these men who loaded your freight in your employ or are they self-employed? I have four large packs to be carried over the Chilkoot."

"Finn has apprised me of your situation, ma'am. Indians around here call their own shots. These men are Tlingits, strong as oxen and sure as mountain goats. I'd be pleased if you came to my cabin where my wife will fix us lunch and we'll all settle on how best to get you over the pass. There's no time to waste if you're going to beat the freeze up."

"I'll take two Indians," said Mitzi. "I have two large bundles."

"Come with us," said Moore. "Your bundles need repacking, if not rethinking altogether."

"We're off," said Leo, pack on his back, heading onto the forest path towards the Chilkoot, along with Pete, Jethro, and the other prospectors. "See you in Dawson City!"

"Good luck, gentlemen," said Meg, watching them go quickly as they could.

The Tlingit were only three-quarters the size of Finn but they slung the hundredweight packs on their backs easier than he did and led the way along the path to Moore's cabin.

"We'll come back for my supply sacks," said Moore. "Let's get all your gear on the way first."

"Is it safe," said Finn, "to leave all these supplies on the wharf?"

"I own the wharf," said Moore. "Nobody steals from me. Besides, there's nobody around here yet." He walked a long-legged, steady, hiker's pace. He was full of talk about the future. "I thought your ship would be full of pirates, gold diggers, claim jumpers, and the like. But they'll be coming. You mark my words. This port will be the new New York City. Gateway to the North. Land of gold. Maybe diamonds too. That could be next. And Dawson City... you watch it. It'll be the Paris of the North. I've been saying this for years. Been sailing the north sea since I was seven. I know this country. And I've seen the world."

"What parts have you seen?" said Meg, trying to keep up with him.

He looked sharply at her to see if she was genuinely interested. "Born in Germany. Had a towboat service on the Mississippi. Fought in the Mexican War. Prospected as far south as Peru and as far north as you can go in Alaska. Only place I didn't prospect was the Klondike."

"Why not? Why didn't you?"

"Because I'm a damned fool. Gave it up too soon. Wanted to be captain of my own ship." He laughed. "Had a whole fleet of steamships at one time. Transported everything from camels to fairies."

"Fairies?" said Meg.

"You know ..." He nodded in the direction of Mad Mitzi who was lagging behind, trying to keep trail mud off her skirt. "Dance hall girls. Then I gave up that life when one of my sons showed me the White Pass. That was ten years ago. And here I stay." He pointed to a big log cabin, nestled amongst some smaller ones, at the foot of the trail. "Ogilvie and a big Indian fella called Skookum Jim helped turn that trail into a good one for pack animals. But, mark my words, with this here coming gold rush, you're soon going to see a train running up that pass, down to Whitehorse and all the way to Ladue's Dawson City.

"John J. Healy, he's another wily old ship's captain. He's banking on the Chilkoot as the main route. He's got a cabin over there in Dyea. But he's wrong. The Chilkoot's too steep for trains and ordinary people. It's here on my land that you're going to see the crowds appear. Mark my words."

✤

*Whooshing around in front of the troupe approaching the small
settlement of mostly vacated cabins and shacks, were the spirits
of Ike and Piji, arguing.*

*"What's the use," grumbled Piji, "of that healer for our dogs, if
she's moving on soon as she can? And likely as not, won't make
it over the pass. She should stay here."*

*"She will! She will! I know her." Ike was too excited to be prop-
erly smug. "Once she sees our dogs ... And the pups. That'll be the
clincher. She'll stay for them."*

Meg could see smoke rising from the chimney of Moore's cabin. As
they drew near to it, there was the sudden loud howling of a big pack
of wolves, many different voices, not sonorous, not all in harmony,
and very close by. Mitzi screamed and ran to hide behind Finn. Meg
stopped in her tracks. The men laughed.

"That's my team," said Moore. "My dogs. My chariot. My cargo
carriers."

"Where?" Meg wanted to run to see them, but her pack weighed
her down.

Moore led her to the other side of the cabin where he had built a
spacious kennel, with separated compartments, all of thick, strong
wire. A dozen huge, wolf-like dogs were standing on hind legs, paw-
ing the wire frantically and howling in various tones.

"Enough!" commanded Moore. "I'm back and you're scaring the
ladies. Settle down."

Some did. Some did not. They stood panting, or paced, or jumped
up at the fencing, staring and vying for the attention of Meg as she
approached their kennel. She saw their white chests and faces, curled
tails, brown to black top coats, and their dark amber eyes.

"They are *so beautiful!*" Meg clapped her hands together.

Mitzi turned to the men. "She's fallen in love with the dogs."

"You'll never see a better team," said Moore. "And there are pups, inside.'

"Isn't it just like I told you!" Ike exclaimed to Piji. He clenched both fists in triumph.

Piji, forever clad in the furs of Yuki and Yukitu, smiled at her Ike. It was good to have him with her again, and looking so pleased at life. "I'm going to Amy," she told him. "I should get behind her on this. You work on Meg."

"Don't need to," said Ike. "The pups will lure her. I even know which one she'll want."

Moore's wife, Amy, an efficient and fit older woman, welcomed everyone into their comfortable cabin and served out plates of hot fish pie. The Tlingit packers took theirs out on the porch because it was too crowded and hot for them inside. Meg could not keep away from the pen in the corner of the cabin. Therein was a mother and five malamute pups.

"Can I have one?" she asked.

"They're only a month old," Amy said, scrutinizing Meg. "Can't leave their mother for another two weeks. I won't let them go for another two weeks after that. And then, one will cost you $50."

"Fifty dollars!" said Mitzi. "That's a good week's wages. No one pays that for a *dog*!"

"I would," said Meg. "If I could get one of these."

"Which one would you take?' asked Amy.

"That one that sits off by itself and stares at me."

"That one there ..." Moore pointed, "with the long legs and big ears?"

Meg nodded. Moore raised his eyebrows and glanced at Finn.

"Not a good choice, Meg," said Finn. "Looks like a throwback. You'll want one more stocky and playful with the others. More dog-like. You'll see lots more dogs. Believe me. Wait until you see mine in Whitehorse."

"This is the one I really want," said Meg, thinking it reminded her most of Ma Wolf's pups. Meg reached slowly into the pen and let the pup sniff her hand. She put her fingers at the base of its ears and massaged them. She picked up the pup, quickly examining the private parts. "She's a girl!" announced Dr. Meg.

"I agree with your choice," said Amy, as Meg helped her clear the table and wash up the dishes. Mitzi was outside with the men trying to repack her wardrobe into packs that could be carried over the Chilkoot. "Men think only about muscle power. You've spotted the natural leader. She could be more trouble than the rest, with her independence, but she's the one that has to be called Yukon Sally."

"Why?"

"Because she's got the most wolf strain in her and legend has it that these dogs go back to wolves called Yukon Sally and Jake."

"It can't be a very old legend with modern English names like that!" Meg laughed.

"You're right," Amy smiled. "Around here stories become legends in no time at all. I've been here a lot of years and believe me, I've heard some doozers. Of course, life is way too dull if you can't make up a story or two. Or have dreams, like my husband. Me, I have the dogs. It was the only thing I could do to keep myself busy and sane in this wilderness that my husband calls the new New York City." Amy turned to scrubbing more dishes as she commented, "When I was your age, I was breeding babies. You not interested in that?"

"Don't have a husband."

"Are you seriously considering taking on a Yukon Sally?"

"I am."

"I had a dear young friend," Amy paused over the wash basin. "Must have been a dozen years ago. She stayed here with her dog team over the summer until ... She was a great storyteller. Liked to write them down too. She left me "The Legend of Yukon Sally and Jake", all written down. It's a good story, but I miss her company." Amy took up the dish cloth again, keeping her eyes averted.

"What happened to your friend?" said Meg, gently.

"Died. Died in childbirth." Amy scrubbed at the pie dish. "No doctor. Only me to tend her. Nothing more I could do. So much blood! Baby died too. Wish I'd had real doctoring experience. Is it true," Amy faced Meg squarely, "that you're a real doctor, of dogs?"

"Dogs and other animals," said Meg. "Not of people. I'm sure you did as well as I could have, for your friend. What was her name?"

"Annie. We called her Inuit Annie because we couldn't pronounce her last name."

"Hmmm," said Meg, wondering if it were possible that Crazy Annie and Inuit Annie ...

"You're looking very thoughtful," said Amy. "You are thoughtful, aren't you? You're not rushing up here after gold or ... like your friend, that Mitzi. If you're really serious about dogs and taking one of mine ... Are you?"

"I would like to."

"Then here's what you should do ..." Amy set the pie dish firmly on the draining board. "You should stay here, stay the entire winter. Dog teams come through here all winter long. You'd have plenty to doctor. And you'd learn everything you need to know about sled dogs. Come spring, your pup would be big enough to travel and you could sail down the Yukon to Dawson in no time at all. Only fools like that Mitzi, or Finn, go on the Chilkoot at this time of year. And if they get over it, they're likely to find the Yukon River frozen up."

"But Finn has his dogs on the other side of the Chilkoot. He'll make it to them, surely."

"Finn can make it, if anyone can. But with her ... ?"

"Where would I live, given that I have to stay and wait until spring to take my pup?"

"There's a log cabin in good condition just over there. It could be your home and your doctoring office." Amy's eyes became very mothering as she appealed to Meg. "I'd love to have your company. Not that I'd make a nuisance of myself with you." She took up a dish towel. "There's always too much to do, what with looking after my man, this place, the dogs. I don't think you know what you're getting into with these dogs and sledding. But I could teach you ... if you'll teach me a bit about doctoring."

"Sounds like a fair deal," said Meg.

"Yay!" Ike clenched his fists in victory and flew off Meg's shoulders to meet Piji who flew off Amy's back, furs floating outward from her head, as she joined in celebratory dance with Ike.

Dishes dried, Meg sat down on the leather sofa to observe the pups cavorting with each other. Her pup joined in, but soon got bored with romping and returned to look curiously over the edge of the pen at what was going on in the rest of the cabin. She stared most intently at Meg. So like Ma Wolf.

"Yukon Sally." Meg knelt down and stroked her head. "My little Yukie."

"Ah!" said Piji, bowing her head in remembrance. Ike put his arm around Piji.

Mad Mitzi flounced into the cabin, flopped onto the sofa, and took out her flask. "Those *idiot* Indians!" She took a swig and offered the flask around. "Anyone want some?"

"What do you mean?" Amy frowned. "There's nothing idiot about those packers."

"They walked off! They refuse to go today."

"Then it's with good reason."

Mitzi ignored Amy. "They charge way too much. Ten cents a pound at the beginning then two *dollars* a pound when they get to the steep part."

"The Scales," said Amy. "The steepest part, nearest the summit, it's called The Scales because most people drop their loads there, can't carry anything but themselves and a small pack up over the summit."

"Finn says he can do it."

Meg went out to talk to Finn. She saw the dark clouds gathering over the mountains.

"What do you think Finn?"

"I think Mitzi's going to have to give up a few of these dresses since she can't afford to pay the packers." He was assembling one pack for her from the contents of her two big bundles. "She hasn't got any *food* in here! Can you sell her some dried food, and socks?" He kept sifting through her things. "And a parka, warm and waterproof?"

"Finn, what about the packers refusing to start today?"

"One day's delay won't hurt. They're right. They've a good sense of the weather patterns here. But I've got to get there, Meg," he looked at her seriously, "before freeze up. Got to get my dogs and go look for a claim. We'll start tomorrow."

"I want to stay here," said Meg, "over winter. I'll come next spring with my pup. Is that all right with you?"

Finn heaved a big sigh. "Figured that might happen. It'll be better for you, Meg. Safer. Wish Mitzi would stay with you, but she's hell-bent on getting to the gold miners."

Meg went to look at the vacated cabins. There were three shacks furnished with bunk beds, a table, and a small stove. The log cabin had more space, a larger table, a stove and a dry sink, even book shelves. Moore rented or loaned these out, according to the means of whoever wanted to stay in them. I could be comfortable enough in that cabin, thought Meg. Could lay dogs out on that table.

It rained heavily for most of the afternoon. The paths turned into mud streams.

"You could set up a store, with all those supplies you brought," said Amy, as Meg helped prepare dinner. "All the mushers coming up from Juneau and down from the Klondike through the winter, they'd buy most of your stuff before spring. Then you wouldn't have to pay packers to take it over the Chilkoot."

"Let's see how it goes," said Meg. "What about food? How do you feed yourselves and the dogs over winter?"

"Lots of game in the woods and fish in the ocean," said Moore.

Deals were made as they sat around the Moore's table eating venison steaks and potatoes, the cabin dimly lit with smelly kerosene lanterns. Moore would transport Mad Mitzi's wardrobe to Dawson by dogsled over the White Pass, once winter set in. Her deposit for the cost of that trip was two bottles of whisky, one of which Moore shared round the table that evening. Finn had no money and had consumed all his booze. In exchange for the Moore's hospitality, he chopped and piled wood, in the rain.

Mitzi was to sleep that night in the cabin with Meg. Mitzi dumped her pack on the cabin floor. Washed her face and various parts in the tin basin then said to Meg, "I'm going to go over a few things with Finn. Don't wait up for me."

Shivering in her cold bedroll, Meg told herself, soon I'll have a wolf pup with me.

Moore rapped on the cabin door an hour before daylight. "Rise and shine," he said. "Bacon's cooking. Breakfast in fifteen minutes."

"Thanks, Captain," said Meg, getting out of her bunk. "I'll be there."

"Where's your mad friend?"

Meg opened the door, wrapped in her parka. "She's with Finn. Prepaying for guide services, I believe."

Moore roared with laughter, throwing his hands into the air and shaking his head as he walked away. Mitzi and Finn were late for breakfast.

"You're welcome to set up your business here for the winter," said Moore when Meg sat down with him and Amy. "Never had a dog doctor on my townsite before."

"Thank you, Captain Moore."

He nodded. "The Chilkoot's cheaper and easier, come May."

Amy scoffed. "The Chilkoot's never easy."

Mitzi was well outfitted in parka, wool socks, mitts, and other items on loan from Meg. All was to be repaid when they met up in Dawson City in the spring.

"Maybe you too should wait until spring," said Meg, holding Yukie in her arms.

"*Chérie*," said Mitzi with a toss of her head, "by spring I'll have made so much money, I'll have diamonds in my dancing shoes." She blew kisses in the air as she set off ahead.

Finn turned to Meg. "I never intended to have you left here."

"Of course not, Finn." She touched his arm. "Just get yourself and Mitzi there safely."

"Sure I will. May have to knock her out and carry her over the summit. But I'll get us to the Klondike. And I'll strike it rich."

4

The Legend of Yukon Sally and Jake

"It's the same handwriting!" Meg looked up from the manuscript Amy had given her. "Your Inuit Annie was a friend of my husband's! I've read her story about Ike and Piji turning wolf pups into sled dogs. I can tell you all about it!"

Amy smiled at all Meg's exclamations. "No need," she said. "Annie told me that story, more than once. You'll find Ike and Piji back in this story, briefly, when they're old. Ike more disgruntled than ever." Amy put wood into the stove then sat down on the couch beside Meg. "I think Annie put a lot of herself into Ike. She had more respect for wolves than mankind. With good reason, given what happened to her! She was attacked by some drunken stranger who leapt out of the darkness after she had tied up her team for the night. She didn't want his baby, but nor did she want it, or herself, to die ... as they did."

Meg put her arm around Amy's shoulder. "She had a good friend in you. And in Randolph, I'm sure."

"Annie did say she liked a man called Randolph, though he wasn't normal. Nor was she!" Amy laughed. "Annie could be right rough on people, and in her language. But she was wonderful with dogs. Taught me every thing I know about these sled dogs." Amy nodded towards the pen where the pups were scrambling to get milk from their mother. "Annie's was not a peaceful death," Amy reflected.

"But she believed her life was important because she passed on the story of 'Ike's Working Wolves' and it was she who brought his line of malamutes to breed with descendants of Yukon Sally and Jake."

"Is that the story in this manuscript?" asked Meg.

"No," said Amy. "But it is the final word of Inuit Annie."

Amy took up her knitting while Meg settled into reading.

Perched upon Meg's shoulder were the spirits of Ike and Piji. They huddled together, the furs of Yuki and Yukitu draped, as ever, over Piji. Ike in his parka, hood down. Both leaned forward, hands clasped in their laps, eager to follow more tales of their progeny.

The Legend of Yukon Sally and Jake

Yukon Sally's Journey to The Klondike

THE ORIGINAL YUKON SALLY belonged to a pack that ranged around the lakes on the north side of the Chilkoot Pass. It was an area of abundance in those ancient times. There were forests for shelter and camouflage, herds of moose and caribou, with many a slow mover to be brought down and feasted upon. In summer, fish were so plentiful they could be swiped up with one paw and gobbled down as a tasty treat. But now at winter's end, the lakes and rivers were still covered in ice, thin ice, ice that was bound to suddenly crack or break up and be rushed downstream in torrents.

Yukon Sally was in her third winter when she decided to leave her pack. Not that she did not like her pack or her home territory. She loved them. Loved romping, teasing and hunting with her siblings.

Their parents growled and snarled most often and most severely at her, but that was because she had grown large as her father and could now outrun her mother, who was a very fast runner. The parents had to be most concerned about her, Yukon Sally, keeping her place within the pack. Order in the pack must be maintained at all costs, that was understood. The order was changed only through death or weakness.

Old Nanny, for instance, whose teeth were brown and fangs broken, whose eyes were murky, eyelashes grown long and white, who dragged herself up slowly from the ground, was sharp enough at keeping pups in line while the pack went hunting. She had a ready cache of small carcasses for them to amuse themselves with while she napped, with one eye open. She had been good for nannying the litter which Yukon Sally was part of and for the following year's litter. And this spring, Old Nanny was there to see the arrival of the new small litter of three pups. She lay down at the entrance to the birthing den and lifted her head to howl in celebration along with the rest of the pack. But soon after, when none were watching, she dragged herself off as far as she could go into the woods, for her final collapse. None were allowed to follow her, but all sensed when she collapsed. They then raised their heads in a howl so plaintive yet so strong that no coyote would dare sneak near her dead body.

A hunting human came along, skinned her carcass, cut out her heart, and ran back to make a great trade with a member of the Wolf Clan. Then bears grabbed and pawed at the meat left on Old Nanny's bones. Ravens and their ilk picked her carcass clean.

Yukon Sally missed Old Nanny. Old Nanny was the only member of the pack who never showed jealousy towards her. But after Old Nanny's death, Yukon Sally had to be concerned about the new order in the pack. There was no opportunity for advancement.

She was top hunter amongst her siblings but she had always to defer to her parents, particularly when it came to grabs at the kill. That she didn't mind, as long as she got her fill and she made sure she did. But there was no one to mate with.

It was a day in late spring, after Yukon Sally's mother nudged her into taking a turn guarding the new pups, that Yukon Sally decided to rebel. She stood her ground, considering her options as she watched the rest of the pack trotting off on the hunt. No way would she stay back from the hunt! She dragged the entire cache of toy bones over to the pups, then left them to play. Unguarded.

Seeing Yukon come loping after them, then veer to the side to overtake them, Yukon Sally's mother lowered her ears and tail, snarled, then raced after Yukon with more speed than she had been able to muster in some time. Yukon's father joined the chase.

Yukon Sally could have stopped, held her ground, and taken on all comers, as was her nature. But fight with her own mother? And father? Go for their jugular? No. Never.

Yukon Sally ran faster than she had ever run.

Then she heard, behind her, the distinctive howl of her mother. High pitched yet mellow. Followed by her father's more bass yet sharp tones. Then all five siblings howled in unison. Yukon heard the reprimand and appeal of each. She stopped and looked back at them. Her family at the edge of the forest near the shore of the largest lake in the territory. They could have chased her out onto the melting and thin ice. But they did not. Nor were they clearly calling for her return. It was a farewell howl that would also provide cover for her, a diversion for hunters and lynx who know a lone wolf is easier prey. Yukon Sally turned and ran the entire length of the lake.

She was hot, panting, slobber flying out the sides of her mouth from the speed of her running. She had not yet thrown all of her winter fur. Clumps remained on her narrow white chest and underbelly, on her reddish brown back and around her large pointed ears.

The sun was at its height above the mountains when Yukon Sally reached the end of the long narrow lake and heard the sound of open rapids ahead. She lay down, cooling her paws in the water that lay on top of the edge of the lake. She slowly slurped water into her mouth. She got up and stood in the water, cooling all four paws. Drank a little more water then started off again, trotting alongside the river whose currents had run over and begun to push away the winter's ice, currents that were gathering pace and strength far greater than a wolf's.

When the sun had sunk, bringing darkness into the forest, Yukon Sally lay down on a remnant of snow under cover of spruce tree boughs. She had never slept alone, away from the companionship and protection of her pack. She lay her head on her front paws, trying to keep her eyes open, trying to stay alert. But soon her eyelids closed over her pale ginger eyes.

She woke several times, looking warily around, listening for the sound of branches breaking. There was only the annoying sound of small animals scurrying, burrowing, in the night. Fools! Hawks and eagles can swoop down upon them by the light of the stars. A rabbit loped by, but Yukon Sally, hungry as she had become, was too tired to chase it down.

The darkness was short-lived at this time of year. Soon, light appeared behind distant mountains, and then the sun. Yukon Sally uncurled her body then lay still, looking silently around. By now her mother would have roused everyone in the pack. Her father, being the slowest to rise, always had to have at least two nudges. They would have stretched and yawned and gathered to take a drink from the water floating over the lake's thinning ice. Who was looking after the pups? Yukon Sally had liked to play with the pups, letting them romp over her back. Then she would growl to make sure they knew who was bigger and could clamp their necks with one quick bite. But no, she would not be left with them while the others went off to the hunt.

Yukon Sally stretched, then came out from under the tree, eyes alert, always. She was very uneasy now, without her pack around her. When on the run, she being the fastest, she had taken the place behind her parents, the others following behind her. Now she had to make her own straight line to the edge of the forest and then along the rocky edge of the river. It narrowed here and rock cliffs rose on the other side. She could hear the strong rumbling of water running swiftly under the ice and she could see wide holes in the ice where rapids had pushed through. Not even a beaver would venture out onto the river in these conditions.

There was a sudden, very loud, cracking sound. Yukon Sally

flinched. It could be lightning. But there was no storm in the air. Another loud cracking sound came from farther upriver. Yukon Sally turned tail and took off along the bank, downriver. She stopped at the height of rock cliffs that formed the narrowest point of a canyon. She stood well back, ready to escape into the forest behind her. The cracking sounds mixed with loud crashing sounds and the rumbling and roar of river water on the move.

Yes. That must be it. The ice on the river was breaking up, bashing and crashing in chunks, jostling and bolting like a herd of caribou put to the chase. She had seen it twice before, under the guidance of her pack. It was why thin ice was so treacherous in their territory. It would break up suddenly like that, a sudden ambush from which there was no escape. You'd be bashed and drowned before you could reach any shore.

Yukon Sally's guard hairs bristled. She sensed, heard, and then saw the cracking and crashing of the ice gathering up at the narrows of the canyon, then bashing its way through the torrents below her. Her ears perked up then lay back and low, as she leapt back from the edge, gave a sharp bark at the deluge of broken ice about to burst through the canyon, and then she took off, following, racing with the great surge of the Yukon River, heading north towards where it would be joined by the Klondike River and flow through Alaska to the Bering Sea.

Yukon Sally kept just ahead of the deluge, exhilarated by its roar and speed, moving with the destructive and creative forces of nature, as it changed the solid roadway of winter into the swift floating channel of summer. Yukon Sally ran and ran until she came up against the junction of another, smaller river. She stood panting on the bank. The deluge passed her by, crashing about in the river below. She paced the river bank, looking for a possible crossing place. None visible. The sun was not yet at its height but it was much too hot for her. She needed to drink. The pads of her paws were heated and sore. She trotted cautiously along the bank of the tributary river until it narrowed and the water nearly overflowed the banks. She lay down to try to reach with her tongue for a drink. A large chunk of ice suddenly bobbed to the surface of the swirling current and banged into the river bank, breaking the ground from beneath Yukon Sally. She tumbled into the current.

She had often swum in the calm cold water of the lake in summer, cooling her body, swimming smoothly along the shoreline, keeping her head above water, until her fur was soaked, her body cooled down, then she would emerge refreshed and strengthened.

But now she was suddenly submerged, head under, being carried by torrents and bashed by pieces of ice. Instinctively, she pointed herself towards the surface and, once her head was above water, she pawed with all her strength to keep herself upright. She was carried round the corner of the tributary river into the mainstream of the mighty Yukon River at its most tumultuous. Tree branches, logs, and ice chunks battered her sides as she tried to point herself towards one river bank. As she neared it, a current suddenly whirled her around and sent her back into the middle. She tried to claw onto a passing log, but it spun over, dunking her below the surface. Again she managed to get her head above water and stay there, her body now numbed by the semi-frozen water. Then she was swept up by the branches of a split tree that carried her beyond the rocky banks to a part of the river which overflowed onto soggy banks. The split tree wedged itself into the mire.

Yukon Sally swam free of the branches, heading towards the forested shore until she felt her paws striking bottom, the water lapping gently, the torrent behind her. She was wading. And then she was on solid ground. She lay down in the warmth of the sun. She rested but did not sleep, eyes closed but nose and ears on the alert, twitching at every scent, every sound, wind and breeze.

When the sun set, Yukon Sally roused herself and lifted her bruised and aching body to a more protected place. She lay down where her back could be against a large rock. She saw a moose and calf in the distance, drinking at the place where she had been cast ashore. Rabbits passed close by, but Yukon hadn't the strength to give chase. And how could she bring down a large moose on her own? There was no one to divert at the front of the moose while she attacked at the rear. It wasn't just lonely being on her own, it was impractical. She wanted to howl in her loneliness, but that would be foolhardy for a weakened and lone wolf. She lay still and quiet through the night.

She rested and licked her bruises all day. There was a place in her side where her tongue couldn't reach that hurt worse than when a caribou hoof had nicked her. If she lay still on one side, it hurt less. When the heat of the sun began to wane, she lifted herself onto her two front paws. That caused jabbing pain. She sprang onto four paws. That was better. Somewhat. As she moved through the woods, following the downriver direction but at a safe distance from the river bank, the pain of the cracked ribs did not cease but she got used to it. She increased her pace to a trot. She would save running for chasing or being chased. She trotted into the darkness, moving lightly as she could on her paws.

The noise of the river in full flood of ice breakup grew dimmer. Yukon Sally came out of the woods. She saw ahead of her the dark blue water of the long narrow lake that would be named Laberge. Its surface was being churned by rubble and ice chunks flowing towards the next junction of the Yukon River.

Yukon Sally went to the pebbly shore of the lake and turned round and round in a small circle until she lay painfully down, watching the water lap the shore, and looking out across the lake. It felt familiar being in the territory of a long narrow lake. She found camouflage under a thicket of bushes and lay there until dawn.

On the other side of the lake she heard the howling of a strange wolf pack. A small pack. Just four different voices. The voices were faint, coming from across and farther up the lake. Yukon Sally ran farther up her side of the lake, ignoring the pain in her side, running at nearly full speed. She stopped to lap up some water then raised her head, in her own peculiar sonorous howl. Silence reigned for so long that, anxiously, she began to run again. Then she heard their answering howls. She raced to reach the far end of the lake where she might see them.

Much farther along she stopped to give a sharp howl, but there was no reply. She raced on. And on. The lake narrowed into the river. The river was wide and raging with currents and the dregs of the ice breakup. She ran farther, looking for manageable narrows, but found instead another formidable junction of a large tributary river. No sign of the wolf pack on the other side. Yukon lay down to wait for its appearance. She lifted her head to howl for them. No answer.

Then Yukon Sally heard on the other side of the river, the sound of a moose being brought down. She felt her own hunger. That pack would not leave its meat or its territory. And Yukon Sally was not willing to dive into the torrents to try to join the pack on the other side. She moaned briefly in frustration, then headed farther down-river in search of food.

Yukon Sally looked up at the sun then quickly away into the forest. The sun was blinding and seemingly ever present in this suddenly hot season. It rose above the purpling mountains, ascending to its height above the rushing river, making the muddied waters shine and spar-kle like safe ice. Yukon Sally moved out of its glare, into the woods, and dug a small pit to rest and cool her body against the soil. But then a swarm of mosquitoes tried to get into her ears, her eyes. She nar-rowed her eyes to slits as she would in a blizzard and pawed and shook the mosquitoes away. Might as well get up and on the move.

She sniffed as she trotted amongst the trees, within the sound of the flooding river. She heard the snap of a twig and then she saw it. A large hare, stopped suddenly, trying to make itself invisible, sitting perfectly still against the background of colours similar to its own. Yukon Sally kept her pace, veering slightly away as though she had not noticed the hare. Then, as she was about to pass it by, she sud-denly swerved and took after it. Chased it down. Grabbed its neck with her four front fangs, killing it instantly.

Yukon Sally was so hungry she almost ate the bones but she had been well taught by her elders to leave the brittle pickings to birds and other scavengers. Yukon Sally lifted her head from the scraps of bleeding flesh, licked her lips, and moved on.

She travelled through the dusk, stopping at a curve in the river that created a sandy beach. Logs and branches had been cast onto the beach. There was the smell of fish. Yukon Sally investigated. Yes. Dead fish. Some still squirming. She put them out of their misery and filled her stomach. The fish smell was so strong, the meat so tasty, Yukon did not see the black bear until it was leaping over a log towards her and the fish heads strewn around her.

Yukon Sally considered taking him on, as she bared her teeth and snarled at him. But she was full enough. She would let him have the fish heads. She snarled and growled. The bear raised himself on two haunches, showing his full height and width, making his peculiar barky, squawky, snorting sound. Yukon snarled and held her ground.

The bear lowered himself onto his front paws, shaking his head threateningly, but did not advance. Yukon's fur and guard hairs bristled on her back as she lowered her head menacingly and put herself into springing position. The bear sat down, perplexed at the behaviour of this lone wolf. A pack of wolves he would run from, but what was to happen with this one large wolf?

They both saw an injured salmon flip up onto the shore. The hungry bear was ready to fight for it. He bared his teeth and began to move sideways towards the fish, keeping an eye on the reaction of Yukon Sally.

It's yours, I've had my fill, Yukon conveyed to him, as she relaxed her fur and trotted off into the woods. She found an old hollow log, quite like the one she and her siblings used for taking flying leaps over, or for playing hide-and-seek. Yukon slept well in that log, her refuelled body recovering from its cracks and bruises.

After a few days, she could run without intense pain, fast and far downriver until she heard the sound of another, smaller river. Reaching the junction, she saw that the smaller river was deep and high-banked where it flowed into the raging Yukon, but farther up it was shallow enough to have rocks showing above water. But there, where it shallowed, was a large pack of humans on the opposite bank. Yukon Sally withdrew behind trees to watch them.

She had observed humans before, when she was with her own pack. The humans tried to disguise their scent, by covering their own hide in the hides of animals. But a human covered in caribou skins, or sleeping under a grizzly bear hide, still has the smell of a human. Yukon Sally had observed with her pack, the peculiar powers of humans. Like lightning, they could create fire. But the fires that lightning created moved, moved in any direction of the wind, burning up trees and bushes, eating up any creature that couldn't outrun it. Humans struck up fires that were small and stayed in one place. Humans sat round their fire, feeding it pieces of trees. They stuck pieces of juicy meat into the fire, lifted them out burned, and ate them, licking their chops in satisfaction.

Humans had sharp things, great flying fangs, that they threw into the chests of caribou, bringing them down faster than a good pack of wolves could. Yukon had learned that humans were to be feared, more than the speed of a cougar or lynx, and more than the strength of a grizzly. They had powers and strategies beyond the power of a wolf's. They felled trees faster than a beaver and turned them into floating things that carried them across lakes and downriver faster than fish.

This very large pack of humans, sitting round a fire on the opposite bank of the river, had several floating things pulled up onto shore. Yukon Sally lay down, resting her head upon her front paws so that she might watch and not be seen. Oh, for some hunks of that juicy moose meat before they burned it in the fire. She watched them gnaw at their meat when they took it out of the fire. The leader of the pack stood up and made a loud burping sound. The others grunted and spread their lips, nodding and deferring. The leader pulled over himself a great bear hide; the bear's head fur, including the ears, he adjusted onto the top of his head. He did not make the sounds of a bear but human sounds, as he held onto a thick stick he had pounded on the ground. When he finished his sounds, others nodded in deference. There was some moving about and pissing in the woods, then all stretched out to sleep on pieces of bear hides.

Yukon Sally moved farther back and dozed off, curled up against an overhanging rock. The scent of a squirrel nearby roused her before the full light of day. The squirrel escaped up a tree, but farther up stream, Yukon Sally caught a beaver who had lumbered too far onto shore. Fortified, Yukon paced the river bank until she found a place so shallow she could wade across. Then she ran on an angle through the forest towards the sound of the rushing Yukon River.

She came up against a steep rise of land where trees did not grow and the river banks rose into high rocky cliffs. The Yukon narrowed there into channels formed by high rock islands that divided the river into five channels of rapids and whirlpools and undertows that neither wolf nor human would want to fall into. Yukon Sally walked cautiously along the edge of the high rocky cliff. The spring ice breakup had passed through the torrents below. Then she saw the bear-hided humans sitting very upright in their floating things, paddling hard, steering through and with the rapids and currents below.

Yukon Sally felt the thrill of moving with the river, began to race alongside over the rocky terrain. It was treacherous. The crevasses, the fallen trees, the too-sharp edges of rocks. She had to slow down and leap carefully from one place to the next until she moved farther away from the cliffs and found herself on an ancient trail following the river downstream. There she picked up speed.

The path eventually turned in towards a pebble and sand beach at a curve in the river. Yukon Sally came to an abrupt stop as she smelled, and then saw, two different packs of humans. On shore were camped humans wearing wolf furs. The pack with bear hides were pulling ashore their floating things. No one snarled or made threatening poses. They were friendly to each other, sharing the territory.

Yukon Sally turned to skirt far around them. Her movement caught the sight of some.

"Come on! Let's head it off!" they said in their own language. "That's a big one. Big prize!"

Several hunters started off.

"Stop!" said the Chief of the Wolf Clan. "Let a lone wolf go in peace. Let it start its own new pack. I have spoken."

Yukon Sally understood nothing but the need to flee. She ran along the banks of the Yukon River heading north for five long days and short nights. Rested only in the high heat of day. When she came up against another and yet another tributary river, she would not be stopped. She waded in at the calmest part and swam on an angle with the current until she reached the other side.

Then she heard ahead of her the rush of a wide river flowing fast into the Yukon as it turned northwestwards. It sounded too large for a weary wolf, weakened with hunger, to cross. She could see a small mountain with a rounded top risen up from the flatland at this junction of rivers. Yukon Sally determined to reach that site. She trotted a good way upstream along the wide tributary river then plunged in, swimming with all her remaining strength to reach the other side, just before it joined with the force of the northward currents of the Yukon. She climbed up onto the marshy flatland and lay down exhilarated and exhausted.

In the cool of the few hours of darkness, Yukon Sally made her way up to the top of the smooth, domed mountain. It was dark below on the other side of dome mountain, except for the moonlight gleaming on the junction of the two rivers, the Yukon and the Klondike. She did not want to fight the strength of either river again.

But she did want to swipe with her paws along the shore of the Klondike. Scoop out the salmon she had felt bumping into her as she crossed the currents. And the flatland below her was marshy, smelling promisingly of moose clumping around, though it also smelled dangerously of human hunters and fishing camps. Yukon Sally wanted to howl with hunger and loneliness and a sense of finality. This was as far as she would go. She knew to keep silent in her weakened and lonely state. She lay down in the shelter of bushes. When dawn came, Yukon Sally was roused by a distant howling. It did not sound like a human imitating a wolf. It was the howl of another lone wolf.

Yukon Sally ran down through the woods on the side of dome mountain and across the marsh to the bank of the Yukon River just before it was joined by the Klondike. Yukon Sally looked cautiously around and then lifted her head to call to the single howl she had heard. Her call was immediately answered by a sharp, eager howl from farther downriver, on the high forested edge of the other side. Yukon Sally howled in frustration. Although the river was clear of great ice chunks, it was so far across, so fast flowing... She howled again in dismay. The wolf on the other side howled with unqualified excitement. The voice had the deeper tones of a male. It was the wolf to be known as Yukon Jake.

Jake's Journey to Yukon Sally

FROM BIRTH, Yukon Jake had been used to much affection, attention and food. He was born in a litter of two, but the other pup did not survive. Jake had his mother's milk all to himself. His pack was dangerously small, only his parents plus two yearling sisters, hence they valued Jake all the more. Jake was a roly-poly, affectionate pup given to goofy, show-off stunts.

His pack's territory was in the Alaskan region of the Yukon River, not far from the village of Ike and Piji, who had become famous for their malamute sled dogs. There were many failed experiments during the generations it took to establish this breed. Yukon Jake got caught up in one of those failed experiments, engineered by some teenagers with too much time on their hands. Or as Ike would put it: "Blubberheads! Hardening their rods."

They were trying to seduce wolves with that age-old temptation, food. It didn't work well with mature wolves because they are not scavengers and will not take bribes. But a young wolf, especially a greedy young wolf, might not know…

Yukon Jake was not yet a yearling when he was taken on the hunt with his pack. Because of a lack of pup sitters, he was taught early the skills of hunting. It was his place to keep to the rear when on the run. On this particular late winter morning, Jake's father suddenly stopped at his place in the lead. He sniffed, then saw a severed, bloody caribou leg near a grove of evergreens. Too odd. There was no scent of other animals who might have abandoned the leg. But there was the peculiar scent of humans in the air. Jake's father moved quickly on.

Jake lingered, for he saw the food and wanted it. His mother turned and threatened to chase him back in line. Jake then took up the pace and followed behind. But the sight of the food remained in his mind. When his pack turned a corner, Jake circled back as fast as he could, to grab a few mouthfuls of that meaty leg.

He was absorbed in swallowing his first chunks, when humans came at him from one side, and his pack from the other. His father sprang at a human and got impaled on a spear. His mother, in a flurry of movement, corraled Jake and his sisters, sending them away from the fray and ran after them. She yelped as something struck her in the belly but she kept running in a direction which Jake and siblings followed.

The humans did not pursue them. They grouped over the dying wolf. They were hushed as they watched him struggle for life. Then Nuvik, whose spear it was, pulled out the spear and put it straight into Jake's father's heart. Nuvik felt no sense of triumph. "Brave wolf," he said in Malamute.

Then he turned accusingly on Tukap. "You threw your knife at the mother in retreat. Bonehead! Coward! You'll be cursed."

"Don't blame me. You killed the father. I only wanted to trap the greedy yearling."

"I told you it wouldn't work," said Nuvik, extracting his spear. "You have to get them soon as they're weaned, like my Uncle Ike."

"Shut up. You're the one who killed the father."

"Kill or be killed. You set the food trap. I only came to watch," said Nuvik, holding his spear dripping with blood.

"Then go home. You're the coward. I'm going after my knife." Tukap began to follow the snow trail of wolf paws and blood, then turned back to the others. "Why are you all staring like a bunch of fish heads!" he shouted at them. "Too scared to come with me?"

"Look what you've done!" said one boy. "We came to trap a yearling with food, but he's escaped and you've killed the father and maybe the mother too."

"It's wrong to kill the parents of a pack," said another. "It'll bring on the death of our own parents."

Tukap shrugged his shoulders and smiled.

"You have the heart of ice that never melts," said Nuvik. "I'll give the heart of this brave wolf to my father, ask him to share some of it with me. Now who's going to help carry this big wolf back to the village?"

Four of the seven teenagers carried Jake's father by his four paws, Nuvik solemnly leading the procession, trying to walk like a chief, hoping his father would be proud of him, knowing his Uncle Ike would not, and hoping above all, not to encounter Aunt Piji who had clearly gone mad with the business of turning wolves into malamute dogs.

The other two boys stayed with Tukap. Tukap knew he was in trouble if he came home without his knife. It was the only one he had and it had been obtained from a carver at significant cost. The mother wolf would surely die with it in her side. Tukap wanted the backup of other boys, with weapons, when he came upon her. You never know what might be surrounding her. Or eating her.

"I was right, wasn't I," he said to the boys who remained with him. "We did lure that greedy yearling with food. Should be all the easier to capture him now. Next time I'll have food *and* one of Ike's dogs in heat, all tied up and ready. Won't that be something to watch! Trouble with today is, we started too small. And parents got in the way. We won't have a problem with that next time."

Tukap led the way with bravado, but the others were dragging their snowshoes, uncomfortable with what they were doing. The time between dawn and dusk was short. Cold caribou that would melt in their mouths awaited them at home. Helping their friend retrieve his knife was loyal and brave. And it wasn't good to leave a wolf in a lingering death. But they weren't prepared to follow this trail of blood and paws beyond dusk.

Jake's mother led her pups to the edge of their territory. She lay down and tried to dislodge the knife thrown into her body. It was in just the spot she could not reach. Blood was oozing from it into the snow. Before she passed out, she growled and snarled at Jake and his two older sisters to leave her, to carry on to safety. Jake whimpered and refused. His sisters took off at a slow trot, then stopped to call him. Jake stayed where he was.

He tried to rouse his mother by yelping at her, by sniffing and licking at her snout. Since neither yelps nor licks aroused her, he nipped at her tail. A mature wolf would never tolerate her tail being touched by any but her mate. But not even that aroused his mother. The instinct for action, the go-for-it attitude that was so strong in Jake, made him dig at the wound with his teeth until he pulled out the carved stone knife. His mother came to.

She rolled over, pressing her wound into the snow. The wound began to freeze. Yukon Jake ate snow, cleansing his mouth of his mother's blood and quenching his thirst. His mother looked him in the eyes, then closed hers, to rest, to fall into the sleep of recovery, or death. Jake lay his head on his paws, close to her snout where he could sense the warm air of her breathing.

His sisters returned. They dropped a headless white hare near him then paced several times around their mother, to see that she was still alive, before settling down to keep watch around her. A fallen wolf was vulnerable to all kinds of scavengers.

The sisters raised their heads in alarm when suddenly, they smelled the scent of humans. Jake began to growl. His sisters rebuked him with stares and a curling of their lips, telling him to shut up, keep silent, keep their whereabouts unknown. Jake kept silent with his ears pulled back in readiness.

Tukap and company had reached a point where they spotted the wolves.

"Stop!" Tukap held up his right mitt. "There they are," he said in hushed tone. "On that far ridge. It's the river bank. They're under the evergreens."

"I see only three. The greedy one. And two full-growns. Where's the mother?"

"They're standing around the mother, Blubberhead!"

"She must be alive. Wolves don't guard dead ones."

"Maybe they do if she hasn't been dead for long, Fishface!"

"You're the Fishface! I'm getting out of here. Those wolves have it in for us."

"Yeah. Let's leave them alone. It's getting dark."

"Cowards! I want my knife. I can't go home without my knife."

"Then you go for it, Braveone! We're going home."

"I'm coming back tomorrow," said Tukap, "for my knife,"

Yukon Jake growled and snarled in the direction of the retreating teenagers. The bristling fur on his sisters' backs settled down.

That night a blizzard swept through the village of the famed Uncle Ike and Aunt Piji. It covered the blood-stained trail of what remained of Yukon Jake's pack.

The trouble is, Ike thought that evening of the blizzard, when he left Piji at home, warm in the furs of Yuki and Yukitu, you can create a great line, but you lose control over what happens to it. Even in his own village, where people had been so co-operative when he had first started the dog business, there were now cheaters, the slipshod, the ones cutting corners, the many who thought they could do it better and faster, and worst of all there were the dog beaters.

His thoughts were heavy as he trudged through the blizzard to the nearby home of his friend Pakak. They all promised when they received his pups they would raise and train them according to his rules. But over time, the tales and the evidence got back to him. Dogs ran off because they were tied up for long periods. They were never seen alive again. Dogs strangled themselves trying to break loose. Some were beaten and became servile to their owners but vicious with others. Dogs were worked too hard, or not exercised enough. They were not fed enough, or fed rotten food. He couldn't bear to think of his dogs being eaten but he knew it happened in far away places, with desperate, cowardly people.

"But Ike," said his friend Pakak who liked to chew the fat and argue with Ike. "I can think of situations where it is right to eat your own dog."

"Never!" said Ike, chewing his own piece of blubber.

"The dogs are starving and you are starving. You have a wife and child. Sacrifice the dog's life for the sake of your child."

"No!" said Ike. "Set the dog free and he'll bring you a rabbit and feed himself on mice."

"Supposing you're lost in a blizzard ..."

"Wait it out. Your dogs are your means of getting through the blizzard."

"Supposing you might be rescued if you don't starve to death first. You must sacrifice your dog to stay alive."

"What good is a few more days of life if you have no certainty of rescue? I would wait it out, or die with my dogs. They're more valuable than me. I can't do the work they do."

Pakak raised his piece of blubber into the air, conceding the point to Ike.

"But it is widely believed," he said, raising his best point, "that eating the heart of a great animal is the best sign of respect and the spirit of the animal will then dwell in you and will not die."

Ike spat on the ground. "And if I eat my own shit, I will live forever."

Pakak burst into laughter, slapped his knee. Ike laughed with him.

"Ike, my friend," said Pakak. "You're a good thinker. We're poor storytellers, but we have good talk." He put his hand on Ike's shoulder.

"I'm not a good man," said Ike.

Pakak heaved a sigh. Here we go again with Ike's melancholy.

"I have stolen wolves," said Ike. "Turned them into good dogs but they have lost their dignity."

"Dignity!" Ike uses words like a chief, thought Pakak.

"I took it from them." Ike went on. "I made Tarak mate with different females. And then Icebarb with different males. I got a fine line of pups from them but they lost the wolf's sense of family. Now any dog will mate with any dog in heat and they hardly mind when they're separated from their pups."

"Ah," Pakak recalled the heat of his own blood when he was young and vigorous, how he wanted to mate at every opportunity. "I remember Icebarb well. She was not unlike my first wife. Icebarb wanted to mate with Tarak. Snowface was not enough for her. Your dogs," Pakak whacked Ike's knee with his blubber, "have been taught the ways of humans."

Ike could not smile in return. It was all too true, what Pakak said.

"People are stupid," said Ike. "They think they're smarter than me and smarter than my dogs. They ruin the pups I give them. When I'm gone, my great line of dogs will disappear."

"We are old men," said Pakak. "We should not speak like babies, whining because they have to give up their mother's breast. Soon we will take the long walk into the night. Sometimes when I see how my children raise my grandchildren I too fear for what will become of my line. They waste time making them too many clothes, take them out on the hunt too soon. Or sometimes not soon enough. They let them play with good tools or carvings when old bones would do. They let them sit listening to stories when they should be sleeping. But what can you do but hope that they will learn from their own mistakes. If they'd ask my advice, or just do it the way we did ..."

Ike got impatient. He stood up. "I have to do something about this latest outrage."

"Which one is that?" Pakak knew what was coming. It was the talk of the village and Ike was bound to react to it.

"That gang of ill-bred boys. My nephew included. They tried to trap a young wolf with the leg of a caribou. Botched. Completely botched the whole thing. An experiment doomed to failure. If they had only asked me ..." Ike gritted his teeth in anger and disgust. "They killed the father of the pack and wounded the mother. That is all I know and I must confront my sister and her husband, make my nephew tell the whole sorry story. Will you come with me, Pakak? You know how my sister and her husband are with me. They will show more respect if you are with me."

"I'm with you, my friend. I saw Nuvik and his friends bring home the dead wolf. They were too pleased with themselves."

The blizzard was over and the night clear with stars as Ike and

Pakak made their way to the home of Ike's sister, Isa, and her husband, Anik. Their home was large, well equipped, and had many carvings on display. Anik was an industrious hunter who spent more hours than most on the job and he thought Ike had an easy time of it. "Plays with wolf pups while we hunters do the hard work of bringing home the meat," he often said to his wife and son and other villagers.

Isa shared her husband's view of her brother, Ike, though she also enjoyed being connected to Ike's fame. Isa's early years of marriage were unhappy because she did not bear a child, and she felt she had been hard done by in life. But then, surprisingly, at a late age, she bore their son, Nuvik, and doted on him beyond all else. He could do no wrong and never be given too much. She found fault with all others compared to him, particularly with girls who interested him. Thus he lived at home beyond the normal age and hung out with the boys in the village.

"My sister's husband shares the common beliefs," Ike said to Pakak as they neared Anik and Isa's dwelling. "Believes in spirits, curses, good luck, bad luck. He questions nothing. The more carvings the better. Their home is stuffed with them. And Isa complains about Piji. Says my wife is an embarrassment because she won't collect more carvings and I let her wear Yuki's hide. They say I look bad and should ..."

"Ike, my friend," Pakak put his foot down in impatience, "your dogs will always make you look good. The rest is unimportant. They will go on when you and your relatives are gone. Now let us get on ..."

"It's precisely because of that that I must get to the bottom of this. And I hate it. I have no time for family feuding. I have given a good team of dogs to my sister and husband. And Nuvik, he loves those dogs. What was he thinking, trying to capture wolves?"

Like uncle, like nephew, Pakak was thinking as they reached Anik and Isa's doorway.

"You first," he said to Ike.

Ike crawled in first.

"Ike!" Anik greeted him with surprise. "What are you doing here? I'm in the middle of sharpening my spears. But come in," he said dutifully, then reached to push Ike's hair out of his eyes and push back his parka hood. "Brother, you could do with a hair comb and a new parka. You're a rich man. Why don't you dress better?"

Pakak then appeared and stood up beside Ike. He was warmly welcomed by Anik and Isa. Nuvik, who had been sitting sharpening his spear, stood up in formal greeting then sat back down, glowering, his hands firmly under his legs. He looked ready for a fight.

"My son had an unlucky experience," said Anik. "He and his friends were observing wolves, just as you and Isa did when you were young, Ike."

Isa, sitting beside Nuvik, nodded in firm agreement.

"They would have been better off hunting for meat," Anik continued. "But boys will be boys. I have no time to waste experimenting. I have to bring home the meat ..."

"What happened?" said Pakak, frowning at Ike, cautioning him to hold his temper. "What was unlucky?"

"They threw a piece of caribou to the young wolf and the old wolves turned vicious and attacked. Nuvik would have been killed were he not so skilled with his spear."

"I brought the wolf home," Nuvik stood up. "I killed it cleanly. And I have shown it great respect. We cut out its heart. My father has shared it. You have no reason to look angrily at me, Uncle. I behaved like a man. Which is more than is always said of you."

"Enough!" said Pakak. "You must speak with respect to your elders."

"I did nothing wrong," Nuvik raised his voice in anger and self-defence. "Don't accuse me. It was all Tukap's fault. It was his stupid idea in the first place. And he's the one who threw his knife in the retreating mother wolf. I would never do that. Now he's lost his knife and he wants to track it down. Go after him, not me."

"Wake up, Ike!" Anik pointed his finger at Ike. "Learn something about people. If you had to hunt for your meat the way I do, you wouldn't be able to spend all your time raising precious dogs!"

Ike turned his back on Anik and spoke in an extremely calm voice to Nuvik. "What was Tukap's idea? What was his plan?"

"Capture the young wolf and mate it to one of your dogs."

"Which one?"

"The bitch his father got from you."

"Tundra. I have a mate for her."

"His father can't afford to use yours."

"That's a lie! He knows I'll take whatever he can afford."

Nuvik shrugged. "Maybe he wants to do his own breeding."

Ike's eyes narrowed. "He wanted to tie them up. Tie up the young wolf and tie up Tundra. Then all you young blubberheads would stand around and watch, wouldn't you! Hardening your rods. That was the plan."

"Ike." Pakak touched his shoulder. "We must go and address our concerns to Tukap and his father. We thank you for your hospitality, Anik. Isa." He nodded to them. "And Nuvik . . . you have much to learn."

"Blubberheads!" Ike kept saying as they made their way to Tukap's dwelling. "It would never work. Even the timing is wrong. It will be another moon before Tundra is in season. What were they planning to do with that poor young wolf until then?" He kicked the snow. "And where is it now? Guarding the dead or dying body of its mother?" Ike's heart felt too old to bear this. "We will find them," he said. "Dead or alive."

The next day was clear and windless. Two teams of malamutes sped to the place where Yukon Jake, his mother, and two older sisters were last seen. One team was driven by Ike, the other by Tukap's father, Tukap guiding them to the spot.

Tukap's father had shaken him by the shoulders when he heard the story from Ike and Pakak. "You will put a curse on our family if you have killed both parents," Tukap's father railed at him. "You do not have the brains of a mouse!"

"It was Nuvik who killed the father."

"And you, you coward! You threw your knife at a fleeing mother.

If we find your knife, I will take it from you and keep it until the sea freezes over."

The knife was not to be found. The blizzard had buried it in a drift far beneath the scent of the dogs. But Ike's team could smell the dead body of Yukon Jake's mother. They led everyone to her.

Ike pushed the snow off her body with his hands. He held onto her two stiff and extended front paws. They were white, as was her snout and around her eyes. The rest of her coat was unusually dark. Was it his blurred, teary-eyed vision, or was it really so like the appearance of Yuki?

Far on the other side of the frozen river, he saw three wolves, two light and one dark, like this dead mother. The three young wolves howled. All of Ike's dogs howled in plaintive harmony. And so did Ike, lifting his chin high.

Yukon Jake and his sisters were accepted into another small pack, farther up the Yukon River. But the following winter, when Jake was fully developed, a good hunter, and too much of a rival to the lead male, Jake was forced to run off alone. He had not felt so abandoned and fearful since he stood in the blizzard near the dead body of his mother.

There was nothing for it, but to get running, and keep running, stopping only for sleep when the sun was at its height. He kept close to the bank of the frozen river, making occasional forays into the forest for a rabbit or other small animals.

He leapt back from the river's edge when the ice suddenly cracked like thunder and lightning. He watched it break up into huge chunks and rush with the roar of released water, faster it seemed and louder than the largest herd of fleeing caribou he had ever seen. It propelled him to run against it, running upriver, against the roaring currents, in a strangely challenging and compelling race.

When the deluge passed and the waters calmed, though did not slow down, he ran at an easier pace. He reached the junction of another big river and stopped to gather his strength. He rested. He howled in desperate loneliness.

That was when he heard the answering call of Yukon Sally. Nothing, not even the currents of the Yukon River at its strongest, could keep him from getting to her. He saw her running and leaping on the other side of the river, directing him to start farther upstream where his angle against the current would have a better chance. She was more of a strategist than he. He did what had to be done. Plunged in and swam with all his might to get to the other side of the Yukon before the curve of land where it was joined by the currents of the Klondike. Yukon Sally yelped and kept pace with him, coaching and coaxing, stopping before the point which he must not go beyond.

Yukon Jake won the battle against the force of the Yukon by going with it just far enough to hit the bank where Yukon Sally had stopped. He struggled up the bank, grabbing with his claws onto roots and earth until he stood firmly on the bank beside her.

He was soaked by the brown water, dripping, looking smooth-coated, slick as a beaver. He shook himself repeatedly and as hard as he could, to regain the appearance of a fine-furred wolf, though since it was spring, he was moulting in scruffy clumps. So was she. Neither of them was looking their best. But ah, at last, another lone wolf. Welcoming. Similar in size. Similar in age. And even better, not similar in sex.

Jake yelped and pranced in front of Yukon Sally. She pranced and bowed her head, swiped her front paw up at him. He swiped his paw at her and let her put her head over the back of his neck. Then she let him do the same to her. They bounced back from each other, then came together, swiping with forepaws, sporting, sniffing at the head, exchanging licks on the snout. Then Yukon Sally lay down, assuming her most regal pose but nodding her head to Jake. He lay down near to her, assuming his most regal pose. Both were exhausted, but no longer driven by the loneliness that is worse than hunger. They drew closer together, Yukon Sally inviting Jake to put his forepaw over hers, his snout on top of hers.

Eventually, Yukon Sally and Jake trotted off together across the moose pasture, towards the domed mountain, to hunt together, to sleep together, to start a new pack of free and wild wolves, together.

The descendants of their pack have ranged that territory for all the centuries since. Many summers ago, two newly weaned pups were stolen from a large litter, and when mature, they were bred with descendents of Ike and Piji's dogs, by ...

Annie Iqalukual

Meg put the last page on the pile of manuscript and looked over at the pups dozing in the pen with their mother. And beautiful creatures they are, she thought. "Yukie!" she called.

"Come here, my little Yukie."

Yukie sat up and looked intently at Meg, considering her command. She stayed put.

"OK." Meg smiled and went over to crouch by the pen, reaching to pet her. The pup lifted her paw towards Meg. Meg shook her paw. "Yukon Sally. It's an honour to know you," said Meg. "I'm sorry your ancestors were stolen."

"See," said Piji to Ike, resting on the back of the sofa. "These pups are in good hands."

"These are," Ike agreed. He thought of Annie's portrayal of him, how substantial a man he had been in life. But burdened and complaining in his old age. Disrespectful of his wife. And he felt how small his spirit had become in immortality. He took off his parka. "I'm tired of me," he said to Piji. "You have wisdom and peace. May I have the hide of Yukitu?"

Piji passed it to him. Ike placed it over his head, letting it drape down his back like a cloak. He sat shoulder to shoulder with Piji. "I'm going to rest with you," he said.

5

WINTER IN THE WILDERNESS

MEG SPENT THE WINTER OF 1896–7 on Moore's unpopulated town
site. It was my time in the wilderness, she thought in retrospect, and
I almost did not get out of it. I was so unaware of what would spring
out of that relentless darkness when alone and unprotected.

In the end it was her Yukon Sally who led her out and up the Chilkoot Pass then on to Dawson City. But in the beginning of that winter,
Yukie, the pup, showed only a wolf-like aloofness and desire to escape
Meg and the confines of her cabin. Food did not entice her. Yukie ate
only part of what was in her dish, then sat down, stared at Meg, went
to the door, scratched, then looked appealingly at Meg to be let out
to rejoin the Moore's malamutes. Amy had to chase Yukie away from
their kennel and eventually carry her back to Meg's. Yukie was so
persistent and looked at Meg so mournfully that the ultimate solution
was to have one of Amy's dogs come to play with Yukie twice a day.
At night Yukie was locked in the cabin with Meg but would not sleep
by her bedside like Poley. Yukie slept by the door.

The long winter hours of northern darkness dominated, arriving
earlier and earlier each afternoon. Candles and oil lamps had to be
used sparingly. Amy insisted upon Meg sharing the evening meal in
the Moore's cabin. They were intelligent company, with interesting
tales to tell. But when Meg returned to her cabin, holding the lan-

tern like a minuscule flickering firefly in the forest of darkness, silent
Yukie seeming reluctant at her side, Meg thought of Amy and Captain
Moore, warm body pressed up against warm body. She got into her
bed alone, having brushed her teeth in a mug of icy water, shivering
from her toque-capped head to her sock-clad feet, she uttered her
repeated prayer; "Please God, a mate someday, a human mate, for
life."

There was little to do throughout winter beyond the survival chores
of gathering wood so the fire in the stove never went out and making
repetitive meals of porridge, stew, or beans. Underwear was washed
and dried in the cabin. Outerwear could wait until spring. In the short
hours of daylight, Meg left Yukie to play with the other growing pups
and went with Amy and her team to exercise on the lower part of the
White Pass. Meg strengthened her legs for the Chilkoot climb and
learned how to operate a dog sled.

Outside Meg's cabin was a rough sign saying, "Dog Doctor," but
there were few takers over the course of the winter. Mushers came
occasionally from Juneau en route to the White Pass and Dawson
City but their dogs were generally in good shape, suffering at worst
from cracked or bleeding paws. The mushers knew as well as Meg
how to bandage them, but they liked to see her and talk to her, so they
asked for her services, paid twenty-five cents, rested their dogs a few
days, then were on their way, the rankness of their unwashed, sweaty
bodies and clothes wafting after them.

It was Christmas, when the days were closest to endless nights,
that one Jon Teskey and his team of wounded dogs staggered onto
Moore's town site. Teskey's parka was torn, his face, arm, and back
bleeding. His four dogs were limping, ears torn, faces torn, their fur
bloody.

"What the hell!" Moore shouted.

"Cougar attacked me from behind,' Teskey managed to say. "Got
two of my dogs. God help me save the rest."

Meg turned her cabin into an infirmary, Amy and Moore into her
staff. Teskey was laid on her bed, the dogs on her table, one by one,
to be cleaned, chloroformed, stitched up, the others lying in pain on

the floor, trying to lick their wounds. Yukie sat pressed up against the foot of Meg's bed and would not be moved. She growled threateningly when Amy tried to order her out of the cabin.

While Moore held down the dogs, Amy held scissors, knives, needles threaded with cat-gut, cloths of chloroform, basins of hot water, clean cloths at the ready. Meg pushed an eyeball back into its socket, not that it would ever again be good for seeing. Ears were sewn back together. Several nostrils were stitched up. A torn-open chest was pulled back together, stitched and bandaged, Meg pulling the length of cat-gut thread and knotting it ... just as the dog expired.

The other three survived, as did Teskey, whose lacerations were not deep, thanks to the density of his beaver parka. He was moved from Meg's bed to a cot in the Moore's cabin, then to another abandoned cabin while his dogs healed. He was a quiet man, in his early thirties, used to the silence of mushing the trail from Wrangell and Juneau up the Alaskan coast. He liked to listen to the conversations in Moore's cabin, telling of himself only that he had fled from an orphanage when he was twelve years old. "I truly appreciate your care, ma'am," he said to Meg and repeated it to Amy. "Yous are fine women."

Late January, it was still dark in the morning when Meg rose from her bed and pulled on her thick wool robe to let Yukie out, then put the kettle on the stove. There was a brief knock, then Teskey opened the door and stepped inside.

"Pardon me," he said, "I've just come to thank you and say goodbye."

"But ..." Meg turned her back to adjust her robe.

Suddenly his hand clamped over her mouth and she was forced onto her bed face down.

"Don't be frightened," he said growling into her ear. "You're gonna like this. I'm gonna give it to you every which way. You never felt a cock like this one."

He pinned her down with the weight of his body as he pulled a snot filled hanky from his pocket and stuffed it in her mouth. She choked and gasped for air as he forced her knees up under her and began his every which way. She blanked out briefly when he rolled her over, yanking her by the hair and drove his knuckle into her temple.

"Now you have my seed," Meg heard as she came to. "Consider yourself lucky."

Frantic yelping and scratching continued at the door until Amy and Moore came running, letting Yukie inside. Meg covered her eyes as Yukie whimpered and licked her head.

"I'll get that bastard!" said Moore and set off after him with a team of seven dogs.

But Teskey gave Moore the slip. It was snowing hard enough for his tracks to be covered and he turned off the trail early on, heading for a trapper's cabin far inland where he held up for a few weeks then headed down to Wrangell.

Meg slowly recovered from the internal and external bruising, and the lacerations of dirty fingernails. But the visual memory, the nightmares and the agonizing over what might be the long term consequence of the attack continued to torment her. What if she were pregnant from that man?

Amy was too fearful to speak of it. She hugged Meg tightly and often.

"What matters is that you *live*!" said Amy and urged upon her the potions of their time.

A bottle of hootch and the hottest bath she could endure.

"Jump from the roof into this snow bank," said Amy. "Land hard as you can."

"Mild food poisoning," Amy further suggested. "A piece of this fish ... tomorrow."

Meg smiled wanly. "I know enough about anatomy to know the digestive tract does not supply the reproductive organs. But too little else we know," she lamented. "Far too little else."

Twenty-three interminable mornings, days, and nights later, Meg had a full menstrual period. "I am so *lucky*!" she said out loud and wept. She came out of the outhouse like a person saved. Yukie leapt up on her. Meg took Yukie's front paws and danced with her in the snow.

"I don't think I've ever felt so grateful for, for 'nothing,'" Meg smiled at Amy as she sat in the Moores' cabin, "ever in my entire life."

"It was a terrible thing," said Amy. "Don't be feeling grateful for what was done to you. It's going to be hard for you to trust men. Nor should you. Dogs are better behaved."

"It's certainly been a turning point for Yukie." Meg patted her as she lay near Meg's chair. "She's been keeping me in sight ever since that morning."

"She's not such a pup any more," said Amy. "You've become her pack."

"Yes," said Meg. "I don't feel quite so alone as I did before..."

"It's not safe for a woman to be alone," said Amy. "You know you can sleep in our cabin until you leave for Dawson. And by that time, Yukie will be big enough to protect you. Not that a malamute is ever a good guard dog... the way they go silent as wolves when someone approaches. And they're far too friendly. But Yukie is attached to you now and if anyone comes at you with evil intentions, she would know and her protective instincts would kick in."

"You can't rely on that!" Captain Moore shouted from his chair in the corner. "You should carry a knife, Meg. Out of sight. In your boot or whatnot. Jon Teskey ain't the only crazy man in the world. They should all have their equipment sliced off. I say put them all on that operating table of yours and put your knife to work!"

"Yes! Knife and spear. Harpoon too!" Ike shouted. Enraged out of his rest, he could find no calm since witnessing what Teskey had done to Meg. But witness is all a spirit can do. Had he had a knife and substance at the time, he would have sliced Teskey

into morsels and fed them to the crows. Piji had also flown into
a flurry of ineffectual attack, kicking, gouging with her nails,
yanking, to no real avail. They were two helpless spirits.

As winter passed, Ike fell into depression. Piji thought deeply
then concluded, "Meg should move on. There are more dogs than
ours in need of her services. Ike," she shook his shoulder. "Let us
go with her."

In spring, when the mail boats were resuming, Meg wrote to Deputy
Chief O'Mara

April 29, 1897
My Dear Mick,
It has been a long, dark and difficult winter. I long to hear from you,
but I realize I gave Dawson City as my next address when I wrote to you
in Vancouver. I got waylaid here at Moore's Landing because I fell in love
with a malamute pup and I have to wait until May to take her over the
Chilkoot Pass. The ice is expected to break up on the Yukon River at the
end of the month, which will enable us to take a quick boat ride to Dawson
City. I have heard so much about the challenge of climbing over the Chilk-
oot and then the dangerous rapids beyond, I am not without trepidation
about this journey. But my hosts, Amy and Captain Moore, who have been
like parents to me, assure me that I am fit for the climb and that I will be
in the care of the best of Chilkoot packers and guides. My party is also to
include a young native woman, with the unexpected name of Daisy, who
is likewise knowledgeable about the trail and will be my companion.

I had a terrible experience this winter. I now carry a knife, ready at the
waist, in its own holster. Like a policeman carrying a gun, I like to think.
I was attacked by a musher, Jon Teskey from Wrangell, whose wounds I
tended and whose dogs' lives I had saved.

I had no inkling of the brutal thoughts of this man until he surprised
and attacked me in my cabin. As you said, men can be a "scurvy lot." Yet
there are men like you. I want you to know I treasure and admire you more

than ever. I've gained more understanding of the ugly scenes you must face during the course of your work and how difficult it is to get these scenes out of one's mind, or at least push them aside, to allow for vision of all that is good and beautiful in life.

I am most fortunate to have survived that attack, apparently without long term physical injury. I do fear "pushing my luck" by going up the Chilkoot and facing whatever awaits a lone woman in Dawson City. But I have come this far and I must not give up out of cowardice. I am determined to make it to Dawson City and hope word from you awaits me there. Whatever happens, know that you have my love.

Meg

6

Taking The Chilkoot

MEG MADE IT OVER THE CHILKOOT TRAIL and down the Yukon River to Dawson City at the beginning of June, 1897. She had followed the trail of the legendary wolf, Yukon Sally, with Yukon Sally's namesake pup, and another companion of ancient stock, the very young woman called Daisy.

Upon arrival, Meg and Daisy set up their tent amidst many, many others on the banks of the Yukon and Klondike rivers. Then Meg pushed her way through the crowds, most of whom were heading for the saloons, to find the post office. There was no letter for her but she was informed that only one load of mail had arrived; much more was expected with the arrival of more boats from the northern river route. Meg swallowed her disappointment and returned to their tent where Daisy awaited impatiently. They sold some of Meg's goods, then, cash in hand, went looking for a saloon to eat and drink with other inhabitants of Dawson City.

Meg, being Meg, left the saloon early to get letters done to go out with next morning's mail bag. She wrote first and quickly to O'Mara, urging him to come to Dawson City, if he possibly could, be it on leave, or on holiday. There was indeed a gold rush. She described the routes and how to get outfitted in Vancouver.

After sealing her heartfelt letter to Mick, Meg directed her pen to

Alice and Jacques, describing her journey in some detail so that Alice might be entertained and Jacques would come fully prepared.

June 6, 1897

My dear sister Alice and Jacques,

I have arrived safely in Dawson City! It is now past midnight and we are in full daylight. The sun is shining and it is very warm. I am sitting in my tent with my "wolf," at the door. She has stuck with me, every arduous and dangerous inch of the way. Never ran off once. Such a change in her, from the moment we stepped onto the Chilkoot! Normally when I hiked with her, she would run way ahead of me and off into the woods after the scent of rabbits or any other creature. But once on the Chilkoot, she became my guard dog, would not be separated from me, would let no harm come to me. Even accompanied me when I had to "go behind the bushes."

Tomorrow morning, a river boat will be going downriver to the steamship port in Alaska, carrying the mail from here, along with a lot of very rich men. "Kings of the Klondike," they are called. They have valises full of gold. Yes! Gold nuggets from the size of peas to the size of large eggs. All panned or dug out of the creek beds along the Klondike River. They have been working their claims since last autumn, gathering up loads of gold this spring, and now they are ready for a vacation, a high time of it, down in a real city, namely Seattle and San Francisco.

Dawson City is actually a makeshift settlement of tents and rough wooden buildings quickly erected on streets of mud. Riverboats began to bring in supplies only a few days ago, after the ice on the Yukon River had broken up, allowing me and company to get here as well. Interestingly, they told me the first boat to arrive is called the Alice.

This is very jumbled because I am so rushed to tell you everything, all that I have seen, before the letter gets put in the mail bag. But I have only one urgent message. JACQUES, COME HERE IMMEDIATELY.

Have the foreman take over the management of Clean Sweepers until you return. Alice, you and Jean can oversee him. Jacques can teach you the ropes quickly. Then send him off. Train to Vancouver. Get outfitted and supplies in Vancouver. I will attach a list. Take a steamer up to The Lynn Canal. Make contact there with Captain Moore, who will introduce you to a Chilkoot packer who will guide and carry supplies over the Chilkoot Pass. It is the fastest route. Make sure that you, Jacques, arrange with the packers to have a boat ride ready at the lake on the other side of the Chilkoot to take you to the Yukon River which will then take you quickly to Dawson. I will be here!

I am building a log cabin here as soon as I have sold the items I brought. That will be very soon. I was pestered from the moment I arrived with my three great packs. Brooms are in high demand! Have as large a load as you can transported here by train and then by steamer and boat up the Yukon River. These suddenly rich prospectors will pay up to twenty dollars for a broom. And almost as much for a toothbrush!

There are many dogs here to tend. There are no horses. This is boom town and dream city for the likes of me. And for you, Alice and Jacques, it could be your gold mine. I know there is much more gold to be discovered. You just have to GET HERE AS SOON AS YOU CAN, hike out to the creeks and stake a claim. It can be hard work, the digging and sluicing, but you can do it Jacques. I know you can.

I will tell you now about the Chilkoot Trail so that you, Jacques, will know what to expect. Thanks to Captain Moore I was able to hire the best of packers. Chilkoot Jack, they call him. I tried to use the native names of the Indians but they laughed at my ineptitude and told me to stick to their white nicknames. So I had Chilkoot Jack, and Clem and Tig carrying my loads. Jack is most impressive and handsome. He's a Chilkat chief. All muscle and bone. Very sculptured high cheek bones and nose. Thick dark eyebrows. Almond-shaped eyes. A rather thin moustache and grim mouth. Over winter I had met Jack a few times. He was quite interested in my "medicine man" work with dogs but more important to him was the fact that I followed his advice of practice-hiking on the White Pass trail.

Clem and Tig, who are not taller than me, but a hundred times stronger, have a more ready sense of humour. They did not fully succeed in smuggling their amusement when they first met me in my hiking outfit. From a distance they had figured I was a young man in trousers and jacket, hiking boots and small pack on my back. Then when I spoke in my female voice ... Oh well, they soon got used to me and they had a natural respect for my Yukon Sally who also carried her own small saddlebag pack.

Amy walked with us along the flat shoreline from Moore's landing to Dyea. There we parted tearfully. We had become such good friends. I expect she and the captain will show up in Dawson come winter, if not sooner.

Back to that one-cabin place called Dyea … There waiting to join us was a very striking young girl, lithe as a ballerina, wearing doeskin boots and a light-weight dark wool coat that buttoned down to her knees. It looked serviceable for hiking. Her hair was black and braided, her eyes an unusual ginger colour. She had arrived from Juneau, called herself Daisy, but was known to Chilkoot Jack by an Indian name that translated as "Looks Like a Wolf." She's a curious combination of spunky yet cautious. She told me she's sixteen but I think she's younger than that. She says her father was a prospector who skipped out on her mother, a Tagish woman, when Daisy was eight years old. She went to school in Juneau, "on and off," as she puts it, lived with her mother in a Tagish village for a while then went to work in a saloon in Juneau. She wants to be a singer in Dawson City. She has a beautiful voice. When she sings, Yukie howls in harmony.

Daisy is an agile hiker and a fearless traveller who made me buck up when I was ready to throw in the towel. Thus, Alice, I seem to have acquired another little sister!

The first day was relatively easy going, about ten miles, over sand, stone, some boggy bits and then the quite sparse forest that grows at the base of the mountains. There we were made to camp for the night. I felt up to doing another mile or so but Jack insisted that was far enough for the first day. He wanted us fresh for the beginning of the Chilkoot's ascent next morning. Wise he was!

We had an excellent supper of fried fish we brought from Dyea and sourdough bread that I have learned to make. Our packers slept in their bedrolls out in the open because the night was clear. On other nights they would wryly use the extra tent I brought to sell in Dawson. I say "wryly" because they have a restrained sense of humour towards most everything I carry and the things we women do on this expedition. But they are glad of the tent when it rains, which is often on the Chilkoot! I am glad of the tent always, as some respite from the black flies and mosquitoes that plague the north at this time of year. I extracted a bit of mosquito netting from my pack to drape over my head, secured by my hat when the pests are at their worst in the morning and evening. Daisy also laughs at that. She has somehow become more immune to this plague of the north. But she was glad to sleep in my tent.

So did Yukie, eventually. She began the night by sleeping outside the front flap. But when darkness came, she scratched on the canvas. I untied the flaps. She gave me a lick and settled to sleep in the corner by my feet. Her only problem on that day's hike was getting too hot. She has thrown most of her fur coat for the summer but still, whenever we came to a stream, she would lie belly down in it to get cooled off.

Next morning I moved quickly to complete my ablutions, cook breakfast of tea, bacon, and bread over the fire, wash up in the stream and pack up, as did Daisy. Jack, Clem, and Tig were ready to take off before breakfast. They sat with their backs to us in disgust, or perhaps muted laughter, at how long we scurried about before being ready to depart. We would go behind the bushes. Then I washed hands, face, neck, and underarms in the stream. Daisy followed suit. Then breakfast, which the men consented to join us in. They packed away the tents then waited for us to finish the dishwashing and pack up. The patience of Jack reached its limit when he saw me proceeding to brush my teeth, offering Daisy a toothbrush, and then to comb our hair into place.

"We move. Now!" Jack commanded.

"Let's hit the trail, Meg, Yukie," said Daisy. "The chief is mushing. Let's hike!"

Ah, but it was no hike, that first mile. It was a climb. Suddenly up. Up. Up! The trail was like a steep earth-and-rock staircase, with no landings for respite, as we followed it ever upwards into the unknown. I had no breath to talk. Yukie was panting heavily, trying to get her footing on earth patches as she moved her body upwards and around rocks. I feared it was harder on her limbs than on mine. She faltered sometimes and so did I. So did Daisy. I thought of turning back, before Yukon twisted a leg. We should have taken the White Pass...

"Hey, Chief," Daisy stopped, panting.

Jack turned around. "Keep moving. Not much further. Then flat. Hurts more if stop."

"The chief has spoken," said Daisy to me, then mouthed: "Let's hope he's not a liar!"

"Hike!" shouted Jack when he noticed Yukie about to lie down.

We all hiked. And sure enough. Just beyond our vision, the path that had felt like an endless staircase turned into a great forested landing. We were allowed to rest briefly. Daisy and I sat down gratefully on a log and massaged our groaning knees. Yukon Sally lay down, keeping her eyes alert to everything around. Jack and the others remove their packs only at midday and the end of the day. They sat with their packs on, propped up against a tree, waiting for us to finish our rest. I checked my pocket watch. Jack has no watch but somehow he instinctively limited our rests to fifteen minutes.

We got ourselves up and followed the path, quite soggy at times as we moved upwards through a lush green forest where every kind of leaf was glistening from recent rains and current dampness. Yukon lay down briefly in the cold-water creeks we had to cross, cooling the pads of her feet and her belly. When climbing the initial steep grade, my boots had felt like small boulders to be lifted at each step. Now that I was numbed to that weight, I had to get numbed to the feeling of squishy wet socks from wading through the creeks. I envied Daisy and the packers' lightweight mukluks. She showed me that they have a double layer of insoles for endurance. But you need very strong ankles to operate in those on stony terrain.

We came to another resting place of spectacular beauty where we sat looking across a river to a great drop and a blindingly sparkling white ice field beyond. But thank the Lord, we weren't required to cross that! Our trail went onward and upward through the forest. It had the awesome atmosphere of a cathedral where one is inspired to look upwards and wonder about the creator of all this. Though I realize that is the influence of my Christian upbringing. For in fact cathedrals are built to resemble the natural grandeur of ancient forests and mountains. And one should keep that difference in mind! Every so often I was brought to my knees by stumbling over tree roots and logs upon the trail when looking upwards instead of down. Daisy, who had never been over the Chilkoot but is used to that kind of terrain, got impatient with my exclamations at the wonder of it all.

"Eyes to the ground," she said. "One foot in front of the other. The chief can't carry your pack and you if you break a leg."

At the end of the day, we came to a waist-deep river that had to be forded. Jack went straight into it, clothes, pack, and all, as did Clem and Tig. The campsite for the night was on the other side. Daisy looked at me. "Come on," she said. "Bath time." And waded in.

Jack had removed his pack, ready to wade in to the rescue if necessary. The current looked quite strong. I put the leash on Yukie and led her in with me. I had seen her swim back at Moore's, in the canal, but I had never seen her swim like this! She pulled ahead going at full force and led me to the other side. Jack gave her a rare nod of approval as she emerged and shook the water from her soaking coat. Then she lay down where we were setting up the tents and fell promptly asleep. Just as Daisy and I wanted to do, but we had to get out of wet clothes, into our alternative set, hang up the wet stuff on branches and stagger around preparing bacon, beans, and tea over the fire Jack had built.

The men didn't bother to change their clothes; in fact, had not brought a change of clothes. They dried themselves by the fire, ate quickly, and disappeared into their tent.

"Jack says it will rain tonight," said Daisy.

I cared not. Got into my bedroll and fell to sleep. Woke up to a nightmare of thunder and lightning, with Yukie lying at my feet and a pile of damp clothes being tossed into our tent by Clem who said something grumpy then closed the flap of our tent. The rain pelted through the trees to the ground, faster and harder than the soil could absorb, forming rivulets and puddles round our tent. I then appreciated why Clem had our tent positioned on the higher ground on top of a platform of pine branches. But then the rain accumulated in the sags of our tent's roof and seeped through in drops upon our bedrolls and faces. A rude awakening! Daisy and I sat up, reached up and heaved the pools of rain out of the sag of the tent and fell back asleep. Until it had to be done again.

In the morning we were roused by the voices of our men and the welcome sound of a crackling fire. "Good men!" said Daisy with a smile.

I certainly agreed. I learned to rely upon them as quite uncannily know-ing and capable. They did not concern themselves much with cleanliness while on the trail. But in that too I learned to follow suit, shortening my morning ablutions to a splash of water on the face, a brushing of teeth. Yukie seemed well rested, eager to hit the trail.

The third day was more of the same, putting one foot in front of the other, again and again. That is all one had to do. But the incline was getting gradually steeper as we moved away from the riverbed and up the rocky trail of a canyon. Up and then down. Up and down and then up again, we trudged upon that trail. I can think of no other word but trudge. The ache in my upper legs as I lifted my feet up and then the surprising shakiness and pain at the knees when I moved downwards was repeated again and again. I looked up at the long steep trail ahead and feared I couldn't make it. I was panting heavily, sometimes gripping rocks desper-ately while Daisy seemed to move surely as a mountain goat. She saw the grim look on my face.

"You're fighting the mountain," she said. "It's not your enemy. Talk to it."

"I can't talk," I gasped, "to anything!" I sat down.

"There!" she said. "It has you in its lap. Relax. It won't throw you off. Just keep your footing and lean into it. Embrace and talk to it in your mind."

What bull, I thought. What nonsense! But the more I thought about it and tried to apply it, the more it worked. Tension and fear had been sap-ping my energy. If I just kept putting one foot in front of the other, eyes on the trail just in front of my feet, relax, repeat, accept the trail as friend, not enemy to be conquered ... it worked! Try it, Jacques. Embrace the mountain and keep a steady pace.

We came to a resting place where we could see above the treeline all the mountain peaks on either side of the Chilkoot Pass summit. They are enormous, dark grey rock peaks, with snow and ice spreading down their crevasses into canyons. The pass itself did not look formidably steep from that distance. It was alluring against the blue sky in the sunny afternoon. I definitely wanted to go up and over it.

"How about you?" I said to Yukie, who was lying panting on the rocky

ground. "You up to it?" She sighed and closed her eyes. Not a moment of rest was to be wasted in stupid talk.

"Tomorrow," said Jack, "we go over summit."

Daisy spoke with him in Chilkoot then said to me. "Another couple of hours then we camp for the night. We should have a long sleep and rise early to make the summit at midday. Those rocks don't look bad from here. But they are. They'll be hardest for Yukie. Dogs have broken legs and died, trying to do that pass."

"I'll look after her," I said. "Right Yukie?" She rose and walked ahead of me.

It was easy going from there to the camp site, the trail winding through brush and trees that grew shorter, thinner, and sparser, but still there was plenty of foliage, including wild geraniums. We saw mountain sheep and goats clambering around on the rocks in the distant heights. We had not heard the call of wolves since the first night on the trail.

"I guess they know better than to come this high up," I said to Yukie after we had finished our dinner of smoked salmon and beans, washed down with mugs of black sweetened tea. Yukie sat up on her haunches and gave a sharp howl. I howled in response. Daisy began to sing.

"That'll keep the grizzlies off our trail," said Clem to the other men.

Jack got up, signalling it was time to get some sleep.

We were up and on the trail at 5 a.m. There was extra determination in our limbs as we climbed up and up beyond the tree line. When we came to an ancient avalanche of mountain boulders, Jack took up the position in front of Yukie, who was in front of me, so that he could show the precise footing on the narrow trail winding around the rocks and boulders. We reached a plateau where, looking upwards, we could see the narrow rocky pass which crawls over the summit of the Chilkoot Pass.

Then suddenly, there was a great creeping chill to the air and a blinding fog moved in. There was nothing for it but to draw close as possible together and keep moving up and up the trail, now treacherously slippery. I could hear Yukie's claws scratching on the rocks trying to maintain her footing. I was literally on her tail, ready to steady her when she faltered. Jack took my pack so that I could be more agile. Clem had Yukie's.

It seemed an eternity but we did get through the fog. Then the trick for *me, was never, never to look back down the trail. It was dizzyingly steep. "Eyes front!" Daisy shouted at me from close behind when she saw the panic in my glance.*

There was one more plateau where Jack made us stop to rest and drink cold tea from the canteen. Yukie slurped from a small puddle, lying flat on her belly in front of it.

And then there was what was actually named The Staircase. A steep rocky vertical to the summit, with no railing to cling to or help you up. Sometimes Daisy and I were on all fours like Yukie. I so feared that she would twist a limb or I would. We did not. We climbed that wretched thing for an hour. Nice mountain, I made my mind say, thank you for this stair- case. We reached the top and literally fell upon the summit in a pelting, freezing rain. But who cared about being soaking wet. We had made it!

"Brave dog. Strong women," Jack congratulated us.

"Great Chief. Strong men," I said to them.

Daisy looked at me as she sometimes did when I talked too affection- ately to Yukie. Then she said something in Chilkoot to the men that made them laugh, but she wouldn't tell me what she had said.

As in the maxim in life, one does not stay at the top for long. Storms of wind, rain, sleet or snow, even in summer, can come whipping up out of the blue. Or so we were warned by Jack. We rested and sheltered under a rocky overhang until the heat generated by that last desperate, vertical climb began to dissipate and I felt shivery. The rain ceased and winds began to push fog around the mountain top. "Hike!" said Jack, waking Yukie and stirring the rest of us to rise and take up our packs. "We go down now. Camp. Rest by lake."

And thus we moved on. Down the winding rocky trail. The fog was swept away and we could see in sunlight the most spectacular view of gorges with glacial snow. Farther down were flowing streams and then the calm sparkling turquoise lake where we could rest and sleep. The lure of that helped take our minds off the ache and shakiness in our legs as they accustomed themselves to descending rather than climbing.

There now! I have described the most difficult part of the long journey to the gold fields of the Klondike. The rest of the route is downhill, all the way to a long narrow lake known as Lindeman. It is twenty-six miles in all, from the beginning of the Chilkoot Trail at Dyea to the point of embarkment at Lake Lindeman, but it feels more like a hundred miles climbing up over the treacherous Chilkoot Pass. Once over the Pass and safely camped in a sheltered place for the night, we all fell quickly into the deep sleep of exhaustion. I slept the other way round in our tent so I could put my arm around Yukie and tell her how proud I was of her for making it over the Chilkoot. She was so tired she didn't stir. But Daisy did.

"Know what your name would be in Tagish?" she said. "Sleeps With Dogs."

Yikes! Just looked at my watch. I must conclude soon or I shall miss the outgoing mail.

We could hike at a more leisurely pace on our last day and night before reaching the shore of Lake Lindeman, which we did, next afternoon. There waiting for us, was a wooden boat, the size of a small lifeboat, plus two Tagish river guides to man it. Tagish Wally and Joe, they introduced themselves. They were well known to Jack and Co., who conversed easily with them. The Tlingit Chilkat have their own language but can make themselves understood to the Tagish and vice versa. I shook hands with them as I had with Jack and Co. Daisy kept her hands to herself as is her custom with her mother's people. Like the others, our Tagish guides were startled then amused at shaking hands with a white woman. Jack then said something to them that further amused them but also seemed to reassure them that I was all right to do business with.

It was a warm sunny day. "We swim," Jack announced but stood motionless.

Daisy and I looked at each other. We too wanted to swim, were desperate for any kind of bath and clean underclothes. "Translation," said Daisy, considering Jack's announcement. "We are invited to clear the scene, or join them."

I started walking to another part of the lake's shore.

"I knew you would do that," said Daisy, following, with annoyance. "Sleeps With Dogs," she muttered. "Won't swim with men."

We stripped, crouched behind some fallen trees and ran with a dive into the shockingly cold water. The ice had not completely disappeared from it. That was our first and our last bath before reaching Dawson City. I tell you of this because I want you and everyone to know what perfect gentlemen these Indian men are, in my experience.

I felt sad to part from Chilkoot Jack and Clem and Tig. I shook their hands again, taking Jack's hand in both of mine, thanking him profusely. He suddenly picked me up, carried me over to the boat and set me down in it. Yukie leapt into the boat and sat down in front of me. Daisy shook her head at my behaviour. She raised her hand in a formal salute of thanks and goodbye and got into the boat. We set off across the long, smooth, turquoise blue lake. Chilkoot Jack, Clem, and Tig walked back up into the mountains.

Yukie settled down with her innate good sense to enjoy this restful part of the journey with Wally and Joe rowing us expertly along Lake Lindeman towards the wider Lake Bennett. The water was turquoise blue, serene. Only the sound of the oars dipping. The shores were forested with thin pine trees and white birches, the mountains forming the horizon in every direction. They were lower and more rounded as we made our way farther into the interior north of this great land.

I wish I had time to tell you how expert our oarsmen were as they took us through the rapids between the lakes and then the really treacherous rapids on the Yukon River, where narrow canyons might have bashed us to smithereens. Daisy loved it. Shouted with glee. Yukie and I, partly tethered to the helm, crouched silent as wolves, braced with all our might. And we all came through, thanks to Tagish Wally and Joe, and floated easily three days downriver to the junction of the Klondike, amazed to find that hundreds of others had already made it to Dawson City. And they say hundreds more are coming. Make sure, Jacques, that you are among them. Hurry!

Attached is the list of essentials to be brought from Vancouver. Any extra quantities will be easily, profitably sold here.

With love to you, dear Alice and Jacques and darling little George, Victoria and Herbie. I long to hug you, each and all.

Auntie Meg

SUPPLIES
Food: flour, oatmeal, rice, beans, coffee, tea, baking powder, soda,

yeast cakes, salt, pepper, bacon, dried fish and meat, evaporated fruit and
onions and potatoes, root vegetables, canned butter

Clothes: rubber boots, leather boots, fur parka and mitts, gloves, sev-
eral pairs wool socks, flannel underwear, thick shirts, trousers and jacket.

Tent, mosquito netting, blankets, shovel, gold pan, cooking utensils,
candles, matches.

It was not until the last week of July that this letter was delivered to
Alice. It was a warm but cloudy day in Halifax. The line full of diapers and children's clothes hung still damp outside the house. The
sudden shower in late morning had soaked them just when they were
almost dry enough to bring in. A day like so many others in the current life of Alice.

She sat, reflecting upon the letter, in the leather chair that used
to be Randolph's, then Meg's. But now it was occupied, like the
house, by her, Alice. She had begun to worry about Meg, not hearing from her in so long. But wouldn't you know it … all that money
Jean Atkins had sent to Meg in Vancouver had turned into another
lucky investment. Everything Meg did paid off. She always turned
up in the right place at the right time. And hooked up with the most
prosperous people. Randolph. And now she was with hundreds of
men carrying around valises of gold. Kings of the Klondike, no less!
Alice re-read the opening and closing paragraphs. The rest was tiresome detail of hiking with one pampered dog and some rather smelly
Indians. Ugh!

The news of a major gold strike in the Yukon was no secret. Tele-
grams and headlines had been proclaiming that news across the continent since July 19, when a second ship loaded with a ton of gold from
the Klondike had landed in Seattle. It was the talk of everyone ever
since. Jacques, like every man of little consequence, had thought of
running off to the Klondike. But as she had pointed out to him, it was
a barefaced excuse to abandon his responsibilities and give in to the
bottle, far from home. She refrained from telling him that with his
luck and general weakness of character, by the time he reached the

gold fields they would all be owned and prospering for others. No, she had refused to permit him to join the great herd of failures, rushing off to the Klondike.

But this letter changed her thinking. It was full of practical instructions. The route described, directions given, list of provisions included. It sounded remarkably easy, if you got better guides. You could probably pay to be carried over the pass on a chair, like Cleopatra. Alice smiled at the image of herself as Cleopatra. Then wrinkled her nose. Those Indian guides sounded too like grunting pigs. Surely better could be found.

Why is she requesting Jacques, and not me? Alice smacked the letter down. Why am I always thought to be of so little account? Alice had half a mind to tear up the letter in anger. But the other half led her to fold and put it away in the desk drawer. Locked. Until she decided what to do about it.

7

INHABITANTS OF DAWSON CITY

"What a ride!" Piji had exclaimed when they landed in Dawson with Meg. "Made me feel alive again, like the good old days, mushing dangerous trails with our wolves."

"Me too," said Ike. "But look what's happened to our best trading grounds! It's the worst-looking city I've ever seen. I didn't bring Meg all this way to see this! Look at all these mangy dogs. They're a disgrace!*" Ike led Piji, flying about town, whooshing around alleys and taverns, crowded with people and dogs laying about or staggering around the streets.* "This is what happens when you bring our wolves to the city!" *Ike howled. He hung his head in defeat, concluding, "Meg won't stay. It's too disgusting. She'll go back to Halifax, marry Mick in Boston. Anywhere is better than this!"*

"You have the eyes of a man," said Piji. "Meg's a woman. She'll want to clean this up."

But Piji couldn't be sure and she hovered anxiously with Ike watching over Meg's arrival in Dawson City.

DAISY AND MEG had set up their tent amidst the many others who arrived after the ice breakup. It was a tight maze of hundreds of weather-beaten canvas tents, hastily erected along the banks of the Yukon and Klondike rivers, with hundreds of small boats banging against each other, tied to the shore. Flat-bottom rowboats, canoes, dugouts, rafts, all rough hewn. Meg could see men passed out from celebrating, snoring open-mouthed in the boats. On her disappointing trek to the post office Meg had seen men and dogs flopped and sleeping on the streets of Dawson. The streets themselves were arranged in orderly numbered avenues running parallel to Front Street on the embankment. The construction of wooden buildings was going on night and day, because it could with the sun providing nearly twenty-four hours of lighting. Along with noise of banging and sawing, people shouting and singing, dogs howling and barking also went on all night. And there was the frequent ringing of a bell. Not a church or school bell, but a ship's bell, rang outside a saloon any time a miner whacked his poke of gold on the bar and shouted, "Free drinks! All around!"

While putting up their tent, Meg and Daisy had been surrounded by curious onlookers. All of them men, prospectors, the kind of men Daisy was used to.

"You men have money?" Daisy had said to them. "This lady," she pointed to Meg, "has things to sell. And I do mean things. Combs, soap, toothbrushes. You look like you could use some."

Meg handled the business end of selling the supplies she unpacked from their bundles and Daisy was not shy of soliciting the business. When Meg's money belt was full to bursting, she called a halt to Daisy's soliciting. "Let's go buy the best dinner we can find," she said as they tidied up their appearance inside the tent.

Daisy had combed her braids out, tied her hair becomingly with a pale blue ribbon and donned a clean white blouse borrowed from Meg. She refused to do up the high neck buttons of the blouse, letting

the frilled collar fall lightly on her neckline. She exchanged her moccasins for a pair of heeled ladies' boots from her own pack. Meg also
wore a wrinkled but clean white blouse, cinched her skirt, and put on
more daintily heeled boots.

"You're very pretty," said Meg as they made their way to Front
Street.

"I know," said Daisy. "But I usually hear that from men."

She was more than at ease with the men around until suddenly she
tugged on Meg's sleeve. "Look out! Some dude's following us. Never
seen one like that." She drew closer to Meg. Meg looked over her
shoulder and saw the red coat Mountie approach them. She turned
and stood smiling at him. Daisy stood cautious and suspicious.

"Hello," said Meg. "How nice to meet a policeman!"

"Constable Wiggins at your service, ladies." He tipped his hat to
each of them. "Handsome dog." He put his hand out for Yukie to
sniff.

"This is Yukon Sally. Answers to Yukie or Yukon. I am Meg Oliphant. And this is my young friend, Daisy Ritter."

Yukie proffered her paw in the same motion she used for scratching on doors. Daisy offered her hand to be shaken by the Mountie
because Meg had and signalled that she should, but Daisy did so in
silence.

"You've arrived at a raucous time in Dawson City," said Constable
Wiggins. "The first supply boats of the season have come in, with
more drink than food. As you can hear."

They heard another gong of a bell and the call: "Drinks all
around"

Wiggins explained that Dawson was full of prospectors on a spree.
Those who had spent the previous months extracting gold from their
claims, by the shovelful, the panful, the sluiceful, and the handful,
were ready to do some spending. "And you ladies?" inquired Wiggins.

"Looking for a square meal," said Meg.

"Song and dance," said Daisy firmly.

"Food first?" Meg looked to Daisy for concurrence.

Daisy conceded with a nod.

"Allow me to escort you to The Pioneer," said Wiggins.

Meg held up her skirt as she stepped over dog turds, tobacco wrappers, sticks, and mud holes. Daisy's skirt was already well above her ankles but she held it yet higher.

"May I handle your malamute for you?" asked Wiggins. "We have two good teams of these at headquarters. But we're always in need of more. Are you willing to sell?"

"Oh no!" said Meg. "Not my Yukon Sally." Though she let Wiggins handle her.

"Keep a close watch on her then," said Wiggins. "She's worth a good two hundred and fifty dollars these days in Dawson. And prices aren't going down."

"How much is a woman worth?" said Daisy.

"Daisy!" Meg then turned to Wiggins. "She's just kidding. Daisy is a wonderful singer. Has a most unusual voice, high soprano. You want a job as a singer, don't you, Daisy?"

"That I do," she said and walked ahead.

"And you, Miss Oliphant? Are you seeking work?"

"It's Mrs., actually. I'm a widow. But do call me Meg. And yes, you bet I'm seeking work. And I think I've found it. *Look* at all these poor dogs!" A tired, mangy team of dogs, with various colour and markings, pulled a wagon across their path. Dogs were hitched to wooden posts, some were sleeping from heat exhaustion on the street. They all resembled wolves in their formation, their ears, eyes, faces, their basic colouring and size. But they carried their tails, when relaxed, high and curled, or plumed like a malamute's. "I think some of these hard-working dogs need tending," Meg said to Wiggins. "I am a dog doctor."

Wiggins started to laugh but then politely suppressed it. "Pardon me." He cleared his throat. "I had you figured for a school ma'am. And I must tell you, there is no school yet in Dawson City. But dogs there are!" They had to step around another sleeping dog. Yukie stepped carefully along, not straining on her leash, keeping her chin up, highly alert in this new situation. "Please tell me about your work," Wiggins continued. "Inspector Constantine will be glad to hear we have a doctor of any species."

Meg explained her mission as Wiggins made way for them through the throngs moving in and out of the few saloons and stores. Men staggered to and from outhouses, spit on the ground, snorted and blew snot from their noses, leaned up against the buildings and posts, or slumped on the bench outside Ladue's mining and building supplies store. Some slept and snored on out-of-use dogsleds. But all who were awake enough to see Wiggins leading the regal-looking malamute and the two new ladies in town, drew to attention and doffed their hats to them.

It was hard to figure these two new women. They did not look like the leather-skinned wives who accompanied miners this far north. And they did not have the look of the dance hall hurdy-gurdies who had come from Circle City and beyond. They were both tall, not dainty-looking, and had pretty good figures. Dressed alike but had completely different colouring and the younger one had a certain waifishness about her. The older one kept an eye on her like a big sister. Some men stood up and whistled at them.

"Take it easy, boys!" Wiggins turned to them as he stepped up onto the wooden platform in front of The Pioneer Saloon. "This is Doctor Meg Oliphant from the city of Halifax and this here is her prize malamute, Yukon Sally. So, now you all know who this malamute belongs to, should she get away. And this here is Miss Daisy Ritter, a fine … What did you say?" He turned to Meg. "Oh yes, a fine soprano singer. They'll be building a residence here in Dawson. Good evening to you all." Wiggins tipped his hat.

Daisy, then Meg, waved politely to all the men standing and lurching around.

"Is this what city means?" Daisy whispered to Meg. "Hundreds of drunks and not enough saloons?"

Outside it was sunny and bright. Inside, The Pioneer, dark from lack of windows, was crowded with men drinking whisky and smoking cigars, roaring with men bragging, laughing, deriding, scoffing, laying wagers, and telling jokes. The odours of cigars, whisky, sweaty clothes, greasy hair, kerosene lamps, and farts blended into one gaseous smell. It overwhelmed Meg and Daisy as they stood in the doorway, eyes adjusting to the darkness. There were only a half-dozen tables and chairs, rough hewn and primitively assembled from thin logs. No table cloths. An apparent shortage of glasses and dishes. Men were drinking from tin mugs. There was a great shortage of women.

The one woman in dance hall attire of red satin with black ruffles caterpillaring over her breasts and shoulders, looked up from leaning upon the shoulders of a man at a table and scrutinized the appearance of Daisy and Meg. Close to the doorway sat two women in modest, closely buttoned dresses, no hats or jewellery. They had been chatting with each other while the several men at the table bantered amongst themselves. The men stopped talking and stood up as Constable Wiggins led Meg and Daisy to their table. Chairs were offered to Meg and Daisy.

"Mrs. Berry. Mrs. Lippy." Wiggins tipped his hat to each of the ladies and then to their husbands on either side of them. "Clarence. Tom. May I introduce these two newcomer ladies to your table? Dr. Meg Oliphant and Daisy Ritter. The Berrys and the Lippys. Two Kings of the Klondike, I might add." Wiggins then stood at perfect attention. "And now, if you'll excuse me, I'll return to my duties. Dr. Meg and Miss Daisy ... if you would please make yourself known to Inspector Constantine tomorrow. He keeps a register of each and every citizen of this fair city."

"I'm Salome Lippy. Welcome to the Klondike." She extended her hand, which was rough, wrinkled, and reddened. Her face was young, friendly, and weather-beaten, as was Mrs. Berry's.

"And I'm Ethel Berry." She shook Daisy's then Meg's hand. "Sit down, shall we? Are you hungry? Clarence, we must order something for these newcomers. When did you arrive? How did you get here?" She paused. "Excuse me. I'm afraid I've lost my civilized manners. Salome and I have been here for two years. Roughing it in the gold fields. Quite an experience. Wouldn't you say, Salome?"

"I'll say! And I'll say I'm looking forward to hot baths, a big bed with a mattress, oranges, fresh eggs, city lights, a horse and carriage ..."

"We're departing for the Outside, tomorrow morning," said Ethel Berry. "We shall set sail for Seattle and the comforts of modern life. Do you know," she turned to pat her husband's arm, "that I was literally dragged here, as a young bride? Not at all kicking and screaming, let me tell you. It was the greatest adventure of my life. My dear Clarence pulled me over the mountains on a sled." She sat back, momentarily beaming. "Over the Chilkoot, no less. In the middle of winter. That was our honeymoon. Now tell us, you must be adventurous women. How did you get here?"

They invited Meg and Daisy to have their first meal in Dawson "on them" while they shared their stories. A meal taken from cans of corned beef, peas, and potatoes, heated up in a frying pan and served with a pot of tea.

"Pretty bad for the price, isn't it?" said Ethel. "But we would have paid anything for a meal like this last winter. It wasn't to be had. We lived on porridge, sourdough bread, and whatever fish or game we could buy from the Indians. Our men kept on digging up gold in those wretched tunnels. I had nightmares about us dying of scurvy while locked in a gold vault. Which was not far from the truth." Ethel suddenly clamped her mouth and turned to Salome.

"Our son died of scurvy," said Salome and looked stonily ahead while Ethel put her arm around her. "I'm so sorry, Sal. I didn't mean to remind you ..."

"We're sorry too," said Meg and prodded Ethel to go on about their lives in a log hut with a sod roof and earth floor. Ethel described the plank table, the two seats carved from tree stumps, the plank bench, and wooden platform with cloth-stuffed mattress for their bed that were the furnishings, only a pot-bellied stove for heat. No windows. Light came from candles and a lantern or the opened door.

"I had a can full of nuggets to pay Clarence's helpers and buy anything I wanted," said Ethel. "But soon there was nothing to buy. Ladue's store ran out of soap for doing laundry. He never did sell a book, or stationery for writing home, wool for knitting, anything that would have helped us keep our sanity over the dark winter months. Sal's cabin was a half mile upstream but we visited back and forth, be it forty below or not, didn't we Sal? We read each other's books over and over again, till we could recite them by heart. Want to hear me recite *Huckleberry Finn*?" Ethel laughed. "I thought not. But don't get me wrong. I'm not complaining. We had our love to keep us warm, in the coldest of times, didn't we Clarence?"

Daisy ate hungrily and listened intently but would not be drawn into the conversation.

"Do you know someone who goes by the name of Finn?" asked Meg.

"Poor Finn?" said Tom Lippy. "That's what he goes by here. Never seen a fella who gets more shafted than him. Poor beggar. There's Lucky Swede who strikes it rich with no effort at all and then there's Poor Finn... combing the creeks with his dogs, having to sell them off one by one. 'Course he blows what he has on booze."

"He got put through the wringer by that woman he brought here," said Salome. "She's a bad sort."

"What's that mean?" Daisy suddenly spoke. "Do you think she's a whore?"

"Daisy!" Meg looked askance at her.

"We don't use that word around here, dear," said Ethel kindly. "Inspector Constantine dealt with her case. He could tell you the circumstances. We only know that she charged Poor Finn with assault, wanted money from him, wanted him in jail."

"She's a dancer," said Meg, "I know her. Mad Mitzi Bonaparte. Where is she?"

Clarence laughed. "She's everywhere. Probably over at Joe Ash's. The Northern Saloon. He's got the only piano in town. Wouldn't be surprised if she's right there dancing on top of it. And my friend Anton paying for her drinks."

"Anton who?" said Meg. "Not Anton Stander?"

Everyone stared at her.

"I met Anton Stander in Vancouver." said Meg, taking some tea to divert attention. "Also Mitzi and Finn. How has Anton fared?"

"He partnered with me," said Clarence. "He too struck it rich."

"Another Klondike King," said Ethel, looking sensitively at Meg.

"Were you very good friends? Shall we try to find him and tell him you're here?"

"Is he too leaving with you, tomorrow?"

"No. Not Anton. He won't take a vacation. He's too … involved … here." Ethel looked at Salome, then both looked away, anywhere, to the moose heads looking down at them from the walls of the saloon.

"Works hard, plays hard, does our Anton," said Clarence. "He just came into town to celebrate the arrival of the *Alice*. He'll be going back to the creeks tomorrow."

"Speaking of 'Alice'…" Meg abruptly changed the subject, not wanting to be seen as chasing after Anton, the Klondike King. If he were interested, he could find her. "I have a sister who's name is Alice. I must write to her tonight if there's a boat going out tomorrow with the mail." She stood up. "It's been a great pleasure meeting you and we thank you most heartily for the meal. We'll see you when you come back from The Outside?" Meg smiled.

"Indeed. Our pleasure." The Berrys and Lippys stood up.

"Daisy?" said Meg.

"I don't have no letters to write," said Daisy. "I'm going to go find that saloon with the piano." Daisy did not return to the tent that night.

Next morning, with the letters she had spent the night writing to Mick, Alice and Jacques, in hand, Meg followed Yukie on the lead as they made their way amongst the tents, towards the makeshift docks where the *Portus B. Weare*, a sternwheeler, was being loaded for its trip back down the Yukon to St. Michael's in Alaska. The *Alice* had left days earlier. The "docks" were heavy planks propped from the river bank up onto the boat's gunnels. The captain, a burly man, stood at the centre of the ship's upper deck railing, observing the commotion.

A throng of men were trying to walk steadily from the Dawson saloons to the docks. They swaggered with their bodies full of whisky and their luggage full of gold. Some dance hall girls accompanied them. They were a merry and noisy bunch, arousing dogs from various quarters, who howled or barked at their singing. Yukie yanked on her leash, trying to get to every dog she saw or heard. In the background was the constant sound of Dawson City, the sawing of lumber, the hammering of nails into boards, the shouting of orders to men and dogs.

"Hey, Meg!" Daisy called from the crowd. She raised one arm to Meg, the other was holding onto a prospector in shirt, breeches, and a new bowler hat. "You missed a good party."

"Yes, Daisy. I can see that. But I haven't missed the mail boat, have I?" She held her letters up, waving them at the captain. He tipped his cap, beckoning her to come aboard.

Back in their tent, Daisy was fending off Yukie who wanted to know, by sniffing, where she had been and with whom. "Look at this!" Daisy pulled out a pouch full of gold dust and nuggets. "Just look at it! Real gold. These miners have so much, they don't know what to do with it. They lay it at your feet for a song. Pour it down your titties for a dance. Put nuggets in your bloomers if you show them ..."

"Daisy, you *didn't*!" Meg folded her arms firmly and frowned like a mother.

Daisy looked sideways at Meg, removed her blouse and skirt, then in camisole and bloomers sat down on her bedroll to unlace her boots. "No, ma'am. Daisy did not. But your friend Mitzi did."

Meg sat down on her own bedroll. Then lay down on it and stared at the tent ceiling.

"Don't you want to hear more?" said Daisy.

Meg rolled over to face Daisy. "What exactly was your job at the saloon in Juneau?"

"Singing and bedding with the boss."

"Why did you leave?"

"Because I hated the boss. Hated what he made me do."

"How old are you, really, Daisy?"

"About a hundred and fourteen compared to you."

"Daisy!"

"Will you quit Daisying me! You sound like my father and I hate him most of all. I'm not half as dumb as you think I am. I learn fast. You know that? I listen and I watch and I learn." She wiped the dirt off her boots and began to shine them with the hem of Meg's skirt.

"I think," said Meg carefully, "I *know,* that you are very smart. What did you learn tonight?"

"That I can get rich here, just by singin' and pretendin' to be prim as them wives. You know I got more gold by keeping my blouse done up than Mitzi did by dancin' in her bloomers." Daisy hiccupped and broke into laughter. "You shoulda seen it. There she was, rakin' in a dollar a dance. Same as me. Can you believe it? They'll pay a dollar just to have one dance with you. 'Course, you have to encourage them to buy a lot of drinks from Joe Ash at the bar. He bein' the owner and all. But Mitzi, she wants more. She wants that friend of yours. Anton what's-his-name. He's drunk as a skunk already. And she gets him drunker. Wants his whole poke. You can tell that. So she throws back her head, lets all those blonde curls fall loose, steps back and out of her skirt. And does a dance for all, in her bloomers. Back in Juneau, that would be nothin' new. The boss made the women strut around in their bloomers. Brought more business. But here in Dawson it's different. In comes that chief of what you call them? Mounties. He comes stompin' into the saloon. Bellows: '*No bloomers in Dawson!* Fine of $100 or ten days in the clinker. Which will it be?'"

"What did she do then?" Meg asked. "Mad Mitzi."

"Your Anton paid the fine for her and Joe Ash kicked them both out. Bein' as that chief Mountie threatened to fine Joe Ash if bloomers was ever shown in his saloon again." Daisy put her head down onto her pillow of clothes. "I'm real tired from all the learnin' I did today." She yawned so long her hiccups stopped. "I got enough money to buy anything I want. And I don't have to suck anybody's anything. I'm gonna buy silk dresses. How about a pink one for you, Mother Meg?"

"Thank you, Daisy, but I don't need more dresses. And I'm worried about what could happen to you. Men can be dangerous. They can take you by surprise and . . . ruin you."

"Ruin me!" Daisy laughed without mirth. "What do you mean by that? You ever been ruined?"

"Came very close, once," said Meg. "Wouldn't want that to happen to you."

"You talk clear as fog," Daisy flung her arm as she rolled over. "I ain't been killed. And it seems I aren't ever goin' to be sent away with a baby. So stop worrying about me. I know when to carry a knife, just like you. Except I got the sense to keep it outa sight, in my bloomers. That's all I got to say tonight."

It was late afternoon when Yukon Sally roused Meg and Daisy by licking their faces and yelping sharply. "Oooow!" Daisy put her hands to her head.

"How's the head, Daisy girl?" said Meg.

"Feels like a woodpecker's trying to get inside it for worms."

"That bad? Come on." Meg extracted herself from her bedroll. "I have the perfect remedy. A bath. You'll feel much better after a soak in a tub. There's bound to be a bath house in Dawson City."

The bath house was a tent erected over a foundation of logs chinked with mud. A sign was hinged to a pole extending over the doorway and another painted onto the tent.

Mrs. Molly Doyle's LAUNDRY & BATH
FORTUNES TOLD $1.

Rope lines of men's shirts, undershirts, under drawers, long johns, and socks were strung out on either side of the tent. Wooden rain barrels and tin pails stood against the log walls. A woman with faded red hair wearing a brightly patterned cotton dress, itself in need of laundering, sat on a wooden bench pulled across the doorway. She looked up from resting her head in her hands as Yukie sprinted towards her.

"*Git!*" She flailed her arms. "No dogs allowed. People only in my tubs."

Meg pulled Yukie back. "She'll stay outside. We'd like to have a bath, Mrs. Doyle. How much is it, please?"

"Well now! Aren't you the polite one! You must be the two new women in town. Dr. Elephant is it? And the singer?" She looked Daisy over. "Heard you sound like something between a wolf and a lark. Heard you're right light on your feet too. Had the miners falling all over you. Heard you made that Mad Mitzi look like the tramp she is."

"I didn't do anything to her."

"Sure an' I will, if she ever comes round here again. You two want one bath or two?"

"One bath each, please," said Meg.

"That'll cost you $5 each and that's for fifteen minutes in the tub. Not a second more."

"Whoa! That's expensive!" said Meg.

"So is clean water. And it costs me twenty-five cents a pail. That's without heating it up. You want hot water?"

"Warm will do."

"Right then. Come back at 8:30."

"But we were hoping to have a bath now."

"You and everyone else. The earliest opening is 8:30 this evening. Take it or leave it."

"We'll take it," said Daisy.

"That's 8:30 to 8:45 and no one but you two in the tubs. Don't think you can pull a Mitzi on me."

"What's a Mitzi?"

"She booked the tubs for an hour, for herself and a friend. The 'friend' turned out to be several men . . . to whom she gave . . . shall we say 'personal baths.' I bet she earned more in that one hour than I earn in a month."

"Where were you?"

"I was fool enough to take her at her word and go do some errands. Left my water boy in charge." Molly snorted. "She gave *him* a good tip."

"And probably an eyeful," said Daisy.

"Couldn't believe she'd do it," said Molly. "Sure an' I wouldn't. Some of them miners are dirty as chimney sweeps. I tell 'em to jump in the river before they use my tubs."

"Wooden tubs!" Meg exclaimed when she saw them. "I thought they would be tin."

"I got tin ones on order," said Molly. "Don't worry. I scrubbed them down for you. You being a doctor and all."

"What's the matter with wooden tubs?" said Daisy as they sat in their lukewarm baths.

"Germs," said Meg. "Other people's germs lodged in the cracks and crannies."

"Other people's germs?" Daisy squirmed in her tub. "Is that like worms?"

"Yes." Meg laughed. "Good analogy. But they're so small they're invisible."

Daisy stood up. "Would you quit using such big words! I'm getting out of here. I want my money back."

"Settle down in there!" Molly shouted through the cracks of the door. "Nobody gets their money back. And nobody gets the clap from my tubs."

"The *clap*! I know what that is!" Daisy was out of the tub reaching for a towel.

"Daisy," said Meg. "Believe me. You don't get disease from clean water."

"How clean is this water?" Daisy demanded of Molly.

"Fresh as a daisy." Molly laughed. "You can trust me. And your dog doctor."

Daisy got back in the tub with a groan. "I hate that," she whispered to Meg. "I had a stupid school teacher who kept saying that. 'Fresh as a Daisy.'"

"And furthermore," said Molly loudly through the cracks, "you can learn more from me than from any school. I've been around. And around longer than all you others who come here with no husbands.

And I've paid for my sins. Got the scars to prove it. But I also got my own sense of honour. I don't lie, steal, or spread disease. But I was fool enough to hook up with a man who did all three to me. So I end up as a washer woman in the Klondike, earning as much as I can to keep myself in old age. Clean and honest. You keep clean and honest, and you'll be all right here in Dawson, or any city."

"Thank you," said Meg. "Good advice, I'm sure."

Daisy held her nose and sank under the water.

Later that night, Meg went with Daisy to The Northern Saloon. She had intended to have a couple of drinks and just watch Daisy's performance. But Joe had rules for his saloon.

"You're an unescorted lady," he pointed out to her. "And mighty good-looking to all the men around here. If you dance with them, they have to pay."

"Are you telling me I have to dance for money?" said Meg indignantly.

"I warned her," said Daisy, "but she wouldn't listen to me."

"It's only fair," said Joe. He nodded in the direction of three dance hall girls who stood challengingly at the bar, watching what transpired between Joe and Meg. "I can't have you taking business away from my girls, now can I? There's Gypsy Rose and Sapphire Star and Mandolin Lily there, they can't dance for free. And Daisy, she's got to be paid for her talent."

"Let me think it over, if you will, Mr. Ash. I have my own moral rules to consider. And perhaps I won't wish to dance at all."

But when the music began and polite men approached her respectfully, Meg accepted.

"All proceeds," she stipulated to them, "will go to the dogs. I am a doctor thereof."

Some of the men were excellent dancers and Meg allowed them to make more than one donation to the dogs. She had more than a couple of drinks and whistled like a man in enthusiastic applause at Daisy's performance. Yukon Sally howled in echo as she waited outside the saloon.

"Over $50! I made over $50!" Meg counted her earnings next day in the tent. "I didn't make that in a *week* as a vet."

"I made over a hundred," said Daisy. "It's time you switched professions."

"Oh no," said Meg. "That was just fun. I want to get to work. Right Yukie? Let's go buy a piece of land. With this on top of the proceeds from selling all the goods we brought here, we should be able to build a very nice dog house and clinic."

While Daisy went shopping for a dressmaker and materials, Meg took Yukie to get registered at the North West Mounted Police headquarters. It was a log barracks at the end of Front Street. The main door was open, letting light into the room where Inspector Charles Constantine presided over three work tables.

"Dr. Meg Oliphant and dog, Yukon Sally, to see you, sir."

"Thank you, Constable. Back to your duties," said Constantine before he looked up.

"Good day, Inspector," said Meg noticing that he was not a tall man, but certainly looked strong, his red serge coat wide shouldered. Silver showed at the temple line of his dark hair. His eyes were sharp when he looked up at her.

"Inspector, yes," said Constantine, facing her squarely. "And chief magistrate, also commander-in-chief and home and foreign secretary. But good day? What's a good day in this poor excuse for a town?" He pondered which table to use. "Haven't figured that one out yet. Maybe when I can get more than three hours sleep in a night." He lifted the chair in front of one table and placed it in front of another. "Please have a seat, Madam Doctor, here at the desk of registrants. I presume you've come to give me your particulars."

"Yes, sir, if that is required." said Meg.

"It is indeed. By the Law of Constantine. Only way to keep a handle on all the outcasts, adventurers, convicts, and general escapees from normal society that find their way to the Klondike. Do you keep a gun?"

"No. Should I?"

"Not allowed. No guns and no bloomers ... ahem ... indecent attire, allowed in Dawson. What is your purpose here, if I may ask, for the records?" He poised his pen.

"Veterinarian," said Meg. "And Chief Cook and Bottle Washer."

Constantine looked her in the eye. "And professional dancer?"

Meg blushed. "That was because of The Law of Joe Ash."

"So I was informed. Just verifying." He laid down his pen.

"I want to buy a plot of land and build a house, right away. And I need to order more supplies. It's urgent ..."

"You and Belinda Mulroney."

"Belinda Mulroney! Is she here?"

Constantine nodded.

"How and when did she ..."

"First to arrive after ice breakup. Came downriver with a raft full of merchandise. Just like you. Only faster off the mark and higher priced. Sold all her goods first day she got here. Cotton goods and hot water bottles. Sold at a hundred times the price they cost her. Then she had some little cabins built and sold them off as fast as a man could fold up his tent. Now she's hauling lumber off to the gold creeks to set up a saloon there. Where she'll no doubt sell drinks at twice the price charged here in Dawson. It's all highway robbery of the first order. But not something the chief magistrate can do anything about. Except I won't let her or the other saloon bandits have the supply ships come loaded with nothing but whisky."

"I need ether," said Meg, "to use in my surgery. And iodine, more chloroform and cat-gut. And how about some chickens to lay fresh eggs? Are they allowed in Dawson? And seeds to plant a garden. Is it too late to get some seeds in?"

Constantine recorded her list of things to be brought in from the Outside. Then he stood up and reached across his table desk to shake her hand. "Welcome to Dawson City," he said. "At last a citizen who is not a hooligan, circus performer, or dry-land pirate."

"Thank you, sir. But the crucial question is: when your dogs are ill or injured, will you bring them to my surgery?"

"That too," said Inspector Constantine, "I will see to."

Over that summer of 1897, Dawson City expanded into several straight avenues running parallel to the Yukon River bank, with streets criss-crossing them in an orderly gridlock design. Meg had a two-storey log house built on the edge of town farthest from the busy waterfront, back near where the landscape rose up into Dome Mountain. There were two bedrooms upstairs, a sitting room, kitchen, and veterinary rooms downstairs, a porch at the front, and attached to the back of the house a high-fence kennel with rocks bolstering its base. The rocks were there to prevent Yukon Sally from digging out.

Dawson City lots were small and over a thousand dollars each. Daisy became one of the highest-paid entertainers, earning up to $500 a week with her singing, dancing, and twenty-five-cent commission on every drink that her admirers bought, and she helped Meg finance their property and building. Every inch of the property was used, with a garden in a narrow strip along the side of the house, leaving just enough room at the end of it for a small chicken coop. The boat bringing seeds and live hens did not arrive until August when it was too late to plant anything, so Meg's two hens had a larger run. But they were so frightened by Yukie's howling and attempts to get into their pen that they would not lay eggs and had to be sold to a restau-rateur who profited hugely from their outlay.

Each time a boat arrived with mail, Meg lined up with a hundred others outside the post office. It was weeks, though it seemed like years, before she received a letter from Mick. Written in late Novem-ber in response to her letter from Vancouver, it was so out of date, Meg could take nothing relevant from it except its cautionary expres-sion of love.

I do not like this helpless situation, Mick wrote, *being here in Boston while you venture into the wilds of the north. I have word that the Alaskan ports are lawless, gunslingers' havens. No one knows anything about your destination in Canada. My darling Meg, I must not burden you with my fears for your well-being, though they torment me. You must exercise the greatest caution in your choice of companions and never venture out alone. If it weren't for my responsibilities here I would be with you. The particular case I'm working on is as yet unsolved. I don't know what else is of importance to say, except: my heart is with you.*

Meg hiked up Dome Mountain with Yukie to savour this letter and compose her reply.

I'm overlooking Dawson City, she wrote, *surely the most unusual of cities. I feel safe, protected by the diligent North West Mounted Police. It is an orderly town, in spite of its dominance of saloons. I am constantly guarded by my Yukon Sally and have the most interesting company in my young housemate, Daisy. Every woman here works hard at some job or other, and I have not found it at all as difficult as I did in Halifax to establish my business. I'm happily surprised by how "at home" I feel here in this boom town of adventurers and genuine free thinkers. And I am devoted to my patients, the hard-working, spirited, wolf-like dogs.*

Most of them are the product of more hapless breeding and training than the malamute line of my Yukon Sally, the famed dogs of Ike and Piji, which I will tell you about ... when we meet again. But all the dogs are hard-working and highly intelligent. I can't wait to see them when they are in their element ... pulling sleds over snow. In summer, they lay around, exhausted by heat, spreading worm infestation by eating their own or others' turds. Yes, I'm sorry, but they do, out of hunger and peculiar habit. I do not always make myself popular by haranguing people to keep the streets clean of such "temptations" for the dogs. But once they understand the consequences, they usually do what they should, for their dog's sake. Here, dogs are indeed valued and respected, as horses are in other parts of the world.

Dawson City is a Mecca for dog doctors. I am in my element! And though the town itself lacks trees and gardens, it is within a most beautiful landscape of great rushing rivers and forested mountains. I enjoy hiking in

early morning, training Yukie to pull a light wagon or carry a saddlebag.
We go along the riverfront and the rocky trail of Moosehide Gulch, often to
the Tagish camp where we purchase fish and caribou from the natives.

Dearest Mick, I keep hoping every day for news from you. Must rush to
get this letter on today's boat. But, all the while, my longing is to see you,
to be in your arms again ...

Meg posted her letter, knowing like everyone else who haunted
the post office of Dawson, that it could take many weeks for a letter
to get from one side of the continent to the other and more to travel
north into the unknown territory of no trains, electricity, telephones,
or telegraphs.

Meg's friendship with Inspector Constantine grew along with her
reputation as a veterinarian. Word spread fast in the small area of
Dawson City once Constantine himself was seen bringing members of
the Mounties' dog teams to, as her sign said: THE DOG DOCTOR.

Dogs with wounds from fighting, with ear infections, worm infes-
tations, cut pads, strained ligaments, splinters in their throats, heat
stroke, colic, the heaves, and hernias were brought to Dr. Meg's. And
since ninety percent of them left in good repair, more were brought.
The two basic veterinary textbooks she had carried all the way from
Halifax were talked about in Dawson as the Dog Doctor's Bibles.

"If you don't believe *me*," Meg said, impatient with the men who
doubted her abilities and knowledge because she was a woman, "look
it up yourself. There!" She pointed to the thick volume on Canine
Surgery. If necessary, she would read to them the pertinent passage.

It was harder to persuade some owners to not hit their dogs or feed
them bones.

"There should be laws," she complained to Constantine, who was
often seen calling in at her premises, with or without a dog in hand.
"How about creating the Constantine Law against Maltreatment of
Animals."

"Wouldn't work with these ruffians," he said, accepting a quick
mug of tea. "But I tell you what does work. The Law of Greed. With
the price of dogs risen from $25 to $250, not even these lunkheads

will knowingly damage their dogs. You just keep telling them how to maintain their dogs' health. The lunkheads can learn. But you have to keep drilling it in."

"I guess that explains why I'm having such a hard time persuading them to change the breeding habits so that the females aren't bred until they're over two years old and then only every other year."

"You got it," said Constantine. "That would be defying the Law of Greed. In a gold rush town, the Law of Greed prevails."

Piji and Ike liked to perch upon The Dog Doctor *sign over Meg's door. They could rest there, with a good view of Dawson City. The streets were cleaner and the dogs were being well maintained. Too wise to say, "I told you so," Piji put her hand on Ike's knee and said, "It's good to see things turn out so well. And our dogs will have a better future with healers like this Meg you brought to our land."*

"Yes." Ike put his arm around Piji, slipping it under Yuki's fur. He was pleased now, very pleased. "I have watched over this creature from birth. She has become like us and more. She is the lead wolf who can nurture and maintain the pack. Even a big wild pack such as we have in this strange city. But she can't do it alone."

"You are right." Piji smiled, knowing what Ike had in mind. "That chief Mountie is the right mate for her. He's very good at keeping order. She will mate with him."

Ike and Piji rocked together, in peace and harmony, on the sign over Meg's door.

Daisy strolled out of Meg's door each late afternoon. Quiet and grumpy in the early hours, Daisy rose late, lounged around the kitchen in her baggy nightgown, leafing through the book of songs she had brought from Juneau or studying Meg's book of poetry. Daisy had been resistant to Meg's urging her to recite Pauline Johnson's poetry as part of her performance and had flatly refused to wear "native dress." Daisy created her own style, hiring the best dressmaker in town to sew her bright-coloured silk dresses with an unusually short hemline that showed off her silk-stockinged ankles and expensive kid leather shoes with high heels. Constantine had ordered the boats coming upriver that summer to bring food and practical items but he couldn't prevent the import of luxury goods that fetched the highest price. Fancy hats and shoes, bolts of satin and worsted wool, powder and rouge, olives and caviar, velvet chaise lounges, pianos and violins. Daisy was a prime purchaser.

"My mother loved silk dresses," she said. "And so do I. And so do the men. They'd never dance with me if I wore stinky hides."

But she found that her audience did like the odd dramatic poem mixed into her repertoire. Daisy worked hard at her job, memorizing the entire book of popular songs and a selection of narrative poems. She developed a rotation of her performances so that regular attendees would not get bored with repetitions of the previous night. She found that if an audience was flagging, she could always rally their sentiments with a soulful rendition of "Danny Boy" and a rowdy one of "Swanee River" with lots of prancing about and skirt flouncing.

Daisy liked a long walk with Yukon Sally as escort in the fresh air and sunlight of late afternoon. Her colleagues often came for a pot-luck supper with her and Meg before they went to work. Sometimes Molly Doyle joined them.

"How's business?" said Meg, doling out her scalloped potatoes and Molly's canned sausages.

"I'm raking it in, ever since I got a box of starch to do the men's fancy shirts. Dollar a shirt I get. And everybody likes the new tin tubs. Less scrubbing for me and higher cost for the customer."

Gypsy Rose poured lemonade. "So about how much would you make in a week?"

"As much as you, I reckon."

"Over a hundred dollars?" said Gypsy. "That's what I got last week."

"Close enough," said Molly. "And I got clean hands."

"Oh quit your braggin', Molly," said Gypsy, "we got jewelled hands, eh girls?" She looked round at Sapphire Star and Mandolin Lily. "Dawson is a gold mine for us too. We can pick and choose the men and what we want to do with them. And they don't want rough stuff, the way some back in real cities do. Here in Dawson, they're hard-working miners who like their whisky and their women straight up and natural. Right girls?" They nodded in agreement. "And then there's our Daisy, who makes a fortune without a private room. But I figure it's all going to change once the rush gets going proper. Then we'll have boatloads of competition. I'm going to make all I can before summer's end, then I'll take the best offer and sail away with him, down the Yukon to luxury ever after in the Outside."

"Maybe I'll do that too," said Mandolin Lily, who wore a Turkish-style headdress and mediaeval belted and tasselled skirt, with a loose blouse that allowed a glimpse of her midriff flesh when she raised her arms.

"I'm nowhere near ready to quit," said Sapphire Star, who didn't have such a pretty face or interesting outfit, but did have an intriguing voice, graceful movements, and much liveliness in her eyes. "I love the stage. Can't wait for a larger audience. I want to own the first great theatre in Dawson. Want to work for me, Daisy, instead of that cheapskate Joe Ash?"

"I might," said Daisy, "if you have a piano."

"Of course I'll have a piano. And electric lights. Red velvet curtains. A mezzanine. And boxes where gentlemen can drink champagne with ladies in Parisian gowns."

"Gentlemen in boxes?" said Daisy. "And what the heck is a mez-zanine?"

After they left for their night shift, Meg had the evening to herself. She checked in on her kennel patient, a young malamute carried in from the gold creeks, emaciated and dehydrated.

"Can't make him eat or drink," the miner had said. "He was vomiting bile and now he don't seem to have nothing left inside him."

"You should have brought him in sooner," said Meg as she gently prodded the belly.

"Yeah, well, we ain't used to having a dog doctor. Couldn't be sure you weren't just some rumour."

Meg cut into the dog's stomach and found the blockage: a chewed boot lace.

"I'll be darned," said the miner. "These dogs eat everything in sight. Who'd a thought my boot lace would do him in! Will he live?"

"I think so," said Meg. "Let me pipe water and soft food into him for a few days."

The young dog sat up and looked intently as a wolf at Meg when she checked in on him. "Good boy," she said, noticing he had drunk a healthy amount from his water bowl. "Back to the gold creeks for you."

Meg closed the door of the infirmary and spoke to Yukie. "Do you know that, as your doctor, I earn far less than the laundress? And those Mounties who look after all of us, earn least of all. So where's the social justice in this City of Dawson? What do you say we take a little trip out to the gold creeks to see what life's like there?"

Yukie murmured, nodding her head and swiping her paw on Meg's knee.

Constantine dropped by during his night rounds. Meg sat on the steps of her front porch while he stood at ease with his hands clasped firmly behind his back, his eyes casting over the town streets.

"Does it ever bother you," said Meg, "that you guardians of society are paid $8 a day and, shall we say, 'entertainers' get a dollar a minute, and more?"

"Would you do what they do?" Constantine looked incredulous.

"No," said Meg, smiling at his shock. "I actually prefer working with animals. But if worst comes to worst in this business, if I need to supplement my income, I'm thinking of doing a little performing myself. I do like to read, and read out loud to others. I have these novels I packed over the Chilkoot. I was thinking of giving readings from them, say a chapter a night. Might charge say twenty-five cents a person, same as it costs to get into a circus. In any city outside Dawson, that is." She smiled.

Constantine laughed. "Dawson is its own circus," he said. "But don't you go worrying about money. All too soon Dawson is going to have more customers than it can possibly manage. I'll let you in on the latest from Outside. Just when I'm getting a little order into this pack of ruffians, this jail yard of a town," he said, "word comes that I can expect some thousands more escapees from normal society. Thousands! Moore's Landing has just been renamed Skagway and boomed into a scrag of a place, far worse than this. No police. Run by a bunch of gunslingers, American style. Several ships a day landing in the narrows. Dumping their cargo overboard at low and high tide. Then rushing back down south for more. Flimsy buildings springing up out of the mud flats like mushrooms after a rain. Poor Moore's having trouble just hanging onto his own plot of land. Some hooligan called Soapy Smith has established the Law of Pay Me for Protection or Get Shot."

"Can't you Mounties help out?"

"Not our territory. American soil. Best we can do is protect our border at the top of the Chilkoot and see to it that those who come over are adequately supplied and not slinging guns. A North West Squadron should be planting the Union Jack and patrolling the top as we speak. But the rich are coming by boat and expecting to buy anything they want here in Dawson. And the other great stupids are trying to come overland. Without a clue as to the distance and impossibility of it."

"Why did you come here?"

"Following orders."

"Surely you could have asked for another posting."

He looked seriously at Meg. "The Yukon is my biggest command. I'm the first Mountie to be called here." He looked away from her, northwards. "Brought the first squadron. Built Fort Constantine, upriver there. It was my duty to hold the border and establish law and order in this territory. Never expected to be caught up in a greedy gold rush. But here I am. Here we are." He looked at her with a soft spot in his eyes. "You're a fine woman."

"Why thank you, Inspector. You're a good man."

"Try to be." He looked at the porch floor. "Can't marry you."

"What!" Meg gasped, then thought and smiled at Constantine. "But I haven't asked you to marry me. What if I did?"

He looked at her. "I'd have to tell you I have a wife. Back in Winnipeg. Had three sons. Only one lived." He hung his head momentarily. "I don't know why I'm telling you this. Not in the line of duty. But I've found myself drawn to you. And I can't be ... Hell and damnation!" He snapped to attention. "Better just shut my trap now. And get on with my duties." He looked at her, deeply embarrassed. "Good night, Dr. ... Meg."

Meg stood up. "You're an admirable man, Inspector ... Charles. May we shake hands, please? To friendship?"

He shook her hand. Saluted. Then walked in his perfect military gait into Dawson City and his duties.

Ike and Piji watched Meg hug Yukon Sally good night, then get into bed alone and lonely, pulling the covers up around her head. Huddled with Ike at the foot of the bed, Piji wanted to weep in sympathy and in disappointment of their hopes for Meg.

Ike shook his head in complete dismay. "You never know," he said to Piji. "With humans, you just never know."

"We'll keep watch," said Piji. "It's all we can do as spirits."

8

AT THE GOLD CREEKS

IT WAS LATE JULY. The ground was hard-packed from lack of rain. The blackflies were gone, the mosquitoes present only in the evening and in shady, marshy places. The sun shone. Wildflowers bloomed in hazes of pink and purple spikes. Shrubs sprouted yellow blossoms. Wild berries ripened on bushes.

Daisy and Meg and Yukon Sally were hiking the long day's journey to the gold creeks, no longer called Rabbit and Gold Bottom, but Bonanza and Eldorado. They all carried packs, including Yukie, who carried their small canvas tent in a bundle on her back. The path to the creeks was well worn but not busy.

Prospectors stayed at the creeks, working their claims or looking for new ones. They went into Dawson only for supplies and the occasional bender. Now that Belinda was building a saloon and store at the fork of the two main creeks, the path coming from the creeks was less used, though the steady trickle of prospectors going to the creeks for the first time continued.

They did not speak of it, but both Meg and Daisy were hoping to discover at the gold creeks certain past acquaintances, now known as Kings of the Klondike.

"I can't go on forever," said Daisy, "playing the innocent virgin, keeping them all at bay. I get proposals all the time."

"But that's your appeal," said Meg. "Once you start doing what Gypsy and the others do, you'll lose your special attraction."

"You don't know men, Meg. Not like I do. They're not going to just dance forever."

"You'd be surprised at what I know about men."

"Oh yeah? So tell me something I don't already know."

"You tell me how old you really are."

"Nope." Daisy shook her head. "Not until I'm old enough not to shock you."

"You're fourteen. And I'm not shocked. I'm just sorry you missed out on childhood."

"I had enough of childhood. I like what I'm doing now. It's better than what I had to do in Juneau."

"Then follow the advice of your older and wiser friend. Stick to singing and dancing."

"Do you know that some people think you're my dyke?"

"Daisy!"

"There, I shocked you. Maybe you don't even know what it means."

"Can we change the subject, Daisy? I'm finding this very distasteful."

"Don't like it much myself. I told Sapphire she was full of moose piss. And I'll never, ever work for her. But I wouldn't mind working for myself. Build my own premises. Run the show. I'm going to do that, soon as I get enough money."

"Not a bad idea," said Meg. "And I owe you plenty. I'll help you as much as I can." Meg squeezed her hand and held it for a little distance.

Behind them on the trail, well out of earshot, a miner observed them curiously. Quite an odd pair. Two females wearing white blouses and sturdy, high, lace-up boots. Prospectors' boots. One in trousers with braces. The other in a skirt hardly covering her knees. One with light brown hair tied back under a fedora. The other with school-girl braids, her hair black as an Indian's. Holding hands. What you didn't see in the Klondike! Wouldn't be allowed in the civilized world.

Daisy and Meg came up a gradual incline through grassy woods that suddenly ended where trees had been cut down to build shelters and sluices for the gold miners, who were digging on every square foot of land along the creeks below. Meg and Daisy looked down upon a scene of ravaged landscape. Only stumps of trees remained. The earth was overturned and cracked, dry, ashen grey. All along the creeks and up the slopes, the land was cordoned off with many stakes, ropes, and trenches, designating the precise claims. They could see men working like a colony of ants, except there was no overall co-operation as they individually swung pickaxes, dug with shovels, panned the sluices built along Bonanza and Eldorado.

"Looks like a forest fire swept through here," said Daisy.

In the distance, where the two creeks met, there were a couple of cabins, tents, and a two-storey building that was under construction. "Must be Belinda's saloon," said Meg. "Let's go. Hike, Yukie! I've acquired a serious thirst."

As they hiked past the claims, making their way to the fork of the two creeks, the thin muscular miners laid down their tools to watch the approach of this peculiar pair with the young malamute. Squaw and husband? No. Two women. In odd apparel.

"Well, blow me down if they ain't good lookin'!" The men took off their sweat-rimmed hats, wiped their mud-smudged faces, swiped their dirt-caked trousers and shirts, grinned.

"Welcome ladies. What can we do you for?"

"Gentlemen." Meg smiled and nodded, taking off her hat, loosening her hair to tumble around her shoulders. "Any claims left here about?"

"Not much left above or below here on Bonanza. Nor on Eldorado. But then you never know till you actually dig in."

"Want to stay awhile?" said his partner. "Water your dog? Fine lookin' malamute. She for sale?"

"Afraid not."

"Dang! I've got good gold to pay."

"And no manners! Pardon the language of my partner, ma'am," said the other. "You and your young friend care to wet your whistle?

Darcy and me could fire up some tea, real quick. Sit yourselves down, won't you?"

He motioned to a rough plank bench and table covered with a large tin pail, two tin mugs, plates, and old silver spoons and forks, all washed and stacked neatly beside a mess of sugar tin, tea tin, bacon fat tin, flour sack, bean sack, corked bottles fermenting some liquid, and a row of canned goods with their labels showing proudly, as in a store of prized goods. A shaving soap mug and brush sat beside a wash basin with a not-very-clean cloth draped over it in a hump, covering rising sourdough. Beneath the table were pots and pans, carefully lidded. The miners' home was a crawl space tent, staked to the ground with tree branch poles, the front flap opened for airing.

"We have apricots." Darcy picked up a tin from the table, offering to share it.

"Thank you. But we won't deprive you of your apricots. Or your time, today. We must move on and set up our camp at the fork."

"We'll help."

"Thank you, but we must press on." Meg and Daisy waved goodbye.

"Come back for supper then."

"Wait! You haven't seen our gold." Darcy lifted a pot from under the table, heavily, using both hands.

His partner miner removed the lid. "See! Full! Pots of gold. We can buy you anything you want. Anything."

The ladies and their dog pressed on, looked at each other, and burst out laughing. "Anything we want! Anything? This doesn't sound too rough to me!"

They were stared at or welcomed at every claim as they moved along Bonanza. The new sites were all makeshift. Some tidier than others. Some with a clothesline of underdrawers, socks, and shirts drying in the sun. Miners caught without their shirts on hastily covered themselves at the approach of Meg and Daisy. Doffed their hats. Buttoned up their waistcoats.

Very few were too socially primitive, damaged, or fundamentally uninterested in women not to halt their work and try to have a con-

versation with Meg and Daisy. Those who found their way to the
Klondike in the summer of '97 were generally seasoned miners, used
to looking after themselves in primitive conditions. Their need was
not for women as housekeepers. They were desperate for female
company and more if they could get it.

Older sites that had been staked in the autumn of '96 and been
worked through the winter and spring had a log cabin and mined
tunnels, wooden sluices and dams built on the creek. The banks of
Bonanza were continuous piles of sifted earth and stones. Gold nuggets had been sifted out in pans, chunks dug out with shovels, veins
of gold hacked away from rock faces by pickaxes.

Meg and Daisy came to a well-established log cabin where a handsome woman sat on a bench out front with her young daughter reading aloud from a children's book. Both mother and daughter were
well dressed, in the latest fashion brought to Dawson. There was
a hand-carved sign over the door saying CARMACK. The mother
stood up, holding her daughter's hand and looked unsmilingly at
Daisy and Meg.

"Must be Shaaw Tl'áa, you know… Kate Carmack and her daughter Graphie," said Daisy. "Dressed to the nines on this dirty old
claim."

It was an orderly cabin, tin wash tub hung up on the outside wall,
blanket airing on a line. When Daisy addressed Kate in Tagish, she
smiled and spoke readily. They conversed in Tagish for some time,
Graphie glancing at Meg and digging her feet into the ground impatiently. Meg heard Daisy mention the name Skookum Jim more than
once. Then Daisy burst out laughing.

"Shaaw Tl'áa tells me she doesn't like our Dawson City. Says it's
full of loud women who lift their skirts and mate for money." She
turned back to Kate. "This is my friend, Meg. She's a medicine man
for animals."

Kate looked nonplussed. "Will you have some tea?" she said,
motioning for them to come into the cabin.

The men, Carmack, Jim, and Charlie, had gone off to Belinda's saloon. Yukon Sally lay down while the women conversed over tea, sitting in the bright light of outdoors. Kate spoke stiffly in English, sometimes narrowing her dark eyes when she addressed Meg's questions. She laughed and relaxed with Daisy in Tagish. But at the end, she smiled warmly at Meg and agreed to come visit her when next she was in Dawson. She would tell Meg what she knew about plant remedies. Graphie sat and fidgeted, treating her book like a precious toy, delving in and out of it, pretending not to be listening to their conversation, sometimes pouting, sometimes perplexed. Kate waved goodbye sadly.

"All that gold sure isn't making her life better, is it?" said Meg.

"She isn't what she used to be," said Daisy. "I never saw much of her. But my mother talked about her more than anyone else in the clan. Which isn't saying much, since my mother wasn't a talker. But she sure admired Shaaw Tl'áa. She could do everything. Cook, trap, hunt, sew, and heal with plants. She was what you call a princess in the Wolf Clan. But she really doesn't know what to do with gold. Or a husband who has suddenly turned himself into the first King of the Klondike. I'd like to meet this Carmack. Seems he's changed. Used to consider himself lucky to have married Shaaw Tl'áa. They say he fitted right into the ways of the clan. Unlike my father. My dad just wanted a woman to cook and screw. Then he left her and me when he got fed up with the territory, the cold, and the mountains."

Meg put her arm on Daisy's shoulder. Daisy removed it.

"Watch it!" she said. "These miners got enough to talk about with you in trousers."

Meg laughed. "I think," she said, "that Shaaw ... however you say it ... Kate, is too trusting. Jim and Charlie too. From what she said, she found the gold. But Carmack has the claims in his name. If it is true that the law wouldn't permit Kate, because she's a woman, and Jim and Charlie because they're Indians, to register their own claims, then the law should be changed. They should take it to court. I'm going to ask Constantine about this."

"What courts?" said Daisy. "There's no such thing around here.

And don't think Kate is stupid. She knows the only real way she has, is to make Carmack *want* to treat her right. She has to keep that pecker happy."

"Daisy!"

"Don't Daisy me. It's true. Kate sees the signs. Now that he's rich, and doesn't need her help to survive in this territory, he wants to drop the Tagish ways and turn her into a 'lady.' She doesn't mind much. Likes the fancy dresses, though not all the time. Too hard to work in. And corsets ... they *hurt*. But she likes an adventure. Wants so see what it's like on the Outside. Carmack says he'll take her and Graphie to San Francisco where he has relatives. Sounds all right to me."

"But he's started yelling at her. That's not a good sign."

"I know. But Skookum Jim would never let him hurt her. Can't wait to see him again. Come on. Hike, Yukon!" Daisy quickened her pace. "Men await us at Belinda's saloon."

"It's unfair that Carmack didn't take Kate to the saloon with them," said Meg.

"Then who would look after that sulky brat?"

"She's just a kid," said Meg. "Reminds me of my niece."

They reached the junction of Bonanza and Eldorado. Set back from the claims along the creeks was a camp of some tents, shacks, and an old log cabin with grass and wild flowers growing on its sod roof top. Nearby was the saloon with carpenters working on the second storey. The sign over the saloon door said unequivocally: BELINDA MULRONEY'S. There was as yet no glass in the window spaces and the front door was opened wide to the warm, still sunlit night. Smoke from cigars, pipes, and cigarettes wafted out the windows. A din of men's voices, hoots, and shouts was coming from within. Outside, sitting on stumps and piles of boards, more men were talking, smoking, drinking from mugs and bottles. They began to rise, put their hands over their eyebrows, the better to see as Meg and Daisy approached.

"Let's pitch our tent and make ourselves more presentable ... to Miss Mulroney, shall we?" said Meg to Daisy.

Meg donned a skirt and ladies boots. Daisy put on her silk stockings and fine boots. They dusted off their blouses and lowered their rolled up sleeves.

"Blue ribbon for you," said Meg, handing it to her after they had brushed their hair. "And red for me."

Several teams of assorted malamutes were tethered to tree stumps near Belinda's saloon, but at strategic distances apart, so they had their own territory and couldn't get at one another to fight. Yukon Sally was straining on the leash to make friends, as long as they wanted to play and not try to dominate her. She knew not to interfere with any team. She held up her chin and tail as she walked regally past, not deigning to answer the yelps and howls that teams set up seeing her pass by. Meg let her greet various miners and dogs en route, then settled her, tethered to a stump in view of the saloon's doorway.

It was Saturday night. Men were spilling out of the doorway to see what was going on. They all stepped back, doffing their hats, making a path for Meg and Daisy into the saloon, through the dim light and smoke-filled air to the large wooden bar behind which stood Belinda Mulroney, also wearing a white blouse and long dark skirt. "Well, if it ain't!" said Belinda, holding a large jug of whisky. "Long time no see, Dr. Oliphant."

"Fancy meeting you here! Belinda, if I may." Meg reached over the bar to shake hands.

"Belinda, it is. And nothing fancy about here," she laughed, shaking hands. "Though there's gold dust on the floor. Who's your friend? And what'll you have? Whisky or water? It's all I got. A dollar a shot. And for you, I have a glass. No extra." She reached under the bar and produced two glasses.

"Pardon me, ladies," said several men at once offering to pay for them. "Allow me."

Meg looked into the crowd around them. She was disappointed that Anton Stander was not in sight. Daisy rose up on her toes when she saw who was standing at the end of the bar. A tall, very broad shouldered man, wearing a brimmed hat with a bright red band around it, a red plaid shirt with a yellow and green silk tie loosely knotted at the collar. A chain of gold nuggets was draped across his chest from his right suspender to a watch in the shirt pocket on his left side. His eyes were dark, cheekbones high, lips full but fringed by a scraggly moustache.

"That's Skookum Jim." Daisy pulled Meg with her as she moved towards him. She greeted him by his Tagish name, Keish.

He smiled at her and raised his hand high above the crowd. "Drinks all around boys." He nodded assent to Belinda to begin pouring at his expense. "Welcome to 'Looks Like a Wolf,'" he said in Tagish, raising his glass, "and friend."

"To what?" said the men.

"Me, Daisy, and my friend Meg." Daisy spoke out and smiled as though on stage.

"Kaa Goox," Jim introduced the man beside him to Daisy and then to Meg. "My cousin, Tagish Charlie."

Charlie was shorter and stockier, with large dark eyes, prominent nose and cheek bones, no facial hair. He too wore a loud plaid shirt and tie with gold nugget watch chain. Both Jim and Charlie had thick black hair, cut and trimmed in the conventional style of George Carmack, who pushed his way forward to stand between Jim and Charlie. He put his arms over their shoulders. Carmack no longer wore moccasins or any Indian adornment. His shirt was military grey with brass buttons up the front, his trousers well fitted to his trim torso, no need for suspenders. His boots were new. He looked at Daisy and Meg as though they would instantly prefer him.

"Boys," he said, "partners. Introduce me to your lady friends."

"I know your wife." Daisy looked coldly at him. "I was raised by the Wolf Clan."

George stood up straight, put his glass on the bar for a refill. "I know her clan. I don't recall having seen you before."

"Shaaw Tl'áa left with you before my time in the clan. But she came back once with your daughter, Graphie."

"Well then," said George, "nice to meet you. And your pretty friend." He took off his dark grey fedora. "Next round is on me." He winked at Meg.

She frowned and turned her attention to Charlie. George collected the drink Belinda poured, giving her a wink, which she ignored, then he turned to Jim and Charlie, who had Daisy and Meg's full attention.

"Well boys, looks like you struck it rich, again. I'll leave you to your fine company. Ladies." He raised his glass to them and elbowed his way back into the crowd.

Daisy, Jim, and Charlie launched into their native language after other men introduced themselves to Meg and escorted her around the saloon. She was introduced to Ogilvie, who had surveyed the White Pass, with Skookum Jim doing the muscle work and Moore spurring them on. Now the government had given Ogilvie the job of surveying and thereby settling any disputes on the gold claims. Meg noticed that the miners deferred to him, showing respect for his honesty and judgment, even when they kidded him.

"Ogilvie," they said, "he's the real boss man around here. Sharp as a tack and honest as the day is long."

"Mr. Ogilvie," Meg asked him, "what if I went prospecting and found some gold, could I stake a claim?"

"No," he said, matter-of-factly, "not according to law. Women can't stake claims, but you can buy or invest in a claim already staked. That's what Belinda does. And Big Alex. They make a pile of money that way, without ever having to lift a shovel. The first prospectors here go crazy just to stake a claim but then they don't have the money, manpower, equipment, or just plain staying power, to work it. So they sell it and stake another, or go begging for investors. Like Alex Mac-Donald. He's that big, sober, silent fellow sitting over there. Look at the size of him! Big Moose from Antigonish, they call him. If you come with me I'll introduce you to him."

The Big Moose had his back to them as they approached.

"Hey, Alex," said Ogilvie.

"No!" Alex shouted without turning to see who it was. "No deal!" Then he looked around. "It's you, Ogilvie." He tipped his cap to him and to Meg. "Ma'am. Pardon me. Thought you was someone else. Pesterin' me for loans. How do you do?"

Meg shook his hand, tried to engage in conversation, but he grunted and shied away.

All these men I'm meeting, Meg mused, scanning the room, but not the one I was really hoping to. Where is Anton? And Mitzi? And Finn? She asked if anyone had seen a man called Finn around the creeks.

"He had a bad winter of it," they said. "Got sick. Had to sell his dogs and team up with that darkie friend of his. What's his name?"

"Jethro?" said Meg.

"That's it. Jethro. He's working a good claim. Finn helping. When he ain't too drunk or sick to stand. If he can stand, expect you'll see him here tonight."

"He owes me," said Alex but would say no more.

"What about Anton Stander?" Meg tried to say casually. "And Mad Mitzi?"

"Oh they'll be here. And there'll be a scene. You betcha."

"What do you mean?"

The man thought of how to put this politely. "She knows how to get a man's goat."

"Amongst other things!" Laughter all around.

"Boys!" It was George Carmack shouting over the crowd. "Let's have a song. Sing my song, why don't you? Let's go."

He launched into singing about himself as the discoverer of gold on Bonanza Creek, with everyone joining in as soon as he got to the chorus. It was a jumble of rhymes, but the gist was clear. Carmack was first and sole discoverer.

Meg had rejoined Daisy with Jim and Charlie when Carmack began the song. Jim sang along as heartily as anyone.

"Your sister Kate told us she was the first to see the gold," said Meg. "Isn't that true?"

"Oh sure," said Jim. "But we were all in on it together. And George had to stake the claim. He figured they wouldn't let us stake, bein' as we're Indians. And he made up the song. So he gives himself the credit." Jim smiled. "It's settled out good enough. Charlie and me are takin' our share. Ogilvie plays fair. He got our claims recorded right and the Mounties back him up. They let us into the saloons too." Jim looked around with a smile of satisfaction.

"They *should*!" Daisy stomped her foot.

"Of course they should," said Meg. "And Kate too. She should be here."

"Down, girls," Jim moved his hand as though he were patting pups. "Settle down. They just want to make sure us Indians don't get too drunk. Charlie and me, we know how to handle ourselves."

"George should change that song," said Meg. "It should be about Kate and you too."

Jim shrugged. Charlie shrugged.

"Meg and I are good singers," said Daisy. "We'll give you a song."

Daisy and Meg were standing on the bar singing "Danny Boy," Belinda herself joining in, though not from on top of the bar, when Anton Stander appeared in the doorway with Mad Mitzi at his side.

Meg faltered mid-song but Daisy carried on with her harmony. Meg picked up and carried on singing to the end of the song. Anton said something to Mitzi then made his way to the bar. Mitzi stood rigidly in the doorway, her shoulders back in regal posture, her chin raised majestically. She tossed a purple stole over her shoulder then let it slide down to catch in the crook of her arms and reveal her bare shoulders and corsetted breasts pushed up to burst over the neckline of her dark pink taffeta dress. A several-strand necklace of gold nuggets hung heavily from her neck.

When they finished singing, men reached up to lift Daisy and Meg down from the bar. Anton caught Meg and pulled her to his chest in an embrace before she could resist. She slowly extricated herself.

"It is you, Margaret." He looked at her intensely, then swooped her into his arms again, whispering into her ears. "I cannot *believe* ..."

There was a shriek from the doorway. Mad Mitzi's arms twirled in the air as she sank to the floor in a faint. The crowd turned to look at her and then back at Anton and Meg.

"Something has happened to your friend," said Meg. "You had better tend to her."

Anton hesitated, turning from one to the other. "All right."

Mitzi would not revive until Anton had carried her outside.

"Take me home," she could be heard screaming hysterically. "Take me *home!*"

Anton came back inside to say to Meg. "I have to leave now. Can I see you tomorrow? Where will you be?"

"I might be here," she said. "Or at our tent."

"What tent? Where?"

"Over there."

"I'll find you. Tomorrow. Noon."

Those in the crowd looked at each other, Skookum Jim at Daisy. Belinda looked to the heavens then wiped her bar top.

Anton did not show up at Meg's tent until the end of the afternoon. Meg was glad to be found returning from walking with Yukon Sally so that it didn't look like she had been waiting all afternoon for him. Daisy, who had slept all day after staying up most of the night, emerged from the tent. She stared at Anton, wondering what it was about him that took such a hold on Meg, who maintained her distance with all the other men.

"He's a wonderful dancer," was all Meg would say about him. "I thought I knew him quite well, in Vancouver."

Anton took his hat off and held it at his side as he approached Meg.

"I'm sorry, Margaret," he said. "I could not be more sorry."

"For what, Anton?" She lifted her chin.

Daisy cleared her throat making her presence known.

"Miss." He nodded to her then said to Meg. "May we take a walk, please?"

"I'll take care of Yukie," said Daisy.

Anton and Meg walked up the hillside bereft of trees and sat down upon rocks overlooking Belinda Mulroney's and the junction of the creeks.

"Where is Mitzi?" said Meg.

"At my cabin. She is not well."

"Oh?" said Meg. "What is her ailment?"

"She faints."

"Yes. We all witnessed that."

"She is nauseous." Anton took his hat off again and laid it on the ground, ran his hand through his dark, tangled hair.

"What is it? The cause?"

"Could be consumption. I've seen more than one die of that around here."

"What does Mitzi say it is?"

"She thinks... It's too soon to say for sure. But she fears... It was very bad this morning. She would not let me near her. But she was outside retching. I couldn't leave her. Eventually she ordered me to go. I must tell you. She fears..."

"Anton, for God's sake tell me." Meg stood up impatiently. "What does Mitzi fear?"

"Ah!" Anton stood up close to her. "My beautiful young widow. So full of purpose. Such fire within. And rhythm..." Anton held out his arms to waltz.

Meg lowered her head and pinched the top of her nose to keep back tears.

Anton put his arms around her. "You have come to me often in my dreams. And now I cannot believe it. You are here. As you were. I feel it. But... how can I know what is true? Madeleine said... I am afraid..."

Meg drew back, dug in her heels. "Of what? Just *tell* me."

"She thinks she is bearing my child."

"Bearing your child! How does she know?"

"She cannot be sure. But she says it runs in her family, that her mother knew immediately when she had conceived. Morning sickness began the next day."

Meg closed her eyes then turned away. "And you believe that."

"Time will tell. A few months. Perhaps one or two."

"Or nine. Or more. Or you may never know."

"I know." Anton took her hand. "I know what you're thinking. She could be deceiving me. She is not like you. She is full of feminine wiles. She can drive a man to distraction. But if you saw her retching today, you would take pity on her. That cannot be faked."

"You think not? Then you had better pick up your hat and proceed. Marry her. Right away. Before she gives birth. Or dies of consumption." Meg started down the hill.

"Meg!" Anton called angrily. "Stop! Tell me how could you do that? You who I thought was so kind, and true ..."

Meg turned around. "Do what?"

"Finn was to be your guide. He told you about everything you needed to get over the Chilkoot and to Dawson. He got you to Moore's and then you found you could do better with the Indian guides. So you rejected Finn, without pay. Abandoned Madeleine who was such a good friend to you in Vancouver. She got you credit at the stores so you could come to the Klondike loaded with supplies to sell at great profit. Then you sent her over the Pass at the worst time of year in the care of Finn who has turned out to be a violent rapist."

Meg stared at him in disbelief. She began to laugh.

"Margaret, how could you ... just laugh?"

"Because you're such a fool, Anton, if you would believe all that. And not check it out! Have you talked to Finn?"

"I have been working my mine."

"And Mitzi has been working you. She fancies herself a great dancer, but really she's an incorrigible actress."

"She's had a hard time in life," said Anton, looking sadly at Meg, who stood firmly with her hands on her hips, "a very hard time, compared to you."

"Really! You know, Anton, you sound like my sister. And you're *wrong*! I have a hard time because I'm trying to do something more with my life than serve myself. Yes I've had wonderful help from some in that, and really stupid jealousy and prejudice from others. Can you imagine Mitzi in vet college? Full of men who will make a good income and think of her only as a potential wife and mother who should not be there distracting them? Some actually hating and fearing her because she is 'abnormal' and bucking convention? I don't think she'd spend her nights with *books*, do you?"

Anton looked perplexed.

He doesn't know what I'm pointing to, thought Meg. He does not have the intelligence of Randolph or Mick or Constantine. But then what am I pointing to? Mitzi also bucks convention. In normal society she is condemned, looked down upon for "selling her body." Here in the Klondike it's an accepted occupation. It's only the risk of disease and pregnancy they worry about. Anton is prepared to do the right thing in the case of pregnancy, so why am I angry at him?

"I don't think I understand you," said Anton.

"Let's hope you understand your Madeleine." Meg started down the hill. "Good luck, Anton. I'm going back to my dog."

Anton accompanied her down the hill in gentlemanly fashion. Yukon Sally, who had broken away from Daisy, came racing up through brush and stumps to find Meg.

Meg sat with two blankets cushioning herself on the hard ground and tree stump she was leaning against. Yukon Sally lay belly up on the ground close by. She was cooling herself in the heat of the early evening sun by exposing her belly and private parts to the air. It was the posture of complete vulnerability and surrender to the environment. Her eyes were closed, her mouth open.

"Yukie!" said Meg, "You look the way I feel. It is undignified."

Yukon opened her eyes and rolled over onto her belly. She sat up.

"I didn't realize I harboured such feelings for Anton until I saw how foolish and misplaced they are."

Yukon gave a brief empathetic howl. The men sawing and banging boards into place over at Belinda Mulroney's stopped to look.

"Thank you," said Meg, putting her arm around Yukon. "But don't let everyone know how bad I feel."

Daisy came from the vicinity of Belinda's carrying a tin mug in each hand, careful not to spill the contents. "She's a tough one," said Daisy, "that Belinda. No free drinks. Not even for the wounded in heart."

"What did she say?"

"I don't think I'll tell you."

"Tell me. No wait. I think I can guess." Meg took a gulp of whisky. "A woman's a fool to get mixed up with men."

"No." Daisy sat down by Meg.

"Then tell me. I want to know."

Daisy pondered.

"Don't give me that Indian silence. Speak. Please. I *hate* not knowing. I *hate* secrets."

"She just said that Anton Stander is a fool for whores. And you're a fool if you're broken-hearted over him. So I told her a dog doctor is nobody's fool. Plunked our money down and took our drinks."

"Thanks, little sister."

They sat in silence for some time.

"Whores and fools," said Meg. "What's the use of talking that way? It's too simple. I don't find it helpful. It's a cover-up. A habit of our times. Like putting cloths and doilies over every piece of furniture. Elaborate hats on our heads. Skirts so long we trip over them. Here it is, 1897, almost the twentieth century and we're talking as though we're in the eighteenth. Whores and fools. Might as well be knaves and slaves. And feminine wiles. Is that a good thing or a bad thing... that I have no feminine wiles?"

Daisy looked over into Meg's tin mug. It was empty.

"You know," said Daisy, "that I have not been able to understand half of what you have just said. I've never seen a doily or a wile. Masculine or feminine. So explain. I *hate* not knowing."

Meg waved her hand in the air, brushing away all concepts. "Psshhst!" she said. "It's all too ordinary. All too human. Lies. Deceits. Greed for gold. People treating people like rags. I gotta go find my old friend Finn. See how he is. Meanwhile..." she leaned woozily over, holding out her empty mug. "Can I have your drink, please Daisy? You're really too young for all this."

Meg woke in the darkness after midnight, slapping at a mosquito buzzing round her face. She could hear fiddling in the distance at

Belinda Mulroney's and the plaintive soprano of Daisy's voice. Then hooting, whistling, stomping, applause, and the chorus of dogs outside. It was deafeningly loud. She pulled the blanket up over her head until it stopped.

Later she wakened to the sound of Skookum Jim and Daisy saying good night to each other in a language she could understand only in its tones of affection. Then Daisy crawled into the tent, Yukon Sally after her. Daisy undressed and got beneath her cover.

"You awake, Meg?"

"Pretending not to be."

"Sober?"

"Too much so."

"I want to stay here and work in Belinda's saloon for a while. I can make twice as much here as in Dawson. Two, not one dollar a dance and ..."

"Be closer to Skookum Jim?"

"That too."

"Where will you live?"

"Belinda will give me free room and board with a room of my own."

"Daisy, you aren't planning to ..."

"No. No whoring. Belinda's orders. It led to too much trouble when Mad Mitzi worked there."

"Explain. Not too many details, please."

"She played the miners off against each other. There'd be fights at the end of the night because she would promise to go home with one but then go with another, whoever offered more. Belinda kicked her out. Then Mitzi set up her own auction. Staged it outdoors. Auctioned herself off to the highest bidder, doing a dance with veils to get them all excited. And Anton won, with the veil down to you know where."

Daisy went with Meg to find Finn.

"Last seen staking on that hopeless hill, north side, above Bonanza," a miner told them. "Sorry sight. Finn's lone tent. Ain't nothin' up there. Finn's a good man, but he lacks horse sense."

They took the hill from a long angle, starting a few claims up from the fork. A lone tent could be seen higher up. Looking down at the creeks, they could see Carmack's claims on Bonanza. Farther away on the banks of Eldorado were the adjacent claims of Clarence Berry and Anton Stander. It was a grey mess of dug-up ground, tents, cabins, and mud heaps unearthed from mine shafts. Mad Mitzi won't last long there, thought Meg. Life in a shack and mud fields is not her style.

It was a hive of activity below but high up the hillside, nothing but tree stumps and Finn's lonely tent. They hiked close up to it. He was not in sight.

"Finn." Meg cupped her hands around her mouth, calling as loud as she could. "Where are you? It's Meg."

They heard a weak voice from within the tent and out came a small, fat malamute pup. Yukon Sally raced over to the pup, sniffing, sporting, dominating it. The pup rolled onto his back and crawled on his belly in submission, but also yelped and bounced against Yukon Sally in delight.

"Finn?" Meg looked into the tent.

Finn was lying on his back, struggling to prop himself up on his elbows. He fell back.

"Meg," he said weakly, "I'm afraid I'm a goner. Look after Jake ..." He passed out.

"Is he dead?" said Daisy, crawling into the tent.

Meg was examining Finn's eyes, the sores round his mouth, trying to listen to his heart.

"Looks like advanced scurvy to me," she concluded.

"I'll go down to Shaaw Tl'áa for help," said Daisy.

Meg searched around. There was a pan of water for Jake the pup and some high smelling bear meat in a cache. A half-full pail of mountain stream water.

Finn came to again. "Did I conk out?" he said. "Am I dreaming or what?"

"Don't try to get up," Meg put her hand firmly on his shoulder. "Save your strength. Help is on its way."

Skookum Jim came up the hill pulling a sled. Along side was Charlie, Daisy, and Kate with a supply of spruce gum.

9

Back in Dawson City

They moved Finn and his tent down the hill to Carmack's cabin. After several days of rest, with Kate administering her remedy of spruce gum and hot tea, and then the gradual consumption of dried fish, beans, some moose meat, Finn was strong enough to stand but could not move very far.

"Get me to Dawson," he said, staggering on his feet. "I got to register my claim."

Daisy rolled her pale eyes skyward. "Your claim on Hopeless Hill," said Daisy. "How urgent can that be?"

"He needs several weeks, would you say, Kate?" Meg turned to her. "Maybe months, to recuperate?"

Kate nodded. "More than one moon."

"She means a month," said Carmack.

"I understood that," said Meg sharply, then turned back to Kate. "If I could purchase a supply of that spruce gum from you, I'll take Finn back to Dawson to recuperate. There should be lots of onions and potatoes shipped in there by now, but this spruce gum works even better than oranges."

Kate gave her a large container of spruce gum. Would take nothing for it.

❁

"So," said Daisy to Meg back in their own tent, "are you going to be shacking up with a man in place of me?"

Meg laughed. "I guess so. Being as there's no hospital yet in Dawson."

"Finn in the bedroom . . . it'll be the talk of the town."

Meg shrugged. "In Halifax, I might care," she said. "Though I'd still do it. In Dawson, it doesn't matter. But how am I going to get him there? That's the problem."

"Big Moose is going back by scow, down the Klondike. Why not hitch a ride with him? Skookum Jim could pull Finn down the creeks to get you to the river."

"That could work," said Meg. "If I could manage to have a conversation with the Moose that doesn't begin and end with '*no!*' My dog is more articulate than he is."

Alex, The Big Moose from Antigonish, was at Belinda's that night.

"He'll do it," Belinda said to Meg. "He's a big softee, really. I can out-bargain him any time."

Meg sallied up to end of the bar where Big Alex stood leaning and watching from his usual post. "Hello Big Moose." She smiled at him. "Do you mind if I call you that?"

He shook his head in a way that could have meant yes, or no, or complete disdain. Then he moved away, excusing himself with a tip of his hat.

"What have I done?" Meg asked Belinda. "He got so offended I couldn't even broach the subject."

"I'll talk to the big oaf," she said. "You just get Finn to the scow. Alex will be there to take you. I'll see to that."

"Doesn't he like being called Big Moose?"

"Would you?"

"Is he afraid of women?"

"Drinking ones? Yes."

☙

Hell and damnation, thought Meg next morning as she walked behind the procession following the creek path to the Klondike. Skookum Jim was in the lead, pulling Finn on a sled. Finn was bumping along, lying on his back, holding the fat pup, Jake, on his chest. Yukon Sally was keeping pace with Jim, and every so often going back to keep Jake in line. Big Moose strode ahead of Meg. I guess I should apologize, Meg said to herself, apologize to this Darwinian ape in front of me. On the other hand, so should he. That was extremely rude to get up and walk away from a lady. A gentleman doesn't do that.

"Mr. McDonald," she said in a clear, frank voice. "I will not apologize for drinking, because that is my pleasure, at times. But I do apologize for calling you Big Moose, if it offends you."

He flapped his hand in the air, brushing the thought away as though it were a mosquito.

Meg quick-stepped to walk beside him. "Mr. McDonald, I do not like walking behind you like a servant. An ill-treated servant."

"Alex."

"Thank you. I'm Meg."

Silence.

"You talk with Belinda. Would you please talk with me, in a similar vein?"

"Business."

"Precisely. My friend Finn has staked a claim and I need ..."

"No!"

"No what?"

"No deal. And don't say please. I can't stand wheedling."

Ahah! thought Meg, a full sentence. "I am not wheedling, Alex. I just need to know how to register the claim for Finn. He's not well enough and he doesn't have so much as a down payment. But I am a businesswoman myself and I do have some capital."

"In gold? Gold is trash."

"Gold is trash?!"

"I bought my first claim for a sack of flour and a half-side of bacon.

Now I'm rich as Croesus. A King of the Klondike. But I don't carry so much as a poke of gold."

"That first claim turned out to be a fortune in gold. How can you say gold is trash? It's the basis of your wealth."

The Big Moose just shrugged.

All right, so he doesn't like to argue. "Alex. Tell me how you got so rich. Everyone knows you are. But how did you start out?"

"Farm boy near Antigonish."

"And then what?"

"Took off. Years in Colorado silver mines."

"And then?"

"Headed north to the Yukon. Not much good at finding anything on my own. Pushed a wheelbarrow around for others. Not much good at talkin', but got good ears. Know where to trade. Bacon turns into a gold mine. But gold is trash if you throw it away." Alex took a deep breath, exhausted by this unusual expenditure of words.

"Gold is trash if you throw it away, eh."

Alex nodded. "Stander throws it away."

"I see."

Silence.

"What does he throw it away on?"

Silence, for many steps.

"I'm not asking for money, or deals, Alex."

"You should. Got a good head on your shoulders. Like Belinda."

"Why, thank you for the compliment. But I was asking your opinion on Anton Stander."

"Throws it away on loose women."

"Well, that doesn't include me ..." Meg fell off weakly, thinking maybe it did.

"Your friend Finn here. He throws it away on booze. He's a bad investment."

"He's still my friend. But if you're trying to tell me I throw myself or my money away on men, you're quite wrong. My money goes to the dogs."

Alex laughed loud as a moose's honk. "That's a good one. Right smart here in the Klondike. I'll loan you some trash for that business if need be."

"Thank you, Alex. I'll bear that in mind."

Finn looked so wobbly as he got up from the sled that Skookum Jim picked him up and carried him to be laid down in the flat-bottom scow.

"You'll look after our young Daisy, won't you please, Jim?" said Meg, shaking his hand.

"She's a Wolf," he said. "One of the clan."

"Good enough," said Meg. "Thank you. See you all back in Dawson?"

"Sure thing," said Jim, who liked to use Carmack's expressions.

It was a quiet ride down the muddy brown currents of the Klondike. Meg was amazed at the number of boats with prospectors heading upriver to the gold creeks. There must have been a big influx into Dawson while she was away. She waved to the people. Yukon Sally sat up, alert and cautious as a wolf guarding her pack and pup in uncertain circumstances. Alex sat silent, Finn was in a doze. Meg thought of what Finn had told her when he became lucid, describing what had actually happened when he took Mad Mitzi over the Chilkoot and downriver.

Finn said Mitzi had thrown hysterics, many times. He tried to coax her. She increased her hysterics. He slapped her cheek and threw her over his back. Carried her up the steepest parts. Told her to wait while he went back to carry up the packs. She came running after him. He took her back up mountain. Tied her to a tree. That made her so truly mad with fear of being attacked by bears and cougars that she fell into a petrified silence. Eventually listened to reason and agreed to wait with his gun in her keeping while he transported the packs, then came back to carry her.

"She got so crazy," Finn said, "I had to worry she would use the gun on me. But in the end, she has a shrewdness about her that gets her around most anything. Makes her hang onto whoever will get her through the worst. And she sure knows how to drive a man wild in the sack. Up against a tree. Wherever ... sorry, Meg. But she sure knows how to use what she has and loves a man using her. Even with no money involved. I don't have any, as you know. But I got her to Whitehorse in spite of some of the worst conditions I've seen. The Chilkoot Stairs were greased with ice and rain and early snow. Everywhere it was filling over so fast with ice that the Indians wouldn't go on the lake and downriver. But I got the loan of their canoe and got us, canoe and all, to Whitehorse.

"Neither Mitzi nor me would get back on that river until it was frozen solid. She had a wild time with the men in Whitehorse. I was busy hunting and ice fishing to feed my dogs, store up a bit for the trip to Dawson. She used my cabin there as her base but spent most time in the other men's cabins. Made enough at her trade to buy herself some finery once I got her to Dawson. But she wouldn't pay me for getting her there. Told me she had paid me more than enough with her 'services.' Told Constantine I was a woman beater and rapist. Wanted me in jail to get rid of me. Figured me being around with a different story wasn't good for her business with the Klondike Kings.

"Constantine wasn't sure who to believe, until my friends arrived and put in some good words for me. Constantine then let me out of the clinker. Wasn't too bad in there. Free food, just had to chop a lot of wood, and they looked after my dogs good. Constantine made Mitzi pay me enough to get out to the creeks with start up supplies. But it was end of winter, ground still frozen, and I guess I'm not much good at prospectin'. Had to team up with Jethro. Sold him my dogs."

Finn's eyes watered and he turned away. "They were in bad shape. I hadn't been able to feed them well enough. Come spring, my bitch, now Jethro's, had a litter of only one. Jake had all the teats to himself. Little fat boy. But he's a good-looking malamute. All my dogs are. Best matched team of malamutes around. Jethro's a good man. He gave me the pup once it was weaned. He'd be a good mate for your Yukon Sally, Meg."

It was mid-August when Meg landed back in Dawson with Big Alex and Finn, Yukon Sally, and Jake. She was astounded by the growth. So many more boats at the floating docks. The streets filling up with buildings and thronging with people.

Constantine in his red serge was superintending the crowds at the docks. The *Alice* had arrived with many passengers. Fashionably dressed men and women were proceeding down the gangplank. It was a new breed of citizens for Dawson City. Not just new prospectors and entrepreneurs of the saloon entertainment business, but entrepreneurs of all trades. Bankers, jewellers, journalists, cobblers, and cabinet makers.

Constantine came over to greet Meg and company. He saw Big Alex hoist himself up onto the dock and begin to step up onto the river bank but then turn, reach down, and lift Meg up by the armpits to a standing position on the dock. She laughed and saluted Constantine. "Beg to report, sir, I have returned from the battlefields with the sick and wounded."

Constantine looked at Finn trying to get himself upright. Then he shouted to Wiggins.

"Ambulance required. Finn's back in town." He turned to Meg. "Finn the Unfortunate. Ever seen a man so prone to trouble? Though he's come back with a better class of escort this time."

Finn was transported to Meg's in the ambulance, a long cart hauled by the Mounties' biggest team of malamutes.

Constantine dropped by later that night. "This town is overloaded," he said, sitting down briefly at Meg's table. "They're coming downriver from Skagway and upriver from Alaska. Costs a thousand dollars for that sternwheeler trip upriver from St. Michael's. They're better dressed, but worse-equipped riff raff. Arrive with no supplies, expecting to find everything here as if Dawson were a real city. I don't know what in Tarnation they're hearing on the Outside. But it's sure not my reports of this escalating situation. In spring, we had just under two thousand so-called citizens registered. Now I reckon we're dealing with five thousand."

But none of them is Jacques or Mick, Meg thought to herself. She had estimated that if her letter arrived in mid- or late July, Jacques could get to Dawson by the end of August, if he acted quickly. Clearly, he had not. There was not so much as a letter of response from Alice. Or from Mick.

"We could do with a medical doctor," Meg said to Constantine. "Any of those arrived?"

"Not a one, though they were on my request list to headquarters. But we do have ourselves one genuine Catholic priest. Father William Judge."

"What's he like?"

"He's not riff raff. I'll tell you that. Figured he was, at first. With such a name . . . Father Judge! Arrived just after you left, coming with the hordes of greeds and grubbers from Skagway. Calls himself Judge. Look at me," Constantine adjusted his hat. "I have to do a judge's work but I don't try to con anyone into thinking I'm the genuine article. Got one on order and I can't wait to hand over a desk to him. But I was wary of this man calling himself Judge, arrives wearing the cloth. Some mighty nasty hustlers can put on the white dog collar and operate in the wilds. You'd be surprised Meg, what strange practices some men have."

"Strange things go on in real cities too," said Meg. "I know more than you think I do."

Constantine looked at her in a way that reminded Meg of one malamute assessing another. She laughed. "Some time, when you have time, Charles, we can tell our own stories. What about Judge?"

"He's a proper priest. Does his job and more. Not a normal man. Goes far and beyond the call of duty. Mans as many desks as I do. He's building a church and the pews within, all with his own hands. Mind you, he's a sorry-looking specimen of a man. Skin and bones. A cannibal would throw him aside."

When the citizens of Dawson saw Finn recover from an advanced case of scurvy under the care of Dr. Meg, some came to her for medical help.

"It wasn't me," said Meg. "It was Kate Carmack's expertise. Spruce gum and bed rest."

"Spruce gum. What's that? Tree sap?"

"It is."

"Why should I have to pay for that?"

"You don't. Go get it yourself if you want."

But they didn't know how. And couldn't be bothered. Or didn't believe her. Or had no respect for "Indian medicine." But others saw, believed, and were willing to pay for the expertise and product. The most influential of these was Father Judge.

He came to her on the recommendation of Finn himself, who when strong enough had walked over to the site of the church under construction and pitched in. Big Alex, also a Catholic, had pitched in a large amount of "trash" to pay for the building materials.

When the church was basically built, Father Judge came knocking on Meg's door. "I understand you're not Catholic," he said. "But you have quite a reputation as a doctor. And I was wondering if you might help me in creating a hospital for people?"

Thus the dog doctor was lured into fundraising and eventually administering at the human hospital of Dawson City.

With his regaining strength, Finn had reached out to Meg and tried to pull her into his bed.

"No, Finn," she said. "You're my friend and guest, only."

"Oh, come on," he said. "I won't hurt you. I just want to thank you, with all I got. You know I'm crazy about you. Always have been. You're through with Stander. You should have someone. What's the matter with me?" He threw off the blankets revealing his thin but strong body and his enlarged private parts.

Meg left the room, but couldn't help smiling as she said through the doorway. "Nothing, Finn. There's nothing the matter with you. You're obviously all cured."

"So I'll have to move out?"

"Yes. As soon as you find a place."

"I'm sorry, Meg. I won't ever show you my pecker again. Forgive me?"

"Of course. You're a well-built male, Finn."

"Thank you, Doctor."

Finn got a room over Ladue's sawmill, where he obtained work as a carpenter.

"You don't have to give me Jake," Meg said when Finn was moving out.

"Oh, yes I do," he said. "He's attached to Yukon Sally and you. And come spring, I'll be back at the creeks, working that claim you so kindly registered for me. Might be broke and unable to feed myself again. He's yours."

"Thank you, Finn." She hugged him. "Yukie and I will take good care of Jake."

Not only potential citizens, but tourists began to arrive in Dawson at the end of that summer of '97. They were wealthy world travellers who wanted to see and contribute to this exotic settlement in the far north that was being advertised worldwide as the site of the last great gold rush on earth. Two such tourists were a female couple who came down the gangplank on the last big passenger boat of the summer, leading two well-groomed Great Danes. The women themselves were an impressive pair. Both wore military-style caps rather than hats. Edith von Born was in a dark, trim dress, Mary E. Hitchcock in a dark tailored suit.

Constable Wiggins was called to the scene. He politely welcomed and interviewed the women then quickly sent word to Constantine about the peculiar nature of their baggage. They had brought an ice cream machine, a magic lantern, a zither, a mandolin, a bowling alley, a score of pigeons, two canaries and a parrot, along with their Great Danes.

"Pigeons and parrots!" Constantine shouted. "What are *they* going to do when it's sixty below! Get those women and their zoo back on the boat." He put his head down to his work at desk number two. "Wait! Pigeons make good pie. And that parrot. We better ask our veterinarian about that."

Misses von Born and Hitchcock said they would be most interested in meeting a woman dog doctor.

"You ladies and your dogs don't want to stay," Constantine said bluntly. "We're going to run out of grub here this winter if the situation doesn't improve. Dogs have been known to be eaten for food in these climes, in desperate circumstances."

"Sir," said Edith von Born, "we ourselves had quickly concluded that this is not a comfortable wintering place. However, we do have the right to dispose of our goods, do we not?"

They did not warm to the Mountie in command of Dawson City but they thought Meg and the teams of sled dogs she introduced them to were a highlight in all their world of travels. Meg had the dogs do "wolf howls" for the ladies. She directed demonstrations of their pulling powers, told them of their Arctic wolf ancestry, pointed to the territory on top of Dome Mountain where a pack of wolves sometimes howled in the night, setting off the dogs of Dawson to howl in response.

"Let us have a photograph of ourselves with these dogs, shall we, Edith?" Mary exclaimed, clapping her hands together. "And we'll tell everyone they are wolves!"

But there were as yet no photographers in Dawson and their boat was giving a warning bell of imminent departure.

"Thank you for this most interesting tour of Dawson City," said Edith. "It would appear we have run out of time to carefully dispose of our goods. And I thought they would be so useful to a burgeoning place like this! I have an idea. I hope you will agree with me, Mary, dear. We could donate our birds and goods to this most unusual veterinary clinic. Could we not? A good cause, wouldn't you agree?"

"Lovely idea," Mary smiled. "I'm sure our dogs agree."

Edith turned to Meg. "The income from the sale of our goods would be at your disposal. Perhaps you could have an auction. What do you say to that?"

"Thank you very, very much. Auctioning is a way of life in Dawson."

There was many an auction at the end of that summer in Dawson City. Saloon girls auctioned themselves off for the winter to the highest bidder for their weight in gold. One girl made it more interesting by presenting herself naked in a tub of wine. Meg presided at the auctions of dogs for breeding and for team work. She added to their value by certifying their health, showing charts of their blood lines, and being the consultant on canine genetics. She advocated selective breeding instead of the *laissez-faire* system in operation, which was the cause of many a dog fight in Dawson City. Her highest recommended male and female dogs sold for over a thousand dollars that season.

But the best-attended auction of all was the one with Father Judge and Doctor Meg auctioning off an ice cream machine, a magic lantern, a zither, a mandolin, a bowling alley, a score of pigeons, two canaries and a parrot, with all proceeds going to the building of a hospital in Dawson City.

"Pigeons," Meg shouted from the balcony of a saloon at the huge crowd gathered below on Front Street. "Trained carrier pigeons. Send a message to your loved ones. Fastest mail out of Dawson City."

"And you'll be wishing this winter you'd saved them for pie," Constantine grumbled.

"Canaries," shouted Meg. "Come on, all you rich Kings of the Klondike. You know there's no better pet in a mine than a singing canary."

"And this handsome parrot," she shouted, while Father Judge held the parrot aloft. "Pope Parrot, is his name; for, he comes with the Church's blessing, to raise money for our hospital. I'm going to start the bidding at $2,000. And that includes one year of free veterinary checkups."

10

A Weak and Feckless Lot

SEPTEMBER BEGAN. Daylight hours decreased quickly in the Yukon. Geese and ducks and small birds gathered themselves into flocks and took off into the southern skies. The caribou herded themselves and followed the scent of warmer air. Two-legged and four-legged hunters tried to intercept as many as they could, wolves attacking the slow and weak, men seeking out the big and meaty.

Green leaves already turned yellow and orange, scattered in winds that chilled from the Arctic. Grizzlies and black bears, seeing the bushes denude of berries and ice beginning to form over their supplies of fish, lumbered into caves to sleep away the oncoming winter. Big game retreated into the mountains. Wolves and dogs of the north grew a thick undercoat of fur. Hares and mice turned white to hide in the snow. Chickadees and snow buntings feathered their nests and sang a cheerful song. "Bring it on."

Constantine paced and frowned. The people of Dawson were his responsibility. He sat down at his correspondence desk and informed Ottawa of the situation:

Approximately 4,000 crazed men, he reported, *chiefly American miners and toughs from the coastal towns, have arrived and aren't about to depart. Winter is fast coming on. The outlook for grub is not good. And all these gold diggers, women included, are apparently blissfully unaware.*

Three-quarters of them have never braved a winter north of Vancouver. And they've come as though expecting to find a proper city with stores full of goods and streets full of furnished houses to rent. What we're going to have on our streets is corpses buried in snow, if supplies don't come through.

Constantine had ordered everyone to chop and lay up a winter's supply of wood. But how could he make them produce a sufficient supply of *food*, damn it! He banged his fist on desk number three. He summoned the general manager of the Alaska Commercial Company. "Captain Healy," he said, "what in Tarnation has happened to your ships? They should be here by now. This town is about to run out of food!"

"Inspector Constantine," said Healy, "I have done my job. I have ordered five steamboats to be loaded with food and clothing. I was informed that these orders have been fulfilled. They are on their way up the Yukon. God knows why they have not arrived yet. But I do not."

"In that case, Captain, the mystery will have to be solved by the North West Mounted Police." Constantine stood up from his desk. He closed the heavy book of daily reports. "I shall be heading down-river to Fortymile at sun-up. If the fate of your steamboats can't be traced from there I'll be stymied. If they're in Alaska, it's beyond my jurisdiction."

Healy considered this. He did not like his company being shown up, even investigated, by the North West Mounted Police. He would send his own investigator. Hansen, his assistant at the Alaska Commercial Company, was always hot to trot.

"Let me talk this over with Captain Hansen," said Healy. "He'll follow the river all through Alaska, right to the ocean if necessary. He's done it many a time."

"Very good then, Captain Healy. I'll expect to see Hansen at the wharf at sun-up. We'll be racing against the freeze over."

Constantine patrolled his way through town that night, finding himself wanting to have a conversation with Meg, say goodbye. The
nights were cold but not yet cold enough for his fur parka. It was too
dark to see as he walked in military stride from the barracks and along
Front Street. He couldn't see them, but he could hear big chunks of
ice crashing into the ice already forming along the river's edge. On
the town side of the street, the saloons were dimly lit but rollicking
with men drinking, fiddles playing, women entertaining with song
and dance. Always plenty of whisky, he observed. Never in short supply of that.

He turned down York Street and worked his way to Meg's. It was
his duty to glance into commercial windows. He glanced into hers.
She too was entertaining. But with a book. And he knew the proceeds
would go to the hospital fund. He watched, feeling like a peeping
Tom. She looked as pretty as his grade-school teacher, hair tied up in
a ribbon, fresh white blouse neatly tucked into that little waist. With a
book held up in one hand, she was animatedly reading, gesturing with
the other hand, looking up dramatically at her audience. Suspense
hanging in the air, he thought, smiling to himself. Then she closed
the book with both hands, bringing it down towards her knees as
she bowed and then looked up with a broad smile at everyone. They
clapped and stomped or rose to their feet shouting for more. She was
laughing as she shook her head and pointed her finger in the air saying, "No more tonight, folks. Come back tomorrow."

Constantine knocked on the door. Meg opened it. "Inspector Constantine! This is an honour. Won't you come in? Well timed, I must
say. The reading is over. Did you so time it?" She smiled.

"Not at all. Sorry to have missed it." Constantine stepped in, tipped
his hat to all. Was amazed to see Big Alex in the crowd, even risen to
his feet in applause. And Kate Carmack with her daughter.

"Just making my rounds. Looks like a peaceful enough gathering.
Might I have a word with you, Dr. Oliphant?" He tipped his hat to all
and stepped back onto the porch.

She stood with the door closed behind her. "What is it?" she said
anxiously.

"Departing tomorrow for Fortymile. Must find out what has happened to our last supply ships. The river is freezing over. Afraid we're going to run out of grub."

"Oh Charles, this sounds serious. And dangerous. Are you sure you should go?"

"It's my duty. No question."

"Well, I won't try to dissuade you of that!" She smiled. "Come back safely." She took his hand in both of hers.

He withdrew his hand, embraced her tightly, kissed her cheek. Then in embarrassment, saluted. In greater embarrassment, he turned and marched down the steps, down the street, no looking back. Damn it! He cursed himself. I should be fired for that. Behaved like a school boy, not a Mountie. Lost control. Lost respect. Damn me ... to hell!

At sun-up, a small crowd waved to Constantine and Hansen as they set off downriver in a sturdy canoe paddled by themselves and two native men. Meg was there on the docks with Yukon Sally and Jake sitting attentively in front of her. Constantine waved once to all then turned and faced the river heading north.

Healy put a lock on the door of the Alaskan Commercial Company, where the remaining food supplies were stored. He had Wiggins and three other constables on hand to enforce the new rules. Only one person at a time would be allowed into the warehouse. And only three day's ration of food could be purchased at a time.

"There's enough for all," he shouted at those gathered around, "so long as no one gets greedy. Now line up, boys. One after the other, neat and tidy. Have your money or poke ready. A fair deal for each and all. Constable Wiggins and company will see to that"

There were dozens ahead of her when Meg took her place in the line up. She looked around at all the newcomers to Dawson, all so ill-equipped for the winter setting in. Pickaxes and shovels aplenty. But their boots were worn out and their packsacks empty. They looked bewildered and discouraged. And so we should, thought Meg. I've never had to line up for rations of food in my life.

"So it is, in Dawson, the city of millionaire miners," she said to the men beside her.

"We should've been told," they complained.

"They should've warned us."

"How can we work the gold fields if we can't have more than a few days' food?"

"Can't buy enough food to go stake a claim, let alone search around for a good one."

"How much longer we supposed to wait for word about them supply ships? I've a good mind to rush this dang warehouse and take the grub to the creeks where we can do some good with it. This is a miners' town. Why don't Miners' Law rule!"

"Constable Wiggins," Meg called out, "this gentleman has a question for you."

Wiggins approached with Healy coming up behind him.

"What is your name, sir?" said Wiggins. "And where are you from?"

"Ely. Ely Doone from Wrangell, Alaska."

"Came up through Moore's place then, did you?" said Healy.

"What you mean Moore's place? Never heard of it. Came up through Skagway. Took the White Pass."

"We don't want no Skagway here." Men stepped forward to stand behind Constable Wiggins and Healy. "This is an orderly town. No guns. No bribery neither. Go back to Skagway if you want your shootouts and lynchings and robberies."

Two newly arrived dance hall girls stepped forward. "We're from Wrangell. It was bad enough. But Skagway! That's real scary! Look what they done to that Frenchman they caught stealing from someone's pack. Lashed him up in front of his tent then filled him with so many gun shots he was nothing but a fountain spouting blood. They left his body, awash in blood and gore, on display for three days. That's Miners' Law, for you. We come to Dawson to get away from that." They sidled up to Constable Wiggins. "Give us a Mountie over Soapy Smith and his gang, any day. Or night."

"Thank you, ladies," said Wiggins. "Now what was your question, Mr. Doone?"

"Clean forgot."

"You haven't forgotten to leave your gun with us at the barracks, have you? I don't recall seeing you report in."

Ely shuffled.

"Are you wearing a gun, Mr. Doone?"

Ely folded his arms over his front, scowling.

"Open your jacket. Now! My man."

Ely opened his jacket and withdrew a pistol which he handed over to Wiggins.

"Thank you, Mr. Doone. It will be kept for you."

"Next!" shouted Healy towards the front of the line. "Let's keep this moving."

The days after Constantine's and Hansen's departure turned into a week. Two weeks. Three. The cold Arctic winds stripped the trees and shrubs of their leaves. The evergreens darkened and the purple-hued mountains seemed to blacken like charcoal. Grass and small plants turned brown. Larger and larger chunks of ice bashed around in the raging currents where the Klondike flowed into the Yukon River.

Each morning, Meg took Yukon Sally and Jake on their run around the outskirts of Dawson. Yukon was over a year old, a large malamute, at her full height, but her body not quite filled out. She was strong enough to pull a sled on her own, sometimes with Jake taking a rest in it. Jake was only a quarter her size but growing fast. He had more black in his coat than Yukon; darker, rounder eyes, and he was growing the broader chest of a malamute. Yukon Sally maintained the long legs and narrower chest of a wolf. Jake was more affectionate than Yukon and could be easily trained with food. He had a goofy playfulness about him that made Meg laugh out loud. The two of them helped to dispel her loneliness.

When she got into her cold bed at night, she wondered about Mick. Why had he not replied to her letters sent from Moore's Landing and upon arrival in Dawson? Had his letter been lost or was he lost to her? She pulled the covers over her head, trying to fend off the dark thoughts. When she got up shivering in the morning, she would reload the stove, make tea, and let the dogs come in to get up on the bed with her while she drank her tea. She missed Daisy and hoped that she would come back into Dawson. Along with Constantine whom she worried about daily.

Three weeks after Constantine's departure, when Meg was running Yukon and Jake part way up the Gulch, she thought she could see something coming upriver from the direction of Fortymile. It was hard to tell, with the river in such a commotion of bashing and jamming ice chunks, but it really did look like there might be something coming against the current towards Dawson. No. Probably just a battered log. But maybe ... "Let's go, Yukie, Jakey. Hike!"

They ran to Front Street and gathered at the wharfs, along with every other person and dog in Dawson City. The word had spread and sent everyone running like wild fire.

"A boat! A boat from the north!" people were shouting. The dogs began to howl and bark.

Meg got to the very edge of the river bank. She could see no boat. There was certainly no big ship of supplies. And no Constantine. Coming round the bend in the river was a much-battered birch-bark canoe, with Hansen and two native men, battling the current and big chunks of ice. All but the dogs fell silent in disappointment and apprehension as they watched Hansen steer into shore. He looked scrawny, wild-eyed, and exhausted, but he sprang up onto the wharf and raised his hand into the air.

"Men of Dawson!" he shouted. "There will be no riverboats here until spring. My Indians and I have come three hundred and fifty miles up the river to tell you this. I advise all of you who are out of provisions or who haven't enough to carry you through the winter to make a dash for the Outside. There is no time to lose! There are some supplies at Fort Yukon that the *Hamilton* brought. Whichever way you go, upriver or downriver, it's hazardous. But you must make the try."

Meg was surrounded by people in panic. They began to shout and scream. Some fainted. Others ran for their belongings to make the dash for the Outside. Meg stood her ground and tried to catch the whole story. She couldn't get near Hansen. Word was passed back that all the supply boats had been stranded and robbed of their cargo, hundreds of miles down the Yukon in Alaska.

"What about Constantine?" she kept asking.

"Probably drowned."

"Strung up. Supply boats got robbed. Mutiny at Fortymile."

"Miners' Law taken over."

"They got him captive at Fortymile."

Various answers were passed head over head in the mob. Yukon Sally's fur was bristling. Jake yelped. "Let's go," said Meg. "Let's get out of this disorderly crowd."

Yukon took off through the dispersing throngs with Jake at her heels and Meg running to catch up. They didn't stop running until they got to their cabin. Yukon and Jake demanded to be let inside. Yukon lay firmly down on the floor, panting, keeping her eyes on Meg. Jake lay down beside her, panting, looking at Meg.

"Well!" said Meg, also panting, "I see we have decided not to make a dash for the Outside."

She stood at the front window observing the street scenes in Dawson. Wiggins and the other constables were patrolling the streets like riot police. Restaurateurs were locking up, guarding what food they had left. People scurried to assess their stocks or clustered to discuss the situation. The dogs of Dawson were eerily silent, watching like wolves for what danger was at hand. Meg recalled stories she'd heard of the previous winter when some dogs were shot because their owners had no food for them. She looked at Yukon Sally and Jake, who looked up at her, inquiringly, trusting, full of readiness for whatever the task at hand.

How could anyone shoot such creatures? I would shoot myself first, she concluded. She drew in her breath as she felt a pang of fear.

"But first of all," she said to Yukon Sally and Jake, "let us find out the truth. What has really happened to our commander-in-chief. And let us see how dire the straits really are. I'm going to find Captain Healy and see what he has to say. He is a practical man. But you malamutes stay put. And keep a low profile. No howling when I'm out of sight. Do not make your presence known. You hear!"

Meg locked them in the back yard. As she set off to find Healy, she calculated what supplies she had on hand. Certainly enough ether and iodine. Constantine had had a good year's supply brought in for her. The cat-gut for sutures might run out but surely that could be brought by dogsled from one of the ports. A month's supply of dried meat and fish for the dogs. That could be replenished with more purchased from the natives at Moosehide. If necessary, I could teach myself to be a hunter. I could certainly learn to ice fish. And I've got enough beans, flour, and tea to share. There's also my secret emergency cache. Tins of corned beef, evaporated milk, and applesauce. I could sell that for a great fortune now. But Big Alex is right. Gold is trash. Food's the treasure.

She encountered Constable Wiggins doing crowd control. "Do you know what has happened to Inspector Constantine?" she asked.

"Constantine will survive," said Wiggins. "You may count on that. But there's been foul play at Fortymile and up at Circle City. Supply ships have been pirated by the fool citizens. But don't believe all you hear. Hansen gets over-excited. Cries wolf before he's actually seen it. Never make a Mountie out of that man. But, rest assured, our man Constantine will come through." Constable Wiggins tipped his hat to her. "You must excuse me now, ma'am. The citizens of Dawson are not at rest."

That answer was more wishful thinking than fact, thought Meg, but she was feeling some relief, if not optimism, by the time she found Captain Healy. He was standing sentinel outside his warehouse, flanked by several muscular citizens, their hands gripping shovels like rifles standing on end. The nearby saloons were noisy with men debating the situation, drinking to one opinion and then to another, as to what to do.

"Captain Healy," said Meg, "do you have enough in your warehouse to get us through the winter?"

"You're a sensible woman," said Healy. "Everyone else comes asking what they can bribe out of me today. 'Every man for himself' is their philosophy. That kind of greedy guts will ensure our extinction. Hence these doors are locked until the citizens of Dawson calm down and listen to me, instead of taking Hansen's word as gospel."

"What is the truth, Captain?"

"The Alaska Commercial Company will see those who stay through the winter. The rations may get meagre but we haven't let a town starve yet."

"Yet, is not a very reassuring word, Captain Healy." Meg smiled.

"I can assure you of another thing, Dr. Oliphant. The *Weare* and the *Bella* have never let me down. Other boats get stranded and never make it. But they always have."

It's not in his interests to have the whole town vacate, thought Meg as she walked towards the waterfront. He and his company can now sell their goods at the highest prices. Must question him sometime on his understanding of "the greatest good for the greatest number." At the wharf, Meg saw more small boats than she could accurately count pushing off in the swift and ice-jumbled currents, full of men determined to make it to the stranded supplies, three hundred and fifty miles downriver.

Meg lay awake that night trying not to think about food and therefore thinking only about food. Roast beef dinners. Breakfasts of fried eggs with bacon. A fresh orange…

There was a scratching at the door. Meg got out of bed. "I'm coming Yukie, I'm coming."

Yukon sat on the back step, Jake beside her. Meg could hear more loudly the commotion on the streets as people discussed or acted upon leaving or staying. Yukon barked a sharp command.

"All right, come in then," said Meg. They followed her up to bed and stood by while she got into it. Yukon placed a paw near Meg's shoulder and spoke. Jake jumped up onto the foot of the bed. "Jake, you sneak!" said Meg. "Get down. Yukon asked first."

Jake growled as she nudged his rump with her foot but he got down from the bed. Yukon Sally got up on the bed, lay down and nuzzled her snout into the crook of Meg's arm. "Oh dear!" Meg patted her. "It's not so worrisome as all that, is it!"

Yukon sat up, ears twitching. Jake jumped back up onto the bed.

"All right, Jakey." She patted him. "Don't you worry, my wolves. All that ruckus out there on the streets, it's just drunk or panicking humans. We'll get through the winter. We're a pack and we'll stick together. Right?"

Yukon gave her face a lick. Jake got up and gave her three licks then settled in with his rump against her shoulder.

"Meg!" The front door had burst open. Daisy's voice sounded. "Meg, I'm back!"

She collided with Yukon and Jake rushing downstairs towards her. "Whooa! What are you spoiled dogs doing inside!" She hugged them. "My! How our fat pup has grown! And so, my braves." She patted each of them. "You're not taking off like all those cowards in boats, are you? No? Good dogs. You have to stay here with us. In case we have to eat you."

"Daisy!" Meg held her arms out to her. "That's not funny. What kept you so long!"

"Skookum Jim," she said. "I'm going to marry him."

"When?"

"As soon as he accepts my proposal. He says I'm too young now."

Meg hugged her. "Now there's a wise man. Worth waiting for!"

Daisy had come in from what was now called Grand Forks in light of all the settlement that had sprung up around Belinda's bar, hotel, and general store. She had come in along with the rush of miners who left their claims unguarded to see what the situation was in Dawson. Belinda herself stayed put, unwilling to leave her cash register unattended.

"That Belinda!" said Daisy. "What a tough! And scrapper! Between her and the Big Moose, they're going to own the whole Klondike. Buying up mines. Buying up supplies before they even get to Dawson."

"What do you mean?"

"It's only hearsay, since you can't get two words out of the Moose and Belinda never shows her hand, but they say the two of them raced downriver back in June to buy up supplies on one of the boats that got stranded. Moose got there first and bought up the foodstuffs. Belinda was mad as hell at losing out on that, but she got the dry goods. Rubber boots and stuff, which she can sell for her usual two hundred per cent mark up come spring cleanup."

"Well! Haven't you picked up on economics out there on the creeks!"

"Economics?" Daisy frowned. "Knock it off, Meg! I'm not even asking what that means. On the other hand, what does it mean? I want to get into some other line of business, besides song and dance. I'm tired of being mauled and ogled by men I don't care about. Belinda doesn't have to do that. And nor do you. Ethel Berry says I could just sing, not dance with the men since I'm such a good singer ..."

"You are. You could go to New York and join the opera."

"I like it here in Dawson."

"So do I. You know in real cities it's much harder for women to get ahead."

"Don't start lecturing, Meg. I'm doing fine and I got a huge poke of gold to prove it."

"Did you see our new hospital? Roof isn't finished and we have no doctor or nurses yet. There's just the priest, me, and Kate as consultant on natural medicines. Lots of openings for you there. Ever thought of becoming a medicine woman?"

"No! I'm going to run a dress and finery shop."

Early next morning, while it was still dark, Molly Doyle came knocking on Meg's door with Sapphire Star, Gypsy Rose, and Mandolin Lily in tow.

"You're a doctor, right?" said Molly, getting straight to the point as soon as they were inside. "Sapphire here needs a potion."

"A potion?" said Meg, inviting them to sit down.

"Either that or an operation," said Molly. "Otherwise she's gotta get out of town for a few months and I say anyone who leaves now is walkin' straight into Hell froze over."

"Certain death," said Lily. "A woman would never make it."

"Molly thinks you could do something for Sapphire," said Rose skeptically. "Though neither she nor us is dogs."

"I don't want any operation." Sapphire looked scared, ready to bolt.

"In your trade," said Molly, "it could be the best guarantee of not having this 'trouble' in future. It worked for me. After my 'operation,' I couldn't have a baby even when I wanted to."

Meg frowned in consternation and pondered. "What exactly are you asking of me?"

"You neuter dogs," said Daisy. "Sounds like these ladies want neutering."

"No!" said Sapphire. "Just a potion. If you can't give me a potion, I'm leaving."

"I have no potions," said Meg. She looked very serious. "They do not work. Believe me, I know from experience. And they could be poisonous. I learned that from medical studies. But I never learned how to do the 'operation' I think you're asking of me. It is not taught in medical or vet school. I'm truly sorry Sapphire but I do not know how. I must tell you all." She looked at each of them in turn. "I haven't the knowledge or expertise to end a human pregnancy. Worse still, neither I nor all the medical texts there are can tell us women how to prevent one, for sure. The best they offer is 'the rhythm method' which ..."

"Doesn't work! Tell it to the men! Surest way to get trapped!" Meg was interrupted by a full chorus of rebukes.

"That's what we used to call, in my time," said Molly, "the fucking lie."

All but Sapphire laughed.

"It's something I want to study more," said Meg resuming her seriousness. "This idea that human ovulation is the same as in mammals. It could be based on a false analogy. Dogs do ovulate when they show blood but maybe it's wrong that women are the same as bitches..."

They all stared at Meg. Molly began to hoot with laughter.

"Time for breakfast," said Daisy. "I'm starving. And Meg..." Daisy wrinkled her nose in disgust. "You better have something better than 'human ovulation' and 'false analogy' to offer our friends."

"Beans," said Meg. "Beans and tea. Let's start with that, then see what else we can do for Sapphire."

The Big Moose from Antigonish sat on the porch of his log cabin, his arms folded over his chest, his large torso pushed heavily against his tipped-back chair. He was wearing his winter sealskin parka but with the hood down and the front undone because it was not yet the winter temperatures of forty to sixty below freezing. Sometimes he stood up and stretched, then leaned against the railing by the steps. But he would not leave his post or talk with anyone who tried to engage him in a deal. Mid-morning, Meg and Daisy stopped in front of his cabin on their way to the rations line-up.

"Hello, Alex," said Meg. "Daisy has a big poke of trash. Got any stores you want to trade?"

"No!" he said. "No deals in fear and desperation."

"Wow!" said Daisy as they moved on. "What was that... seven words and one of them real big! Is he panic-stricken or what? The hoarder! He's hiding it all away for himself."

"I don't think so," said Meg. "He's not a serious hoarder. He'll sell when everyone calms down. He's a decent man. And secretly very generous."

"Oh yeah? How do you know that?"

"Father Judge told me. Alex gave a huge amount to the hospital. And you know the Catholic church Father Judge built..."

"No, I do not. You forget that I've been out of town. And I do not like missionaries."

"Missionaries. Why not?"

"I was taught in a mission school. And I think they're all off their rockers."

"But they gave you a good education?"

"One of them taught me a lot about his dick."

"Oh Daisy, no!"

"Oh Daisy, yes! And you think you know more than me."

Meg put her arm around Daisy's shoulders.

"I warned you about doing that in public," said Daisy, but did not push Meg's arm away. "Tell me more about St. Alex."

"The church burned down. On a Sunday, no less. It was heart-breaking for Father Judge."

"Sounds like a message for him. Didn't he get it?"

"No." Meg laughed. "Everyone pitched in to help rebuild. And Alex quietly paid for most of it."

Meg and Daisy took their place in the long line-up at the Alaskan Commercial Company. Only one day's rations was being allowed. Healy was taking things a day at a time until it was certain what had happened to the supply boats. One cup of dried beans was the ration permitted for that day, September 27th.

"A cup of beans!" A woman was shrieking at the end of the line. "I'm not standing in line for a cup of beans!"

Mad Mitzi flounced past Meg and Daisy and everyone else to get to the front of the line. She lifted her purple velvet skirt, trying to keep it above the mud formed from thousands of boots trampling on partly frozen earth. Her chin raised, turning her head angrily this way and that, her blonde ringlets tossing from side to side, her fur cape billowing, she drew to a halt in front of Captain Healy. "I have money for more than beans!"

"Beans are all you get. And if you don't get back in line, you'll have none of them."

Mad Mitzi wouldn't deign to give him another word. She turned and gave him her back, flouncing off into town.

Daisy had told Meg about Mitzi coming frequently for meals and entertainment in Belinda's saloon, usually with Anton. But sometimes not. She and Anton quarrelled, often. Mitzi would get bored or take umbrage at something Anton said. Then she would leave his table and drink at the bar, flirting and dancing with other men. Anton would react by drinking more, eventually grabbing her by the arm and demanding she go home with him. Usually this would excite her, make her turn her charms fully upon him and persuade him to waltz with her. Or she would turn on him with a temper to match his and demand that he leave her, forever. She would then rent a room at Belinda's for a night or two. If Anton did not come and seek her forgiveness, she would go to his cabin and apparently obtain his.

"She is not pregnant?"

"Who knows," said Daisy, "what she's done with that act."

When Meg and Daisy returned to their cabin with their two cups of beans, they found Mad Mitzi sitting at their table.

"*Chérie!*" Mitzi laughed and opened her arms to Meg. "At last we have a chance to talk! Oh, hello." She turned briefly to Daisy, then back to Meg. "Your door was unlocked so I let myself in. Your dogs went crazy at the back door, scratching and howling like savages to get in. But I didn't dare let them. They're frightening as wolves. I don't know why you keep them."

"I'm not afraid of wolves," said Meg.

"I'll take them for a run." Daisy went out the back door, slamming it loudly behind her.

"She's not well raised, is she! Quite primitive. *Mais, excusez-moi.* She is your friend. I'll say nothing against her."

"There's nothing *to* say. There is nothing bad about her. I love her like a daughter."

Mitzi put her face in her hands. "Don't remind me. Oh, the child I might have had." She looked up with watery eyes and sniffed. "With Anton. He is such a handsome man! *N'est-ce pas?* But I must tell you Meg, he has a wicked temper. He gets drunk and turns into a fiend, I tell you. A *fiend!*" She covered her face as though to prevent the memory of it. Then she looked up at Meg, touched her arm sympathetically. "I know. I know, my innocent friend. He told me. You were once *trés* in love with him. But when he saw me dance, he … well, he begged me to come live with him.

"But really, my *chérie*, those miners' cabins are dreadful. *Dreadful* places. I wanted to come back into town immediately. *Immediatement!* But then word came that a widow called Mrs. Elephant and her half-breed young sister, who looked like a wolf, had arrived in Dawson. Isn't that *comique!*" Mitzi laughed. "I had no idea it was you. We had great laughs over the arrival of a Mrs. Elephant and her wolf. But then Anton wondered and became moody. It took all my wiles to extract from him that you had had a petite rendezvous in Vancouver. Still, we could not know that the widow Elephant was actually you, until we saw you in Belinda's. But it was too late. Oh, *chérie*, I was with child. It was such a shock to see you and feel the inevitable, the inevitable tragedy of love's triangle." She clasped Meg's arm.

"For heaven's sake, Mitzi, where's the tragedy? He simply chose you over me. There's no tragedy. I'm still alive. And kicking."

"Ah yes. But my heart, my mind, my body could not stand the conflict. The shock and conflict. I lost the child. Our love child. *L'enfant d'amour.* And with it went the perfect love that we had. We began to quarrel. Anton turned to drink. His *beautiful,* romantic nature, changed. We have had to part." Mitzi drew in a sorrowful breath.

"When did you lose …" Meg felt herself gagging over Mitzi's terms, "this love child?"

"Weeks ago, *chérie.* Tragic weeks ago. But you are right. It is time to recover. To kick up one's heels. I need to live. And dance again. Do you have a drink? Let's share some whisky. Drink to friendship." Mitzi stood up, heading for the whisky cupboard she had already been into. "And then you must tell me how to get a meal in this wretched town. I have a room at the hotel but they have closed all the restaurants. Imagine! A city without restaurants. And they say this will be the Paris of the north. I think not, *chérie. Je pense pa*s."

"What does it mean," said Daisy when Meg was recounting the scene to her, "*je pense pas?*"

"If I remember my French correctly," Meg laughed, "it means 'I don't think.' I believe she should have said, *je pense que non.* But her English is no better. How can you accurately call a conception, *if* there ever was one, that lasted only a number of days, a *child?* And a love child, for heaven's sake! That was no *l'enfant d'amour.* I call that the oldest ploy in the books."

"Ploy?" said Daisy, then stood up impatiently. "No don't bother explaining that to me. I've had enough of your Mad Mitzi. She treats people like shit wipes. And you should not have shared your beans with her."

"Ah but this is the Klondike. We leave our door open and share our food. Besides, she gave me a big gold nugget. Her parting gift. She's leaving town."

"Not even malamutes can eat gold," said Daisy.

It was dark the next night, September 28th, when again the cry, "*A boat! A boat is coming!*" brought everyone running to Front Street. This time it was not a small craft, no canoe. It was the large bow of the Alaskan Commercial Company's cargo boat, the *Portus B. Weare.* People and dogs crowded along the shoreline, encouraging its struggle against the currents and ice flows by lighting bonfires, waving, shouting, dancing up and down.

Captain Healy forced his way to the front of the crowd. "That's our boat, boys!" he shouted. "Our supplies have come through. I told you! I knew they would. The Alaskan Commercial Company won't let you starve, boys. Make way. Make way."

People cheered and threw their hats into the air. The dogs howled and barked and leapt up on whatever was at hand. Jake sent Daisy stumbling into Meg. Those in the front ranks of the thousands whooping it up on the banks of the Yukon, saw Captain Weare of the *Weare* step forward to shake the hand of Captain Healy.

"*Whisky and hardware!*" They heard Captain Healy shouting.

"What in God's name has happened to all the *food and clothing* that was ordered?" His voice grew louder and angrier. "Circle City, what do you mean they took it from you at Circle City! This isn't the high seas, my man. You're a riverboat captain. Don't tell me they're a bunch of pirates at Circle. They're just a few hopeless miners. And you let them take *our* supplies?"

Captain Weare's replies could not be heard above the roar of Captain Healy and the growing rumble of the crowd along the banks.

"What do you mean you had no choice! I'll give you no choice!" shouted Healy.

Captain Healy had to be bodily restrained from throttling Captain Weare in front of nearly four thousand witnesses. The full story came out and was bandied about from person to person as the throngs made their way back to the saloons or to their beds, hungry.

Meg sat in The Pioneer Saloon listening to the tales of what had happened. Other cargo ships were stranded for the winter in Alaska. But the *Bella* and the *Weare* had gotten farther upriver towards Dawson City. The *Weare* made it to Circle City, where it was boarded by a delegation of residents who pulled out their guns and forced Captain Weare and his small crew to stand aside while they removed food and clothing they wanted for getting through the winter. They then paid what they considered a fair price for the provisions they took.

Then Meg heard that Constantine, who had no jurisdiction beyond Fortymile, was seen waiting there for the arrival of the *Bella*. Because of the Yukon River freezing over, his request for reinforcement of supplies and officers had to be sent south, over the mountains, by dog-sled.

"When it comes to the crunch, in the Klondike," said Meg, who, like the others in The Pioneer, was fortifying herself on whisky, "meaning … when the way in and the way out gets frozen over, it's the dogs we have to rely on, isn't it? I want everyone to remember that, if the food runs out. *We need our dogs!*" She banged on the bar top.

Ike and Piji stomped in accord, hard as they could in their mukluks.

✶

Next day, Dawson was a city with a hangover and growing fear. Some went to church and prayed. Others lulled about or carried on with chores of gathering wood and water, portioning their food, considering hiding or hoarding, sharing or selling.

Meg and friends were occupied trying to console and reassure Sapphire Star.

"The baby could be taken to an orphanage on the boats going out next summer."

"If I knew the father," said Sapphire, with a spark of anger. "I'd get *him* to take it to the Outside."

"You can't trust a man," said Molly Doyle. "Specially when it comes to children."

"Since you couldn't be a mother," said Daisy to Molly, "here's your chance to be a grandmother."

"You could make an honest child of it," said Meg.

"And now that you're so rich ..." said Gypsy Rose.

"With a respectable occupation ..." said Lily.

"Don't you hurdy-gurdies think you can bamboozle me into something I don't want to do," said Molly. "First I've got to see what comes out, don't I?"

Everyone hoped for a sighting of the *Bella* coming upriver, but none had the heart to stand and wait for it. And when the following day, September 30th, a man saw it churning through the ice at the bend of river, few believed him when he yelled, "I see it! I see it. The *Bella*, she's a comin' through."

But when Meg heard the call, she started running, shouting, "Yukie, Jake, Daisy. Come on. Let's go!"

They were in the forefront of the crowd. It was a more muted crowd, clapping hesitantly after the experience with the *Weare*, except for Meg, who cheered loudly when she spotted Constantine standing firmly at the helm of the *Bella*. As it came to a full stop at the dock, Constantine raised his hand for silence.

"Men of Dawson," he shouted, "law and order will prevail. Discipline and co-operation are required. Due to misfortune and lawlessness beyond our borders, further provisions for the winter have been held up and confiscated. In other words, there will be no more grub coming our way by boat until spring. For those who have not laid in a winter's supply, to remain longer is to court death from starvation, or at least the certainty of sickness from scurvy and other troubles. Starvation now stares everyone in the face who is hoping and waiting for relief from the Outside."

There was no point in speaking further. The crowd had gotten the message. The *Bella* too had been waylaid in Circle City, a large part of its food stock "purchased" at gunpoint.

Men of Dawson shook their fists and kicked in the direction of Circle City. They shouted, murmured, stomped their boots, or trudged off in various directions. Constantine disembarked to maintain order and direct lines of action.

"Welcome back!" Meg shouted and waved.

He looked in her direction. Nodded. Then determinedly went about his duty. He nailed a poster up on Front Street with the full text of his speech

His strategy was to thin out the pack, persuade those who should and could vacate to do so. They could board the *Weare* and *Bella* for their final voyage back down through Alaska to Fort Yukon and hopefully beyond to the seaport of St. Michael. It would be risky as any wolf setting off into the wilderness alone, but if he or she had no comfortable place staying within the pack, it was the thing to do.

Constantine hoped to reduce Dawson City by about one thousand. He had assessed that three thousand had the means and strength, or could be provided for, with a rational distribution of the supplies on hand.

Hansen ran around town, fairly jumping up and down, circling groups gathered on Front Street discussing what to do, and barking at them, "Go! Go! Flee for your lives."

Calmer leaders of the community, like the collector of customs and the gold commissioner, reinforced Constantine's directive by addressing people gathered on corners, advising them to take this last chance to escape starvation. To recent arrivals who had not yet staked a claim, set up a business, or put up anything more than a tent, this made eminent sense, except for the factor of losing face, giving up all hope of wealth or fame, and returning to the misery or boredom of the situation which had driven them over the mountains to the Klondike.

And then there was Captain Healy, who confused the deliberators by saying on the one hand that Hansen was a panicking fool, that there was enough grub to get Dawson City through the winter, but then adding, on the other hand, that he was offering the extremely reduced fare of fifty dollars to encourage anyone to board the *Bella* and get out of Dawson as quickly as possible. As a final push, Constantine then made the exodus option as attractive as he possibly could by offering free passage on the *Bella* along with five days allowance of food.

And so it was, the next afternoon, October 1st at 4 p.m., Meg and Daisy stood with others on Front Street watching the departure of the *Bella*. One hundred and sixty had received their five-day free food allowance and were to have boarded the ship. There had been much to-ing and fro-ing on the gangplank, but now it was quiet. The crowd was hushed. They watched Constantine having a few last words with the captain, saluting him, then marching, on the double, down the gangplank and onto the dock where he summoned Wiggins and the other officers who were maintaining order on the waterfront.

"Forty!" Constantine shouted, and in his indignation at the lowliness of human nature, informed the entire gathering: "Forty have absconded with their food allowance. They got on board. Took the five days food and ran off with it. Find them! We'll find every one of them."

But the departure could not be delayed. The ice was growing denser and the darkness gathering.

"I simply changed my mind. Get your hands off me!" It was the distinct voice of Mad Mitzi. She, plus two men, were brought forward as the gangplank was being raised.

"Face jail for fraudulent obtaining of government supplies or get back on the *Bella*," Constantine yelled at them.

The officers held up the sacks of food that had been found on their persons, for the crowd to witness. The gangplank was lowered.

"Back aboard!" shouted the crowd.

Mad Mitzi held up her chin and raised her skirt as she stepped up onto the gangplank.

"You'll be wanting this." Constantine handed her sack of food back to her.

Mitzi opened her carpet bag and put the food back into it.

The gangplank raised, the *Bella* sounded her foghorn and set off in the currents. Her rudder got caught in the ice such that she was spun round and carried downriver stern first, until Captain Dixon could right her. Meg and Daisy had a last glimpse of Madeleine Mitzi Bonaparte standing at the railing waving to them, mouthing the words, "*Au revoir, mes amies.*"

It was late at night when Constantine knocked on Meg's cabin door.

"Ah!" Meg stood aside to invite him in. "Our commander-in-chief. It's good to see you."

"I beg your pardon for calling in so late, but I saw your lamplight."

"I couldn't sleep. I was just reading."

"You're not afraid, like the rest?"

"We were all afraid for your safety. But apart from that, and my dogs', no. And now that you are back, with law and order restored ..." she smiled.

"What a weak and feckless lot," he said removing his fur hat. "Turncoats every one of them, down at Fortymile. Hard to find an honourable man amongst them. But I guess I'm not much better myself." He looked at his feet, briefly.

"Inspector Constantine. Weak and feckless, you are not."

"I stepped over the line when I said goodbye to you. It was weak and dishonourable of me. A Mountie and a married man. I apologize."

"You regret it? I don't."

"I must never do it again."

"I see. All right. I'll try to help you in that by not being too ... feckless myself."

"Thank you. I do enjoy your conversation. I hope ..."

"Of course. Your view of the human race ..." She smiled and kept her hands tightly to herself. " ... I must hear more of that."

Constantine drew to attention. "There was a curious supply aboard the *Bella*. Came all the way from Halifax. Addressed to you. Did you order a hundred brooms?"

11

THE HUMAN STAMPEDE

ALSO ON THE *Bella* was a bag of crumpled mail that had been way-laid for several weeks. In it was a letter to Meg from Mick. It had been written in Boston on July 28, 1897.

My darling Meg,

Your two letters written before and after you climbed the Chilkoot arrived both at once, today! I dare not delay my response and so I am writing, somewhat surreptitiously from my office desk. I must be brief. I thank the Almighty and your own impressive strength that you arrived safely in Dawson City. I am going to wrap things up here as fast as I can and take a leave of absence.

I will find that Jon Teskey of Wrangell and then I will find you. I can only trust you will be there in Dawson City and not unhappy to see me.

I cannot think at this moment where you might write to me, delivery being clearly completely unreliable, but I will check for a letter at Hotel Vancouver and at the post office in Wrangell, assuming they have one.

I have heard your call, Meg, my love. I am coming to protect you for life, if I may.

Mick.

Meg quickly wrote several letters, all of them saying the same thing: *Do not come to Dawson City now. Wait until spring. We lack provisions. Do not worry about me. I shall be here, awaiting you, Mick, my love.*

Half of them she addressed to Hotel Vancouver, half to Wrangell Post Office, then she ran to the docks and the trail exiting Dawson seeking those who were still deciding to flee by small boat or on foot for the Outside, begging them to post her letters. Their looks of panic and desperation filled her with fear for their lives and hopelessness that they, or her letters, would ever reach their destination.

As winter set in, Meg harboured a small hope that Mick would arrive after all, since Dawson City fared much better than was feared, thanks to the good government of Inspector Constantine and company. But Deputy Chief O'Mara did not appear and no letter arrived from him. Meg could only guess that he might have reached what was now called Skagway and found his way down to Wrangell before freeze up. She so deeply regretted having mentioned Teskey's name and anything else about him that she couldn't bear to think about it. She had nightmares about Teskey killing Mick in various forms of surprise attack.

After Christmas, Meg composed a letter to Mick to be delivered by mail dogsled to Wrangell, with a copy to the post office in Skagway, just in case he checked in there.

I fear I have sent you to your death, she wrote to him, *I should have known it is in your nature to go after someone who has done me, or indeed anyone, harm. I can only pray that no harm will come to you. Though given what I have seen of life, it makes no sense to me that there exists a personally caring God who spares one individual's life and not another's; still, I have faith in a God of ultimate goodness, to whom we should direct our prayers and actions. In that faith I await you.*

You should feel quite at home in Dawson, for half the population in this so-called city is from your side of the border. And we are all getting through the months of darkness and severe cold, amazingly well. At the beginning of the winter, it looked as though we were in danger of starvation. About a thousand people were persuaded to head back from whence they had come, after it was discovered that several of our winter supply

boats had been stranded and pirated. Our population was about four thou-
sand. And still is! Because most of those who fled, have come back, includ-
ing ones who carried my letter warning you not to come until spring.

The few hundred who left with free passage on the last big river boats
on October 1st made it to the Outside, as we call it. But for two weeks after
that, people panicked again and sneaked off individually, by boat or on
foot. It was alarming and pitiful to see. Then came the sudden onslaught
of snow storms and the freeze-up of the rivers. We were knee deep and
waist deep in snow. The rivers were solid but not smooth. Great boulders
of ice rammed up against each other creating formidable obstacles to get
around. The individuals who had fled so ill-equipped, returned. Bedrag-
gled. Frozen. Starved. Injured. Snow-blinded. And then the diseases of
consumption and scurvy crept in.

Fortunately, we had built a hospital. Unfortunately, with no better doc-
tors than me and a plant doctor, Kate Carmack, and a priest called Judge.
I have had the busiest winter of my life! Dog doctoring, people doctoring.
No one seems to know or care any more that all my training has been on
pigs, rabbits, horses, dogs, and cats. I douse my human patients with ether
in the same manner I use with the dogs. An ether-soaked rag over their
nose. But it must be used very sparingly, for I fear running out before more
supply arrives.

Our food supply is lasting, just! No one will starve to death. After the
panic, calm and a sense of the common good has reigned. My good friend
and informant, General Commander and Chief of all Policing, Inspector
Constantine, remains in a fury over the seemingly endless stock of whisky
that appears in the saloons, compared to the limited supply of food that
got through to Dawson. The Alaskan Commercial Company's store of food
continues to be carefully rationed out, at a hefty profit to themselves, I'm
sure. And our reigning monarchs of the free-enterprise system that oper-
ates here in the extreme, King Big Moose Alex MacDonald and Queen
Belinda Mulroney, have somehow managed to keep turning up with goods
to sell. The restaurants re-opened before Christmas. Some enterprising
mushers have come from Skagway with items that have been auctioned
off for sizable fortunes. Twenty dollars for a frozen orange. Hundreds for a
turkey. Daisy bought a fancy hat for two hundred and has since sold it for

nearly five hundred. And, oh yes, we have caviar and olives. An acquaintance of mine, Anton Stander, bought a diamond for his new love, a dancer,
called Violet of the Veils. The cost of that diamond, set into a gold pen-
dent, was no more than the turkey.

I have to laugh, as I'm sure you must shake your head, at the values
here. Yet when it comes to the common good, people do rise to the occasion
and pass the hat. We will have all the money we need to pay for some doctors and nurses once the throngs arrive at ice breakup. Constantine ordered
that no more people be allowed to come to Dawson until practical supplies
can be brought in. He even wrote to Washington before Christmas, alert-
ing them to the situation. Their response was to have a herd of reindeer
rounded up in Norway... Norway!... and brought to Canada by sea, to
be herded overland to the Klondike. I could not believe the ignorance, well-
intentioned as it is, that would lead them to do this. The poor reindeer! It
would be kinder just to slaughter them where they are. But Constantine
was informed, note not consulted, but informed, that about five hundred
reindeer are on their way. What's the matter with our own government that
they don't commission our native people to round up caribou locally!

Constantine works twenty-hour days, just keeping the peace and order
here. He is not a man of great vision but of great practicality. Mounted
Police headquarters has ordered that priority be given to the Canadian
border crossing, where the swarms of people are coming up from Skagway.
There's a huge camp of people who have made it to the shores of Lake
Lindeman and are cutting down the forest to make boats to take them
downriver at ice breakup.

Captain Moore's dream of making his townsite the New York of the
north has turned into the nightmare called Skagway. His wife, Amy, has
written me telling that, by the end of the summer, Skagway's bay was a
mass of overloaded and decrepit ships, literally dropping their cargo over
the sides. Horses and dogs, even teams of goats, dropped or thrown over
the sides to swim to shore ... if they survived the drop! Oh dear, I cannot
bear the thought or description of this.

A gangster called Soapy Smith rules the town. People who cross him
are shot. Moore's wharfs were taken over without payment. As was his
land. He and Amy have managed to keep only their cabin and fenced-in

yard. They have to maintain armed guard over it. They say hundreds of
horses are being forced up the White Pass. They're thin and weak, sick
from the voyage, undernourished, their backs overloaded. He says they
look like they wouldn't make it across a pasture, let alone up a mountain
pass. Moore warns and rants at the people driving these poor creatures, but
they pay no heed.

Oh dear. What is the human race coming to? All for the sake of gold!

No. It's more complex and interesting than that. Neither I nor people
like Constantine, Father Judge, or Kate Carmack came here for the gold.
I'm sure it was Kate and not her husband George who first discovered the
gold, though he now takes all credit and has become ashamed of the mate
to whom he owes just about everything. Kate saw a letter George was writ-
ing to his sister in San Francisco, in which he said he would bring his wife
for a visit and described her, Kate, as being Irish, with a broad accent!

What think you of that Mick O'Mara! Sure an' ye must come now and
teach George Carmack what Irish be.

Wherever you are, may you be well and have a smile when you know I
am here, longing for you.

Meg gave her letters to the musher, including one to Alice and
Jacques, for though she had received a load of brooms, no other evidence of Jacques appeared. Lingering on the snow-packed trail with
Yukon Sally and Jake at her side, Meg watched the musher, standing
on his sled driving his team, until they were out of sight. She couldn't
know what would happen to them or her letters.

During that winter of 1897–8, when the land was covered in whitest
snow and the light was not from the sun, but from moon and stars,
Sapphire Star disappeared from her job in the saloon and was not
seen again until spring when she emerged from Molly Doyle's, in the
shape of her old self, but with less sparkle for her old job. Simultaneously, Molly Doyle acquired a grandson, "out of the blue," as they
said. Davey Doyle was a bright healthy baby. But, raising a child
on your own and giving up a child because you're on your own, are

difficult things. It wasn't long before Molly and Sapphire formed an unusual partnership to deal with their human project. Sapphire Star moved in again with Molly Doyle, washed diapers and such by day, sang and danced by night.

It was in the longer daylight of March that a mail musher brought the news to Constantine.

"Headquarters has sent in the big gun," Constantine reported the news to Meg. "Sam Steele. He's built a barracks and raised the flag on top of the Chilkoot. No one is getting through if they don't have the requisite year's supply, 1,150 pounds of food, plus a tent and tools. You'd think that would slow them down. But they're coming through by the thousands. *Thousands!* Says there's no end to the line-up. Trudging up through seven, eight feet of snow." Constantine shook his head, put his fur hat back on his head and marched out into the snow-packed streets of Dawson.

The sun brought more light and warmth to the mountains, to the frozen lakes and rivers. The streets of Dawson turned to slush and mud. Avalanches rumbled down mountains. At the end of April, the Chilkoot packers refused to carry. There was an unusual dump of snow looming close to the trail. "Too dangerous now," they said. "Wait."

Those who did not wait it out were buried in a sudden avalanche. Many were rescued, but fifty-three people died.

Sam Steele, a Mountie more calm and measured in his words than Constantine, went down to the camps on the still-frozen lakes and registered every man, woman, and child there. He would know the names of those who got lost or died en route to Dawson City. He painted an identifying number on every boat, scow, and canoe being built.

"Thirty to forty thousand!" Constantine raged. He did not know which desk to slap the letter upon. "Thirty to forty thousand escapees, on their way to Dawson!"

His boots pounded heavily on Meg's porch when he came to tell her.

"Do sit down, Inspector Constantine, please," said Meg. "Have some tea. Just think ... Dawson will qualify as a real city, at last."

From their point of view, the pack of wolves that roamed the top of Dome Mountain, watched the great rush of people seeking various forms of gold in the Klondike. They stared at the human stampede and could make no good sense of it. One thing they did sense. Danger. Danger had been present ever since the moose pasture was taken over by white humans. Humans who felled trees faster than beavers, humans who howled so noisily all night, and fought so readily within their own pack. This massive pack of human beings carried guns up into the forest and brought down big meat or small, whatever came in sight. Bears, mountain sheep, rabbits, caribou, or wolves. Four young wolves had been ambushed while they romped in what used to be their safe place.

The remainder of the pack left the territory, running north to find more forest and safer territory for the birth of their pups.

The human stampede came from all the continents on earth. They had heard that the Klondike was full of gold and single men. It appealed to the adventurous, the optimistic, and the fortune hunters of both sexes and all ranks of society at the turn of the twentieth century. They expected to launch the new century with great adventure and fortune. They wanted to get out of the cities, which had become polluted with coal smoke, horse dung, and an overhead net of electrical and telegraphic wires. Compared to all that, the Klondike sounded like a sportive winter camp. Canoeing, hiking, and skating were the popular sports of the time. Just the skills required, they thought, to make one's way over mountain trails and downriver to the Klondike. It was rumoured one might be able to do it on a bicycle. And who couldn't drive a stake into a piece of ground that sparkled with gold! Some said you could *smell* the gold, it was that peculiar and abundant in the Klondike.

Prospectors not having much luck in New Zealand decided to board a ship that would take them to Seattle and up the coast to Skagway. A dock worker in Japan decided to change his vocation and hop a ship heading across the north Pacific. An Oxford don and a few wealthy students had their valets pack trunks with sporting clothes, champagne, and foie gras. They set off, with valets and all, across the Atlantic on a luxury steamer. They had put their heads together over a map of the Dominion of Canada and decided upon an overland route starting from Montreal.

Chinese entrepreneurs were already on their way. An Indian merchant considered taking his elephants to the Rockies but backed away at the description of snow. Those well acquainted with snow, such as the Swiss chef, tired of cooking for people who wanted schnitzel, schnitzel, schnitzel, set off for the Klondike with his St. Bernard. A club of widows in New York was persuaded by an enterprising gentleman to pay him a grand sum to organize passage to the Klondike on a luxury ship. The widows could take their cats, dogs, and all. But they had to go the long ocean route, down the east coast of North and South America, to Antarctica, and back up the west coast of the continents. Only one of the women stayed the course and reached Skagway.

A young photographer, Frank Quigley, carefully packed up his equipment in Lucan, Ontario, and sensibly took a train to Vancouver, where he outfitted himself lightly and caught an old boat, jammed with people and horses, a team of goats, and various dogs, all bound for Skagway and the Klondike. A photographer, A.E. Hegg from Sweden, did likewise. They photographed the human stampede of hatters and cobblers, street car drivers and butchers, inventors of flying machines and bricklayers, teachers, doctors, lawyers, and policemen.

They took photos of the human chain moving laboriously up over the Chilkoot Pass in sunny winter days, tens of thousands of footsteps carrying heavy packs, creating what they called the Golden Staircase. Photos of the piles of packs at the top, buried in snow storms. The camp of forty thousand people building boats at the edge of the lakes, waiting to sail in one armada, the moment the ice went out. And there were photos of the few oxen, goats, and pet dogs that went with five thousand horses up the White Pass. The fifty-year-old woman, fit as a man and dressed like a man, who drove a team of goats up the Pass, made it to Dawson with her goats and became Molly Doyle's rival in business. Some of the pet dogs, who were fed and not overburdened with packs, made it with their owners to Dawson.

But the oxen and five thousand horses were all driven to an agonizing death on the White Pass. Death from exhaustion. Death by starvation. Death from whippings by humans gone mad. The horses had broken legs. Pneumonia. They were driven over cliffs. They were terrorized into suicide over cliffs. The long route of their death became known as Dead Horse Gulch.

The last musher of winter arrived in Dawson from Skagway. He reported to Constantine some of the things he had seen on the White Pass.

Constantine listened to what he had to say, ranted in outrage at the descriptions of what he had witnessed, paced in consternation, then took the musher with him to consult with Meg. "But don't tell her about the man drowning his dogs," said Constantine. "Let me take care of the general description."

"We've got horses in trouble on the White Pass," Constantine said to Meg. "Riff raff mistreating them. You have any remedies for horse colic and such that Fritz here might take back with him, maybe give some relief to those he finds in trouble on his way back?"

"Stop the horses from coming!" Meg shouted. "Don't let them on the trail! Outlaw it. Send in reinforcements."

"It's foreign territory." Constantine tried to calm her. "We have no jurisdiction there."

Meg turned to Daisy. "Can you look after Yukie and Jake? I'm going back with Fritz."

"No!" Constantine ordered her to stay.

But she would not obey him.

Fritz was a tall, lean, sixty-year-old musher who took good care of his team.

"It's too hot," Fritz tried to dissuade Meg, "and the snow is too soft. I have to keep my dogs at an easy pace and I can't let you ride the sled unless it's downhill."

"No argument from me," she said. "I'm a fast walker."

Yukon Sally and Jake looked at Meg in hurt and disbelief when she said goodbye to them. They looked as though she had suddenly turned and hit them.

"I'll be back," she said.

Yukon sat down, staring at her. Jakey lay down and looked up sorrowfully.

"Oh, come on, you two spoiled kids," said Daisy, "I'll let you sleep on her bed."

Meg, Fritz, and his sled dogs took off at a steady pace. From the outskirts of town, Meg could hear the frantic and plaintive howl of Yukon Sally. Then it stopped and Jake's even more frantic howls sounded. Then stopped.

Meg asked Fritz to halt. It wasn't long before Yukon Sally came bounding up to Meg, nearly knocking her over as she put her forepaws on Meg's shoulders and licked her face. Meg looked at Fritz.

He shrugged. "Ain't surprisin' since you won't chain your malamutes up."

They set off again with Yukon Sally running alongside. Then they heard Constantine shouting as he came up the trail with his team at high speed and Jake running alongside.

"You'll have to let him come with you," said Constantine as he threw a pack of dried fish onto Fritz's sled. "Yukon jumped the fence and Jake was going to injure himself trying. Meg, you keep them back of Fritz's team and they should be all right."

"But Jake's too young to do the White Pass," Meg worried.

"He's not carrying anything," said Fritz. "He can do it. Or my team will carry him. Come on. Trail's melting. Let's hike!"

Constantine saluted as Meg waved goodbye to him.

"Never seen anything like it my entire life," said Fritz as they sat round the campfire at night, Yukon and Jake sticking close to Meg, Fritz's team curled up together in the shadows. "Are you sure you have the stomach for it? Men gone mad. Men who brought horses they have no feeling for, dogs they don't understand. They do terrible things to those animals. I think you should turn back when we get to the lakes. Take a ride back on the boats. I reckon it's too late to be of any help in any case."

"I'll stay the course. Have to see if I can give any relief."

"I saw a man gone mad, start pushing three malamutes, one by one, through a hole in the ice. He'd bought them for a high price and had no clue how to handle them."

"What do you mean, you saw? You just *watched?*"

"No. I ran and grabbed him as he was shoving the third dog. I put his own head down into the hole but then I yanked him out, just in time. Let him live. His first two dogs died a terrible death. People saw that but did nothing to stop it. They just trudged on up the trail in their own madness. Human nature! Rather be with dogs any day."

He saw tears well up in Meg's eyes but nothing he said succeeded in making her turn back. "Would an army doctor refuse to go to the battlefield?" she said.

"It's man's work," said Fritz. "It'll make you tough and … indelicate."

Meg laughed. "I've never been delicate. Nor wanted to be."

"No Achilles' heel? Don't kid yourself. Everyone has one."

"You're well read, Mr. Fritz."

Fritz laughed. "A gentleman of the first order. And I can see your dogs wouldn't let me be otherwise. They're good-looking malamutes. Good breeding stock."

"I know," said Meg. "Next year when Yukie is going on three, I'll let them mate."

"And what about you? You ever going to mate?"

Meg looked into the darkness. "I'm awaiting the right male."

Meg and Fritz came down onto the wide trail from the summit of the White Pass. All the way, they encountered the dregs of the human stampede, moving slowly, steadily, wearily, up and over the summit. The slow human stampede had every kind of character: the vociferous and the quiet, the solemn and the jesters, the tedious and the bizarre. A young man played a fiddle at the summit. A woman sold cigars. Another offered fortune-telling for five dollars. Absent from the slow motion stampede were the delicate, the fearful, the indecisive, the shysters, and some of the smart business people. They remained in Skagway selling their wares, or had taken the ship to go back home.

Meg could smell the dead horses long before she could see them. She could hear the dying before she could see the pain and terror or surrender in their eyes. The large round, expressive eyes of horses. Their bony bodies, heaving, or still. The broken limbs and smashed heads of those who had stumbled or fallen or been wilfully pushed off the trail and over cliffs.

Meg put a cloth over her nose. Her malamutes kept closer to her, Jake falling in line behind Yukon Sally, both moving in most apprehensive silence, their tails held low. Fritz's dogs pulled ahead down the trail, wanting to get away from the sick and dying and groaning, the smell of the dead.

"There's nothing can be done," Meg said when she could speak, "but put them out of their misery. How much ammunition do you have?"

"I'm saving it for the bastards who brought them here."

Meg grabbed his gun and aimed it at a horse in agony. She put five out of their misery before she let Fritz regain his gun. It was out of ammunition.

"Now, let's get to the beginning of the trail," said Meg. "See if we can do anything preventative. Anything to stop this massacre!"

Yukon and Jake stuck with her as she sped down Dead Horse Gulch, yelling to those who were still trying to bring horses up, "*Stop. Turn around. Certain death! No horses allowed on this trail!*"

"I'll shoot you if you don't turn back!" Fritz pointed his gun and tried to herd men back.

"What the hell! Not more of you bleeding hearts trying to stop us!" one shouted threateningly at both Fritz and Meg. "Get the hell out of my way!"

"It's a free country. You can't stop us," said another.

"I'll shoot you in the knees!" Fritz informed them.

They pulled their own guns. "It's a free country! You'll go down first if you don't get out of my fuckin' way."

"If it's gonna be like this all the way up the trail … !" said another, reconsidering but keeping his hand on his gun.

Meg and Fritz carried on past them, down the trail, shouting at everyone with horses, to take them back.

Then, down near the beginning of the White Pass, Meg and Fritz spotted Moore and another man, trying to stop anyone from going up with a horse.

"Police! Stop!" the other man was commanding, with the gestures and authority of an officer, though he wore no uniform or gun.

"I'm Deputy Chief O'Mara, from the Boston Constabulary," he shouted. "You men listen to reason. Carry your own goods or don't proceed. No horse can make it up the Pass."

Meg ran to him. "Mick!" She buried her face in his chest. Held onto him so tightly that her sobs were pushed back down into her chest.

"Meg, my darling," he said into her ear as he rocked her for a moment. Then he let her extricate herself. Yukon Sally, then Jake, sat down attentively as Meg turned to address those gathering around.

"Chief O'Mara is telling you the truth," she spoke loudly. "No horse can make it up the trail. Your horse will die a terrible death. And it will be your doing. Then you'll have to carry your own gear, or abandon it there. You might as well repack here and start off without your horse. Let it live. I'm a veterinarian, better known to you as a horse doctor. I have seen the carnage on the trail. Do you have any particular questions?"

Back in Moore's cabin, they sat round the table, Mick and Meg with arms around each other talking with Captain Moore and Amy, while Yukon Sally and Jake curled up patiently near the doorstep outside. They had sniffed and pawed Mick, found him acceptable.

"What I found in Wrangell," Mick told Meg, "was the gravestone of Teskey. He had been shot dead for cheating at poker. That's the way it is in that town. Just wish it hadn't taken me so long to get there and back up here."

Amy leaned across the table to Meg. "Your sister, Alice. She came in on a luxury steamer last week. Sent word to us, asking to meet her at the Star Hotel. Skagway's finest. She's a mighty stylish woman, your sister..."

"*Alice!*" Meg sat upright. "I don't believe it! *Alice*...on her own? What about Jacques...and the kids?"

"Jacques is looking after the business and the kids. Alice said she's taking a vacation. Wants to see a bit of the world. Just like you."

Meg sank back into Mick's arm. She gripped his hand on her shoulder, feeling suddenly sickened and sad. The children. The horses. The dogs. How could human beings abandon them like that?

"But your sister took one look at the Chilkoot," said Amy, "and decided she wouldn't follow you over that. She got back on the steamer. Is on her way up to St. Michael's. She'll arrive in Dawson by riverboat."

"As will we," said Mick, decisively, taking Meg's other hand in his, beaming as he announced. "In our own style...married, with dogs."

EPILOGUE

THE SPIRITS OF IKE AND PIJI dwell on in Dawson City. They met up with the spirit of Inuit Annie who had come to rest on the shoulders of the great writers of that city: the poet, Robert Service, and the popular historian, Pierre Berton.

Ike and Piji witnessed the fate of people and dogs, whom Ike can see only in terms of wolves, more or less, like and un-like. They rejoiced at the return of Meg and Mick to Dawson, married, with Yukon Sally and Jake leading them down the gangplank. But their greatest celebration was when the O'Maras soon produced children and Yukon Sally and Jake eventually had many pups.

The Klondike Gold Rush was the glory days for malamute sled dogs. When Dawson became a qualified city of forty thousand, after the human stampede of summer 1898, a team of matched malamutes, with a whisky bar built into the sled, was worth about $10,000. That particular team was owned by Jethro, the black Klondike King who got his first dogs from Finn.

During that summer of '98, when the largest influx of humans came to Dawson City, there was bewilderment, confusion, and much milling about the streets of the city, rather than getting down to work or digging for gold.

Meg took advantage of the situation by organizing dog weight-pulling contests for the amusement of those with money in their pockets. Proceeds went to the building of a school for young humans. The weight-pulling contests in summer were held at dawn when it was coolest and the citizens of Dawson were still up at 3 a.m. Yukon Sally and Jake went on to become the champion freight pullers of Dawson City. In her prime, Yukon Sally could pull a wagon filled with a thousand pounds of gold for an impressive distance along Front Street. Jake in his prime could pull thirty pounds more.

Mick was recruited as a policeman in Dawson. He was good at keeping order in the pack. Liked working in a town where no guns were allowed, though gambling and prostitution were. His first year in Dawson, that peculiar time of the human stampede, was hectic. Constantine, with whom Mick got on well, though sometimes felt a bristling of the fur, was his first boss. Mick knew how to keep his place, but he could see that things were often on the edge of disorder with Constantine.

Typhoid plagued the town before the sewers were installed. A boatload of professional girls from Belgium, set loose amongst the thousands of men from everywhere, resulted in a rash of venereal diseases. Constantine managed to have his request for doctors and nurses to staff the hospital of Dawson fulfilled. Belinda Mulroney moved back into town, built luxury hotels, and profited yet more by investing in electricity for Dawson City.

Constantine snarled about the enormous increase of riff raff in 1898. It was not of the kind he liked to cope with. He went willingly to another post, farther into the wilderness, when Sam Steele came to relieve him of his several leadership duties in September 1898. Constantine left Dawson City with his chin held high and a large crowd saluting him. Meg wiped tears from her eyes, missed him, and was distrustful of his replacement, Sam Steele, until he proved himself worthy.

More than half the population departed voluntarily before winter set in. Some slunk away, returning home with their tail between their legs, not even having gone to look at the gold creeks. But they had their adventure in getting there. Others, like Alice, had a fine time of it, vacationing from their normal lives. They left with a smile and had no desire to tough out a winter in Dawson City.

Alice stayed that summer of 1898 in one of the new hotels that were quickly built and furnished with the many shipments coming upriver all summer long. She paraded in her fine new dresses. She had brought a parasol. She flirted with the richest men and was well treated by them. But that is not all she did. She kept a daily, vividly descriptive journal, with a sharp sense of the manners and foibles of the residents of Dawson, as well as descriptive accounts of the landscape she had travelled over, in the comfort of train and boat. She had arrived with another load of brooms plus a clever assembly of goods that she sold in Dawson at great profit. Much of it was women's personal effects, cosmetics, items of hygiene. She paid her own way and more. Went home with a goodly sum.

Back in Halifax, Alice began her new career. She had had a taste of independence, of not being with her children day and night, and she was determined to get her fill of it. She submitted her writing to newspapers and magazines. She became one of the New Women travel writers and journalists. She hosted elegant parties in the house that Randolph had built and Meg eventually sold to her and Jacques, along with the broom business. Alice was never sufficiently pleased with her mate, Jacques. When he died after a long illness, their children then grown up, Alice took to travelling more than ever, but found no one who could love her as Jacques did.

Finn, that vigorous yet benign kind of wolf, surprised everyone by striking it rich on Hopeless Hill. He had discovered the last large veins of gold. But he lacked the aggression and discipline to develop his claim and acquire more. He drank himself into stupors and into spasms of exhilaration. At a party on the *Bella*, he was showing how well he could balance on the railings. Before anyone could stop him, he fell over, hit his head on the way down and drowned in the river. Meg took Yukon Sally and Jake to his funeral. They howled along with the ringing of the church bell and the weeping of Meg.

Kate of the Wolf Clan was taken to San Francisco by Carmack.

Skookum Jim and Charlie went along, as the adventurous reinforcements they had always been for Kate and Carmack.

"I'll go on the next trip," said Daisy, "if there is one."

Daisy was involved at the time with her new business project. Meg invested money from the sale of her Halifax properties in Daisy's project. It was the first and most-lasting Opera House in Dawson City. It was a theatre for musicals and operettas. It rivalled the crowds that went to Diamond Tooth Gertie's saloon and dancehall.

Kate's first trip to San Francisco was short-lived but not the disaster her second trip with Carmack was. He left her there, with their daughter Graphie, supposedly in the care of Carmack's sister. Carmack came back to Dawson and without benefit of divorce from Kate, he married a woman in Dawson who operated a cigar store.

Daisy, Meg, and others tried to drive Carmack off in shame. When that didn't work, Meg and Daisy used the law. With the aid of Skookum Jim, they brought Kate back to Dawson and helped Kate sue for divorce and settlement. Carmack argued that he had never been legally married to Kate, the Wolf Clan ceremony he had felt honoured by, he now rejected as "Indian" and of no account. For several years, Kate and her supporters sued but the case was eventually dropped.

Carmack left with his cigar store bride and never looked back on the welfare of his first mate and partner in the discovery of gold in the Klondike. He provided some schooling for their daughter but then she eventually took off into the nether life of southern cities.

Daisy lived out her life in Dawson City, enjoying the company of Skookum Jim when he was willing to give it, and trying to enjoy the company of others when he returned to the life of a prospector, though there were no more big gold strikes after 1899.

Skookum Jim was an easy-going kind of wolf with an extraordinary amount of strength. He managed to run in two packs, but he used most of the gold he got out of the Klondike to aid and support his original pack, his Chilkat family.

The great human stampede had gone from Dawson City before the winter of 1899. They went when they heard of gold in Nome,

Alaska, but there wasn't much there and they dwindled into a weak and feckless lot, dispersing over the world.

That Norwegian herd of reindeer never did reach Dawson. A number of wolves benefited from it on route.

In the early twentieth century, Ike and Piji saw the development of the great sled-dog races, held along the Yukon River route, through Alaska and the Yukon. The first was the Iditarod but the longest and most arduous is The Yukon Quest, from Whitehorse to Nome, Alaska. A new breed of dog, the blue-eyed Siberian husky, was imported to compete in the Iditarod. The huskies were smaller and sometimes faster than the malamutes. Not prone to jealousy, Ike cared only that his dogs survive and be cared for.

His soul felt serenity at last, when in 1935, he and Piji accompanied Meg and Mick on a long trip back down to the East Coast, where, with a prize descendent of Yukon Sally and Jake, they attended a meeting of the American Kennel Club. It was the meeting that recognized the Alaskan Malamute as an established breed and the Alaskan Malamute Club was formed. The dogs were to be protected by law and maintained by breeders and vets like Meg.

Thus, after many centuries, Piji felt Ike's spirit at rest with hers.

"It is good to be dead," she rubbed noses with Ike, "when we can witness such things."

Non-fictional Characters

MEG WILKINSON is a fictional character based on women who were finding their way into medical and veterinary professions in the 1890s. The real persons bearing their actual names in *City Wolves* include:

Dr. William Osler and Principal Duncan McEachran of the Faculty of Comparative Medicine and Veterinary Science of McGill University did pioneer this vet college. Aline Cust, whom they refer to in deciding to grant Meg her degree, was the first woman in the British Isles to complete veterinary studies, actually in 1900. But the Royal Veterinary College in Edinburgh did not grant her a degree until 1923 after the Sex Disqualification Act was passed. Meanwhile Dr. Cust had been practising veterinary medicine in Ireland since 1900.

Pauline Johnson (1861–1913), daughter of a Mohawk chief of The Six Nations Reserve and his English wife, was Canada's famous poet and performer of the late 19th century.

Shaaw Tl'áa (also known as Kate Carmack) was arguably the first to discover gold along with her husband, George Washington Carmack, their daughter "Graphie," Shaaw Tl'áa's brothers Keish (Skookum Jim), Kaa Goox (Charlie), and young cousin Koolsen (Patsy). Robert Henderson also claimed to be the first discoverer.

Joseph Ladue was the supplies store owner and founder of Dawson City

Belinda Mulroney became the richest businesswoman of the Klondike. Anton Stander became one of the Klondike kings, along with Jethro the "darkie" who owned the best team of matched malamutes, Clarence and Ethel Berry, Tom and Salome Lippy, Alex MacDonald the "Big Moose" from Antigonish, Lucky Swede, and Joe Ash the tavern boss.

Captain William and Amy Moore did found Moore's landing which became Skagway. William Ogilvie was the respected surveyor.

Superintendent Charles Constantine of the North West Mounted Police kept order in Dawson City. He was eventually replaced by the more famous Colonel Sam Steele.

Captain Healy ran the Alaska Commercial Company along with Captain Hansen.

Father William Judge was "the saint" of Dawson City. Edith von Born and companion Mary E. Hitchcock did visit with their strange entourage.

Soapy Smith was indeed the notorious killer gangster who controlled Skagway until he died in a shootout.

CREDITS

THERE WOULD HAVE BEEN NO YUKON SALLY or Yukon's Jake, Yukitu, or Tundra, were it not for Alison Postma, owner of Wolfrunner Kennels and a model breeder of Alaskan malamutes. Gratitude to her and all sled-dog breeders everywhere, for maintaining our heritage breeds. They are not in it for the money!

Dr. Ardiss Ardeil and her dedicated staff inspired me to imagine the first woman veterinarian and research the history of the profession. She lent me reference books, answered all questions, and expertly vetted the manuscript for this book. When the time had come, she helped us lay our Yukon Sally to rest with utmost compassion.

Dr. John Overell, a veterinarian in great demand at Dawson City, also checked the manuscript and advised me on veterinary work. Barry Gunn, Ontario Veterinary College, and Janice Mercer, Montreal Veterinary College, were prompt and helpful in my research, as were the staff and volunteers at L.E. Shore Memorial Library.

Mushers in the Yukon generously, and often uproariously, invited me and Yukon Sally to meet their dogs, tell us their stories, and teach us tricks of the trade. Outstanding thanks to Stacy Williams, Braden Bennett, William Kleedehn of Limp-a-Long Racing, and Alaskan malamute breeders Hans and Reggie Ottli of Amuyok Kennels.

Having no luck meeting up with wolves directly in the Yukon, I relied on secondary research through documentary films, articles, and books, notably those by R.D. Lawrence. Eileen and Jos Wintermans helped find wolf documentaries.

Amidst the stacks of books and papers read after returning from the Yukon, Pierre Berton's enduringly popular history book *Klondike* told me most about the gold rush. I had known Pierre and his talented wife Janet long before that, since I went to high school with some of their children, and when I became a writer we were both active members of The Writers' Union of Canada. Like other writers who attended the Union's annual meetings and enjoyed hospitality at the Berton's spectacularly Canadian home, I was enriched by every conversation with him. Pierre Berton finished his very great life before I completed *City Wolves*, but I gave Janet Berton an early draft for interest's sake and in response she kindly gave me succinct and astute editorial advice. I thank her for that, and the warm Berton friendship.

Amongst many books about the late nineteenth century, I was most influenced by Charlotte Gray's always reliable and insightful biographies, especially *Flint and Feather* on the life of Pauline Johnson, and *Reluctant Genius* about Alexander Graham Bell. Jennifer Duncan's engrossing biographies of women who went to the Klondike, *Frontier Spirit*, was most illuminating about the variety of adventurous women who wound up in Dawson City. I was persuaded by her view that it was indeed a woman, Kate Carmack, who most likely first discovered the gold that triggered the spectacular rush.

Robert Kroetsch's novel *The Man from the Creeks* gave the most vivid picture of Dawson City gold rush life. I found Jack Hodgin's *Innocent Cities* helpful in recreating Vancouver of that earlier era.

I thank John Heinrich, Dr. Elizabeth Robinson, Su Penny, Liz Kane, and Noel Lomer for their helpful input as "real people" test readers of early drafts.

Rhoda Innuksuk, President of Pauktuutit, helped with Inuit names and culture.

Sheila Watson, agent for my first three novels while I lived in England, now retired, gave the most helpful and encouraging professional advice. I also benefited from the time spent and expert opinion of Canadian agents Denise Bukowski and Anne McDermid. Always gracious, eminent editor Louise Dennys helped with a professional reader's very positive report.

I couldn't do without the support of my wild pack of writer friends. It's an extensive pack of essentially lone wolves who nevertheless share a common territory and follow the Wolf Credo. The call for help will always be answered and we are on the lookout for each other. It's unfair to single any out because everyone counts, but I'm especially grateful for Carol Shield's assurance that "someday you'll look up from your desk and it will be done." The day I did, tears ran down my cheeks, for she was right but she had lost the battle with cancer some months earlier.

All told, *City Wolves* became a ten-year project. I felt the support of all the Writers' Union pack but especially my closest cohorts who leaned in with companionship and ready good advice: Brian Brett, Erika Ritter, Ann Ireland, Andrew Pyper, Lawrence Hill, Erna Paris, Iris Nowell, Merilyn Simonds, Wayne Grady, Michelle Berry, Ken McGoogan and Anne Fine from the old Oxford days territory. Michael Gilbert remains my writer-friend and consultant on trans-gender understanding. And friends of longstanding faith: Anne Powlesland, Shirley Tilghman, Nesta Scott, Peggotty Graham, and Catharine Spenser. Mohawk Mike Robbins fed me pertinent books. Mary Muir helped me climb the Chilkoot trail. Sarah Sheard gave good psychological counsel. Jennifer Varah kept me sane by keeping my computer working.

It's not easy for a human family to run with a writer in its pack and vice versa. My children, now grown up, have made things easy for me, all four being upstanding citizens and rewarding me with grandchildren. My husband, Don Gauer, has supported my writing for nearly thirty years. He was the first to read *City Wolves*, believes in it like no other, and in retirement learned to man the phones and proofread. My daughter Rain, extracted the manuscript from me and gave remarkably objective advice. Daughter Apple gave her sharp professional counsel. Malcolm Jolley was the voice of creative experience from

Gremolata.com. Sage advice came from Alec Jolley. Empathy always from my dogs, Yukon Jake, Yukitu, and QC.

I have literary consultant, Sally Cohen, working with literary lawyer, Marian Hebb, to thank for encouragement through discouragement in the submission of this novel's unusual mix of animal and human characters, history and fiction, until it found its right match with the new, innovative publisher, Blue Butterfly Books. President Patrick Boyer's creativity, true rationality, integrity and realistic optimism are superb to work with. As is Blue Butterfly's alert and professional designer Gary Long, adept at everything from jacket design to maps and mixed fonts. The novel's characters Meg, Alice, Daisy, Mick, and Anton Stander found their look-alikes in real-life persons: Jessie Taylor, Deanna Furnival, Chanel Grist-Algie, John McCollum, and Malcolm Jolley. Chanel took the photographs.

The most crucial relationship in the publishing pack is between author and editor. Ideally it is one of mutual respect and that is what I found with Dominic Farrell. He recognized the soul in *City Wolves* while diligently spotting the sore thumbs. At first I baulked at his advice regarding restructuring, but given time to think deeply I could see a way of doing it that would indeed make the novel more artful and engrossing. Thank you, Dominic, for nudging me into doing what I'm now so glad to have done.

DORRIS HEFFRON was born in Noranda, Quebec, and raised in various Ontario communities. She has an honours B.A. and an M.A. in literature and philosophy from Queen's University. She lived in Oxford, England from 1968 to 1980, where she was a tutor for Oxford University and the Open University giving courses in literature. She has taught creative writing at the University of Malaysia, travelled extensively in Europe, Asia, and South America, and resided while writing and teaching in Holland, France, and Cape Breton Island.

Dorris wrote three novels about teenagers, regarded as pioneers in the genre of young adult fiction, that were translated and put on high school courses in Europe, Japan, and Canada: *Rain and I* (1982); *Crusty Crossed* (1976), and *A Nice Fire and Some Moonpennies* (1971).

A Shark in the House (1996), Dorris's first adult fiction novel, continues its widespread appeal to individuals and book clubs. In *City Wolves*, Dorris now deftly embraces the human and the wild, legends and realities, and the primal spiritual bond that connects us beyond time and place.

Dorris now lives at "Little Creek Wolf Range" near Thornbury, Ontario.

Photo: Dorris with "Yukon Sally", by Barbara Nettleton

Interview with the Author

 You have written successful books and also kept dogs as companions for many years, but until now you always managed to keep your writing and your dogs separate. What happened to bring your two passions together in City Wolves*?*

DORRIS HEFFRON: Something very strange. My previous novels, even though animals were present in them, were inspired by real people and real life situations. *City Wolves* was inspired, I should even say driven, by a sled dog whose name was "Yukon Sally." That must sound quite weird coming from a writer of realistic fiction.

 It does, but that's what I'm trying to get at. What happened?

HEFFRON: Well, my previous novel was in the process of being published when our beloved collie mutt "Frauzie" died of old age. I was bereft. My youngest child had just gone off to university so I was suddenly too alone. I knew I needed another dog right away since I couldn't function, was weepy, didn't want to get out of bed

439

without Frauzie to share my breakfast, walk and talk with, lie by my desk, greet me when I came home. I was in bad shape.

I didn't dare go to the pound for a dog as I always had because I knew I'd come home with every one of them. I decided it was time to spring for a purebred and wanted to have an indigenous Canadian dog. Thought first of a Newfoundlander so I could have a swimming companion. My husband vetoed that on account of its size.

"My second choice is an Alaskan malamute," I then responded, "A dog I can ski with."

"Oh, all right," he said, having no idea about the difficulty of malamutes.

I had come across this breed reading the catalogue *Dogs in Canada*. But our vet warned me that sled dogs, particularly the Alaskan malamute and Siberian husky, are "independent thinking." They're more like wolves than any other dogs, he added. That intrigued me. As I lay awake the night before our appointment to see the one remaining pup for sale at Wolfrunner Kennels, the name Yukon Sally occurred to me.

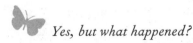 *Yes, but what happened?*

HEFFRON: It was love at first sight on my part. But it took some time for Yukon Sally to honour me with hers. She was a very regal malamute yet could never become a show dog because she was too much of a "throwback." Yukon Sally had more features of the wolf: ginger eyes, narrow chest, long legged, not to mention her character!

She enthralled me. I sought to learn all about her, her ancestry in sled dogs and wolves, the land and people of her origins. I travelled with her throughout the Yukon and Alaska. I read books, interviewed and researched more than I care to remember.

But Yukon Sally kept leading me on. We sold our house in Toronto and bought fifty-two acres in Beaver Valley in central

Ontario so she could have space and a companion pup, "Yukon Jake." I named this property "Little Creek Wolf Range." You might say I had moved from enthralled to obsessed, or even possessed, by Yukon Sally.

Over the course of her ten-year life she led me into ancient times of the Arctic, across the life of the first dog doctor, and up to the Klondike gold rush in the glory days of the malamute sled dogs. Then she dragged me through the most challenging and arduous writing time of my life. When the full story had been researched, verified as to both the imagined and the historical, the manuscript completed and the work sent off—the finish line of our own peculiar kind of Yukon quest finally reached—Yukon Sally expired in my arms. That was on the 21st of December, the darkest day indeed.

That is an unusual story of "inspiration." But how did you actually go about doing all the research? You depict the Klondike gold rush with a real flavour of authenticity.

HEFFRON: Thanks for bringing me back to the practical! I flew to Whitehorse with Yukon Sally in the pet compartment. Then we rented a van and travelled to all the places the gold rush people had gone, camping along the Yukon River route, taking boat trips, hiking the trails, renting a cabin in Dawson City where much has been preserved of the Klondike gold rush days.

Yukon Sally was like having an entry ticket. When seeing her with me, the mushers, breeders, native people, local historians, bartenders, everyone, trusted me and opened up more than they would have if I had shown up on my own as yet another wacky writer snooping around and asking questions.

So your wolf-like dog became a research assistant as well as an inspiration for this story?

HEFFRON: She did. I also took a lot of photos and kept a relevant journal as well as the usual research notes. But I think it was being there, not just seeing the spectacular landscape and hokey towns, but actually feeling the atmosphere, experiencing first hand the spell of the Yukon. There's also fear in the Yukon. I'll never forget hiking up into the mountains, fearing an encounter with a grizzly bear. Maybe it was Yukon Sally who kept them away.

After that personal experience of the Yukon I did all the usual researching in books, papers, museums. The most illuminating accounts I found of the gold rush were in Pierre Berton's history book, *Klondike*, and Jennifer Duncan's *Frontier Spirit*, biographies of women who went to the Klondike.

Your novels have been more contemporary in themes and locales. What caused you to switch now to "historical fiction"?

HEFFRON: I think what is common in all my novels is a strong sense of people within the context of their times. We are products of our time and place.

Although my second novel was set in the Second World War, that is not very far back in time. The cause was, as I said, Yukon Sally. It was she who led me so far back in time with this book.

But the sweep of history always lurks in my thinking. I studied literature at university in the context of the history of writing, from the Middle Ages through each century. Because I write realistic fiction, I strive hard to get the real details right. And I don't like to mess with history. I try to be true to what happened and what real people actually did. So it was a lot of work getting everything accurate in *City Wolves*.

I often cursed myself for attempting something so difficult and of such wide scope. But then Yukon Sally would give me that look of "a wolf doesn't give up" and on I'd trudge.

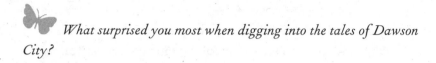

What surprised you most when digging into the tales of Dawson City?

HEFFRON: Discovering how adventurous, entrepreneurial, free-thinking and, in modern terms, "liberated" women of that time and place were. They were also exceptionally achieving. Women like Belinda Mulroney built much of Dawson City, including putting in electricity. She became as rich as the Klondike Kings. Women wore boots and trousers if it was more practical.

Anything else?

HEFFRON: I was also amazed at the international mix of people who made their way to the Klondike. Fifty percent were Americans, and of course there were Canadians, but others came looking for gold from as far away as New Zealand, Asia, Europe. The place had a truly international cast of characters.

And how valued the sled dogs were! A black prospector owned a team of matched malamutes with a "bar," I'm talking booze bar, attached to the sled. That "limousine" was worth about $10,000 in the 1890s, a huge amount of money.

The law and order that the Northwest Mounted Police managed to maintain in Dawson City, largely through the prohibition of guns, was astounding, particularly compared to the violence and corruption that reigned in the Alaskan town of Skagway.

And sex trade workers in Dawson were respected and well paid.

*Meg Wilkinson, the strong and independent woman at the cen-
tre of your story, has decidedly modern views about many things. She
may not conform to some readers' traditional view of "the Victorian
Woman." Do you yourself see her as modern or Victorian?*

HEFFRON: I think the big difference between modern and Victorian women is access to birth control. So much of the Victorian
woman's life depended on the fact that if she had sex she was likely
to get pregnant. If she got married she was expected to have babies
every year or so until she was too old. In the late nineteenth century
women were getting into universities, becoming doctors, running
small businesses, travelling with guides, becoming famous as writers and entertainers. There was a common term, "the New Woman,"
to describe this liberated ideal.

At the turn of the century, as a result, it was quite commonly said,
"Now women can do anything!" Except have reliable control over
their fertility.

Meg is certainly one of the strong-minded, adventurous, liberal-
thinking women of her time, but she is helped in this by her husband,
Randolph. He helps her financially, intellectually, socially—and
he doesn't make her pregnant. That is what really facilitates Meg's
becoming a veterinarian in Victorian times. Meg's sister Alice sees
that and is very jealous of it, because Alice cannot continue teaching after marriage, and she got pregnant on her wedding night. That
curtails her ambitions and fuels her bitterness.

I see as a stereotype the modern woman presented as someone
driven by the need for sex much more than love. I'm sceptical of
that take on women. I certainly don't believe it when a contemporary author depicts a Victorian or earlier woman as obsessed with
sex. Meg is truly Victorian in her avoidance of completed sexual
intercourse until she's with a man she would marry. Her need for
love and interest in men is, shall we say, timeless.

The Inuit couple, Ike and Piji, play an important role in City Wolves, *even though they are long since dead by the time Meg reads their story and their spirits follow her in the Yukon in the 1890s. What is it like writing a novel where a couple of the characters have become spirits?*

HEFFRON: A lot of fun, actually! It involved the creative, imaginative part of writing fiction that I love. Those passages with Ike and Piji, as ancient spirits commenting on Meg's life and times, arose so naturally and humorously out of the main story that I sometimes shrieked and laughed out loud as the wording came to me. Sometimes the passages had to be really worked at, for truth and word perfection, but when I got them right it was the most delightful eureka part of creative fiction. I doubt that I'll ever come up with a better final line than Piji's at the end of the epilogue.

Their role in this story is so significant you could say it wouldn't exist without them. Does that parallel your own approach off the pages of fiction in real life?

HEFFRON: The reality basis of these spirit characters is something I've come to believe is profoundly true and helps me to deal with death. Bodies die. That's for sure. But I think the character, the influence, what amounts to the soul or spirit of that creature, does live on, in what they have created or continue to influence.

I grew to love Ike and Piji and their whole community of people and wolves and dogs when I created their story. My characters do live on in my mind. Real people and animals I have had to lay to rest likewise live on in my mind.

So when I was steered by my very good editor, Dominic Farrell, to make some structural change in the final editing of *City Wolves* and the concept of Ike and Piji as spirit characters came to mind,

I suddenly realized they were the only true and profoundly real means to do what was required. My realist sense of spirits is that they are in no way tangible; they can't actually speak to us. They can just "be," and watch and accompany us. That must be pretty frustrating to them when they see us going off the rails! Hence Ike's tirades, and Piji's sense of sorrow.

Turning from spirits to wolves and sled dogs, because they are also essential to this story, what is the risk of humans writing about animals and ascribing human attributes to them, or thinking for animals with a human brain? Did you encounter that challenge?

HEFFRON: Oh yes! As a child I read many books in which animals spoke and thought as human beings. Those books help children sympathize with and understand animals as fellow creatures. But I also grew up with a strong determination to "tell it like it is," to be a realistic writer. I love and admire animals as they are. I do not want to turn them into human beings.

As Emily Dickinson said, the wonderful thing about dogs is that they know but they don't talk. There are, very intentionally, no talking animals in *City Wolves*.

But I did extensive research and observation of wolves and sled dogs so that I could portray some of their inner life, as a writer should, in portraying any characters in their full dimensions.

Is it a stretch to say wolves are like humans and humans like wolves?

HEFFRON: In European culture there's a lingering image of the wolf as dominantly ferocious. This is underscored in the Grimm fairytale about the wolf eating an old woman and child, Little Red

Riding Hood. But there are counterbalances, such as the legend of Rome being founded by Romulus and Rimus who, as children, had been lovingly raised by wolves. In North America, we're more aware of the intelligence, strength and tenderness of wolves. Though we, too, have poisoned and slaughtered them. Governments here placed bounties on wolves to financially encourage people to kill them.

What we might emulate about wolves is nicely summed up in Del Goetz's *The Wolf Credo*:

> Respect the elders
> Teach the young
> Cooperate with the pack
> Play when you can
> Hunt when you must
> Share your affections
> Voice your feelings
> Leave your mark

With that approach, it is easier to see why City Wolves *is an exploration of the deep natural connection between wolves, dogs and people.*

HEFFRON: Yes, because it looks at their behaviour when they are brought together in a community. There's Ike's village. There's Halifax and Boston, Vancouver and the unusual community called Dawson City.

As an author, I refuse to be explicit. Readers will make their own conclusions as to what is important and meaningful. But I have my own bent and some playful manipulations. It's there in the title and in some chapter titles. I want the readers to enjoy making their own interpretations of what is meant by "city wolves."

Well, without being explicit then, you must at least have observed some similarities between wolf pack behaviour and human family and social behaviour?

HEFFRON: Yes, there are strong similarities and they are implicit in *City Wolves*, but so are the important differences.

For instance, there are some trans-gendered people and there are some trans-gendered wolves. What might be learned from that? The important thing in my mind is that wolves and humans are ultimately integral to the order of things. I see dogs as the loveliest link. But let's not forget the big differences. Wolves could not invent the atom bomb or penicillin. Wolf packs are not egalitarian or democratic. Don't we think that human societies should be, and haven't we worked to make them so?

Your first three books, in pioneering a new genre of novels about teenagers for teenagers, reached a wide audience in different language editions in many countries. Now you are pioneering in City Wolves, *too. How would you describe the fresh ground you are breaking here?*

HEFFRON: I don't think I'm turning up essentially new ground. Profound psychoanalysts like Carl Jung and all the great religions recognize the interconnection of people and animals. This is a very universal theme.

There is a long tradition in literature of portraying animals and people. It's particularly appropriate in a country like Canada where wilderness fortunately remains.

But where ground did have to be broken is that contemporary publishers tend not to be open to the mix these days. *City Wolves* is an unusual combination. It's not old-fashioned allegory or new-fashioned fantasy fiction. It's not suspenseful contemporary fiction including animals separated from people, like the bears in Andrew

Pyper's *The Wildfire Season*, a novel I much admire set in the contemporary Yukon. *City Wolves* is realistic historical fiction portraying animals with people and spirits. It implies similarities but also differences. That's a new kind of mix which a "Think free ... be free!" publisher like Blue Butterfly Books, I'm most happy to say, is open to.

That's nice of you to say. That's what blue butterflies are all about—a new kind of mix. But getting back to your writing, in addition to confronting such barriers in literature as you just described, City Wolves *also celebrates a woman who demolished social barriers. Is it important that she was a first female veterinarian in Canada?*

HEFFRON: Pioneering women today, such as the first woman astronaut, object to being described as "the first woman" to do this or that. It seems they want to emphasize that they are great astronauts or whatever their profession or calling may be, and play down being the first woman at it.

But as for Meg, it was obviously of huge importance that she was seen as the first woman trying to get into the profession. That is what made it so difficult for her. She had to be not just courageous, but doubly qualified, more persistent, a skilled diplomat, a better negotiator, well supported, and fortunate enough to have men at the top who had their own good reasons for wanting her to succeed—just as male lead wolves seek out female lead wolves. Oops! I'm being explicit. Time to stop.

ABOUT THIS BOOK

A tale of ventures and loves, *City Wolves* follows Meg Wilkinson, one of Canada's first female veterinarians, from a restricting life in Nova Scotia to the wild confusion of gold rush Yukon with its fascinating characters and world of licence. Amidst Mounties, dance hall girls, Klondike kings, mushers, priests, and swindlers—all the mangy and magnificent people, dogs, and spirits that suddenly populate raucous Dawson City—Meg finds more than most prospectors. She discovers deep satisfaction caring for the dogs that are so like the wolves who, from earliest days, inspired her into veterinary service.

Yet Meg had also learned a much older story about the wolves, the ancestors of the sled dogs, and about Ike and Piji, an Inuit couple who had been among the first to bridge the wolf-human divide. Their spirits haunt this story as they inspire and observe Meg throughout her adventures. While their story speaks to Meg and strengthens a passion for her work, it also helps stir her desire for love.

Brimming with colourful characters, drama, humour, and rich historical detail, *City Wolves* is lively, insightful historical fiction that brilliantly reveals the wolf-like nature of humans and the human nature of wolves.